Sources for Library Materials in FY10
Albany County Public Library

- Cash Gifts
- Public Money
- Donated Items

18%

50%

32%

The Rosary

**Center Point
Large Print**

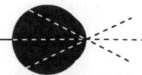

**This Large Print Book carries the
Seal of Approval of N.A.V.H.**

The Rosary

Florence L. Barclay

CENTER POINT PUBLISHING
THORNDIKE, MAINE

Originally published by
G. P. Putnam's Sons in 1910.

The text of this Large Print edition is unabridged.
In other aspects, this book may vary
from the original edition.
Printed in the United States of America
on permanent paper.
Set in 16-point Times New Roman type.

ISBN: 978-1-60285-859-6

Library of Congress Cataloging-in-Publication Data

Barclay, Florence L. (Florence Louisa), 1862–1921.
  The rosary / Florence L. Barclay.
    p. cm.
  Originally published: New York : G.P. Putnam's Sons, 1910.
  ISBN 978-1-60285-859-6 (library binding : alk. paper)
  1. Large type books. I. Title.
  PR6003.A66R6 2010
  823′.912—dc22

                                                    2010017357

CONTENTS

CHAPTER I

Enter the Duchess

The peaceful stillness of an English summer afternoon brooded over the park and gardens at Overdene. A hush of moving sunlight and lengthening shadows lay upon the lawn, and a promise of refreshing coolness made the shade of the great cedar tree a place to be desired.

The old stone house, solid, substantial, and unadorned, suggested unlimited spaciousness and comfort within; and was redeemed from positive ugliness without, by the fine ivy, magnolia trees, and wistaria, of many years' growth, climbing its plain face, and now covering it with a mantle of soft green, large white blooms, and a cascade of purple blossom.

A terrace ran the full length of the house, bounded at one end by a large conservatory, at the other by an aviary. Wide stone steps, at intervals, led down from the terrace on to the soft springy turf of the lawn. Beyond—the wide park; clumps of old trees, haunted by shy brown deer; and, through the trees, fitful gleams of the river, a narrow silver ribbon, winding gracefully in and out between long grass, buttercups, and cow-daisies.

The sun-dial pointed to four o'clock.

7

The birds were having their hour of silence. Not a trill sounded from among the softly moving leaves, not a chirp, not a twitter. The stillness seemed almost oppressive. The one brilliant spot of colour in the landscape was a large scarlet macaw, asleep on his stand under the cedar.

At last came the sound of an opening door. A quaint old figure stepped out on to the terrace, walked its entire length to the right, and disappeared into the rose-garden. The Duchess of Meldrum had gone to cut her roses.

She wore an ancient straw hat, of the early-Victorian shape known as "mushroom," tied with black ribbons beneath her portly chin; a loose brown holland coat; a very short tweed skirt, and Engadine "gouties." She had on some very old gauntlet gloves, and carried a wooden basket and a huge pair of scissors.

A wag had once remarked that if you met her Grace of Meldrum returning from gardening or feeding her poultry, and were in a charitable frame of mind, you would very likely give her sixpence. But, after you had thus drawn her attention to yourself and she looked at you, Sir Walter Raleigh's cloak would not be in it! Your one possible course would be to collapse into the mud, and let the ducal "gouties" trample on you. This the duchess would do with gusto; then accept your apologies with good nature; and keep your sixpence, to show when she told the story.

The duchess lived alone; that is to say, she had no desire for the perpetual companionship of any of her own kith and kin, nor for the constant smiles and flattery of a paid companion. Her pale daughter, whom she had systematically snubbed, had married; her handsome son, whom she had adored and spoiled, had prematurely died, before the death, a few years since, of Thomas, fifth Duke of Meldrum. He had come to a sudden and, as the duchess often remarked, very suitable end; for, on his sixty-second birthday, clad in all the splendours of his hunting scarlet, top hat, and buff corduroy breeches, the mare he was mercilessly putting at an impossible fence suddenly refused, and Thomas, Duke of Meldrum, shot into a field of turnips; pitched upon his head, and spoke no more.

This sudden cessation of his noisy and fiery life meant a complete transformation in the entourage of the duchess. Hitherto she had had to tolerate the boon companions, congenial to himself, with whom he chose to fill the house; or to invite those of her own friends to whom she could explain Thomas, and who suffered Thomas gladly, out of friendship for her, and enjoyment of lovely Overdene. But even then the duchess had no pleasure in her parties; for, quaint rough diamond though she herself might appear, the bluest of blue blood ran in her veins; and, though her manner had the off-hand abruptness and disregard of other people's feelings not unfrequently found in old ladies of high rank, she was at heart a true gentle-woman, and could always be trusted to say and do the right thing in moments of importance: The late duke's language had been sulphurous and his manners Georgian; and when he had been laid in the unwonted quiet of his ancestral vault—"so unlike him, poor dear," as the duchess remarked, "that it is quite a comfort to know he is not really there"—her Grace looked around her, and began to realise the beauties and possibilities of Overdene.

At first she contented herself with gardening, making an aviary, and surrounding herself with all sorts of queer birds and beasts; upon whom she lavished the affection which, of late years, had known no human outlet.

But after a while her natural inclination to hospitality, her humorous enjoyment of other people's foibles, and a quaint delight in parading her own, led to constant succession of house-parties at Overdene, which soon became known as a Liberty Hall of varied delights where you always met the people you most wanted to meet, found every facility for enjoying your favourite pastime, were fed and housed in perfect style, and spent some of the most ideal days of your summer, or cheery days of your winter, never dull, never bored, free to come and go as you pleased, and everything seasoned everybody with the delightful "sauce piquante" of never being quite sure what the duchess would do or say next.

She mentally arranged her parties under three heads—"freak parties," "mere people parties," and "best parties." A "best party" was in progress on the lovely June day when the duchess, having enjoyed an unusually long siesta, donned what she called her "garden togs" and sallied forth to cut roses.

As she tramped along the terrace and passed through the little iron gate leading to the rose-garden, Tommy, the scarlet macaw, opened one eye and watched her; gave a loud kiss as she reached the gate and disappeared from view, then laughed to himself and went to sleep again.

Of all the many pets, Tommy was prime favourite. He represented the duchess's one concession to morbid sentiment. After the demise of the duke she had found it so depressing to be invariably addressed with suave deference by every male voice she heard. If the butler could have snorted, or the rector have rapped out an uncomplimentary adjective, the duchess would have felt cheered. As it was, a fixed and settled melancholy lay upon her spirit until she saw in a dealer's list an advertisement of a prize macaw, warranted a grand talker, with a vocabulary of over five hundred words.

The duchess went immediately to town, paid a visit to the dealer, heard a few of the macaw's words and the tone in which he said them, bought him on the spot, and took him down to Overdene. The first evening he sat crossly on the perch of his grand new stand, declining to say a single one of his five hundred words, though the duchess spent her evening in the hall, sitting in every possible place; first close to him; then, away in a distant corner; in an arm-chair placed behind a screen; reading, with her back turned, feigning not to notice him; facing him with concentrated attention. Tommy merely clicked his tongue at her every time she emerged from a hiding-place; or, if the rather worried butler or nervous under-footman passed hurriedly through the hall, sent showers of kisses after them, and then went into fits of ventriloquial laughter. The duchess, in despair, even tried reminding him in a whisper of the remarks he had made in the shop; but Tommy only winked at her and put his claw over his beak. Still, she enjoyed his flushed and scarlet appearance, and retired to rest hopeful and in no wise regretting her bargain.

The next morning it became instantly evident to the house-maid who swept the hall, the footman who sorted the letters, and the butler who sounded the breakfast gong, that a good night's rest had restored to Tommy the full use of his vocabulary. And when the duchess came sailing down the stairs, ten minutes after the gong had sounded, and Tommy, flapping his wings angrily, shrieked at her: "Now then, old girl! Come on!" she went to breakfast in a more cheerful mood than she had known for months past.

CHAPTER II

Introduces the Honourable Jane

The only one of her relatives who practically made her home with the duchess was her niece and former ward, the Honourable Jane Champion; and this consisted merely in the fact that the Honourable Jane was the one person who might invite herself to Overdene or Portland Place, arrive when she chose, stay as long as she pleased, and leave when it suited her convenience. On the death of her father, when her lonely girlhood in her Norfolk home came to an end, she would gladly have filled the place of a daughter to the duchess. But the duchess did not require a daughter; and a daughter with pronounced views, plenty of back-bone of her own, a fine figure, and a plain face, would have seemed to her Grace of Meldrum a peculiarly undesirable acquisition. So Jane was given to understand that she might come whenever she liked, and stay as long as she liked, but on the same footing as other people. This meant liberty to come and go as she pleased; and no responsibility towards her aunt's guests. The duchess preferred managing her own parties in her own way.

Jane Champion was now in her thirtieth year. She had once been described, by one who saw below the surface, as a perfectly beautiful woman in an absolutely plain shell; and no man had as yet looked beneath the shell, and seen the woman in her perfection. She would have made earth heaven for a blind lover who, not having eyes for the plainness of her face or the massiveness of her figure, might have drawn nearer, and apprehended the wonder of her as a woman, experiencing the wealth of tenderness of which she was capable, the blessed comfort of the shelter of her love, the perfect comprehension of her sympathy, the marvellous joy of winning and wedding her. But as yet, no blind man with far-seeing vision had come her way; and it always seemed to be her lot to take a second place, on occasions when she would have filled the first to infinite perfection.

She had been bridesmaid at weddings where the charming brides, notwithstanding their superficial loveliness, possessed few of the qualifications for wifehood with which she was so richly endowed.

She was godmother to her friends' babies, she, whose motherhood would have been a thing for wonder and worship.

She had a glorious voice, but her face not matching it, its existence was rarely suspected; and as she accompanied to perfection, she was usually in requisition to play for the singing of others.

In short, all her life long Jane had filled second places, and filled them very contentedly. She had never known what it was to be absolutely first with any one. Her mother's death had occurred during her infancy, so that she had not even the most shadowy remembrance of that maternal love and tenderness which she used sometimes to try to imagine, although she had never experienced it.

Her mother's maid, a faithful and devoted woman, dismissed soon after the death of her mistress, chancing to be in the neighbourhood some twelve years later, called at the manor, in the hope of finding some in the household who remembered her.

After tea, Fraulein and Miss Jebb being out of the way, she was spirited up into the schoolroom to see Miss Jane, her heart full of memories of the "sweet babe" upon whom she and her dear lady had lavished so much love and care.

She found awaiting her a tall, plain girl with a frank, boyish manner and a rather disconcerting way as she afterwards remarked, of "taking stock of a body the while one was a-talking," which at first checked the flow of good Sarah's reminiscences, poured forth so freely in the housekeeper's room below, and reduced her to looking tearfully around the room, remarking that she remembered choosing the blessed wall-paper with her dear lady now gone, whose joy had been so great when the dear babe first took notice and reached up for the roses. "And I can show you, miss, if you care to know it just which bunch of roses it were."

But before Sarah's visit was over, Jane had heard many undreamed-of-things; amongst others, that her mother used to kiss her little hands, "ah, many a time she did, miss; called them little rose-petals, and covered them with kisses."

The child, utterly unused to any demonstrations of affection, looked at her rather ungainly brown hands and laughed, simply because she was ashamed of the unwonted tightening at her throat and the queer stinging of tears beneath her eyelids. Thus Sarah departed under the impression that Miss Jane had grown up into a rather heartless young lady. But Fraulein and Jebbie never knew why, from that day onward, the hands, of which they had so often had cause to complain, were kept scrupulously clean; and on her birthday night, unashamed in the quiet darkness, the lonely little child kissed her own hands beneath the bedclothes, striving thus to reach the tenderness of her dead mother's lips.

And in after years, when she became her own mistress, one of her first actions was to advertise for Sarah Matthews and engage her as her own maid, at a salary which enabled the good woman eventually to buy herself a comfortable annuity.

Jane saw but little of her father, who had found it difficult to forgive her, firstly, for being a girl when he desired a son; secondly, being a girl, for having inherited his plainness rather than her mother's beauty. Parents are apt to see no injustice in the fact that they are often annoyed with their offspring for possessing attributes, both of character and appearance, with which they themselves have endowed them.

The hero of Jane's childhood, the chum of her girlhood and the close friend of her maturer years, was Deryck Brand, only son of the rector of the parish, and her senior by nearly ten years. But even in their friendship, close though it was, she had never felt herself first to him. As a medical student, at home during vacations, his mother and his profession took precedence in his mind of the lonely child, whose devotion pleased him and whose strong character and original mental development interested him. Later on he married a lovely girl, as unlike Jane as one woman could possibly be to another; but still their friendship held and deepened; and now, when he was rapidly advancing to the very front rank of his profession, her appreciation of his work, and sympathetic understanding of his aims and efforts, meant more to him than even the signal mark of royal favour, of which he had lately been the recipient.

Jane Champion had no close friends amongst the women of her set. Her lonely girlhood had bred in her an absolute frankness towards herself and other people which made it difficult for her to understand or tolerate the little artificialities of society, or the trivial weaknesses of her own sex. Women to whom she had shown special kindness—and they were many—maintained an attitude of grateful admiration in her presence, and of cowardly silence in her absence when she chanced to be under discussion.

But of men friends she had many, especially among a set of young fellows just through college, of whom she made particular chums; nice lads, who wrote to her of their college and mess-room scrapes, as they would never have dreamed of doing to their own mothers. She knew perfectly well that they called her "old Jane" and "pretty Jane" and "dearest Jane" amongst themselves, but she believed in the harmlessness of their fun and the genuineness of their affection, and gave them a generous amount of her own in return.

Jane Champion happened just now to be paying one of her long visits to Overdene, and was playing golf with a boy for whom she had long had a rod in pickle on this summer afternoon when the duchess went to cut blooms in her rose-garden. Only, as Jane found out, you cannot decorously lead up to a scolding if you are very keen on golf, and go golfing with a person who is equally enthusiastic, and who all the way to the links explains exactly how he played every hole the last time he went round, and all the way back gloats over, in retrospection, the way you and he have played every hole this time.

So Jane considered her afternoon, didactically, a failure. But, in the smoking-room that night, young Cathcart explained the game all over again to a few choice spirits, and then remarked: "Old Jane was superb! Fancy! Such a drive as that, and doing number seven in three and not talking about it! I've jolly well made up my mind to send no more bouquets to Tou-Tou. Hang it, boys! You can't see yourself at champagne suppers with a dancing-woman, when you've walked round the links, on a day like this, with the Honourable Jane. She drives like a rifle shot, and when she lofts, you'd think the ball was a swallow; and beat me three holes up and never mentioned it. By Jove, a fellow wants to have a clean bill when he shakes hands with her!"

CHAPTER III

The Surprise Packet

The sun-dial pointed to half past four o'clock. The hour of silence appeared to be over. The birds commenced twittering; and a cuckoo, in an adjacent wood, sounded his note at intervals.

The house awoke to sudden life. There was an opening and shutting of doors. Two footmen, in the mulberry and silver of the Meldrum livery, hurried down from the terrace, carrying folding tea-tables, with which they supplemented those of rustic oak standing permanently under the cedar. One promptly returned to the house; while the other remained behind, spreading snowy cloths over each table.

The macaw awoke, stretched his wings and flapped them twice, then sidled up and down his perch, concentrating his attention upon the footman.

"Mind!" he exclaimed suddenly, in the butler's voice, as a cloth, flung on too hurriedly, fluttered to the grass.

"Hold your jaw!" said the young footman irritably, flicking the bird with the table-cloth, and then glancing furtively at the rose-garden.

"Tommy wants a gooseberry!" shrieked the macaw, dodging the table-cloth and hanging, head downwards, from his perch.

"Don't you wish you may get it?" said the footman viciously.

"Give it him, somebody," remarked Tommy, in the duchess's voice.

The footman started, and looked over his shoulder; then hurriedly told Tommy just what he thought of him, and where he wished him; cuffed him soundly, and returned to the house, followed by peals of laughter, mingled with exhortations and imprecations from the angry bird, who danced up and down on his perch until his enemy had vanished from view.

A few minutes later the tables were spread with the large variety of eatables considered necessary at an English afternoon tea; the massive silver urn and teapots gleamed on the buffet-table, behind which the old butler presided; muffins, crumpets, cakes, and every kind of sandwich supplemented the dainty little rolled slices of white and brown bread-and-butter, while heaped-up bowls of freshly gathered strawberries lent a touch of colour to the artistic effect of white and silver. When all was ready, the butler raised his hand and sounded an old Chinese gong hanging in the cedar tree. Before the penetrating boom had died away, voices were heard in the distance from all over the grounds.

Up from the river, down from the tennis courts, out from house and garden, came the duchess's guests, rejoicing in the refreshing prospect of tea, hurrying to the welcome shade of the cedar;— charming women in white, carefully guarding their complexions beneath shady hats and pictur-esque parasols;—delightful girls, who had long ago sacrificed complexions to comfort, and now walked across the lawn bareheaded, swinging their rackets and discussing the last hard-fought set; men in flannels, sunburned and handsome, joining in the talk and laughter; praising their part-ners, while remaining unobtrusively silent as to their own achievements.

They made a picturesque group as they gathered

under the tree, subsiding with immense satisfaction into the low wicker chairs, or on to the soft turf, and helping themselves to what they pleased. When all were supplied with tea, coffee, or iced drinks, to their liking, conversation flowed again.

"So the duchess's concert comes off to-night," remarked someone. "I wish to goodness they would hang this tree with Chinese lanterns and have it out here. It is too hot to face a crowded function indoors."

"Oh, that's all right," said Garth Dalmain, "I'm stage-manager, you know; and I can promise you that all the long windows opening on to the terrace shall stand wide. So no one need be in the concert-room, who prefers to stop outside. There will be a row of lounge chairs placed on the terrace near the windows. You won't see much; but you will hear, perfectly."

"Ah, but half the fun is in seeing," exclaimed one of the tennis girls. "People who have remained on the terrace will miss all the point of it afterwards when the dear duchess shows us how everybody did it. I don't care how hot it is. Book me a seat in the front row!"

"Who is the surprise packet to-night?" asked Lady Ingleby, who had arrived since luncheon.

"Velma," said Mary Strathern. "She is coming for the week-end, and delightful it will be to have her. No one but the duchess could have worked it, and no place but Overdene would have tempted her. She will sing only one song at the concert; but she is sure to break forth later on, and give us plenty. We will persuade Jane to drift to the piano accidentally and play over, just by chance, the opening bars of some of Velma's best things, and we shall soon hear the magic voice. She never can resist a perfectly played accompaniment."

"Why call Madame Velma the 'surprise packet'?" asked a girl, to whom the Overdene "best parties" were a new experience.

"That, my dear," replied Lady Ingleby, "is a little joke of the duchess's. This concert is arranged for the amusement of her house party, and for the gratification and glorification of local celebrities. The whole neighbourhood is invited. None of you are asked to perform, but local celebrities are. In fact they furnish the entire programme, to their own delight, the satisfaction of their friends and relatives, and our entertainment, particularly afterwards when the duchess takes us through every item, with original notes, comments, and impersonations. Oh, Dal! Do you remember when she tucked a sheet of white writing-paper into her tea-gown for a dog collar, and took off the high-church curate nervously singing a comic song? Then at the very end, you see—and really some of it is quite good for amateurs—she trots out Velma, or some equally perfect artiste, to show them how it really can be done; and suddenly the place is full of music, and a great hush falls on the audience, and the poor complacent amateurs realise that the noise they have been making was, after all, not music; and they go dumbly home. But they have forgotten all about it by the following year; or a fresh contingent of willing performers steps into the breach. The duchess's little joke always comes off."

"The Honourable Jane does not approve of it," said young Ronald Ingram; "therefore she is generally given marching orders and departs to her next visit before the event. But no one can accompany Madame Velma so perfectly, so this time she is commanded to stay. But I doubt if the 'surprise packet' will come off with quite such a shock as usual, and I am certain the fun won't be so good afterwards. The Honourable Jane has been known to jump on the duchess for that sort of thing. She is safe to get the worst of it at the time, but it has a restraining effect afterwards."

"I think Miss Champion is quite right," said a bright-faced American girl, bravely, holding a gold spoon poised for a moment over the strawberry ice-cream with which Garth Dalmain had supplied her.

"In my country we should call it real mean to laugh at people who had been our guests and performed in our houses."

"In your country, my dear," said Myra Ingleby, "you have no duchesses."

"Well, we supply you with quite a good few,"

replied the American girl calmly, and went on with her ice.

A general laugh followed; and the latest Anglo-American match came up for discussion.

"Where is the Honourable Jane?" inquired someone presently.

"Golfing with Billy," said Ronald Ingram. "Ah, here they come."

Jane's tall figure was seen, walking along the terrace, accompanied by Billy Cathcart, talking eagerly. They put their clubs away in the lower hall; then came down the lawn together to the tea-tables.

Jane wore a tailor-made coat and skirt of grey tweed, a blue and white cambric shirt, starched linen collar and cuffs, a silk tie, and a soft felt hat with a few black quills in it. She walked with the freedom of movement and swing of limb which indicate great strength and a body well under control. Her appearance was extraordinarily unlike that of all the pretty and graceful women grouped beneath the cedar tree. And yet it was in no sense masculine—or, to use a more appropriate word, mannish; for everything strong is masculine; but a woman who apes an appearance of strength which she does not possess, is mannish;—rather was it so truly feminine that she could afford to adopt a severe simplicity of attire, which suited admirably the decided plainness of her features, and the almost massive proportions of her figure.

She stepped into the circle beneath the cedar, and took one of the half-dozen places immediately vacated by the men, with the complete absence of self-consciousness which always characterised her.

"What did you go round in, Miss Champion?" inquired one of the men.

"My ordinary clothes," replied Jane; quoting Punch, and evading the question.

But Billy burst out: "She went round in—"

"Oh, be quiet, Billy," interposed Jane. "You and I are practically the only golf maniacs present. Most of these dear people are even ignorant as to who 'bogie' is, or why we should be so proud of beating him. Where is my aunt? Poor Simmons was toddling all over the place when we went in to put away our clubs, searching for her with a telegram."

"Why didn't you open it?" asked Myra.

"Because my aunt never allows her telegrams to be opened. She loves shocks; and there is always the possibility of a telegram containing startling news. She says it completely spoils it if someone else knows it first, and breaks it to her gently."

"Here comes the duchess," said Garth Dalmain, who was sitting where he could see the little gate into the rose-garden.

"Do not mention the telegram," cautioned Jane. "It would not please her that I should even know of its arrival. It would be a shame to take any of the bloom off the unexpected delight of a wire on this hot day, when nothing unusual seemed likely to happen."

They turned and looked towards the duchess as she bustled across the lawn; this quaint old figure, who had called them together; who owned the lovely place where they were spending such delightful days; and whose odd whimsicalities had been so freely discussed while they drank her tea and feasted off her strawberries. The men rose as she approached, but not quite so spontaneously as they had done for her niece.

The duchess carried a large wooden basket filled to overflowing with exquisite roses. Every bloom was perfect, and each had been cut at exactly the right moment.

CHAPTER IV

Jane Volunteers

The duchess plumped down her basket in the middle of the strawberry table.

"There, good people!" she said, rather breathlessly. "Help yourselves, and let me see you all wearing roses to-night. And the concert-room is to be a bower of roses. We will call it *'La Fete des Roses.'* . . . No, thank you, Ronnie. That tea has been made half an hour at least, and you ought to love me too well to press it upon me. Besides, I never take tea. I have a whiskey and soda when I wake from my nap, and that sustains me until dinner. Oh yes, my dear Myra, I know I came to your interesting meeting, and signed that excellent pledge *'Pour Encourager les Autres'*; but I drove straight to my doctor when I left your house, and he gave me a certificate to say I *must* take something when I needed it; and I always need it when I wake from my nap. . . . Really, Dal, it is positively wicked for any man, off the stage, to look as picturesque as you do, in that pale violet shirt, and dark violet tie, and those white flannels. If I were your grandmother I should send you in to take them off. If you turn the heads of old dowagers such as I am, what chance have all these chickens? . . . Hush, Tommy! That was a very naughty word! And you need not be jealous of Dal. I admire you still more. Dal, will you paint my scarlet macaw?"

The young artist, whose portraits in that year's Academy had created much interest in the artistic world, and whose violet shirt had just been so severely censured, lay back in his lounge-chair, with his arms behind his head and a gleam of amusement in his bright brown eyes.

"No, dear Duchess," he said. "I beg respectfully to decline the commission, Tommy would require a Landseer to do full justice to his attitudes and expression. Besides, it would be demoralising to an innocent and well-brought-up youth, such as you know me to be, to spend long hours in Tommy's society, listening to the remarks that sweet bird would make while I painted him. But I will tell you what I will do. I will paint you, dear Duchess, only not in that hat! Ever since I was quite a small boy, a straw hat with black ribbons tied under the chin has made me feel ill. If I yielded to my natural impulses now, I should hide my face in Miss Champion's lap, and kick and scream until you took it off. I will paint you in the black velvet gown you wore last night, with the Medici collar; and the jolly arrangement of lace and diamonds on your head. And in your hand you shall hold an antique crystal mirror, mounted in silver."

The artist half closed his eyes, and as he described his picture in a voice full of music and mystery, an attentive hush fell upon the gay group around him. When Garth Dalmain described his pictures, people saw them. When they walked into the Academy or the New Gallery the following year, they would say: "Ah, there it is! just as we saw it that day, before a stroke of it was on the canvas."

"In your left hand, you shall hold the mirror, but you shall not be looking into it; because you never look into mirrors, dear Duchess, excepting to see whether the scolding you are giving your maid, as she stands behind you, is making her cry; and whether that is why she is being so clumsy in her manipulation of pins and things. If it is, you promptly promise her a day off, to go and see her old mother; and pay her journey there and back. If it isn't, you scold her some more. Were I the maid, I should always cry, large tears warranted to show in the glass; only I should not sniff, because sniffing is so intensely aggravating; and I should be most frightfully careful that my tears did not run down your neck."

"Dal, you ridiculous *child!*" said the duchess. "Leave off talking about my maids, and my neck, and your crocodile tears, and finish describing the portrait. What do I do, with the mirror?"

"You do not look into it," continued Garth Dalmain, meditatively; "because we *know* that is a thing you never do. Even when you put on that hat, and tie those ribbons—Miss Champion, I wish you would hold my hand—in a bow under your chin, you don't consult the mirror. But you shall sit with it in your left hand, your elbow resting on an Eastern table of black ebony inlaid with mother-of-pearl. You will turn it from you, so that it reflects something exactly in front of you in the imaginary foreground. You will be looking at this unseen object with an expression of sublime affection. And in the mirror I will paint a vivid, brilliant, complete reflection, minute, but perfect in every detail, of your scarlet macaw on his perch. We will call it 'Reflections,' because one must always give a silly up-to-date title to pictures, and just now one nondescript word is the fashion, unless you feel it needful to attract to yourself the eye of the public, in the catalogue, by calling your picture twenty lines of Tennyson. But when the portrait goes down to posterity as a famous picture, it will figure in the catalogue of the National Gallery as 'The Duchess, the Mirror, and the Macaw.'"

"Bravo!" said the duchess, delighted. "You shall paint it, Dal, in time for next year's Academy, and we will all go and see it."

And he did. And they all went. And when they saw it they said: "Ah, of course! There it is; just as we saw it under the cedar at Overdene."

"Here comes Simmons with something on a salver," exclaimed the duchess. "How that man waddles! Why can't somebody teach him to step out? Jane! You march across this lawn like a grenadier. Can't you explain to Simmons how it's done? . . . Well? What is it? Ha! A telegram. Now what horrible thing can have happened? Who would like to guess? I hope it is not merely some idiot who has missed a train."

Amid a breathless and highly satisfactory silence, the duchess tore open the orange envelope.

Apparently the shock was of a thorough, though not enjoyable, kind; for the duchess, at all times highly coloured, became purple as she read, and absolutely inarticulate with indignation. Jane rose quietly, looked over her aunt's shoulder, read the long message, and returned to her seat.

"Creature!" exclaimed the duchess, at last. "Oh, creature! This comes of asking them as friends. And I had a lovely string of pearls for her, worth far more than she would have been offered, professionally, for one song. And to fail at the last minute! Oh, *creature!*"

"Dear aunt," said Jane, "if poor Madame Velma has a sudden attack of laryngitis, she could not possibly sing a note, even had the Queen commanded her. Her telegram is full of regrets."

"Don't argue, Jane!" exclaimed the duchess, crossly. "And don't drag in the Queen, who has nothing to do with my concert or Velma's throat. I do abominate irrelevance, and you know it! *Why* must she have her what-do-you-call-it, just when she was coming to sing here? In my young days people never had these new-fangled complaints. I have no patience with all this appendicitis and what not—cutting people open at every possible excuse. In my young days we called it a good old-fashioned stomach-ache, and gave them Turkey rhubarb!"

Myra Ingleby hid her face behind her garden hat; and Garth Dalmain whispered to Jane: "I do abominate irrelevance, and you know it!" But Jane shook her head at him, and refused to smile.

"Tommy wants a gooseberry!" shouted the

macaw, having apparently noticed the mention of rhubarb.

"Oh, give it him, somebody!" said the worried duchess.

"Dear aunt," said Jane, "there are no gooseberries."

"Don't argue, girl!" cried the duchess, furiously; and Garth, delighted, shook his head at Jane. "When he says 'gooseberry,' he means anything *green,* as you very well know!"

Half a dozen people hastened to Tommy with lettuce, water-cress, and cucumber sandwiches; and Garth picked one blade of grass, and handed it to Jane with an air of anxious solicitude; but Jane ignored it.

"No answer, Simmons," said the duchess. "Why don't you go? . . . Oh, how that man waddles! Teach him to walk, somebody! Now the question is, What is to be done? Here is half the county coming to hear Velma, by my invitation; and Velma in London pretending to have appendicitis—no, I mean the other thing. Oh, 'drat the woman!' as that clever bird would say."

"Hold your jaw!" shouted Tommy. The duchess smiled, and consented to sit down.

"But, dear Duchess," suggested Garth in his most soothing voice, "the county does not know Madame Velma was to be here. It was a profound secret. You were to trot her out at the end. Lady Ingleby called her your 'surprise packet.'"

Myra came out from behind her garden hat, and the duchess nodded at her approvingly.

"Quite true," she said. "That was the lovely part of it. Oh, creature!"

"But, dear Duchess," pursued Garth persuasively, "if the county did not know, the county will not be disappointed. They are coming to listen to one another, and to hear themselves, and to enjoy your claret-cup and ices. All this they will do, and go away delighted, saying how cleverly the dear duchess discovers and exploits local talent."

"Ah, ha!" said the duchess, with a gleam in the hawk eye, and a raising of the hooked nose—which Mrs. Parker Bangs of Chicago, who had met the duchess once or twice, described as "genuine Plantagenet"—"but they will go away wise in their own conceits, and satisfied with their own mediocre performances. My idea is to let them do it, and then show them how it should be done."

"But Aunt 'Gina," said Jane, gently; "surely you forget that most of these people have been to town and heard plenty of good music, Madame Velma herself most likely, and all the great singers. They know they cannot sing like a prima donna; but they do their anxious best, because you ask them. I cannot see that they require an object lesson."

"Jane," said the duchess, "for the third time this afternoon I must request you not to argue."

"Miss Champion," said Garth Dalmain, "if I

were your grandmamma, I should send you to bed."

"What is to be done?" reiterated the duchess. "She was to sing *The Rosary*. I had set my heart on it. The whole decoration of the room is planned to suit that song—festoons of white roses; and a great red-cross at the back of the platform, made entirely of crimson ramblers. Jane!"

"Yes, aunt."

"Oh, don't say 'Yes, aunt,' in that senseless way! Can't you make some suggestion?"

"Drat the woman!" exclaimed Tommy, suddenly.

"Hark to that sweet bird!" cried the duchess, her good humour fully restored. "Give him a strawberry, somebody. Now, Jane, what do you suggest?"

Jane Champion was seated with her broad back half turned to her aunt, one knee crossed over the other, her large, capable hands clasped round it. She loosed her hands, turned slowly round, and looked into the keen eyes peering at her from under the mushroom hat. As she read the half-resentful, half-appealing demand in them, a slow smile dawned in her own. She waited a moment to make sure of the duchess's meaning, then said quietly: "I will sing *The Rosary* for you, in Velma's place, to-night, if you really wish it, aunt."

Had the gathering under the tree been a party of

"mere people," it would have gasped. Had it been a "freak party," it would have been loud-voiced in its expressions of surprise. Being a "best party," it gave no outward sign; but a sense of blank astonishment, purely mental, was in the air. The duchess herself was the only person present who had heard Jane Champion sing.

"Have you the song?" asked her Grace of Meldrum, rising, and picking up her telegram and empty basket.

"I have," said Jane. "I spent a few hours with Madame Blanche when I was in town last month; and she, who so rarely admires these modern songs, was immensely taken with it. She sang it, and allowed me to accompany her. We spent nearly an hour over it. I obtained a copy afterwards."

"Good," said the duchess. "Then I count on you. Now I must send a sympathetic telegram to that poor dear Velma, who will be fretting at having to fail us. So 'au revoir,' good people. Remember, we dine punctually at eight o'clock. Music is supposed to begin at nine. Ronnie, be a kind boy, and carry Tommy into the hall for me. He will screech so fearfully if he sees me walk away without him. He is so very loving, dear bird!"

Silence under the cedar.

Most people were watching young Ronald, holding the stand as much at arm's length as possible; while Tommy, keeping his balance wonderfully, sidled up close to him, evidently making confidential remarks into Ronnie's terrified ear. The duchess walked on before, quite satisfied with the new turn events had taken.

One or two people were watching Jane.

"It is very brave of you," said Myra Ingleby, at length. "I would offer to play your accompaniment, dear; but I can only manage *Au Clair de la Lune*, and *Three Blind Mice*, with one finger."

"And I would offer to play your accompaniment, dear," said Garth Dalmain, "if you were going to sing Lassen's *Allerseelen*, for I play that quite beautifully with ten fingers! It is an education only to hear the way I bring out the tolling of the cemetery chapel bell right through the song. The poor thing with the bunch of purple heather can never get away from it. Even in the grand crescendo, appassionata, fortissimo, when they discover that 'in death's dark valley this is Holy Day,' I give them no holiday from that bell. I don't know what it did 'once in May.' It tolls all the time, with maddening persistence, in my accompaniment. But I have seen *The Rosary*, and I dare not face those chords. To begin with, you start in every known flat; and before you have gone far you have gathered unto yourself handfuls of known and unknown sharps, to which you cling, not daring to let them go, lest they should be wanted again the next moment. Alas, no! When it is a question of accompanying *The Rosary*, I must say, as the old farmer at the tenants' dinner the other day said to the duchess when she pressed upon him a third helping of pudding: 'Madam, I *cannot!*' "

"Don't be silly, Dal," said Jane. "You could accompany *The Rosary* perfectly, if I wanted it done. But, as it happens, I prefer accompanying myself."

"Ah," said Lady Ingleby, sympathetically, "I quite understand that. It would be such a relief all the time to know that if things seemed going wrong, you could stop the other part, and give yourself the note."

The only two real musicians present glanced at each other, and a gleam of amusement passed between them.

"It certainly would be useful, if necessary," said Jane.

"*I* would 'stop the other part' and 'give you the note,'" said Garth, demurely.

"I am sure you would," said Jane. "You are always so very kind. But I prefer to keep the matter in my own hands."

"You realise the difficulty of making the voice carry in a place of that size unless you can stand and face the audience?" Garth Dalmain spoke anxiously. Jane was a special friend of his, and he had a man's dislike of the idea of his chum failing in anything, publicly.

The same quiet smile dawned in Jane's eyes and

passed to her lips as when she had realised that her aunt meant her to volunteer in Velma's place. She glanced around. Most of the party had wandered off in twos and threes, some to the house, others back to the river. She and Dal and Myra were practically alone. Her calm eyes were full of quiet amusement as she steadfastly met the anxious look in Garth's, and answered his question.

"Yes, I know. But the acoustic properties of the room are very perfect, and I have learned to throw my voice. Perhaps you may not know—in fact, how should you know?—but I have had the immense privilege of studying with Madame Marchesi in Paris, and of keeping up to the mark since by an occasional delightful hour with her no less gifted daughter in London. So I ought to know all there is to know about the management of a voice, if I have at all adequately availed myself of such golden opportunities."

These quiet words were Greek to Myra, conveying no more to her mind than if Jane had said: "I have been learning Tonic sol-fa." In fact, not quite so much, seeing that Lady Ingleby had herself once tried to master the Tonic sol-fa system in order to instruct her men and maids in part-singing. It was at a time when she owned a distinctly musical household. The second footman possessed a fine barytone. The butler could "do a little bass," which is to say that, while the other parts soared to higher regions, he could stay on the bottom note if carefully placed there, and told to remain. The head housemaid sang what she called "seconds"; in other words, she followed along, slightly behind the trebles as regarded time, and a major third below them as regarded pitch. The housekeeper, a large, dark person with a fringe on her upper lip, unshaven and unashamed, produced a really remarkable effect by singing the air an octave below the trebles. Unfortunately Lady Ingleby was apt to confuse her with the butler. Myra herself was the first to admit that she had not "much ear"; but it was decidedly trying, at a moment when she dared not remove her eyes from the accompaniment of Good King Wenceslas, to have called out: "Stay where you are, Jenkins!" and then find it was Mrs. Jarvis who had been travelling upwards. But when a new footman, engaged by Lord Ingleby with no reference to his musical gifts, chanced to possess a fine throaty tenor, Myra felt she really had material with which great things might be accomplished, and decided herself to learn the Tonic sol-fa system. She easily mastered mi, re, do, and so, fa, fa, mi, because these represented the opening lines of *Three Blind Mice*, always a musical landmark to Myra. But when it came to the fugue-like intricacies in the theme of "They all ran after the farmer's wife," Lady Ingleby was lost without the words to cling to, and gave up the Tonic sol-fa system in despair.

So the name of the greatest teacher of singing of this age did not convey much to Myra's mind. But Garth Dalmain sat up.

"I say! No wonder you take it coolly. Why, Velma herself was a pupil of the great madame."

"That is how it happens that I know her rather well," said Jane. "I am here to-day because I was to have played her accompaniment."

"I see," said Garth. "And now you have to do both. 'Land's sake!' as Mrs. Parker Bangs says when you explain who's who at a Marlborough House garden party. But you prefer playing other people's accompaniments, to singing yourself, don't you?"

Jane's slow smile dawned again.

"I prefer singing," she said, "but accompanying is more useful."

"Of course it is," said Garth. "Heaps of people can sing a little, but very few can accompany properly."

"Jane," said Myra, her grey eyes looking out lazily from under their long black lashes, "if you have had singing lessons, and know some songs, why hasn't the duchess turned you on to sing to us before this?"

"For a sad reason," Jane replied. "You know her only son died eight years ago? He was such a handsome, talented fellow. He and I inherited our love of music from our grandfather. My cousin got into a musical set at college, studied with enthu-

41

siasm, and wanted to take it up professionally. He had promised, one Christmas vacation, to sing at a charity concert in town, and went out, when only just recovering from influenza, to fulfil this engagement. He had a relapse, double pneumonia set in, and he died in five days from heart failure. My poor aunt was frantic with grief; and since then any mention of my love of music makes her very bitter. I, too, wanted to take it up professionally, but she put her foot down heavily. I scarcely ever venture to sing or play here."

"Why not elsewhere?" asked Garth Dalmain. "We have stayed about at the same houses, and I had not the faintest idea you sang."

"I do not know," said Jane slowly. "But—music means so much to me. It is a sort of holy of holies in the tabernacle of one's inner being. And it is not easy to lift the veil."

"The veil will be lifted to-night," said Myra Ingleby.

"Yes," agreed Jane, smiling a little ruefully, "I suppose it will."

"And we shall pass in," said Garth Dalmain.

CHAPTER V

Confidences

The shadows silently lengthened on the lawn.

The home-coming rooks circled and cawed around the tall elm trees.

The sun-dial pointed to six o'clock.

Myra Ingleby rose and stood with the slanting rays of the sun full in her eyes, her arms stretched over her head. The artist noted every graceful line of her willowy figure.

"Ah, bah!" she yawned. "It is so perfect out here, and I must go in to my maid. Jane, be advised in time. Do not ever begin facial massage. You become a slave to it, and it takes up hours of your day. Look at me."

They were both looking already. Myra was worth looking at.

"For ordinary dressing purposes, I need not have gone in until seven; and now I must lose this last, perfect hour."

"What happens?" asked Jane. "I know nothing of the process."

"I can't go into details," replied Lady Ingleby, "but you know how sweet I have looked all day? Well, if I did not go to my maid now, I should look less sweet by the end of dinner, and at the close of the evening I should appear ten years older."

"You would always look sweet," said Jane, with frank sincerity; "and why mind looking the age you are?"

"My dear, 'a man is as old as he feels; a woman is as old as she looks,' " quoted Myra.

"I *feel* just seven," said Garth.

"And you *look* seventeen," laughed Myra.

"And I *am* twenty-seven," retorted Garth; "so the duchess should not call me 'a ridiculous child.' And, dear lady, if curtailing this mysterious process is going to make you one whit less lovely to-night, I do beseech you to hasten to your maid, or you will spoil my whole evening. I shall burst into tears at dinner, and the duchess hates scenes, as you very well know!"

Lady Ingleby flapped him with her garden hat as she passed.

"Be quiet, you ridiculous child!" she said. "You had no business to listen to what I was saying to Jane. You shall paint me this autumn. And after that I will give up facial massage, and go abroad, and come back quite old."

She flung this last threat over her shoulder as she trailed away across the lawn.

"How lovely she is!" commented Garth, gazing after her. "How much of that was true, do you suppose, Miss Champion?"

"I have not the slightest idea," replied Jane. "I am completely ignorant on the subject of facial massage."

"Not much, I should think," continued Garth, "or she would not have told us."

"Ah, you are wrong there," replied Jane, quickly. "Myra is extraordinarily honest, and always inclined to be frank about herself and her foibles. She had a curious upbringing. She is one of a large family, and was always considered the black sheep, not so much by her brothers and sisters, as by her mother. Nothing she was, or said, or did, was ever right. When Lord Ingleby met her, and I suppose saw her incipient possibilities, she was a tall, gawky girl, with lovely eyes, a sweet, sensitive mouth, and a what-on-earth-am-I-going-to-do-next expression on her face. He was twenty years her senior, but fell most determinedly in love with her and, though her mother pressed upon him all her other daughters in turn, he would have Myra or nobody. When he proposed to her it was impossible at first to make her understand what he meant. His meaning dawned on her at length, and he was not kept waiting long for her answer. I have often heard him tease her about it. She looked at him with an adorable smile, her eyes brimming over with tears, and said: 'Why, of course. I'll marry you *gratefully,* and I think it is perfectly sweet of you to like me. But what a blow for mamma!' They were married with as little delay as possible, and he took her off to Paris, Italy, and Egypt, had six months abroad, and brought her back—this! I was staying with them once, and her mother was also there. We were sitting in the morning room,—no men, just half a dozen women,—and her mother began finding fault about something, and said: 'Has not Lord Ingleby often told you of it?' Myra looked up in her sweet, lazy way and answered: 'Dear mamma, I know it must seem strange to you, but, do you know, my husband thinks everything I do perfect.' 'Your husband is a fool!' snapped her mother. 'From *your* point of view, dear mamma,' said Myra, sweetly."

"Old curmudgeon!" remarked Garth. "Why are people of that sort allowed to be called 'mothers'? We, who have had tender, perfect mothers, would like to make it law that the other kind should always be called 'she-parents,' or 'female progenitors,' or any other descriptive title, but not profane the sacred name of mother!"

Jane was silent. She knew the beautiful story of Garth's boyhood with his widowed mother. She knew his passionate adoration of her sainted memory. She liked him best when she got a glimpse beneath the surface, and did not wish to check his mood by reminding him that she herself had never even lisped that name.

Garth rose from his chair and stretched his slim figure in the slanting sun-rays, much as Myra had done. Jane looked at him. As is often the case with plain people, great physical beauty appealed to her strongly. She only allowed to that appeal its right proportion in her estimation of her friends. Garth Dalmain by no means came first among her particular chums. He was older than most of them, and yet in some ways younger than any, and his remarkable youthfulness of manner and exuberance of spirits sometimes made him appear foolish to Jane, whose sense of humour was of a more sedate kind. But of the absolute perfection of his outward appearance, there was no question; and Jane looked at him now, much as his own mother might have looked, with honest admiration in her kind eyes.

Garth, notwithstanding the pale violet shirt and dark violet tie, was quite unconscious of his own appearance; and, dazzled by the golden sunlight, was also unconscious of Jane's look.

"Oh, I say, Miss Champion!" he cried, boyishly. "Isn't it nice that they have all gone in? I have been wanting a good jaw with you. Really, when we all get together we do drivel sometimes, to keep the ball rolling. It is like patting up air-balls; and very often they burst, and one realises that an empty, shrivelled little skin is all that is left after most conversations. Did you ever buy air-balls at Brighton? Do you remember the wild excitement of seeing the man coming along the parade, with a huge bunch of them—blue, green, red, white, and yellow, all shining in the sun? And one used to wonder how he ever contrived to pick them all up—I don't know how!—and what would happen if he put them all down. I always knew exactly which one I wanted, and it was generally on a very inside string and took a long time to disentangle. And how maddening it was if the grown-ups grew tired of waiting, and walked on with the penny. Only I would rather have had none, than not have the one on which I had fixed my heart. Wouldn't you?"

"I never bought air-balls at Brighton," replied Jane, without enthusiasm. Garth was feeling seven again, and Jane was feeling bored.

For once he seemed conscious of this. He took his coat from the back of the chair where he had hung it, and put it on.

"Come along, Miss Champion," he said; "I am so tired of doing nothing. Let us go down to the river and find a boat or two. Dinner is not until eight o'clock, and I am certain you can dress, even for the *role* of Velma, in half an hour. I have known you do it in ten minutes, at a pinch. There is ample time for me to row you within sight of the minster, and we can talk as we go. Ah, fancy! the grey old minster with this sunset behind it, and a field of cowslips in the fore-ground!"

But Jane did not rise.

"My dear Dal," she said, "you would not feel much enthusiasm for the minster or the sunset, after you had pulled my twelve stone odd up the river. You would drop exhausted among the cowslips. Surely you might know by now that I am not the sort of person to be told off to sit in the stern of a tiny skiff and steer. If I am in a boat, I like to row; and if I row, I prefer rowing stroke. But I do not want to row now, because I have been playing golf the whole afternoon. And you know perfectly well it would be no pleasure to you to have to gaze at me all the way up and all the way down the river; knowing all the time, that I was mentally criticising your stroke and marking the careless way you feathered."

Garth sat down, lay back in his chair, with his arms behind his sleek dark head, and looked at her with his soft shining eyes, just as he had looked at the duchess.

"How cross you are, old chap," he said, gently. "What is the matter?"

Jane laughed and held out her hand. "Oh, you dear boy! I think you have the sweetest temper in the world. I won't be cross any more. The truth is, I hate the duchess's concerts, and I don't like being the duchess's 'surprise-packet.'"

"I see," said Garth, sympathetically. "But, that being so, why did you offer?"

"Ah, I had to," said Jane. "Poor old dear! She so rarely asks me anything, and her eyes besought. Don't you know how one longs to have something to do for someone who belongs to one? I would black her boots if she wished it. But it is so hard to stay here, week after week, and be kept at arm's length. This one thing she asked of me, and her proud old eyes pleaded. Could I refuse?"

Garth was all sympathy. "No, dear," he said thoughtfully; "of course you couldn't. And don't bother over that silly joke about the 'surprise packet.' You see, you won't be that. I have no doubt you sing vastly better than most of them, but they will not realise it. It takes a Velma to make such people as these sit up. They will think *The Rosary* a pretty song, and give you a mild clap, and there the thing will end. So don't worry."

Jane sat and considered this. Then: "Dal," she said, "I do hate singing before that sort of audience. It is like giving them your soul to look at, and you don't want them to see it. It seems indecent. To my mind, music is the most *revealing* thing in the world. I shiver when I think of that song, and yet I daren't do less than my best. When the moment comes, I shall live in the song, and forget the audience. Let me tell you a lesson I once had from Madame Blanche. I was singing Bemberg's *Chant Hindou*, the passionate prayer of an Indian woman to Brahma. I began: *'Brahma! Dieu des croyants,'* and sang it as I might have sung *'do, re, mi.'* Brahma was nothing to me. 'Stop!' cried Madame Blanche in her most imperious manner. 'Ah, vous Anglais! What are you doing? *Brahma*, c'est un Dieu! He may not be *your* God. He may not be *my* God. But he is some-

50

body's God. He is the God of the song. Ecoutez!' And she lifted her head and sang: 'Brahma! Dieu des croyants! Maitre des cites saintes!' with her beautiful brow illumined, and a passion of religious fervour which thrilled one's soul. It was a lesson I never forgot. I can honestly say I have never sung a song tamely, since."

"Fine!" said Garth Dalmain. "I like enthusiasm in every branch of art. I never care to paint a portrait, unless I adore the woman I am painting."

Jane smiled. The conversation was turning exactly the way she had hoped eventually to lead it.

"Dal, dear," she said, "you adore so many in turn, that we old friends, who have your real interest at heart, fear you will never adore to any definite purpose."

Garth laughed. "Oh bother!" he said. "Are you like all the rest? Do you also think adoration and admiration must necessarily mean marriage. I should have expected you to take a saner and more masculine view."

"My dear boy," said Jane, "your friends have decided that you need a wife. You are alone in the world. You have a lovely home. You are in a fair way to be spoiled by all the silly women who run after you. Of course we are perfectly aware that your wife must have every incomparable beauty under the sun united in her own exquisite person. But each new divinity you see and paint appar-

51

ently fulfils, for the time being, this wondrous ideal; and, perhaps, if you wedded one, instead of painting her, she might continue permanently to fulfil it."

Garth considered this in silence, his level brows knitted. At last he said: "Beauty is so much a thing of the surface. I see it, and admire it. I desire it, and paint it. When I have painted it, I have made it my own, and somehow I find I have done with it. All the time I am painting a woman, I am seeking for her soul. I want to express it on my canvas; and do you know, Miss Champion, I find that a lovely woman does not always have a lovely soul."

Jane was silent. The last things she wished to discuss were other women's souls.

"There is just one who seems to me perfect," continued Garth. "I am to paint her this autumn. I believe I shall find her soul as exquisite as her body."

"And she is—?" inquired Jane.

"Lady Brand."

"Flower!" exclaimed Jane. "Are *you* so taken with Flower?"

"Ah, she is lovely," said Garth, with reverent enthusiasm. "It positively is not right for any one to be so absolutely flawlessly lovely. It makes me ache. Do you know that feeling, Miss Champion, of perfect loveliness making you ache?"

"No, I don't," said Jane, shortly. "And I do not

think other people's wives ought to have that effect upon you."

"My dear old chap," exclaimed Garth, astonished; "it has nothing to do with wives or no wives. A wood of bluebells in morning sunshine would have precisely the same effect. I ache to paint her. When I have painted her and really done justice to that matchless loveliness as I see it, I shall feel all right. At present I have only painted her from memory; but she is to sit to me in October."

"From memory?" questioned Jane.

"Yes, I paint a great deal from memory. Give me one look of a certain kind at a face, let me see it at a moment which lets one penetrate beneath the surface, and I can paint that face from memory weeks after. Lots of my best studies have been done that way. Ah, the delight of it! Beauty—the worship of beauty is to me a religion."

"Rather a godless form of religion," suggested Jane.

"Ah no," said Garth reverently. "All true beauty comes from God, and leads back to God. 'Every good gift and every perfect gift is from above, and cometh down from the Father of lights.' I once met an old freak who said all sickness came from the devil. I never could believe that, for my mother was an invalid during the last years of her life, and I can testify that her sickness was a blessing to many, and borne to the glory of God.

But I am convinced all true beauty is God-given, and that is why the worship of beauty is to me a religion. Nothing bad was ever truly beautiful; nothing good is ever really ugly."

Jane smiled as she watched him, lying back in the golden sunlight, the very personification of manly beauty. The absolute lack of self-consciousness, either for himself or for her, which allowed him to talk thus to the plainest woman of his acquaintance, held a vein of humour which diverted Jane. It appealed to her more than buying coloured air-balls, or screaming because the duchess wore a mushroom hat.

"Then are plain people to be denied their share of goodness, Dal?" she asked.

"Plainness is not ugliness," replied Garth Dalmain simply. "I learned that when quite a small boy. My mother took me to hear a famous preacher. As he sat on the platform during the pre-liminaries he seemed to me quite the ugliest man I had ever seen. He reminded me of a grotesque gorilla, and I dreaded the moment when he should rise up and face us and give out a text. It seemed to me there ought to be bars between, and that we should want to throw nuts and oranges. But when he rose to speak, his face was transfigured. Goodness and inspiration shone from it, making it as the face of an angel. I never again thought him ugly. The beauty of his soul shone through, trans-figuring his body. Child though I was, I could differentiate even then between ugliness and plainness. When he sat down at the close of his magnificent sermon, I no longer thought him a complicated form of chimpanzee. I remembered the divine halo of his smile. Of course his actual plainness of feature remained. It was not the sort of face one could have wanted to live with, or to have day after day opposite to one at table. But then one was not called to that sort of discipline, which would have been martyrdom to me. And he has always stood to my mind since as a proof of the truth that goodness is never ugly; and that divine love and aspiration shining through the plainest features may redeem them temporarily into beauty; and, permanently, into a thing one loves to remember."

"I see," said Jane. "It must have often helped you to a right view to have realised that so long ago. But now let us return to the important question of the face which you *are* to have daily opposite you at table. It cannot be Lady Brand's, nor can it be Myra's; but, you know, Dal, a very lovely one is being suggested for the position."

"No names, please," said Garth, quickly. "I object to girls' names being mentioned in this sort of conversation."

"Very well, dear boy. I understand and respect your objection. You have made her famous already by your impressionist portrait of her, and I hear you are to do a more elaborate picture 'in the fall.' Now, Dal, you know you admire her immensely. She is lovely, she is charming, she hails from the land whose women, when they possess charm, unite with it a freshness and a piquancy which place them beyond compare. In some ways you are so unique yourself that you ought to have a wife with a certain amount of originality. Now, I hardly know how far the opinion of your friends would influence you in such a matter, but you may like to hear how fully they approve your very open allegiance to—shall we say—the beautiful 'Stars and Stripes'?"

Garth Dalmain took out his cigarette case, carefully selected a cigarette, and sat with it between his fingers in absorbed contemplation.

"Smoke," said Jane.

"Thanks," said Garth. He struck a match and very deliberately lighted his cigarette. As he flung away the vesta the breeze caught it and it fell on the lawn, flaming brightly. Garth sprang up and extinguished it, then drew his chair more exactly opposite to Jane's and lay back, smoking meditatively, and watching the little rings he blew mount into the cedar branches, expand, fade, and vanish.

Jane was watching him. The varied and characteristic ways in which her friends lighted and smoked their cigarettes always interested Jane. There were at least a dozen young men of whom she could have given the names upon hearing a description of their method. Also, she had learned from Deryck Brand the value of silences in an important conversation, and the art of not weakening a statement by a postscript.

At last Garth spoke.

"I wonder why the smoke is that lovely pale blue as it curls up from the cigarette, and a greyish-white if one blows it out."

Jane knew it was because it had become impregnated with moisture, but she did not say so, having no desire to contribute her quota of pats to this airball, or to encourage the superficial workings of his mind just then. She quietly awaited the response to her appeal to his deeper nature which she felt certain would be forthcoming. Presently it came.

"It is awfully good of you, Miss Champion, to take the trouble to think all this and to say it to me. May I prove my gratitude by explaining for once where my difficulty lies? I have scarcely defined it to myself, and yet I believe I can express it to you." Another long silence. Garth smoked and pondered.

Jane waited. It was a very comprehending, very companionable silence. Garth found himself parodying the last lines of an old sixteenth-century song:

"Then ever pray that heaven may send
Such weeds, such chairs, and such a friend."

Either the cigarette, or the chair, or Jane, or perhaps all three combined were producing in him a sublime sense of calm, and rest, and well-being; an uplifting of spirit which made all good things seem better; all difficult things, easy; and all ideals, possible. The silence, like the sunset, was golden; but at last he broke it.

"Two women—the only two women who have ever really been in my life—form for me a standard below which I cannot fall,—one, my mother, a sacred and ideal memory; the other, old Margery Graem, my childhood's friend and nurse, now my housekeeper and general tender and mender. Her faithful heart and constant remembrance help to keep me true to the ideal of that sweet presence which faded from beside me when I stood on the threshold of manhood. Margery lives at Castle Gleneesh. When I return home, the sight which first meets my eyes as the hall door opens is old Margery in her black satin apron, lawn kerchief, and lavender ribbons. I always feel seven then, and I always hug her. You, Miss Champion, don't like me when I feel seven; but Margery does. Now, this is what I want you to realise. When I bring a bride to Gleneesh and present her to Margery, the kind old eyes will try to see nothing but good; the faithful old heart will yearn to love and serve. And yet I shall know she knows the standard, just as I know it; I shall know she remembers the ideal of gentle, tender, Christian womanhood, just as I remember it; and I must not, I dare not, fall short. Believe me, Miss Champion, more than once, when physical attraction has been strong, and I have been tempted in the worship of the outward loveliness to disregard or forget the essentials,—the things which are unseen but eternal,—then, all unconscious of exercising any such influence, old Margery's clear eyes look into mine, old Margery's mittened hand seems to rest upon my coat sleeve, and the voice which has guided me from infancy, says, in gentle astonishment: 'Is this your choice, Master Garthie, to fill my dear lady's place?' No doubt, Miss Champion, it will seem almost absurd to you when you think of our set and our sentiments, and the way we racket round that I should sit here on the duchess's lawn and confess that I have been held back from proposing marriage to the women I have most admired, because of what would have been my old nurse's opinion of them! But you must remember her opinion is formed by a memory, and that memory is the memory of my dead mother. Moreover, Margery voices my best self, and expresses my own judgment when it is not blinded by passion or warped by my worship of the beautiful. Not that Margery would disapprove of loveliness; in fact, she would approve of nothing else for me, I know very well. But her penetration rapidly goes beneath the surface. According to one of Paul's sublime paradoxes, she looks at the things that are not seen. It seems queer that I can tell you all this, Miss Champion, and really it is the first time I have actually formulated it in my own mind. But I think it so extremely friendly of you to have troubled to give me good advice in the matter."

Garth Dalmain ceased speaking, and the silence which followed suddenly assumed alarming proportions, seeming to Jane like a high fence which she was vainly trying to scale. She found herself mentally rushing hither and thither, seeking a gate or any possible means of egress. And still she was confronted by the difficulty of replying adequately to the totally unexpected. And what added to her dumbness was the fact that she was infinitely touched by Garth's confession; and when Jane was deeply moved speech always became difficult. That this young man—adored by all the girls for his good looks and delightful manners; pursued for his extreme eligibility by mothers and chaperons; famous already in the world of art; flattered, courted, sought after in society—should calmly admit that the only woman really left *in* his life was his old nurse, and that her opinion and expectations held him back from a worldly, or unwise marriage, touched Jane deeply, even while in her heart she smiled at what their set would say could they realise the situation. It revealed Garth in a new light; and suddenly Jane understood him, as she had not understood him before.

And yet the only reply she could bring herself to frame was: "I wish I knew old Margery."

Garth's brown eyes flashed with pleasure.

"Ah, I wish you did," he said. "And I should like you to see Castle Gleneesh. You would enjoy the view from the terrace, sheer into the gorge, and away across the purple hills. And I think you would like the pine woods and the moor. I say, Miss Champion, why should not *I* get up a 'best party' in September, and implore the duchess to come and chaperon it? And then you could come, and any one else you would like asked. And—and, perhaps—we might ask—the beautiful 'Stars and Stripes,' and her aunt, Mrs. Parker Bangs of Chicago; and then we should see what Margery thought of her!"

"Delightful!" said Jane. "I would come with pleasure. And really, Dal, I think that girl has a sweet nature. Could you do better? The exterior is perfect, and surely the soul is there. Yes, ask us all, and see what happens."

"I will," cried Garth, delighted. "And what will Margery think of Mrs. Parker Bangs?"

"Never mind," said Jane decidedly. "When you marry the niece, the aunt goes back to Chicago."

"And I wish her people were not millionaires."

"That can't be helped," said Jane. "Americans are so charming, that we really must not mind their money."

"I wish Miss Lister and her aunt were here,"

remarked Garth. "But they are to be at Lady Ingleby's, where I am due next Tuesday. Do you come on there, Miss Champion?"

"I do," replied Jane. "I go to the Brands for a few days on Tuesday, but I have promised Myra to turn up at Shenstone for the week-end. I like staying there. They are such a harmonious couple."

"Yes," said Garth, "but no one could help being a harmonious couple, who had married Lady Ingleby."

"What grammar!" laughed Jane. "But I know what you mean, and I am glad you think so highly of Myra. She is a dear! Only do make haste and paint her and get her off your mind, so as to be free for Pauline Lister."

The sun-dial pointed to seven o'clock. The rooks had circled round the elms and dropped contentedly into their nests.

"Let us go in," said Jane, rising. "I am glad we have had this talk," she added, as he walked beside her across the lawn.

"Yes," said Garth. "Air-balls weren't in it! It was a football this time—good solid leather. And we each kicked one goal,—a tie, you know. For your advice went home to me, and I think my reply showed you the true lie of things; eh, Miss Champion?"

He was feeling seven again; but Jane saw him now through old Margery's glasses, and it did not annoy her.

"Yes," she said, smiling at him with her kind, true eyes; "we will consider it a tie, and surely it will prove a tie to our friendship. Thank you, Dal, for all you have told me."

Arrived in her room, Jane found she had half an hour to spare before dressing. She took out her diary. Her conversation with Garth Dalmain seemed worth recording, particularly his story of the preacher whose beauty of soul redeemed the ugliness of his body. She wrote it down verbatim.

Then she rang for her maid, and dressed for dinner, and the concert which should follow.

CHAPTER VI

The Veil Is Lifted

"MISS CHAMPION! Oh, here you are! Your turn next, please. The last item of the local programme is in course of performance, after which the duchess explains Velma's laryngitis—let us hope she will not call it 'appendicitis'—and then I usher you up. Are you ready?"

Garth Dalmain, as master of ceremonies, had sought Jane Champion on the terrace, and stood before her in the soft light of the hanging Chinese lanterns. The crimson rambler in his button-hole, and his red silk socks, which matched it, lent an artistic touch of colour to the conventional black and white of his evening clothes.

Jane looked up from the comfortable depths of her wicker chair; then smiled at his anxious face.

"I am ready," she said, and rising, walked beside him. "Has it gone well?" she asked. "Is it a good audience?"

"Packed," replied Garth, "and the duchess has enjoyed herself. It has been funnier than usual. But now comes the event of the evening. I say, where is your score?"

"Thanks," said Jane. "I shall play it from memory. It obviates the bother of turning over."

They passed into the concert-room and stood behind screens and a curtain, close to the half-dozen steps leading, from the side, up on to the platform.

"Oh, hark to the duchess!" whispered Garth. " '*My niece, Jane Champion, has kindly consented to step into the breach—*' Which means that you will have to step up on to that platform in another half-minute. Really it would be kinder to you if she said less about Velma. But never mind; they are prepared to like anything. There! *Appendicitis!* I told you so. Poor Madame Velma! Let us hope it won't get into the local papers. Oh, goodness! She is going to enlarge on new-fangled diseases. Well, it gives us a moment's breathing space. . . . I say, Miss Champion, I was chaffing this afternoon about sharps and flats. I can play that accompaniment for you if you like. No? Well, just as you think best. But remember, it takes a lot of voice to make much effect in this concert-room, and the place is crowded. Now—the duchess has done. Come on. Mind the bottom step. Hang it all! How dark it is behind this curtain!"

Garth gave her his hand, and Jane mounted the steps and passed into view of the large audience assembled in the Overdene concert-room. Her tall figure seemed taller than usual as she walked alone across the rather high platform. She wore a black evening gown of soft material, with old lace at her bosom and one string of pearls round her neck. When she appeared, the audience gazed at her and applauded doubtfully. Velma's name on the programme had raised great expectations; and here was Miss Champion, who certainly played very nicely, but was not supposed to be able to sing, volunteering to sing Velma's song. A more kindly audience would have cheered her to the echo, voicing its generous appreciation of her effort, and sanguine expectation of her success. This audience expressed its astonishment, in the dubiousness of its faint applause.

Jane smiled at them good-naturedly; sat down at the piano, a Bechstein grand; glanced at the festoons of white roses and the cross of crimson ramblers; then, without further preliminaries, struck the opening chord and commenced to sing.

The deep, perfect voice thrilled through the room.

A sudden breathless hush fell upon the audience.

Each syllable penetrated the silence, borne on a tone so tender and so amazingly sweet, that casual hearts stood still and marvelled at their own emotion; and those who felt deeply already, responded with a yet deeper thrill to the magic of that music.

> "The hours I spent with thee, dear heart,
> Are as a string of pearls to me;
> I count them over, ev'ry one apart,
> My rosary,—my rosary."

Softly, thoughtfully, tenderly, the last two words were breathed into the silence, holding a world of reminiscence—a large-hearted woman's faithful remembrance of tender moments in the past.

The listening crowd held its breath. This was not a song. This was the throbbing of a heart; and it throbbed in tones of such sweetness, that tears started unbidden.

Then the voice, which had rendered the opening lines so quietly, rose in a rapid crescendo of quivering pain.

> "Each hour a pearl, each pearl a prayer,
> To still a heart in absence wrung;
> I tell each bead unto the end, and there—
> A cross is hung!"

The last four words were given with a sudden power and passion which electrified the assembly. In the pause which followed, could be heard the tension of feeling produced. But in another moment the quiet voice fell soothingly, expressing a strength of endurance which would fail in no crisis, nor fear to face any depths of pain; yet gathering to itself a poignancy of sweetness, rendered richer by the discipline of suffering.

> "O memories that bless and burn!
> O barren gain and bitter loss!
> I kiss each bead, and strive at last to learn
> To kiss the cross . . . to kiss the cross."

Only those who have heard Jane sing *The Rosary* can possibly realise how she sang *"I kiss each bead."* The lingering retrospection in each word breathed out a love so womanly, so beautiful, so tender, that her identity was forgotten—even by those in the audience who knew her best—in the magic of her rendering of the song.

The accompaniment, which opens with a single chord, closes with a single note.

Jane struck it softly, lingeringly; then rose, turned from the piano, and was leaving the platform, when a sudden burst of wild applause broke from the audience. Jane hesitated, paused, looked at her aunt's guests as if almost surprised to find them there. Then the slow smile dawned in her eyes and passed to her lips. She stood in the centre of the platform for a moment, awkwardly, almost shyly; then moved on as men's voices began to shout "Encore! 'core!" and left the platform by the side staircase.

But there, behind the scenes, in the semi-darkness of screens and curtains, a fresh surprise awaited Jane, more startling than the enthusiastic tumult of her audience.

At the foot of the staircase stood Garth Dalmain. His face was absolutely colourless, and his eyes shone out from it like burning stars. He remained motionless until she stepped from the last stair and stood close to him. Then with a sudden movement he caught her by the shoulders and turned her round.

"Go back!" he said, and the overmastering need quivering in his voice drew Jane's eyes to his in mute astonishment. "Go back at once and sing it all over again, note for note, word for word, just as before. Ah, don't stand here waiting! Go back now! Go back at once! Don't you know that you *must?*"

Jane looked into those shining eyes. Something she saw in them excused the brusque command of his tone. Without a word, she quietly mounted the steps and walked across the platform to the piano. People were still applauding, and redoubled their demonstrations of delight as she appeared; but

Jane took her seat at the instrument without giving them a thought.

She was experiencing a very curious and unusual sensation. Never before in her whole life had she obeyed a peremptory command. In her childhood's days, Fraulein and Miss Jebb soon found out that they could only obtain their desires by means of carefully worded requests, or pathetic appeals to her good feelings and sense of right. An unreasonable order, or a reasonable one unexplained, promptly met with a point-blank refusal. And this characteristic still remained, though modified by time; and even the duchess, as a rule, said "please" to Jane.

But now a young man with a white face and blazing eyes had unceremoniously swung her round, ordered her up the stairs, and commanded her to sing a song over again, note for note, word for word, and she was meekly going to obey.

As she took her seat, Jane suddenly made up her mind not to sing *The Rosary* again. She had many finer songs in her repertoire. The audience expected another. Why should she disappoint those expectations because of the imperious demands of a very highly excited boy?

She commenced the magnificent prelude to Handel's "Where'er you walk," but, as she played it, her sense of truth and justice intervened. She had not come back to sing again at the bidding of a highly excited boy, but of a deeply moved man;

and his emotion was of no ordinary kind. That Garth Dalmain should have been so moved as to forget even momentarily his punctilious courtesy of manner was the highest possible tribute to her art and to her song. While she played the Handel theme—and played it so that a whole orchestra seemed marshalled upon the key-board under those strong, firm fingers—she suddenly realised, though scarcely understanding it, the *must* of which Garth had spoken, and made up her mind to yield to its necessity. So; when the opening bars were ended, instead of singing the grand song from Semele she paused for a moment; struck once more *The Rosary*'s opening chord; and did as Garth had bidden her to do.

"The hours I spent with thee, dear heart,
Are as a string of pearls to me;
I count them over, ev'ry one apart,
My rosary,—my rosary.

"Each hour a pearl, each pearl a prayer,
To still a heart in absence wrung;
I tell each bead unto the end, and there—
A cross is hung!

"O memories that bless and burn!
O barren gain and bitter loss!
I kiss each bead, and strive at last to learn
To kiss the cross . . . to kiss the cross."

When Jane left the platform, Garth was still standing motionless at the foot of the stairs. His face was just as white as before, but his eyes had lost that terrible look of unshed tears, which had sent her back, at his bidding, without a word of question or remonstrance. A wonderful light now shone in them; a light of adoration, which touched Jane's heart because she had never before seen anything quite like it. She smiled as she came slowly down the steps, and held out both hands to him with an unconscious movement of gracious friendliness. Garth stepped close to the bottom of the staircase and took them in his, while she was still on the step above him.

For a moment he did not speak. Then in a low voice, vibrant with emotion: "My God!" he said, "Oh, my God!"

"Hush," said Jane; "I never like to hear that name spoken lightly, Dal."

"Spoken lightly!" he exclaimed. "No speaking lightly would be possible for me to-night. 'Every perfect gift is from above.' When words fail me to speak of the gift, can you wonder if I apostrophise the Giver?"

Jane looked steadily into his shining eyes, and a smile of pleasure illumined her own. "So you liked my song?" she said.

"Liked—liked your song?" repeated Garth, a shade of perplexity crossing his face. "I do not know whether I liked your song."

"Then why this flattering demonstration?" inquired Jane, laughing.

"Because," said Garth, very low, "you lifted the veil, and I—I passed within."

He was still holding her hands in his; and, as he spoke the last two words, he turned them gently over and, bending, kissed each palm with an indescribably tender reverence; then, loosing them, stood on one side, and Jane went out on to the terrace alone.

CHAPTER VII

Garth Finds His Rosary

Jane spent but a very few minutes in the drawing-room that evening. The fun in progress there was not to her taste, and the praises heaped upon herself annoyed her. Also she wanted the quiet of her own room in order to think over that closing episode of the concert, which had taken place between herself and Garth, behind the scenes. She did not feel certain how to take it. She was conscious that it held an element which she could not fathom, and Garth's last act had awakened in herself feelings which she did not understand. She extremely disliked the way in which he had kissed her hands; and yet he had put into the action such a passion of reverent worship that it gave her a sense of consecration—of being, as it were, set apart to minister always to the hearts of men in that perfect gift of melody which should uplift and ennoble. She could not lose the sensation of the impress of his lips upon the palms of her hands. It was as if he had left behind something tangible and abiding. She caught herself looking at them anxiously once or twice, and the third time this happened she determined to go to her room.

The duchess was at the piano, completely hidden from view by nearly the whole of her house party, crowding round in fits of delighted laughter. Ronnie had just broken through from the inmost circle to fetch an antimacassar; and Billy, to dash to the writing-table for a sheet of note-paper. Jane knew the note-paper meant a clerical dog collar, and she concluded something had been worn which resembled an antimacassar.

She turned rather wearily and moved towards the door. Quiet and unobserved though her retreat had been, Garth was at the door before her. She did not know how he got there; for, as she turned to leave the room, she had seen his sleek head close to Myra Ingleby's on the further side of the duchess's crowd. He opened the door and Jane passed out. She felt equally desirous of saying two things to him,—either: "How dared you behave in so unconventional a way?" or: "Tell me just what you want me to do, and I will do it."

She said neither.

Garth followed her into the hall, lighted a

candle, and threw the match at Tommy; then handed her the silver candlestick. He was looking absurdly happy. Jane felt annoyed with him for parading this gladness, which she had unwittingly caused and in which she had no share. Also she felt she must break this intimate silence. It was saying so much which ought not to be said, since it could not be spoken. She took her candle rather aggressively and turned upon the second step.

"Good-night, Dal," she said. "And do you know that you are missing the curate?"

He looked up at her. His eyes shone in the light of her candle.

"No," he said. "I am neither missing nor missed. I was only waiting in there until you went up. I shall not go back. I am going out into the park now to breathe in the refreshing coolness of the night breeze. And I am going to stand under the oaks and tell my beads. I did not know I had a rosary, until to-night, but I have—I have!"

"I should say you have a dozen," remarked Jane, dryly.

"Then you would be wrong," replied Garth. "I have just one. But it has many hours. I shall be able to call them all to mind when I get out there alone. I am going to 'count each pearl.'"

"How about the cross?" asked Jane.

"I have not reached that yet," answered Garth. "There is no cross to my rosary."

"I fear there is a cross to every true rosary, Dal,"

said Jane gently, "and I also fear it will go hard with you when you find yours."

But Garth was confident and unafraid.

"When I find mine," he said, "I hope I shall be able to"— Involuntarily Jane looked at her hands. He saw the look and smiled, though he had the grace to colour beneath his tan,—"to *face* the cross," he said.

Jane turned and began to mount the stairs; but Garth arrested her with an eager question.

"Just one moment, Miss Champion! There is something I want to ask you. May I? Will you think me impertinent, presuming, inquisitive?"

"I have no doubt I shall," said Jane. "But I am thinking you all sorts of unusual things to-night; so three adjectives more or less will not matter much. You may ask."

"Miss Champion, have *you* a rosary?"

Jane looked at him blankly; then suddenly understood the drift of his question.

"My dear boy, *no!*" she said. "Thank goodness, I have kept clear of 'memories that bless and burn.' None of these things enter into my rational and well-ordered life, and I have no wish that they should."

"Then," deliberated Garth, "how came you to sing *The Rosary* as if each line were your own experience; each joy or pain a thing—long passed, perhaps—but your own?"

"Because," explained Jane, "I always live in a

song when I sing it. Did I not tell you the lesson I learned over the *Chant Hindou*? Therefore I had a rosary undoubtedly when I was singing that song to-night. But, apart from that, in the sense you mean, no, thank goodness, I have none."

Garth mounted two steps, bringing his eyes on a level with the candlestick.

"But *if* you cared," he said, speaking very low, "that is how you would care? that is as you would feel?"

Jane considered. "Yes," she said, "*if* I cared, I suppose I should care just so, and feel as I felt during those few minutes."

"Then it was *you* in the song, although the circumstances are not yours?"

"Yes, I suppose so," Jane replied, "if we can consider ourselves apart from our circumstances. But surely this is rather an unprofitable 'air-ball.' Goodnight, 'Master Garthie!'"

"I say, Miss Champion! Just one thing more. Will you sing for me to-morrow? Will you come to the music-room and sing all the lovely things I want to hear? And will you let me play a few of your accompaniments? Ah, promise you will come. And promise to sing whatever I ask, and I won't bother you any more now."

He stood looking up at her, waiting for her promise, with such adoration shining in his eyes that Jane was startled and more than a little troubled. Then suddenly it seemed to her that she had found the key, and she hastened to explain it to herself and to him.

"Oh, you dear boy!" she said. "What an artist you are! And how difficult it is for us commonplace, matter-of-fact people to understand the artistic temperament. Here you go, almost turning my steady old head by your rapture over what seemed to you perfection of sound which has reached you through the ear; just as, again and again, you worship at the shrine of perfection of form, which reaches you through the eye. I begin to understand how it is you turn the heads of women when you paint them. However, you are very delightful in your delight, and I want to go up to bed. So I promise to sing all you want and as much as you wish to-morrow. Now keep your promise and don't bother me any more to-night. Don't spend the whole night in the park, and try not to frighten the deer. No, I do not need any assistance with my candle, and I am quite used to going upstairs by myself, thank you. Can't you hear what personal and appropriate remarks Tommy is making down there? Now do run away, Master Garthie, and count your pearls. And if you suddenly come upon a cross—remember, the cross can, in all probability, be persuaded to return to Chicago!"

Jane was still smiling as she entered her room and placed her candlestick on the dressing-table.

Overdene was lighted solely by lamps and

candles. The duchess refused to modernise it by the installation of electric light. But candles abounded, and Jane, who liked a brilliant illumination, proceeded to light both candles in the branches on either side of the dressing-table mirror, and in the sconces on the wall beside the mantelpiece, and in the tall silver candlesticks upon the writing-table. Then she seated herself in a comfortable arm-chair, reached for her writing-case, took out her diary and a fountain pen, and prepared to finish the day's entry. She wrote, *"Sang 'The Rosary' at Aunt 'Gina's concert in place of Velma, failed (laryngitis),"* and came to a full stop.

Somehow the scene with Garth was difficult to record, and the sensations which still remained therefrom, absolutely unwritable. Jane sat and pondered the situation, content to allow the page to remain blank.

Before she rose, locked her book, and prepared for rest, she had, to her own satisfaction, clearly explained the whole thing. Garth's artistic temperament was the basis of the argument; and, alas, the artistic temperament is not a very firm foundation, either for a theory, or for the fabric of a destiny. However, *faute de mieux*, Jane had to accept it as main factor in her mental adjustment, thus: This vibrant emotion in Garth, so strangely disturbing to her own solid calm, was in no sense personal to herself, excepting in so far as her voice and musical gifts were concerned. Just as the sight of paintable beauty crazed him with delight, making him wild with alternate hope and despair until he obtained his wish and had his canvas and his sitter arranged to his liking; so now, his passion for the beautiful had been awakened, this time through the medium, not of sight, but of sound. When she had given him his fill of song, and allowed him to play some of her accompaniments, he would be content, and that disquieting look of adoration would pass from those beautiful brown eyes. Meanwhile it was pleasant to look forward to to-morrow, though it behooved her to remember that all this admiration had in it nothing personal to herself. He would have gone into even greater raptures over Madame Blanche, for instance, who had the same timbre of voice and method of singing, combined with a beauty of person which delighted the eye the while her voice enchanted the ear. Certainly Garth must see and hear her, as music appeared to mean so much to him. Jane began planning this, and then her mind turned to Pauline Lister, the lovely American girl, whose name had been coupled with Garth Dalmain's all the season. Jane felt certain she was just the wife he needed. Her loveliness would content him, her shrewd common-sense and straightforward, practical ways would counterbalance his somewhat erratic temperament, and her adaptability would enable her to suit herself to his surroundings, both in his northern home and amongst his large circle of friends down south. Once married, he would give up raving about Flower and Myra, and kissing people's hands in that—"absurd way," Jane was going to say, but she was invariably truthful, even in her thoughts, and substituted "extraordinary" as the more correct adjective—in that extraordinary way.

She sat forward in her chair with her elbows on her knees, and held her large hands before her, palms upward, realising again the sensations of that moment. Then she pulled herself up sharply. "Jane Champion, don't be a fool! You would wrong that dear, beauty-loving boy, more than you would wrong yourself, if you took him for one moment seriously. His homage to-night was no more personal to you than his appreciation of the excellent dinner was personal to Aunt Georgina's chef. In his enjoyment of the production, the producer was included; but that was all. Be gratified at the success of your art, and do not spoil that success by any absurd sentimentality. Now wash your very ungainly hands and go to bed." Thus Jane to herself.

And under the oaks, with soft turf beneath his feet, stood Garth Dalmain, the shy deer sleeping around unconscious of his presence; the planets above, hanging like lamps in the deep purple of the sky. And he, also, soliloquised.

"I have found her," he said, in low tones of rapture, "the ideal woman, the crown of womanhood, the perfect mate for the spirit, soul, and body of the man who can win her.—Jane! Jane! Ah, how blind I have been! To have known her for years, and yet not realised her to be this. But she lifted the veil, and I passed in. Ah grand, noble heart! She will never be able to draw the veil again between her soul and mine. And she has no rosary. I thank God for that. No other man possesses, or has ever possessed, that which I desire more than I ever desired anything upon this earth, Jane's love, Jane's tenderness. Ah, what will it mean? 'I count each pearl.' She *will* count them some day—her pearls and mine. God spare us the cross. Must there be a cross to every true rosary? Then God give me the heavy end, and may the mutual bearing of it bind us together. Ah, those dear hands! Ah, those true steadfast eyes! . . . Jane!— Jane! Surely it has always been Jane, though I did not know it, blind fool that I have been! But one thing I know: whereas I was blind, now I see. And it will always be Jane from this night onward through time and—please God—into eternity."

The night breeze stirred his thick dark hair, and his eyes, as he raised them, shone in the starlight.

And Jane, almost asleep, was roused by the tapping of her blind against the casement, and murmured "Anything you wish, Garth, just tell me, and I will do it." Then awakening suddenly to the consciousness of what she had said, she sat up in the darkness and scolded herself furiously. "Oh, you middle-aged donkey! You call yourself staid and sensible, and a little flattery from a boy of whom you are fond turns your head completely. Come to your senses at once; or leave Overdene by the first train in the morning."

CHAPTER VIII

Added Pearls

The days which followed were golden days to Jane. There was nothing to spoil the enjoyment of a very new and strangely sweet experience.

Garth's manner the next morning held none of the excitement or outward demonstration which had perplexed and troubled her the evening before. He was very quiet, and seemed to Jane older than she had ever known him. He had very few lapses into his seven-year-old mood, even with the duchess; and when someone chaffingly asked him whether he was practising the correct deportment of a soon-to-be-married man,

"Yes," said Garth quietly, "I am."

"Will she be at Shenstone?" inquired Ronald; for several of the duchess's party were due at Lady Ingleby's for the following week-end.

"Yes," said Garth, "she will."

"Oh, lor'!" cried Billy, dramatically. "Prithee, Benedict, are we to take this seriously?"

But Jane, who wrapped in the morning paper, sat near where Garth was standing, came out from behind it to look up at him and say, so that only he heard it, "Oh, Dal, I am so glad! Did you make up your mind last night?"

"Yes," said Garth, turning so that he spoke to her alone, "last night."

"Did our talk in the afternoon have something to do with it?"

"No, nothing whatever."

"Was it *The Rosary*?"

He hesitated; then said, without looking at her: "The revelation of *The Rosary*? Yes."

To Jane his mood of excitement was now fully explained, and she could give herself up freely to the enjoyment of this new phase in their friendship, for the hours of music together were a very real delight. Garth was more of a musician than she had known, and she enjoyed his clean, masculine touch on the piano, unblurred by slur or pedal; more delicate than her own, where delicacy was required. What her voice was to him during those wonderful hours he did not express in words, for after that first evening he put a firm restraint upon his speech. Under the oaks he had made up his mind to wait a week before speaking, and he waited.

But the new and strangely sweet experience to

Jane was that of being absolutely first to someone. In ways known only to himself and to her Garth made her feel this. There was nothing for any one else to notice, and yet she knew perfectly well that she never came into the room without his being instantly conscious that she was there; that she never left a room, without being at once missed by him. His attentions were so unobtrusive and tactful that no one else realised them. They called forth no chaff from friends and no "Hoity-toity! What now?" from the duchess. And yet his devotion seemed always surrounding her. For the first time in her life Jane was made to feel herself *first* in the whole thought of another. It made him seem strangely her own. She took a pleasure and pride in all he said, and did, and was; and in the hours they spent together in the music-room she learned to know him and to understand that enthusiastic beauty-loving, irresponsible nature, as she had never understood it before.

The days were golden, and the parting at night was sweet, because it gave an added zest to the pleasure of meeting in the morning. And yet during these golden days the thought of love, in the ordinary sense of the word, never entered Jane's mind. Her ignorance in this matter arose, not so much from inexperience, as from too large an experience of the travesty of the real thing; an experience which hindered her from recognising love itself, now that love in its most ideal form was drawing near.

Jane had not come through a dozen seasons without receiving nearly a dozen proposals of marriage. An heiress, independent of parents and guardians, of good blood and lineage, a few proposals of a certain type were inevitable. Middle-aged men—becoming bald and grey; tired of racketing about town; with beautiful old country places and an unfortunate lack of the wherewithal to keep them up—proposed to the Honourable Jane Champion in a business-like way, and the Honourable Jane looked them up and down, and through and through, until they felt very cheap, and then quietly refused them, in an equally business-like way.

Two or three nice boys, whom she had pulled out of scrapes and set on their feet again after hopeless croppers, had thought, in a wave of maudlin gratitude, how good it would be for a fellow always to have her at hand to keep him straight and tell him what he ought to do, don't you know? and—er—well, yes—pay his debts, and be a sort of mother-who-doesn't-scold kind of person to him; and had caught hold of her kind hand, and implored her to marry them. Jane had slapped them if they ventured to touch her, and recommended them not to be silly.

One solemn proposal she had had quite lately from the bachelor rector of a parish adjoining

Overdene. He had often inflicted wearisome conversations upon her; and when he called, intending to put the momentous question, Jane, who was sitting at her writing-table in the Overdene drawing-room, did not see any occasion to move from it. If the rector became too prosy, she could surreptitiously finish a few notes. He sank into a deep arm-chair close to the writing-table, crossed his somewhat bandy legs one over the other, made the tips of his fingers meet with unctuous accuracy, and intoned the opening sentences of his proposition. Jane, sharpening pencils and sorting nibs, apparently only caught the drift of what he was saying, for when he had chanted the phrase, "Not alone from selfish motives, my dear Miss Champion; but for the good of my parish; for the welfare of my flock, for the advancement of the work of the church in our midst," Jane opened a despatch-box and drew out her cheque-book.

"I shall be delighted to subscribe, Mr. Bilberry," she said. "Is it for a font, a pulpit, new hymn-books, or what?"

"My dear lady," said the rector tremulously, "you misunderstand me. My desire is to lead you to the altar."

"Dear Mr. Bilberry," said Jane Champion, "that would be quite unnecessary. From any part of your church the fact that you need a new altar-cloth is absolutely patent to all comers. I will, with the greatest pleasure, give you a cheque for ten pounds towards it. I have attended your church rather often lately because I enjoy a long, quiet walk by myself through the woods. And now I am sure you would like to see my aunt before you go. She is in the aviary, feeding her foreign birds. If you go out by that window and pass along the terrace to your left, you will find the aviary and the duchess. I would suggest the advisability of not mentioning this conversation to my aunt. She does not approve of elaborate altar-cloths, and would scold us both, and insist on the money being spent in providing boots for the school children. No, please do not thank me. I am really glad of an opportunity of helping on your excellent work in this neighbourhood."

Jane wondered once or twice whether the cheque would be cashed. She would have liked to receive it back by post, torn in half; with a few wrathful lines of manly indignation. But when it returned to her in due course from her bankers, it was indorsed *P. Bilberry*, in a neat scholarly hand, without even a dash of indignation beneath it; and she threw it into the waste-paper basket, with rather a bitter smile.

These were Jane's experiences of offers of marriage. She had never been loved for her own sake; she had never felt herself really first in the heart and life of another. And now, when the adoring love of a man's whole being was tenderly, cautiously beginning to surround and envelop her, she did not recognise the reason of her happiness or of his devotion. She considered him the avowed lover of another woman, with whose youth and loveliness she would not have dreamed of competing; and she regarded this closeness of intimacy between herself and Garth as a development of a friendship more beautiful than she had hitherto considered possible.

Thus matters stood when Tuesday arrived and the Overdene party broke up. Jane went to town to spend a couple of days with the Brands. Garth went straight to Shenstone, where he had been asked expressly to meet Miss Lister and her aunt, Mrs. Parker Bangs. Jane was due at Shenstone on Friday for the week-end.

CHAPTER IX

Lady Ingleby's House Party

As Jane took her seat and the train moved out of the London terminus she leaned back in her corner with a sigh of satisfaction. Somehow these days in town had seemed insufferably long. Jane reviewed them thoughtfully, and sought the reason. They had been filled with interests and engagements; and the very fact of being in town, as a rule, contented her. Why had she felt so restless and dissatisfied and lonely?

From force of habit she had just stopped at the railway book-stall for her usual pile of literature. Her friends always said Jane could not go even the shortest journey without at least half a dozen papers. But now they lay unheeded on the seat in front of her. Jane was considering her Tuesday, Wednesday, and Thursday, and wondering why they had merely been weary stepping-stones to Friday. And here was Friday at last, and once in the train en route for Shenstone, she began to feel happy and exhilarated. What had been the matter with these three days? Flower had been charming; Deryck, his own friendly, interesting self; little Dicky, delightful; and Baby Blossom, as sweet as only Baby Blossom could be. What was amiss?

"I know," said Jane. "Of course! Why did I not realise it before? I had too much music during those last days at Overdene; and *such* music! I have been suffering from a surfeit of music, and the miss of it has given me this blank feeling of loneliness. No doubt we shall have plenty at Myra's, and Dal will be there to clamour for it if Myra fails to suggest it."

With a happy little smile of pleasurable anticipation, Jane took up the *spectator,* and was soon absorbed in an article on the South African problem.

Myra met her at the station, driving ponies tandem. A light cart was also there for the maid and baggage; and, without losing a moment, Jane and her hostess were off along the country lane at a brisk trot.

The fields and woods were an exquisite restful green in the afternoon sunshine. Wild roses clustered in the hedges. The last loads of hay were being carted in. There was an ecstasy in the songs of the birds and a transporting sense of sweetness about all the sights and scents of the country, such as Jane had never experienced so vividly before. She drew a deep breath and exclaimed, almost involuntarily: "Ah! it is good to be here!"

"You dear!" said Lady Ingleby, twirling her whip and nodding in gracious response to respectful salutes from the hay-field. "It is a comfort to have you! I always feel you are like the bass of a tune—something so solid and satisfactory and beneath one in case of a crisis. I hate crises. They are so tiring. As I say: Why can't things always go on as they are? They are as they were, and they were as they will be, if only people wouldn't bother. However, I am certain nothing could go far wrong when *you* are anywhere near."

Myra flicked the leader, who was inclined to "sugar," and they flew along between the high hedges, brushing lightly against overhanging masses of honeysuckle and wild clematis. Jane snatched a spray of the clematis, in passing. " 'Traveller's joy,' " she said, with that same quiet smile of glad anticipation, and put the white blossom in her buttonhole.

"Well," continued Lady Ingleby, "my house party is going on quite satisfactorily. Oh, and, Jane, there seems no doubt about Dal. How pleased I shall be if it comes off under my wing! The American girl is simply exquisite, and so vivacious and charming. And Dal has quite given up being silly—not that *I* ever thought him silly, but I know *you* did—and is very quiet and pensive; really were it any one but he, one would almost say 'dull.' And they roam about together in the most approved fashion. I try to get the aunt to make all her remarks to me. I am so afraid of her putting Dal off. He is so fastidious. I have promised Billy anything, up to the half of my kingdom, if he will sit at the feet of Mrs. Parker Bangs and listen to her wisdom, answer her questions, and keep her away from Dal. Billy is being so abjectly devoted in his attentions to Mrs. Parker Bangs that I begin to have fears lest he intends asking me to kiss him; in which case I shall hand him over to you to chastise. You manage these boys so splendidly. I fully believe Dal will propose to Pauline Lister tonight. I can't imagine why he didn't last night. There was a most perfect moon, and they went on the lake. What more *could* Dal want?—a lake, and a moon, and that lovely girl! Billy took Mrs. Parker Bangs in a double canoe and nearly upset her through laughing so much at the things she said about having to sit flat on the bottom. But he paddled her off to the opposite side of the lake from Dal and her niece, which was all we wanted. Mrs. Parker Bangs asked me afterwards whether Billy is a widower. Now what do you suppose she meant by that?"

"I haven't the faintest idea," said Jane. "But I am delighted to hear about Dal and Miss Lister. She is just the girl for him, and she will soon adapt herself to his ways and needs. Besides, Dal *must* have flawless loveliness, and really he gets it there."

"He does indeed," said Myra. "You should have seen her last night, in white satin, with wild roses in her hair. I cannot imagine why Dal did not rave. But perhaps it is a good sign that he should take things more quietly. I suppose he is making up his mind."

"No," said Jane. "I believe he did that at Overdene. But it means a lot to him. He takes marriage very seriously. Whom have you at Shenstone?"

Lady Ingleby told off a list of names. Jane knew them all.

"Delightful!" she said. "Oh! how glad I am to be here! London has been so hot and so dull. I never thought it hot or dull before. I feel a renegade. Ah! there is the lovely little church! I want to hear the new organ. I was glad your nice parson remembered me and let me have a share in it. Has it two manuals or three?"

"Half a dozen I think," said Lady Ingleby, "and you work them up and down with your feet. But I judged it wiser to leave them alone when I played for the children's service one Sunday. You never know quite what will happen if you touch those mechanical affairs."

"Don't you mean the composition pedals?" suggested Jane.

"I dare say I do," said Myra placidly. "Those things underneath, like foot-rests, which startle you horribly if you accidentally kick them."

Jane smiled at the thought of how Garth would throw back his head and shout, if she told him of this conversation. Lady Ingleby's musical remarks always amused her friends.

They passed the village church on the green, ivy-clad, picturesque, and, half a minute later, swerved in at the park gates. Myra saw Jane glance at the gate-post they had just shaved, and laughed. "A miss is as good as a mile," she said, as they dashed up the long drive between the elms, "as I told dear mamma, when she expostulated wrathfully with me for what she called my 'furious driving' the other day. By the way, Jane, dear mamma has been quite *cordial* lately. By the time I am seventy and she is ninety-eight I think she will begin to be almost fond of me. Here we are. Do notice Lawson. He is new, and such a nice man. He sings so well, and plays the concertina a little, and teaches in the Sunday-school, and speaks really quite excellently at temperance meetings. He is extremely fond of mowing the lawns, and my maid tells me he is studying French with her. The only thing he seems really incapable of being is an efficient butler; which is so unfortunate, as I like him far too well ever to part with him. Michael says I have a perfectly fatal habit of *liking people,* and of encouraging them to do the things they do well and enjoy doing, instead of the things they were engaged to do. I suppose I have; but I do like my household to be happy."

They alighted, and Myra trailed into the hall with a lazy grace which gave no indication of the masterly way she had handled her ponies, but rather suggested stepping from a comfortable seat in a barouche. Jane looked with interest at the man-servant who came forward and deftly assisted them. He had not quite the air of a butler but neither could she imagine him playing a concertina or haranguing a temperance meeting and he acquitted himself quite creditably.

"Oh, that was not Lawson," explained Myra, as she led the way upstairs. "I had forgotten. He had to go to the vicarage this afternoon to see the vicar about a 'service of song' they are getting up. That was Tom, but we call him 'Jephson' in the house. He was one of Michael's stud grooms, but he is engaged to one of the housemaids, and I found he so very much preferred being in the house, so I have arranged for him to understudy Lawson, and he is growing side whiskers. I shall have to break it to Michael on his return from Norway. This way, Jane. We have put you in the Magnolia room. I knew you would enjoy the view of the lake. Oh, I forgot to tell you, a tennis tournament is in progress. I must hasten to the courts. Tea will be going on there, under the chestnuts. Dal and Ronnie are to play the final for the men's singles. It ought to be a fine match. It was to come on at about half-past four. Don't wait to do any changings. Your maid and your luggage can't be here just yet."

"Thanks," said Jane; "I always travel in country clothes, and have done so to-day, as you see. I will just get rid of the railway dust, and follow you."

Ten minutes later, guided by sounds of cheering and laughter, Jane made her way through the shrubbery to the tennis lawns. The whole of Lady Ingleby's house party was assembled there, forming a picturesque group under the white and scarlet chestnut-trees. Beyond, on the beautifully kept turf of the court, an exciting set was in progress. As she approached, Jane could distinguish Garth's slim, agile figure, in white flannels and the violet shirt; and young Ronnie, huge and powerful, trusting to the terrific force of his cuts and drives to counterbalance Garth's keener eye and swifter turn of wrist.

It was a fine game. Garth had won the first set

by six to four, and now the score stood at five to four in Ronnie's favour; but this game was Garth's service, and he was almost certain to win it. The score would then be "games all."

Jane walked along the line of garden chairs to where she saw a vacant one near Myra. She was greeted with delight, but hurriedly, by the eager watchers of the game.

Suddenly a howl went up. Garth had made two faults.

Jane found her chair, and turned her attention to the game. Almost instantly shrieks of astonishment and surprise again arose. Garth had served *into* the net and *over* the line. Game and set were Ronnie's.

"One all," remarked Billy. "Well! I never saw Dal do *that* before. However, it gives us the bliss of watching another set. They are splendidly matched. Dal is lightning, and Ronnie thunder."

The players crossed over, Garth rather white beneath his tan. He was beyond words vexed with himself for failing in his service, at that critical juncture. Not that he minded losing the set; but it seemed to him it must be patent to the whole crowd, that it was the sight, out of the tail of his eye, of a tall grey figure moving quietly along the line of chairs, which for a moment or two set earth and sky whirling, and made a confused blur of net and lines. As a matter of fact, only one of the onlookers connected Garth's loss of the game with

Jane's arrival, and she was the lovely girl, seated exactly opposite the net, with whom he exchanged a smile and a word as he crossed to the other side of the court.

The last set proved the most exciting of the three. Nine hard-fought games, five to Garth, four to Ronnie. And now Ronnie was serving, and fighting hard to make it games-all. Over and over enthusiastic partisans of both shouted "Deuce!" and then when Garth had won the "vantage," a slashing over-hand service from Ronnie beat him, and it was "deuce" again.

"Don't it make one giddy?" said Mrs. Parker Bangs to Billy, who reclined on the sward at her feet. "I should say it has gone on long enough. And they must both be wanting their tea. It would have been kind in Mr. Dalmain to have let that ball pass, anyway."

"Yes, wouldn't it?" said Billy earnestly. "But you see, Dal is not naturally kind. Now, if I had been playing against Ronnie, I should have let those over-hand balls of his pass long ago."

"I am sure you would," said Mrs. Parker Bangs, approvingly; while Jane leaned over, at Myra's request, and pinched Billy.

Slash went Ronnie's racket. "Deuce! deuce!" shouted half a dozen voices.

"They shouldn't say that," remarked Mrs. Parker Bangs, "even if they are mad about it."

Billy hugged his knees, delightedly; looking up

at her with an expression of seraphic innocence.

"No. Isn't it sad?" he murmured. "I never say naughty words when I play. I always say 'Game love.' It sounds so much nicer, I think."

Jane pinched again, but Billy's rapt gaze at Mrs. Parker Bangs continued.

"Billy," said Myra sternly, "go into the hall and fetch my scarlet sunshade. Yes, I dare say you *will* miss the finish," she added in a stern whisper, as he leaned over her chair, remonstrating; "but you richly deserve it."

"I have made up my mind what to ask, dear queen," whispered Billy as he returned, breathless, three minutes later and laid the parasol in Lady Ingleby's lap. "You promised me anything, up to the half of your kingdom. I will have the head of Mrs. Parker Bangs in a charger."

"Oh, shut up, Billy!" exclaimed Jane, "and get out of the light! We missed that last stroke. What is the score?"

Once again it was Garth's vantage, and once again Ronnie's arm swung high for an untakable smasher.

"Play up, Dal!" cried a voice, amid the general hubbub.

Garth knew that dear voice. He did not look in its direction, but he smiled. The next moment his arm shot out like a flash of lightning. The ball touched ground on Ronnie's side of the net and shot the length of the court without rising.

Ronnie's wild scoop at it was hopeless. Game and set were Garth's.

They walked off the ground together, their rackets under their arms, the flush of a well-contested fight on their handsome faces. It had been so near a thing that both could sense the thrill of victory.

Pauline Lister had been sitting with Garth's coat on her lap, and his watch and chain were in her keeping. He paused a moment to take them up and receive her congratulations; then, slipping on his coat, and pocketing his watch, came straight to Jane.

"How do you do, Miss Champion?"

His eyes sought hers eagerly; and the welcoming gladness he saw in them filled him with certainty and content. He had missed her so unutterably during these days. Tuesday, Wednesday, and Thursday had just been weary stepping-stones to Friday. It seemed incredible that one person's absence could make so vast a difference. And yet how perfect that it should be so; and that they should both realise it, now the day had come when he intended to tell her how desperately he wanted her always. Yes, that they should *both* realise it—for he felt certain Jane had also experienced the blank. A thing so complete and overwhelming as the miss of her had been to him could not be one-sided. And how well worth the experience of these lonely days if they had thereby learned something of what *together* meant, now the words were to be spoken which should insure forever no more such partings.

All this sped through Garth's mind as he greeted Jane with that most commonplace of English greetings, the everlasting question which never receives an answer. But from Garth, at that moment, it did not sound commonplace to Jane, and she answered it quite frankly and fully. She wanted above all things to tell him exactly how she did; to hear all about himself, and compare notes on the happenings of these three interminable days; and to take up their close comradeship again, exactly where it had left off. Her hand went home to his with that firm completeness of clasp, which always made a hand shake with Jane such a satisfactory and really friendly thing.

"Very fit, thank you, Dal," she answered. "At least I am every moment improving in health and spirits, now I have arrived here at last."

Garth stood his racket against the arm of her chair and deposited himself full length on the grass beside her, leaning on his elbow.

"Was anything wrong with London?" he asked, rather low, not looking up at her, but at the smart brown shoe, planted firmly on the grass so near his hand.

"Nothing was wrong with London," replied Jane frankly; "it was hot and dusty of course, but delightful as usual. Something was wrong with *me;* and you will be ashamed of me, Dal, if I confess what it was."

Garth did not look up, but assiduously picked little blades of grass and laid them in a pattern on Jane's shoe. This conversation would have been exactly to the point had they been alone. But was Jane really going to announce to the assembled company, in that dear, resonant, carrying voice of hers, the sweet secret of their miss of one another?

"Liver?" inquired Mrs. Parker Bangs suddenly.

"Muffins!" exclaimed Billy instantly, and, rushing for them, almost shot them into her lap in the haste with which he handed them, stumbling headlong over Garth's legs at the same moment.

Jane stared at Mrs. Parker Bangs and her muffins; then looked down at the top of Garth's dark head, bent low over the grass.

"I was dull," she said, "intolerably dull. And Dal always says 'only a dullard is dull.' But I diagnosed my dulness in the train just now and found it was largely his fault. Do you hear, Dal?"

Garth lifted his head and looked at her, realising in that moment that it was, after all, possible for a complete and overwhelming experience to be one-sided. Jane's calm grey eyes were full of gay friendliness.

"It was your fault, my dear boy," said Jane.

"How so?" queried Garth; and though there was a deep flush on his sunburned face, his voice was quietly interrogative.

"Because, during those last days at Overdene, you led me on into a time of musical dissipation such as I had never known before, and I missed it to a degree which was positively alarming. I began to fear for the balance of my well-ordered mind."

"Well," said Myra, coming out from behind her red parasol, "you and Dal can have orgies of music here if you want them. You will find a piano in the drawing-room and another in the hall, and a Bechstein grand in the billiard-room. That is where I hold the practices for the men and maids. I could not make up my mind which makers I really preferred, Erard, Broadwood, Collard, or Bechstein; so by degrees I collected one of each. And after all I think I play best upon the little cottage piano we had in the school-room at home. It stands in my boudoir now. I seem more accustomed to its notes, or it lends itself better to my way of playing."

"Thank you, Myra," said Jane. "I fancy Dal and I will like the Bechstein."

"And if you want something really exciting in the way of music," continued Lady Ingleby, "you might attend some of the rehearsals for this 'service of song' they are getting up in aid of the organ deficit fund. I believe they are attempting great things."

"I would sooner pay off the whole deficit, than go within a mile of a 'service of song,'" said Jane emphatically.

"Oh, no," put in Garth quickly, noting Myra's look of disappointment. "It is so good for people to work off their own debts and earn the things they need in their churches. And 'services of song' are delightful if well done, as I am sure this will be if Lady Ingleby's people are in it. Lawson outlined it to me this morning, and hummed all the principal airs. It is highly dramatic. Robinson Crusoe—no, of course not! What's the beggar's name? 'Uncle Tom's Cabin'? Yes, I knew it was something black. Lawson is Uncle Tom, and the vicar's small daughter is to be little Eva. Miss Champion, you will walk down with me to the very next rehearsal."

"Shall I?" said Jane, unconscious of how tender was the smile she gave him; conscious only that in her own heart was the remembrance of the evening at Overdene when she felt so inclined to say to him: "Tell me just what you want me to do, and I will do it."

"Pauline will just love to go with you," said Mrs. Parker Bangs. "She dotes on rural music."

"Rubbish, aunt!" said Miss Lister, who had slipped into an empty chair near Myra. "I agree with Miss Champion about 'services of song,' and I don't care for any music but the best."

Jane turned to her quickly, with a cordial smile and her most friendly manner. "Ah, but you must come," she said. "We will be victimised together. And perhaps Dal and Lawson will succeed in converting us to the cult of the 'service of song.' And anyway it will be amusing to have Dal explain it to us. He will need the courage of his convictions."

"Talking of something 'really exciting in the way of music,'" said Pauline Lister, "we had it on board when we came over. There was a nice friendly crowd on board the *Arabic*, and they arranged a concert for half-past eight on the Thursday evening. We were about two hundred miles off the coast of Ireland, and when we came up from dinner we had run into a dense fog. At eight o'clock they started blowing the fog-horn every half-minute, and while the fog-horn was sounding you couldn't hear yourself speak. However, all the programmes were printed, and it was our last night on board, so they concluded to have the concert all the same. Down we all trooped into the saloon, and each item of that programme was punctuated by the stentorian *boo* of the fog-horn every thirty seconds. You never heard anything so cute as the way it came in, right on time. A man with a deep bass voice sang *Rocked in the Cradle of the Deep*, and each time he reached the refrain, 'And calm and peaceful is my sle-eep,' *boo* went the fog-horn, casting a certain amount of doubt on our expectations of peaceful sleep that night, anyway. Then a man with a sweet tenor sang *Oft in the Stilly Night*, and the fog-horn showed us just how oft, namely, every thirty seconds. But the queerest effect of all was when a girl had to play a piano-forte solo. It was something of Chopin's, full of runs and trills and little silvery notes. She started all right; but when she was half-way down the first page, *boo* went the fog-horn, a longer blast than usual. We saw her fingers flying, and the turning of the page, but not a note could we hear; and when the old horn stopped and we could hear the piano again, she had reached a place half-way down the second page, and we hadn't heard what led to it. My! it was funny. That went on all through. She was a plucky girl to stick to it. We gave her a good round of applause when she had finished, and the fog-horn joined in and drowned us. It was the queerest concert experience I ever had. But we all enjoyed it. Only we didn't enjoy that noise keeping right on until five o'clock next morning."

Jane had turned in her chair, and listened with appreciative interest while the lovely American girl talked, watching, with real delight, her exquisite face and graceful gestures, and thinking how Dal must enjoy looking at her when she talked with so much charm and animation. She glanced down, trying to see the admiration in his eyes; but his head was bent, and he was apparently absorbed in the occupation of tracing the broguing of her shoes with the long stalk of a chestnut leaf. For a moment she watched the slim brown hand, as carefully intent on this useless task, as if working on a canvas; then she suddenly withdrew her foot, feeling almost vexed with him for his inattention and apparent indifference.

Garth sat up instantly. "It must have been awfully funny," he said. "And how well you told it. One could hear the fog-horn, and see the dismayed faces of the performers. Like an earthquake, a fog-horn is the sort of thing you don't ever get used to. It sounds worse every time. Let's each tell the funniest thing we remember at a concert. I once heard a youth recite Tennyson's *Charge of the Light Brigade* with much dramatic action. But he was extremely nervous, and got rather mixed. In describing the attitude of mind of the noble six hundred, he told us impressively that it was

" 'Theirs not to make reply;
Theirs not to do or die;
Theirs *but to reason why*.'

"The tone and action were all right, and I doubt whether many of the audience noticed anything wrong with the words."

"That reminds me," said Ronald Ingram, "of quite the funniest thing I ever heard. It was at a Thanksgiving service when some of our troops returned from South Africa. The proceedings concluded by the singing of the national anthem right through. You recollect how recently we had

106

had to make the change of pronoun, and how difficult it was to remember not to shout: 'Send *her* victorious'? Well, there was a fellow just behind me, with a tremendous voice, singing lustily, and taking special pains to get the pronouns correct throughout. And when he reached the fourth line of the second verse he sang with loyal fervour:

" 'Confound *his* politics,
Frustrate *his* knavish tricks!' "

"That would amuse the King," said Lady Ingleby. "Are you sure it is a fact, Ronnie?"

"Positive! I could tell you the church, and the day, and call a whole pewful of witnesses who were convulsed by it."

"Well, I shall tell his Majesty at the next opportunity, and say you heard it. But how about the tennis? What comes next? Final for couples? Oh, yes! Dal, you and Miss Lister play Colonel Loraine and Miss Vermount; and I think you ought to win fairly easily. You two are so well matched. Jane, this will be worth watching."

"I am sure it will," said Jane warmly, looking at the two, who had risen and stood together in the evening sunlight, examining their rackets and discussing possible tactics, while awaiting their opponents. They made such a radiantly beautiful couple; it was as if nature had put her very best and loveliest into every detail of each. The only fault which could possibly have been found with the idea of them wedded, was that her dark, slim beauty was so very much just a feminine edition of his, that they might easily have been taken for brother and sister; but this was not a fault which occurred to Jane. Her whole-hearted admiration of Pauline increased every time she looked at her; and now she had really seen them together, she felt sure she had given wise advice to Garth, and rejoiced to know he was taking it.

Later on, as they strolled back to the house together,—she and Garth alone,—Jane said, simply: "Dal, you will not mind if I ask? Is it settled yet?"

"I mind nothing you ask," Garth replied; "only be more explicit. Is what settled?"

"Are you and Miss Lister engaged?"

"No," Garth answered. "What made you suppose we should be?"

"You said at Overdene on Tuesday—*Tuesday!* oh! doesn't it seem weeks ago?—you said we were to take you seriously."

"It seems years ago," said Garth; "and I sincerely hope you will take me—seriously. All the same I have not proposed to Miss Lister; and I am anxious for an undisturbed talk with you on the subject. Miss Champion, after dinner to-night, when all the games and amusements are in full swing, and we can escape unobserved, will you come out onto the terrace with me, where I shall be able to speak to you without fear of interruption? The moonlight on the lake is worth seeing from the terrace. I spent an hour out there last night—ah, no; you are wrong for once—I spent it alone, when the boating was over, and thought of—how —to-night—we might be talking there together."

"Certainly I will come," said Jane; "and you must feel free to tell me anything you wish, and promise to let me advise or help in any way I can."

"I will tell you everything," said Garth very low, "and you shall advise and help as *only* you can."

Jane sat on her window-sill, enjoying the sunset and the exquisite view, and glad of a quiet half-hour before she need think of summoning her maid. Immediately below her ran the terrace, wide and gravelled, bounded by a broad stone parapet, behind which was a drop of eight or ten feet to the old-fashioned garden, with quaint box-bordered flower-beds, winding walks, and stone fountains. Beyond, a stretch of smooth lawn sloping down to the lake, which now lay, a silver mirror, in the soft evening light. The stillness was so perfect; the sense of peace, so all-pervading. Jane held a book on her knee, but she was not reading. She was looking away to the distant woods beyond the lake; then to the pearly sky above, flecked with rosy clouds and streaked with gleams of gold; and a sense of content, and gladness, and well-being, filled her.

Presently she heard a light step on the gravel below and leaned forward to see to whom it belonged. Garth had come out of the smoking-room and walked briskly to and fro, once or twice. Then he threw himself into a wicker seat just beneath her window, and sat there, smoking meditatively. The fragrance of his cigarette reached Jane, up among the magnolia blossoms. " 'Zenith, Marcovitch,' " she said to herself, and smiled. "Packed in jolly green boxes, twelve shillings a hundred! I must remember in case I want to give him a Christmas present. By then it will be difficult to find anything which has not already been showered upon him."

Garth flung away the end of his cigarette, and commenced humming below his breath; then gradually broke into words and sang softly, in his sweet barytone:

" 'It is not mine to sing the stately grace,
The great soul beaming in my lady's face.' "

The tones, though quiet, were so vibrant with passionate feeling, that Jane felt herself an eavesdropper. She hastily picked a large magnolia leaf and, leaning out, let it fall upon his head. Garth started, and looked up. "Hullo!" he said. "*You*—up there?"

"Yes," said Jane, laughing down at him, and speaking low lest other casements should be open,

"I—up here. You are serenading the wrong window, dear 'devout lover.'"

"What a lot you know about it," remarked Garth, rather moodily.

"Don't I?" whispered Jane. "But you must not mind, Master Garthie, because you know how truly I care. In old Margery's absence, you must let me be mentor."

Garth sprang up and stood erect, looking up at her, half-amused, half-defiant.

"Shall I climb the magnolia?" he said. "I have heaps to say to you which cannot be shouted to the whole front of the house."

"Certainly not," replied Jane. "I don't want any Romeos coming in at my window. 'Hoity-toity! What next?' as Aunt 'Gina would say. Run along and change your pinafore, Master Garthie. The 'heaps of things' must keep until to-night, or we shall both be late for dinner."

"All right," said Garth, "all right. But you will come out here this evening, Miss Champion? And you will give me as long as I want?"

"I will come as soon as we can possibly escape," replied Jane; "and you cannot be more anxious to tell me everything than I am to hear it. Oh! the scent of these magnolias! And just look at the great white trumpets! Would you like one for your buttonhole?"

He gave her a wistful, whimsical little smile; then turned and went indoors.

"Why do I feel so inclined to tease him?" mused Jane, as she moved, from the window. "Really it is I who have been silly this time; and he, staid and sensible. Myra is quite right. He is taking it very seriously. And how about her? Ah! I hope she cares enough, and in the right way.—Come in, Matthews! And you can put out the gown I wore on the night of the concert at Overdene, and we must make haste. We have just twenty minutes. What a lovely evening! Before you do anything else, come and see this sunset on the lake. Ah! it is good to be here!"

CHAPTER X

The Revelation

All the impatience in the world could not prevent dinner at Shenstone from being a long function, and two of the most popular people in the party could not easily escape afterwards unnoticed. So a distant clock in the village was striking ten, as Garth and Jane stepped out on to the terrace together. Garth caught up a rug in passing, and closed the door of the lower hall carefully behind him.

They were quite alone. It was the first time they had been really alone since these days apart, which had seemed so long to both.

They walked silently, side by side, to the wide

stone parapet overlooking the old-fashioned garden. The silvery moonlight flooded the whole scene with radiance. They could see the stiff box-borders, the winding paths, the queerly shaped flower-beds, and, beyond, the lake, like a silver mirror, reflecting the calm loveliness of the full moon.

Garth spread the rug on the coping, and Jane sat down. He stood beside her, one foot on the coping, his arms folded across his chest, his head erect. Jane had seated herself sideways, turning towards him, her back to an old stone lion mounting guard upon the parapet; but she turned her head still further, to look down upon the lake, and she thought Garth was looking in the same direction.

But Garth was looking at Jane.

She wore the gown of soft trailing black material she had worn at the Overdene concert, only she had not on the pearls or, indeed, any ornament save a cluster of crimson rambler roses. They nestled in the soft, creamy old lace which covered the bosom of her gown. There was a quiet strength and nobility about her attitude which thrilled the soul of the man who stood watching her. All the adoring love, the passion of worship, which filled his heart, rose to his eyes and shone there. No need to conceal it now. His hour had come at last, and he had nothing to hide from the woman he loved.

Presently she turned, wondering why he did not begin his confidences about Pauline Lister. Looking up inquiringly, she met his eyes.

"Dal!" cried Jane, and half rose from her seat. "Oh, Dal,—don't!"

He gently pressed her back. "Hush, dear," he said. "I must tell you everything, and you have promised to listen, and to advise and help. Ah, Jane, Jane! I shall need your help. I want it so greatly, and not only your help, Jane—but *you*— you, yourself. Ah, how I want you! These three days have been one continual ache of loneliness, because you were not there; and life began to live and move again, when you returned. And yet it has been so hard, waiting all these hours to speak. I have so much to tell you, Jane, of all you are to me—all you have become to me, since the night of the concert. Ah, how can I express it? I have never had any big things in my life; all has been more or less trivial—on the surface. This need of you—this wanting you—is so huge. It dwarfs all that went before; it would overwhelm all that is to come,—were it not that it will be the throne, the crown, the summit, of the future.—Oh, Jane! I have admired so many women. I have raved about them, sighed for them, painted them, and for- gotten them. But I never *loved* a woman before; I never knew what womanhood meant to a man, until I heard your voice thrill through the still- ness—'I count each pearl.' Ah, beloved, I have learned to count pearls since then, precious hours in the past, long forgotten, now remembered, and at last understood. 'Each hour a pearl, each pearl a prayer,' ay, a passionate plea that past and present may blend together into a perfect rosary, and that the future may hold no possibility of pain or parting. Oh, Jane—Jane! Shall I ever be able to make you understand—all—how much—Oh, *Jane!*"

She was not sure just when he had come so near; but he had dropped on one knee in front of her, and, as he uttered the last broken sentences, he passed both his arms around her waist and pressed his face into the soft lace at her bosom. A sudden quietness came over him. All struggling with explanations seemed hushed into the silence of complete comprehension—an all-pervading, enveloping silence.

Jane neither moved nor spoke. It was so strangely sweet to have him there—this whirlwind of emotion come home to rest, in a great stillness, just above her quiet heart. Suddenly she realised that the blank of the last three days had not been the miss of the music, but the miss of *him;* and as she realised this, she unconsciously put her arms about him. Sensations unknown to her before, awoke and moved within her,—a heavenly sense of aloofness from the world, the loneliness of life all swept away by this dear fact—just he and she together. Even as she thought it, felt it, he lifted his head, still holding her, and looking into her face, said: "You and I together, my own—my own."

But those beautiful shining eyes were more than Jane could bear. The sense of her plainness smote her, even in that moment; and those adoring eyes seemed lights that revealed it. With no thought in her mind but to hide the outward part from him who had suddenly come so close to the shrine within, she quickly put both hands behind his head and pressed his face down again, into the lace at her bosom. But, to him, those dear firm hands holding him close, by that sudden movement, seemed an acceptance of himself and of all he had to offer. For ten, twenty, thirty exquisite seconds, his soul throbbed in silence and rapture beyond words. Then he broke from the pressure of those restraining hands; lifted his head, and looked into her face once more.

"My wife!" he said.

Into Jane's honest face came a look of startled wonder; then a deep flush, seeming to draw all the blood, which had throbbed so strangely through her heart, into her cheeks, making them burn, and her heart die within her. She disengaged herself from his hold, rose, and stood looking away to where the still waters of the lake gleamed silver in the moonlight.

Garth Dalmain stood beside her. He did not

touch her, nor did he speak again. He felt sure he had won; and his whole soul was filled with a gladness unspeakable. His spirit was content. The intense silence seemed more expressive than words. Any ordinary touch would have dimmed the sense of those moments when her hands had held him to her. So he stood quite still and waited.

At last Jane spoke. "Do you mean that you wish to ask me to be—to be *that*—to you?"

"Yes, dear," he answered, gently; but in his voice vibrated the quiet of strong self-control. "At least I came out here intending to ask it of you. But I cannot ask it now, beloved. I can't ask you *to be* what you *are* already. No promise, no ceremony, no giving or receiving of a ring, could make you more my wife than you have been just now in those wonderful moments."

Jane slowly turned and looked at him. She had never seen anything so radiant as his face. But still those shining eyes smote her like swords. She longed to cover them with her hands; or bid him look away over the woods and water, while he went on saying these sweet things to her. She put up one foot on the low parapet, leaned her elbow on her knee, and shielded her face with her hand. Then she answered him, trying to speak calmly.

"You have taken me absolutely by surprise, Dal. I knew you had been delightfully nice and attentive since the concert evening, and that our mutual understanding of music and pleasure in it, coupled with an increased intimacy brought about by our confidential conversation under the cedar, had resulted in an unusually close and delightful friendship. I honestly admit it seems to have—it has—meant more to me than any friendship has ever meant. But that was partly owing to your temperament, Dal, which tends to make you always the most vivid spot in one's mental landscape. But truly I thought you wanted me out here in order to pour out confidences about Pauline Lister. Everybody believes that her loveliness has effected your final capture, and truly, Dal, truly— I thought so, too." Jane paused.

"Well?" said the quiet voice, with its deep undertone of gladness. "You know otherwise now."

"Dal—you have so startled and astonished me. I cannot give you an answer to-night. You must let me have until to-morrow—to-morrow morning."

"But, beloved," he said tenderly, moving a little nearer, "there is no more need for you to answer than I felt need to put a question. Can't you realise this? Question and answer were asked and given just now. Oh, my dearest—come back to me. Sit down again."

But Jane stood rigid.

"No," she said. "I can't allow you to take things for granted in this way. You took me by surprise, and I lost my head utterly—unpardonably, I admit. But, my dear boy, marriage is a serious thing. Marriage is not a mere question of sentiment. It has to wear. It has to last. It must have a solid and dependable foundation, to stand the test and strain of daily life together. I know so many married couples intimately. I stay in their homes, and act sponsor to their children; with the result that I vowed never to risk it myself. And now I have let you put this question, and you must not wonder if I ask for twelve hours to think it over."

Garth took this silently. He sat down on the stone coping with his back to the lake and, leaning backward, tried to see her face; but the hand completely screened it. He crossed his knees and clasped both hands around them, rocking slightly backward and forward for a minute while mastering the impulse to speak or act violently. He strove to compose his mind by fixing it upon trivial details which chanced to catch his eye. His red socks showed clearly in the moonlight against the white paving of the terrace, and looked well with black patent-leather shoes. He resolved always to wear red silk socks in the evening, and wondered whether Jane would knit some for him. He counted the windows along the front of the house, noting which were his and which were Jane's, and how many came between. At last he knew he could trust himself, and, leaning back, spoke very gently, his dark head almost touching the lace of her sleeve.

"Dearest—tell me, didn't you feel just now—"

"Oh, hush!" cried Jane, almost harshly, "hush, Dal! Don't talk about feelings with this question between us. Marriage is fact, not feeling. If you want to do really the best thing for us both, go straight indoors now and don't speak to me again to-night. I heard you say you were going to try the organ in the church on the common at eleven o'clock to-morrow morning. Well—I will come there soon after half-past eleven and listen while you play; and at noon you can send away the blower, and I will give you my answer. But now— oh, go away, dear; for truly I cannot bear anymore. I must be left alone."

Garth loosed the strong fingers clasped so tightly round his knee. He slipped the hand next to her along the stone coping, close to her foot. She felt him take hold of her gown with those deft, masterful fingers. Then he bent his dark head quickly, and whispering: "I kiss the cross," with a gesture of infinite reverence and tenderness, which Jane never forgot, he kissed the hem of her skirt. The next moment she was alone.

She listened while his footsteps died away. She heard the door into the lower hall open and close. Then slowly she sat down just as she had sat when he knelt in front of her. Now she was quite alone. The tension of these last hard moments relaxed. She pressed both hands over the lace at her bosom where that dear, beautiful, adoring face had been hidden. Had she *felt,* he asked. Ah! what had she not felt?

Tears never came easily to Jane. But to-night she had been called a name by which she had never thought to be called; and already her honest heart was telling her she would never be called by it again. And large silent tears overflowed and fell upon her hands and upon the lace at her breast. For the wife and the mother in her had been wakened and stirred, and the deeps of her nature broke through the barriers of stern repression and almost masculine self-control, and refused to be driven back without the womanly tribute of tears.

And around her feet lay the scattered petals of crushed rambler roses.

Presently she passed indoors. The upper hall was filled with merry groups and resounded with "good-nights" as the women mounted the great staircase, pausing to fling back final repartees, or to confirm plans for the morrow.

Garth Dalmain was standing at the foot of the staircase, held in conversation by Pauline Lister and her aunt, who had turned on the fourth step. Jane saw his slim, erect figure and glossy head the moment she entered the hall. His back was towards her, and though she advanced and stood quite near, he gave no sign of being aware of her presence. But the joyousness of his voice seemed to make him hers again in this new sweet way.

She alone knew what had caused it, and unconsciously she put one hand over her bosom as she listened.

"Sorry, dear ladies," Garth was saying, "but to-morrow morning is impossible. I have an engagement in the village. Yes—really! At eleven o'clock."

"That sounds so rural and pretty, Mr. Dalmain," said Mrs. Parker Bangs. "Why not take Pauline and me along? We have seen no dairies, and no dairy-maids, nor any of the things in Adam Bede, since we came over. I would just love to step into Mrs. Poyser's kitchen and see myself reflected in the warming-pans on the walls."

"Perhaps we would be *de trop* in the dairy," murmured Miss Lister archly.

She looked very lovely in her creamy-white satin gown, her small head held regally, the brilliant charm of American womanhood radiating from her. She wore no jewels, save one string of perfectly matched pearls; but on Pauline Lister's neck even pearls seemed to sparkle.

All these scintillations, flung at Garth, passed over his sleek head and reached Jane where she lingered in the background. She took in every detail. Never had Miss Lister's loveliness been more correctly appraised.

"But it happens, unfortunately, to be neither a dairy-maid nor a warming-pan," said Garth. "My appointment is with a very grubby small boy, whose rural beauties consist in a shock of red hair and a whole pepper-pot of freckles."

"Philanthropic?" inquired Miss Lister.

"Yes, at the rate of threepence an hour."

"A caddy, of course," cried both ladies together.

"My! What a mystery about a thing so simple!" added Mrs. Parker Bangs. "Now we have heard, Mr. Dalmain, that it is well worth the walk to the links to see you play. So you may expect us to arrive there, time to see you start around."

Garth's eyes twinkled. Jane could hear the twinkle in his voice. "My dear lady," he said, "you overestimate my play as, in your great kindness of heart, you overestimate many other things connected with me. But I shall like to think of you at the golf links at eleven o'clock to-morrow morning. You might drive there, but the walk through the woods is too charming to miss. Only remember, you cross the park and leave by the north gate, not the main entrance by which we go to the railway station. I would offer to escort you, but duty takes me, at an early hour, in quite another direction. Besides, when Miss Lister's wish to see the links is known, so many people will discover golf to be the one possible way of spending to-morrow morning, that I should be but a unit in the crowd which will troop across the park to the north gate. It will be quite impossible for you to miss your way."

Mrs. Parker Bangs was beginning to explain

elaborately that never, under any circumstances, could he be a unit, when her niece peremptorily interposed.

"That will do, aunt. Don't be silly. We are all units, except when we make a crowd; which is what we are doing on this staircase at this present moment, so that Miss Champion has for some time been trying ineffectually to pass us. Do you golf to-morrow, Miss Champion?"

Garth stood on one side, and Jane began to mount the stairs. He did not look at her, but it seemed to Jane that his eyes were on the hem of her gown as it trailed past him. She paused beside Miss Lister. She knew exactly how effectual a foil she made to the American girl's white loveliness. She turned and faced him. She wished him to look up and see them standing there together. She wanted the artist eyes to take in the cruel contrast. She wanted the artist soul of him to realise it. She waited.

Garth's eyes were still on the hem of her gown, close to the left foot; but he lifted them slowly to the lace at her bosom, where her hand still lay. There they rested a moment, then dropped again, without rising higher.

"Yes," said Mrs. Parker Bangs, "are you playing around with Mr. Dalmain to-morrow forenoon, Miss Champion?"

Jane suddenly flushed crimson, and then was furious with herself for blushing, and hated the circumstances which made her feel and act so unlike her ordinary self. She hesitated during the long dreadful moment. How dared Garth behave in that way? People would think there was something unusual about her gown. She felt a wild impulse to stoop and look at it herself to see whether his kiss had materialised and was hanging like a star to the silken hem. Then she forced herself to calmness and answered rather brusquely: "I am not golfing to-morrow; but you could not do better than go to the links. Good-night, Mrs. Parker Bangs. Sleep well, Miss Lister. Good-night, Dal."

Garth was on the step below them, handing Pauline's aunt a letter she had dropped.

"Good-night, Miss Champion," he said, and for one instant his eyes met hers, but he did not hold out his hand, or appear to see hers half extended.

The three women mounted the staircase together, then went different ways. Miss Lister trailed away down a passage to the right, her aunt trotting in her wake.

"There's been a tiff there," said Mrs. Parker Bangs.

"Poor thing!" said Miss Lister softly. "I like her. She's a real good sort. I should have thought she would have been more sensible than the rest of us."

"A real plain sort," said her aunt, ignoring the last sentence.

"Well, she didn't make her own face," said Miss Lister generously.

"No, and she don't pay other people to make it for her. She's what Sir Walter Scott calls: 'Nature in all its ruggedness.'"

"Dear aunt," remarked Miss Lister wearily, "I wish you wouldn't trouble to quote the English classics to me when we are alone. It is pure waste of breath, because you see I *know* you have read them all. Here is my door. Now come right in and make yourself comfy on that couch. I am going to sit in this palatial arm-chair opposite, and do a little very needful explaining. My! How they fix one to the floor! These ancestral castles are all right so far as they go, but they don't know a thing about rockers. Now I have a word or two to say about Miss Champion. She's a real good sort, and I like her. She's not a beauty; but she has a fine figure, and she dresses right. She has heaps of money, and could have rarer pearls than mine; but she knows better than to put pearls on that brown skin. I like a woman who knows her limitations and is sensible over them. All the men adore her, not for what she looks but for what she is, and, my word, aunt, that's what pays in the long run. That is what lasts. Ten years hence the Honourable Jane will still be what she is, and I shall be trying to look what I'm not. As for Garth Dalmain, he has eyes for all of us and a heart for none. His pretty speeches and admiring looks don't mean marriage, because he is a man with an ideal of womanhood and he can't see himself marrying below it. If the Sistine Madonna could step down off those clouds and hand the infant to the young woman on her left, he might marry *her;* but even then he would be afraid he might see someone next day who did her hair more becomingly, or that her foot would not look so well on his Persian rugs as it does on that cloud. He won't marry money, because he has plenty of it. And even if he hadn't, money made in candles would not appeal to him. He won't marry beauty, because he thinks too much about it. He adores so many lovely faces, that he is never sure for twenty-four hours which of them he admires most, bar the fact that, as in the case of fruit trees, the unattainable are usually the most desired. He won't marry goodness—virtue—worth—whatever you choose to call the sterling qualities of character—because in all these the Honourable Jane Champion is his ideal, and she is too sensible a woman to tie such an epicure to her plain face. Besides, she considers herself his grandmother, and doesn't require him to teach her to suck eggs. But Garth Dalmain, poor boy, is so sublimely lacking in self-consciousness that he never questions whether he can win his ideal. He possesses her already in his soul, and it will be a fearful smack in the face when she says 'No,' as she assuredly will do, for reasons aforesaid.

These three days, while he has been playing around with me, and you and other dear match-making old donkeys have gambolled about us, and made sure we were falling in love, he has been worshipping the ground she walks on, and counting the hours until he should see her walk on it again. He enjoyed being with me more than with the other girls, because I understood, and helped him to work all conversations round to her, and he knew, when she arrived here, I could be trusted to develop sudden anxiety about you, or have important letters to write, if she came in sight. But that is all there will ever be between me and Garth Dalmain; and if you had a really careful regard for my young affections you would drop your false set on the marble wash-stand, or devise some other equally false excuse for our immediate departure for town to-morrow.—And now, dear, don't stay to argue; because I have said exactly all there is to say on the subject, and a little more. And try to toddle to bed without telling me of which cute character in Dickens I remind you, because I am cuter than any of them, and if I stay in this tight frock another second I can't answer for the consequences.—Oui, Josephine, entrez!—Good-night, dear aunt. Happy dreams!"

But after her maid had left her, Pauline switched off the electric light and, drawing back the curtain, stood for a long while at her window, looking out at the peaceful English scene bathed in moonlight. At last she murmured softly, leaning her beautiful head against the window frame:

"I stated your case well, but you didn't quite deserve it, Dal. You ought to have let me know about Jane, weeks ago. Anyway, it will stop the talk about you and me. And as for you, dear, you will go on sighing for the moon; and when you find the moon is unattainable, you will not dream of seeking solace in more earthly lights—not even poppa's best sperm," she added, with a wistful little smile, for Pauline's fun sparkled in solitude as freely as in company, and as often at her own expense as at that of other people, and her brave American spirit would not admit, even to herself, a serious hurt.

Meanwhile Jane had turned to the left and passed slowly to her room. Garth had not taken her half-proffered hand, and she knew perfectly well why. He would never again be content to clasp her hand in friendship. If she cut him off from the touch which meant absolute possession, she cut herself off from the contact of simple comradeship. Garth, to-night, was like a royal tiger who had tasted blood. It seemed a queer simile, as she thought of him in his conventional evening clothes, correct in every line, well-groomed, smart almost to a fault. But out on the terrace with him she had realised, for the first time, the primal elements which go to the making of a man—a forceful determined, ruling man—creation's king. They echo of primeval forests. The roar of the lion is in them, the fierceness of the tiger; the instinct of dominant possession, which says: "Mine to have and hold, to fight for and enjoy; and I slay all comers!" She had felt it, and her own brave soul had understood it and responded to it, unafraid; and been ready to mate with it, if only—ah! if only—

But things could never be again as they had been before. If she meant to starve her tiger, steel bars must be between them for evermore. None of those sentimental suggestions of attempts to be a sort of unsatisfactory cross between sister and friend would do for the man whose head she had unconsciously held against her breast. Jane knew this. He had kept himself magnificently in hand after she put him from her, but she knew he was only giving her breathing space. He still considered her his own, and his very certainty of the near future had given him that gentle patience in the present. But even now, while her answer pended, he would not take her hand in friendship. Jane closed her door and locked it. She must face this problem of the future, with all else locked out excepting herself and him. Ah! if she could but lock herself out and think only of him and of his love, as beautiful, perfect gifts laid at her feet, that she might draw them up into her empty arms and clasp them there for evermore. Just for a little while she would do this. One hour of realisation was her right. Afterwards she must bring *herself* into the problem,—her possibilities; her limitations; herself, in her relation to him in the future; in the effect marriage with her would be likely to have upon him. What it might mean to her did not consciously enter into her calculations. Jane was self-conscious, with the intense self-consciousness of all reserved natures, but she was not selfish.

At first, then, she left her room in darkness, and, groping her way to the curtains, drew them back, threw up the sash, and, drawing a chair to the window, sat down, leaning her elbows on the sill and her chin in her hands, and looked down upon the terrace, still bathed in moonlight. Her window was almost opposite the place where she and Garth had talked. She could see the stone lion and the vase full of scarlet geraniums. She could locate the exact spot where she was sitting when he—Memory awoke, vibrant.

Then Jane allowed herself the most wonderful mental experience of her life. She was a woman of purpose and decision. She had said she had a right to that hour, and she took it to the full. In soul she met her tiger and mated with him, unafraid. He had not asked whether she loved him or not, and she did not need to ask herself. She surrendered her proud liberty, and tenderly, humbly, wistfully, yet with all the strength of her strong nature, promised to love, honour, and obey him. She met the adoration of his splendid eyes without a tremor. She had locked her body out. She was alone with her soul; and her soul was all-beautiful—perfect for him.

The loneliness of years slipped from her. Life became rich and purposeful. He needed her always, and she was always there and always able to meet his need. "Are you content, my beloved?" she asked over and over; and Garth's joyous voice, with the ring of perpetual youth in it, always answered: "Perfectly content." And Jane smiled into the night, and in the depths of her calm eyes dawned a knowledge hitherto unknown, and in her tender smile trembled, with unspeakable sweetness, an understanding of the secret of a woman's truest bliss. "He is mine and I am his. And because he is mine, my beloved is safe; and because I am his, he is content."

Thus she gave herself completely; gathering him into the shelter of her love; and her generous heart expanded to the greatness of the gift. Then the mother in her awoke and realised how much of the maternal flows into the love of a true woman when she understands how largely the child-nature predominates in the man in love, and how the very strength of his need of her reduces to unaccustomed weakness the strong nature to which she has become essential.

Jane pressed her hands upon her breast. "Garth,"

she whispered, "Garth, I *understand*. My own poor boy, it was so hard to you to be sent away just then. But you had had all—all you wanted, in those few wonderful moments, and nothing can rob you of that fact. And you have made me *so* yours that, whatever the future brings for you and me, no other face will ever be hidden here. It is yours, and I am yours—to-night, and henceforward, forever."

Jane leaned her forehead on the window-sill. The moonlight fell on the heavy coils of her brown hair. The scent of the magnolia blooms rose in fragrance around her. The song of a nightingale purled and thrilled in an adjacent wood. The lonely years of the past, the perplexing moments of the present, the uncertain vistas of the future, all rolled away. She sailed with Garth upon a golden ocean far removed from the shores of time. For love is eternal; and the birth of love frees the spirit from all limitations of the flesh.

A clock in the distant village struck midnight. The twelve strokes floated up to Jane's window across the moonlit park. Time was once more. Her freed spirit resumed the burden of the body.

A new day had begun, the day upon which she had promised her answer to Garth. The next time that clock struck twelve she would be standing with him in the church, and her answer must be ready.

She turned from the window without closing it, drew the curtains closely across, switched on the electric light over the writing-table, took off her evening gown, hung up bodice and skirt in the wardrobe, resolutely locking the door upon them. Then she slipped on a sage-green wrapper, which she had lately purchased at a bazaar because every one else fled from it, and the old lady whose handiwork it was seemed so disappointed, and, drawing a chair near the writing-table, took out her diary, unlocked the heavy clasp, and began to read. She turned the pages slowly, pausing here and there, until she came to those she sought. Over them she pondered long, her head in her hands. They contained a very full account of her conversation with Garth on the afternoon of the day of the concert at Overdene; and the lines upon which she specially dwelt were these: "His face was transfigured. . . . Goodness and inspiration shone from it, making it as the face of an angel. . . . I never thought him ugly again. Child though I was, I could differentiate even then between ugliness and plainness. I have associated his face ever since with the wondrous beauty of his soul. When he sat down, at the close of his address, I no longer thought him a compli-cated form of chimpanzee. I remembered the divine halo of his smile. Of course it was not the sort of face one *could* have wanted to live with, or to have day after day opposite one at table, but then one was not called to that sort of discipline, which would have been martyrdom to me. And he has always stood to my mind since as a proof of the truth that goodness is never ugly, and that divine love and aspiration, shining through the plainest features, may redeem them, temporarily, into beauty; and permanently, into a thing one loves to remember."

At first Jane read the entire passage. Then her mind focussed itself upon one sentence: "Of course it was not the sort of face one *could* have wanted to live with, or to have day after day opposite one at table, . . . which would have been martyrdom to me."

At length Jane arose, turned on all the lights over the dressing-table, particularly two bright ones on either side of the mirror, and, sitting down before it, faced herself honestly.

When the village clock struck one, Garth Dalmain stood at his window taking a final look at the night which had meant so much to him. He remembered, with an amused smile, how, to help himself to calmness, he had sat on the terrace and thought of his socks, and then had counted the windows between his and Jane's. There were five of them. He knew her window by the magnolia tree and the seat beneath it where he had chanced to sit, not knowing she was above him. He leaned far out and looked towards it now.

The curtains were drawn, but there appeared still to be a light behind them. Even as he watched, it went out.

He looked down at the terrace. He could see the stone lion and the vase of scarlet geraniums. He could locate the exact spot where she was sitting when he—

Then he dropped upon his knees beside the window and looked up into the starry sky.

Garth's mother had lived long enough to teach him the holy secret of her sweet patience and endurance. In moments of deep feeling, words from his mother's Bible came to his lips more readily than expressions of his own thought. Now, looking upward, he repeated softly and reverently: " 'Every good gift and every perfect gift is from above, and cometh down from the Father of lights, with whom is no variableness, neither shadow of turning.' And oh, Father," he added, "keep us in the light—she and I. May there be in us, as there is in Thee, no variableness, neither shadow which is cast by turning."

Then he rose to his feet and looked across once more to the stone lion and the broad coping. His soul sang within him, and he folded his arms across his chest. "My wife!" he said. "Oh! my wife!"

And, as the village clock struck one, Jane arrived at her decision.

Slowly she rose, and turned off all the lights; then, groping her way to the bed, fell upon her knees beside it, and broke into a passion of desperate, silent weeping.

CHAPTER XI

Garth Finds the Cross

The village church on the green was bathed in sunshine as Jane emerged from the cool shade of the park. The clock proclaimed the hour half-past eleven, and Jane did not hasten, knowing she was not expected until twelve. The windows of the church were open, and the massive oaken doors stood ajar.

Jane paused beneath the ivy-covered porch and stood listening. The tones of the organ reached her as from an immense distance, and yet with an all-pervading nearness. The sound was disassociated from hands and feet. The organ seemed breathing, and its breath was music.

Jane pushed the heavy door further open, and even at that moment it occurred to her that the freckled boy with a red head, and Garth's slim proportions, had evidently passed easily through an aperture which refused ingress to her more massive figure. She pushed the door further open, and went in.

Instantly a stillness entered into her soul. The

sense of unseen presences, often so strongly felt on entering an empty church alone, the impress left upon old walls and rafters by the worshipping minds of centuries, hushed the insistent beating of her own perplexity, and for a few moments she forgot the errand which brought her there, and bowed her head in unison with the worship of ages.

Garth was playing the *Veni, Creator Spiritus* to Attwood's perfect setting; and, as Jane walked noiselessly up to the chancel, he began to sing the words of the second verse. He sang them softly, but his beautifully modulated barytone carried well, and every syllable reached her.

"Enable with perpetual light
The dulness of our blinded sight;
Anoint and cheer our soiled face
With the abundance of Thy grace;
Keep far our foes; give peace at home;
Where Thou art Guide, no ill can come."

Then the organ swelled into full power, pealing out the theme of the last verse without its words, and allowing those he had sung to repeat themselves over and over in Jane's mind: "Where Thou art Guide, no ill can come." Had she not prayed for guidance? Then surely all would be well.

She paused at the entrance to the chancel. Garth

had returned to the second verse, and was singing again, to a waldflute accompaniment, "Enable with perpetual light—."

Jane seated herself in one of the old oak stalls and looked around her. The brilliant sunshine from without entered through the stained-glass windows, mellowed into golden beams of soft amber light, with here and there a shaft of crimson. What a beautiful expression—perpetual light! As Garth sang it, each syllable seemed to pierce the silence like a ray of purest sunlight. "The dulness of—" Jane could just see the top of his dark head over the heavy brocade of the organ curtain. She dreaded the moment when he should turn, and those vivid eyes should catch sight of her—"our blinded sight." How would he take what she must say? Would she have strength to come through a long hard scene? Would he be tragically heart-broken?—"Anoint and cheer our soiled face"—Would he argue, and insist, and override her judgment?—"With the abundance of Thy grace"—Could she oppose his fierce strength, if he chose to exert it? Would they either of them come through so hard a time without wounding each other terribly?—"Keep far our foes; give peace at home"—Oh! what could she say? What would he say? How should she answer? What reason could she give for her refusal which Garth would ever take as final?— "Where Thou art Guide, no ill can come."

And then, after a few soft, impromptu chords; the theme changed.

Jane's heart stood still. Garth was playing *The Rosary*. He did not sing it; but the soft insistence of the organ pipes seemed to press the words into the air, as no voice could have done. Memory's pearls, in all the purity of their gleaming preciousness, were counted one by one by the flute and dulciana; and the sadder tones of the waldflute proclaimed the finding of the cross. It all held a new meaning for Jane, who looked helplessly round, as if seeking some way of escape from the sad sweetness of sound which filled the little church.

Suddenly it ceased. Garth stood up, turned, and saw her. The glory of a great joy leaped into his face.

"All right, Jimmy," he said; "that will do for this morning. And here is a bright sixpence, because you have managed the blowing so well. Hullo! It's a shilling! Never mind. You shall have it because it is such a glorious day. There never was such a day, Jimmy; and I want you to be happy also. Now run off quickly, and shut the church door behind you, my boy."

Ah! how his voice, with its ring of buoyant gladness, shook her soul.

The red-headed boy, rather grubby, with a whole pepper-pot of freckles, but a beaming face of pleasure, came out from behind the organ, clattered down a side aisle; dropped his shilling on the way and had to find it; but at last went out, the heavy door closing behind him with a resounding clang.

Garth had remained standing beside the organ, quite motionless, without looking at Jane, and now that they were absolutely alone in the church, he still stood and waited a few moments. To Jane those moments seemed days, weeks, years, an eternity. Then he came out into the centre of the chancel, his head erect, his eyes shining, his whole bearing that of a conqueror sure of his victory. He walked down to the quaintly carved oaken screen and, passing beneath it, stood at the step. Then he signed to Jane to come and stand beside him.

"Here, dearest," he said; "let it be here."

Jane came to him, and for a moment they stood together, looking up the chancel. It was darker than the rest of the church, being lighted only by three narrow stained-glass windows, gems of colour and of significance. The centre window, immediately over the communion table, represented the Saviour of the world, dying upon the cross. They gazed at it in reverent silence. Then Garth turned to Jane.

"My beloved," he said, "it is a sacred Presence and a sacred place. But no place could be too sacred for that which we have to say to each other, and the Holy Presence, in which we both believe, is here to bless and ratify it. I am waiting for your answer."

Jane cleared her throat and put her trembling hands into the large pockets of her tweed coat.

"Dal," she said; "my answer is a question. How old are you?"

She felt his start of intense surprise. She saw the light of expectant joy fade from his face. But he replied, after only a momentary hesitation: "I thought you knew, dearest. I am twenty-seven."

"Well," said Jane slowly and deliberately, "I am thirty; and I look thirty-five, and feel forty. You are twenty-seven, Dal, and you look nineteen, and often feel nine. I have been thinking it over, and—you know—I cannot marry a mere boy."

Silence—absolute.

In sheer terror Jane forced herself to look at him. He was white to the lips. His face was very stern and calm—a strange, stony calmness. There was not much youth in it just then. *"Anoint and cheer our soiled face"*—The silent church seemed to wail the words in bewildered agony.

At last he spoke. "I had not thought of myself," he said slowly. "I cannot explain how it comes to pass, but I have not thought of myself at all, since my mind has been full of you. Therefore I had not realised how little there is in me that you could care for. I believed you had felt as I did, that we were—just each other's." For a moment he put out his hand as if he would have touched her. Then it dropped heavily to his side. "You are quite right," he said. "You could not marry any one whom you consider a mere boy."

He turned from her and faced up the chancel. For the space of a long silent minute he looked at the window over the holy table, where hung the suffering Christ. Then he bowed his head. "I accept the cross," he said, and, turning, walked quietly down the aisle. The church door opened, closed behind him with a heavy clang, and Jane was alone.

She stumbled back to the seat she had left, and fell upon her knees.

"O, my God," she cried, "send him back to me, oh, send him back! . . . Oh, Garth! It is I who am plain and unattractive and unworthy, not you. Oh, Garth—come back! come back! come back! . . . I will trust and not be afraid . . . Oh, my own Dear—come back!"

She listened, with straining ears. She waited, until every nerve of her body ached with suspense. She decided what she would say when the heavy door reopened and she saw Garth standing in a shaft of sunlight. She tried to remember the *Veni*, but the hollow clang of the door had silenced even memory's echo of that haunting music. So she waited silently, and as she waited the silence grew and seemed to enclose her within cruel, relentless walls which opened only to allow her glimpses into the vista of future lonely years. Just once more she broke that silence. "Oh, darling, come back! *I will risk it,*" she said. But no step drew near, and, kneeling with her face buried in her clasped hands, Jane suddenly realised that Garth Dalmain had accepted her decision as final and irrevocable, and would not return.

How long she knelt there after realising this, she never knew. But at last comfort came to her. She felt she had done right. A few hours of present anguish were better than years of future disillusion. Her own life would be sadly empty, and losing this newly found joy was costing her more than she had expected; but she honestly believed "she had done rightly towards him, and what did her own pain matter?" Thus comfort came to Jane.

At last she rose and passed out of the silent church into the breezy sunshine.

Near the park gates a little knot of excited boys were preparing to fly a kite. Jimmy, the hero of the hour, the centre of attraction, proved to be the proud possessor of this new kite. Jimmy was finding the day glorious indeed, and was being happy. "Happy *also,*" Garth had said. And Jane's eyes filled with tears, as she remembered the word and the tone in which it was spoken.

"There goes my poor boy's shilling," she said to

herself sadly, as the kite mounted and soared above the common; "but, alas, where is his joy?"

As she passed up the avenue a dog-cart was driven swiftly down it. Garth Dalmain drove it; behind him a groom and a portmanteau. He lifted his hat as he passed her, but looked straight before him. In a moment he was gone. Had Jane wanted to stop him she could not have done so. But she did not want to stop him. She felt absolutely satisfied that she had done the right thing, and done it at greater cost to herself than to him. He would eventually—ah, perhaps before so very long—find another to be to him all, and more than all, he had believed she could be. But she? The dull ache at her bosom reminded her of her own words the night before, whispered in the secret of her chamber to him who, alas, was not there to hear: "Whatever the future brings for you and me, no other face will ever be hidden here." And, in this first hour of the coming lonely years, she knew them to be true.

In the hall she met Pauline Lister.

"Is that you, Miss Champion?" said Pauline. "Well now, have you heard of Mr. Dalmain? He has had to go to town unexpectedly, on the 1.15 train; and aunt has dropped her false teeth on her marble wash-stand and must get to the dentist right away. So we go to town on the 2.30. It's an uncertain world. It complicates one's plans, when they have to depend on other people's teeth. But I would sooner break false teeth than true hearts, any day. One can get the former mended, but I guess no one can mend the latter. We are lunching early in our rooms; so I wish you good-by, Miss Champion."

CHAPTER XII

The Doctor's Prescription

The Honourable Jane Champion stood on the summit of the Great Pyramid and looked around her. The four exhausted Arabs whose exertions, combined with her own activity, had placed her there, dropped in the picturesque attitudes into which an Arab falls by nature. They had hoisted the Honourable Jane's eleven stone ten from the bottom to the top in record time, and now lay around, proud of their achievement and sure of their "backsheesh."

The whole thing had gone as if by clock-work. Two mahogany-coloured, finely proportioned fellows, in scanty white garments, sprang with the ease of antelopes to the top of a high step, turning to reach down eagerly and seize Jane's upstretched hands. One remained behind, unseen but indispensable, to lend timely aid at exactly the right moment. Then came the apparently impossible task for Jane, of placing the sole of her foot on the edge of a stone four feet above the one upon which she was standing. It seemed rather like stepping up on to the drawing-room mantel-piece. But encouraged by cries of "Eiwa! Eiwa!" she did it; when instantly a voice behind said, "Tyeb!" two voices above shouted, "Keteer!" the grip on her hands tightened, the Arab behind hoisted, and Jane had stepped up, with an ease which surprised herself. As a matter of fact, under those circumstances the impossible thing would have been not to have stepped up.

Arab number four was water-carrier, and offered water from a gourd at intervals; and once, when Jane had to cry halt for a few minutes' breathing space, Schehati, handsomest of all, and leader of the enterprise, offered to recite English Shakespeare-poetry. This proved to be:

"Jack-an-Jill
Went uppy hill,
To fetchy paily water;
Jack fell down-an
Broke his crown-an
Jill came tumbling after."

Jane had laughed; and Schehati, encouraged by the success of his attempt to edify and amuse, used lines of the immortal nursery epic as signals for united action during the remainder of the climb. Therefore Jane mounted one step to the fact that Jack fell down, and scaled the next to infor-

mation as to the serious nature of his injuries, and
at the third, Schehati, bending over, confidentially
mentioned in her ear, while Ali shoved behind,
that "Jill came tumbling after."

The familiar words, heard under such novel circumstances, took on fresh meaning. Jane commenced speculating as to whether the downfall of
Jack need necessarily have caused so complete a
loss of self-control and equilibrium on the part of
Jill. Would she not have proved her devotion
better by bringing the mutual pail safely to the
bottom of the hill, and there attending to the
wounds of her fallen hero? Jane, in her time, had
witnessed the tragic downfall of various delightful
jacks, and had herself ministered tenderly to their
broken crowns; for in each case the Jill had
remained on the top of the hill, flirting with that
objectionable person of the name of Horner,
whose cool, calculating way of setting to work—
so unlike poor Jack's headlong method—invariably secured him the plum; upon which he
remarked "What a good boy am I!" and was usually taken at his own smug valuation. But Jane's
entire sympathy on these occasions was with the
defeated lover, and more than one Jack was now
on his feet again, bravely facing life, because that
kind hand had been held out to him as he lay in his
valley of humiliation, and that comprehending
sympathy had proved balm to his broken crown.

"Dickery, dickery, dock!" chanted Schehati

solemnly, as he hauled again; "Moses ran up the clock. The clock struck 'one'—"

The clock struck "one"?—It was nearly three years since that night at Shenstone when the clock had struck "one," and Jane had arrived at her decision,—the decision which precipitated her Jack from his Pisgah of future promise. And yet—no. He had not fallen before the blow. He had taken it erect, and his light step had been even firmer than usual as he walked down the church and left her, after quietly and deliberately accepting her decision. It was Jane herself, left alone, who fell hopelessly over the pail. She shivered even now when she remembered how its icy waters drenched her heart. Ah, what would have happened if Garth had come back in answer to her cry during those first moments of intolerable suffering and loneliness? But Garth was not the sort of man who, when a door has been shut upon him, waits on the mat outside, hoping to be recalled. When she put him from her, and he realised that she meant it he passed completely out of her life. He was at the railway station by the time she reached the house, and from that day to this they had never met. Garth evidently considered the avoidance of meetings to be his responsibility, and he never failed her in this. Once or twice she went on a visit to houses where she knew him to be staying. He always happened to have left that morning, if she arrived in time for luncheon; or by an early afternoon train, if she was due for tea. He never timed it so that there should be tragic passings of each other, with set faces, at the railway stations; or a formal word of greeting as she arrived and he departed,—just enough to awaken all the slumbering pain and set people wondering. Jane remembered with shame that this was the sort of picturesque tragedy she would have expected from Garth Dalmain. But the man who had surprised her by his dignified acquiescence in her decision, continued to surprise her by the strength with which he silently accepted it as final and kept out of her way. Jane had not probed the depth of the wound she had inflicted.

Never once was his departure connected, in the minds of others, with her arrival. There was always some excellent and perfectly natural reason why he had been obliged to leave, and he was openly talked of and regretted, and Jane heard all the latest "Dal stories," and found herself surrounded by the atmosphere of his exotic, beauty-loving nature. And there was usually a girl—always the loveliest of the party—confidentially pointed out to Jane, by the rest, as a certainty, if only Dal had had another twenty-four hours of her society. But the girl herself would appear quite heart-whole, only very full of an evidently delightful friendship, expressing all Dal's ideas on art and colour, as her own, and confi-

dently happy in an assured sense of her own loveliness and charm and power to please. Never did
he leave behind him traces which the woman who
loved him regretted to find. But he was always
gone—irrevocably gone. Garth Dalmain was not
the sort of man to wait on the door-mat of a
woman's indecision.

Neither did this Jack of hers break his crown.
His portrait of Pauline Lister, painted six months
after the Shenstone visit, had proved the finest bit
of work he had as yet accomplished. He had
painted the lovely American, in creamy white
satin, standing on a dark oak staircase, one hand
resting on the balustrade, the other, full of yellow
roses, held out towards an unseen friend below.
Behind and above her shone a stained-glass
window, centuries old, the arms, crest, and mot-
toes of the noble family to whom the place
belonged, shining thereon in rose-coloured and
golden glass. He had wonderfully caught the
charm and vivacity of the girl. She was gaily up-
to-date, and frankly American, from the crown of
her queenly little head, to the point of her satin
shoe; and the suggestiveness of placing her in surroundings which breathed an atmosphere of the
best traditions of England's ancient ancestral
homes, the fearless wedding of the new world
with the old, the putting of this sparkling gem
from the new into the beautiful mellow setting of
the old and there showing it at its best,—all this

was the making of the picture. People smiled, and said the painter had done on canvas what he shortly intended doing in reality; but the tie between artist and sitter never grew into anything closer than a pleasant friendship, and it was the noble owner of the staircase and window who eventually persuaded Miss Lister to remain in surroundings which suited her so admirably.

One story about that portrait Jane had heard discussed more than once in circles where both were known. Pauline Lister had come to the first sittings wearing her beautiful string of pearls, and Garth had painted them wonderfully, spending hours over the delicate perfecting of each separate gleaming drop. Suddenly one day he seized his palette-knife, scraped the whole necklace off the canvas with a stroke, and declared she must wear her rose-topazes in order to carry out his scheme of colour. She was wearing her rose-topazes when Jane saw the picture in the Academy, and very lovely they looked on the delicate whiteness of her neck. But people who had seen Garth's painting of the pearls maintained that that scrape of the palette-knife had destroyed work which would have been the talk of the year. And Pauline Lister, just after it had happened, was reported to have said, with a shrug of her pretty shoulders: "Schemes of colour are all very well. But he scraped my pearls off the canvas because some one who came in hummed a tune while looking at the picture. I would be obliged if people who walk around the studio while I am being painted will in future refrain from humming tunes. I don't want him to scoop off my topazes and call for my emeralds. Also I feel like offering a reward for the discovery of that tune. I want to know what it has to do with my scheme of colour, anyway."

When Jane heard the story, she was spending a few days with the Brands in Wimpole Street. It was told at tea, in Lady Brand's pretty boudoir. The duchess's Concert, at which Garth had heard her sing *The Rosary*, was a thing of the past. Nearly a year had elapsed since their final parting, and this was the very first thought or word or sign of his remembrance, which directly or indirectly, had come her way. She could not doubt that the tune hummed had been *The Rosary*.

> "The hours I spent with thee, dear heart,
> Are as a string of pearls to me;
> I count them over, every one, apart."

She seemed to hear Garth's voice on the terrace, as she heard it in those first startled moments of realising the gift which was being laid at her feet—"I have learned to count pearls, beloved."

Jane's heart was growing cold and frozen in its emptiness. This incident of the studio warmed and woke it for the moment, and with the waking came sharp pain. When the visitors had left, and

Lady Brand had gone to the nursery, she walked over to the piano, sat down, and softly played the accompaniment of *The Rosary*. The fine unexpected chords, full of discords working into harmony, seemed to suit her mood and her memories.

Suddenly a voice behind her said: "Sing it, Jane." She turned quickly. The doctor had come in, and was lying back luxuriously in a large armchair at her elbow, his hands clasped behind his head. "Sing it, Jane," he said.

"I can't, Deryck," she answered, still softly sounding the chords. "I have not sung for months."

"What has been the matter—for months?"

Jane took her hands off the keys, and swung round impulsively.

"Oh, boy," she said. "I have made a bad mess of my life! And yet I know I did right. I would do the same again; at least—at least, I hope I would."

The doctor sat in silence for a minute, looking at her and pondering these short, quick sentences. Also he waited for more, knowing it would come more easily if he waited silently.

It came.

"Boy—I gave up something, which was more than life itself to me, for the sake of another, and I can't get over it. I know I did right, and yet—I can't get over it."

The doctor leaned forward and took the clenched hands between his.

"Can you tell me about it, Jeanette?"

"I can tell no one, Deryck; not even you."

"If ever you find you must tell someone, Jane, will you promise to come to me?"

"Gladly."

"Good! Now, my dear girl, here is a prescription for you. Go abroad. And, mind, I do not mean by that, just to Paris and back, or Switzerland this summer, and the Riviera in the autumn. Go to America and see a few big things. See Niagara. And all your life afterwards, when trivialities are trying you, you will love to let your mind go back to the vast green mass of water sweeping over the falls; to the thunderous roar, and the upward rush of spray; to the huge perpetual onwardness of it all. You will like to remember, when you are bothering about pouring water in and out of teacups, 'Niagara is flowing still.' Stay in a hotel so near the falls that you can hear their great voice night and day, thundering out themes of power and progress. Spend hours walking round and viewing it from every point. Go to the Cave of the Winds, across the frail bridges, where the guide will turn and shout to you: 'Are your rings on tight?' Learn, in passing, the true meaning of the Rock of Ages. Receive Niagara into your life and soul as a possession, and thank God for it.

"Then go in for other big things in America. Try spirituality and humanity; love and life. Seek out Mrs. Ballington Booth, the great 'Little Mother' of all American prisoners. I know her well, I am proud to say, and can give you a letter of introduction. Ask her to take you with her to Sing-Sing, or to Columbus State Prison, and to let you hear her address an audience of two thousand convicts, holding out to them the gospel of hope and love,—her own inspired and inspiring belief in fresh possibilities even for the most despairing.

"Go to New York City and see how, when a man wants a big building and has only a small plot of ground, he makes the most of that ground by running his building up into the sky. Learn to do likewise.—And then, when the great-souled, large-hearted, rapid-minded people of America have waked you to enthusiasm with their bigness, go off to Japan and see a little people nobly doing their best to become great.—Then to Palestine, and spend months in tracing the footsteps of the greatest human life ever lived. Take Egypt on your way home, just to remind yourself that there are still, in this very modern world of ours, a few passably ancient things,—a well-preserved wooden man, for instance, with eyes of opaque white quartz, a piece of rock crystal in the centre for a pupil. These glittering eyes looked out upon the world from beneath their eyelids of bronze, in the time of Abraham. You will find it in the museum at Cairo. Ride a donkey in the Mooskee if you want real sport; and if you feel a little slack, climb the Great Pyramid. Ask for an Arab named

Schehati, and tell him you want to do it one minute quicker than any lady has ever done it before.

"Then come home, my dear girl, ring me up and ask for an appointment; or chance it, and let Stoddart slip you into my consulting-room between patients, and report how the prescription has worked. I never gave a better; and you need not offer me a guinea! I attend old friends gratis."

Jane laughed, and gripped his hand. "Oh, boy," she said, "I believe you are right. My whole ideas of life have been focussed on myself and my own individual pains and losses. I will do as you say; and God bless you for saying it.—Here comes Flower. Flower," she said, as the doctor's wife trailed in, wearing a soft tea-gown, and turning on the electric lights as she passed, "will this boy of ours ever grow old? Here he is, seriously advising that a stout, middle-aged woman should climb the Great Pyramid as a cure for depression, and do it in record time!"

"Darling," said the doctor's wife, seating herself on the arm of his chair, "whom have you been seeing who is stout, or depressed, or middle-aged? If you mean Mrs. Parker Bangs, she is not middle-aged, because she is an American, and no American is ever middle-aged. And she is only depressed because, even after painting her lovely niece's portrait, Garth Dalmain has failed to propose to her. And it is no good advising her to climb the Great Pyramid, though she is doing Egypt this winter, because I heard her say yesterday that she should never think of going up the pyramids until the children of Israel, or whoever the natives are who live around those parts, have the sense to put an elevator right up the centre."

Jane and the doctor laughed, and Flower, settling herself more comfortably, for the doctor's arm had stolen around her, said: "Jane, I heard you playing *The Rosary* just now, such a favourite of mine, and it is months since I heard it. Do sing it, dear."

Jane met the doctor's eyes and smiled reassuringly; then turned without any hesitation and did as Flower asked. The prescription had already done her good.

At the last words of the song the doctor's wife bent over and laid a tender little kiss just above his temple, where the thick dark hair was streaked with silver. But the doctor's mind was intent on Jane, and before the final chords were struck he knew he had diagnosed her case correctly. "But she had better go abroad," he thought. "It will take her mind off herself altogether, giving her a larger view of things in general, and a better proportioned view of things in particular. And the boy won't change; or, if he does, Jane will be proved right, to her own satisfaction. But, if this is *her* side, good heavens, what must *his* be! I had wondered what was sapping all his buoyant youthfulness. To care for Jane would be an education; but to have made Jane care! And then to have lost her! He must have nerves of steel, to be facing life at all. What is this cross they are both learning to kiss, and holding up between them? Perhaps Niagara will sweep it away, and she will cable him from there."

Then the doctor took the dear little hand resting on his shoulder and kissed it softly, while Jane's back was still turned. For the doctor had had past experience of the cross, and now the pearls were very precious.

So Jane took the prescription, and two years went by in the taking; and here she was, on the top of the Great Pyramid, and, moreover, she had done it in record time, and laughed as she thought of how she should report the fact to Deryck.

Her Arabs lay around, very hot and shiny, and content. Large backsheesh was assured, and they looked up at her with pleased possessive eyes, as an achievement of their own; hardly realising how large a part her finely developed athletic powers and elastic limbs had played in the speed of the ascent.

And Jane stood there, sound in wind and limb, and with the exhilarating sense, always helpful to the mind, of a bodily feat accomplished.

She was looking her best in her Norfolk coat and skirt of brown tweed with hints of green and orange in it, plenty of useful pockets piped with leather, leather buttons, and a broad band of leather round the bottom of the skirt. A connoisseur would have named at once the one and only firm from which that costume could have come, and the hatter who supplied the soft green Tyrolian hat—for Jane scorned pith helmets—which matched it so admirably. But Schehati was no connoisseur of clothing, though a pretty shrewd judge of ways and manners, and he summed up Jane thus: "Nice gentleman-lady! Give good backsheesh, and not sit down halfway and say: 'No top'! But real lady-gentleman! Give backsheesh with kind face, and not send poor Arab to Assouan."

Jane was deeply tanned by the Eastern sun. Burning a splendid brown, and enjoying the process, she had no need of veils or parasols; and her strong eyes faced the golden light of the desert without the aid of smoked glasses. She had once heard Garth remark that a sight which made him feel really ill, was the back view of a woman in a motor-veil, and Jane had laughingly agreed, for to her veils of any kind had always seemed superfluous. The heavy coils of her brown hair never blew about into fascinating little curls and wisps, but remained where, with a few well-directed hairpins, she each morning solidly placed them.

Jane had never looked better than she did on this March day, standing on the summit of the Great Pyramid. Strong, brown, and well-knit, a reliable mind in a capable body, the undeniable plainness of her face redeemed by its kindly expression of interest and enjoyment; her wide, pleasant smile revealing her fine white teeth, witnesses to her perfect soundness and health, within and without.

"Nice gentleman-lady," murmured Schehati again: and had Jane overheard the remark it would not have offended her; for, though she held a masculine woman only one degree less in abhorrence than an effeminate man, she would have taken Schehati's compound noun as a tribute to the fact that she was well-groomed and independent, knowing her own mind, and, when she started out to go to a place, reaching it in the shortest possible time, without fidget, fuss, or flurry. These three feminine attributes were held in scorn by Jane, who knew herself so deeply womanly that she could afford in minor ways to be frankly unfeminine.

The doctor's prescription had worked admirably. That look of falling to pieces and ageing prematurely—a general dilapidation of mind and body—which it had grieved and startled him to see in Jane as she sat before him on the music-stool, was gone completely. She looked a calm, pleasant thirty; ready to go happily on, year by year, towards an equally agreeable and delightful forty; and not afraid of fifty, when that time should come. Her clear eyes looked frankly out upon the world, and her sane mind formed sound opinions and pronounced fair judgments, tempered by the kindliness of an unusually large and generous heart.

Just now she was considering the view and finding it very good. Its strong contrasts held her.

On one side lay the fertile Delta, with its groves of waving palm, orange, and olive trees, growing in rich profusion on the banks of the Nile, a broad band of gleaming silver. On the other, the Desert, with its far-distant horizon, stretching away in undulations of golden sand; not a tree, not a leaf, not a blade of grass, but boundless liberty, an ocean of solid golden glory. For the sun was setting, and the sky flamed into colour.

"A parting of the ways," said Jane; "a place of choice. How difficult to know which to choose—liberty or fruitfulness. One would have to consult the Sphinx—wise old guardian of the ages, silent keeper of Time's secrets, gazing on into the future as It has always gazed, while future became present, and present glided into past.—Come, Schehati, let us descend. Oh, yes, I will certainly sit upon the stone on which the King sat when he was Prince of Wales. Thank you for mentioning it. It will supply a delightful topic of conversation next time I am honoured by a few minutes of his gracious Majesty's attention, and will save me from floundering into trite remarks about the weather.—And now take me to the Sphinx, Schehati. There is a question I would ask of It, just as the sun dips below the horizon."

CHAPTER XIII

The Answer of the Sphinx

Moonlight in the desert.

Jane ordered her after-dinner coffee on the piazza of the hotel, that she might lose as little as possible of the mystic loveliness of the night. The pyramids appeared so huge and solid, in the clear white light; and the Sphinx gathered unto itself more mystery.

Jane promised herself a stroll round by moonlight presently. Meanwhile she lay back in a low wicker chair, comfortably upholstered, sipping her coffee, and giving herself up to the sense of dreamy content which, in a healthy body, is apt to follow vigorous exertion.

Very tender and quiet thoughts of Garth came to her this evening, perhaps brought about by the associations of moonlight.

> "The moon shines bright:—in such a night as this,
> When the sweet wind did gently kiss the trees,
> And they did make no noise—"

Ah! the great poet knew the effect upon the heart of a vivid reminder to the senses. Jane now passed beneath the spell.

To begin with, Garth's voice seemed singing everywhere:

"Enable with perpetual light
The dulness of our blinded sight."

Then from out the deep blue and silvery light, Garth's dear adoring eyes seemed watching her. Jane closed her own, to see them better. To-night she did not feel like shrinking from them, they were so full of love.

No shade of critical regard was in them. Ah! had she wronged him with her fears for the future? Her heart seemed full of trust to-night, full of confidence in him and in herself. It seemed to her that if he were here she could go out with him into this brilliant moonlight, seat herself upon some ancient fallen stone, and let him kneel in front of her and gaze and gaze in his persistent way, as much as he pleased. In thought there seemed to-night no shrinking from those dear eyes. She felt she would say: "It is all your own, Garth, to look at when you will. For your sake, I could wish it beautiful; but if it is as you like it, my own Dear, why should I hide it from you?"

What had brought about this change of mind? Had Deryck's prescription done its full work? Was this a saner point of view than the one she had felt constrained to take when she arrived, through so much agony of renunciation, at her decision?

Instead of going up the Nile, and then to Constantinople and Athens, should she take the steamer which sailed from Alexandria to-morrow, be in London a week hence, send for Garth, make full confession, and let him decide as to their future?

That he loved her still, it never occurred to Jane to doubt. At the very thought of sending for him and telling him the simple truth, he seemed so near her once more, that she could feel the clasp of his arms, and his head upon her heart. And those dear shining eyes! Oh, Garth, Garth!

"One thing is clear to me to-night," thought Jane. "If he still needs me—wants me—I cannot live any longer away from him. I must go to him." She opened her eyes and looked towards the Sphinx. The whole line of reasoning which had carried such weight at Shenstone flashed through her mind in twenty seconds. Then she closed her eyes again and clasped her hands upon her bosom.

"I will risk it," she said; and deep joy awoke within her heart.

A party of English people came from the dining-room on to the piazza with a clatter. They had arrived that evening and gone in late to dinner. Jane had hardly noticed them,—a handsome woman and her daughter, two young men, and an older man of military appearance. They did not interest Jane, but they broke in upon her reverie; for they seated themselves at a table near by and, in truly British fashion, continued a loud-voiced conversation, as if no one else were present. One or two foreigners, who had been peacefully dreaming over coffee and cigarettes, rose and strolled away to quiet seats under the palm trees. Jane would have done the same, but she really felt too comfortable to move, and afraid of losing the sweet sense of Garth's nearness. So she remained where she was.

The elderly man held in his hand a letter and a copy of the *Morning Post*, just received from England. They were discussing news contained in the letter and a paragraph he had been reading aloud from the paper.

"Poor fellow! How too sad!" said the chaperon of the party.

"I should think he would sooner have been killed outright!" exclaimed the girl. "I know I would."

"Oh, no," said one of the young men, leaning towards her. "Life is sweet, under any circumstances."

"Oh, but blind!" cried the young voice, with a shudder. "Quite blind for the rest of one's life. Horrible!"

"Was it his own gun?" asked the older woman. "And how came they to be having a shooting party in March?"

Jane smiled a fierce smile into the moonlight. Passionate love of animal life, intense regard for all life, even of the tiniest insect, was as much a religion with her as the worship of beauty was with Garth. She never could pretend sorrow over these accounts of shooting accidents, or falls in the hunting-field. When those who went out to inflict cruel pain were hurt themselves; when those who went forth to take eager, palpitating life, lost their own; it seemed to Jane a just retribution. She felt no regret, and pretended none. So now she smiled fiercely to herself, thinking: "One pair of eyes the less to look along a gun and frustrate the despairing dash for home and little ones of a terrified little mother rabbit. One hand that will never again change a soaring upward flight of spreading wings, into an agonised mass of falling feathers. One chance to the good, for the noble stag, as he makes a brave run to join his hinds in the valley."

Meanwhile the military-looking man had readjusted his eye-glasses and was holding the sheets of a closely written letter to the light.

"No," he said after a moment, "shooting parties are over. There is nothing doing on the moors now. They were potting bunnies."

"Was he shooting?" asked the girl.

"No," replied the owner of the letter, "and that seems such hard luck. He had given up shooting altogether a year or two ago. He never really enjoyed it, because he so loved the beauty of life and hated death in every form. He has a lovely place in the North, and was up there painting. He happened to pass within sight of some fellows rabbit-shooting, and saw what he considered cruelty to a wounded rabbit. He vaulted over a gate to expostulate and to save the little creature from further suffering. Then it happened. One of the lads, apparently startled, let off his gun. The charge struck a tree a few yards off, and the shot glanced. It did not strike him full. The face is only slightly peppered and the brain quite uninjured. But shots pierced the retina of each eye, and the sight is hopelessly gone."

"Awful hard luck," said the young man.

"I never can understand a chap not bein' keen on shootin'," said the youth who had not yet spoken.

"Ah, but you would if you had known him," said the soldier. "He was so full of life and vivid vitality. One could not imagine him either dying or dealing death. And his love of the beautiful was almost a form of religious worship. I can't explain it; but he had a way of making you see beauty in things you had hardly noticed before. And now, poor chap, he can't see them himself."

"Has he a mother?" asked the older woman.

"No, he has no one. He is absolutely alone. Scores of friends of course; he was a most popular man about town, and could stay in almost any house in the kingdom if he chose to send a post-card to say he was coming. But no relations, I believe, and never would marry. Poor chap! He will wish he had been less fastidious, now. He might have had the pick of all the nicest girls, most seasons. But not he! Just charming friendships, and wedded to his art. And now, as Lady Ingleby, says, he lies in the dark, helpless and alone."

"Oh, do talk of something else!" cried the girl, pushing back her chair and rising. "I want to forget it. It's too horribly sad. Fancy what it must be to wake up and not know whether it is day or night, and to have to lie in the dark and wonder. Oh, do come out and talk of something cheerful."

They all rose, and the young man slipped his hand through the girl's arm, glad of the excuse her agitation provided.

"Forget it, dear," he said softly. "Come on out and see the old Sphinx by moonlight."

They left the piazza, followed by the rest of the party; but the man to whom the *Morning Post* belonged laid it on the table and stayed behind, lighting a cigar.

Jane rose from her chair and came towards him.

"May I look at your paper?" she said abruptly.

"Certainly," he replied, with ready courtesy. Then, looking more closely at her: "Why, certainly, Miss Champion. And how do you do? I did not know you were in these parts."

"Ah, General Loraine! Your face seemed familiar, but I had not recognised you, either. Thanks, I will borrow this if I may. And don't let

169

me keep you from your friends. We shall meet again by and by."

Jane waited until the whole party had passed out of sight and until the sound of their voices and laughter had died away in the distance. Then she returned to her chair, the place where Garth had seemed so near. She looked once more at the Sphinx and at the huge pyramid in the moonlight.

Then she took up the paper and opened it.

"Enable with perpetual light
The dulness of our blinded sight."

Yes—it was Garth Dalmain—*her* Garth, of the adoring shining eyes—who lay at his house in the North; blind, helpless, and alone.

CHAPTER XIV

In Deryck's Safe Control

The white cliffs of Dover gradually became more solid and distinct, until at length they rose from the sea, a strong white wall, emblem of the undeniable purity of England, the stainless honour and integrity of her throne, her church, her parliament, her courts of justice, and her dealings at home and abroad, whether with friend or foe. "Strength and whiteness," thought Jane as she paced the steamer's deck; and after a two years' absence her heart went out to her native land. Then Dover Castle caught her eye, so beautiful in the pearly light of that spring afternoon. Her mind leaped to enjoyment, then fell back stunned by the blow of quick remembrance, and Jane shut her eyes.

All beautiful sights brought this pang to her heart since the reading of that paragraph on the piazza of the Mena House Hotel.

An hour after she had read it, she was driving down the long straight road to Cairo; embarked at Alexandria the next day; landed at Brindisi, and this night and day travelling had brought her at last within sight of the shores of England. In a few minutes she would set foot upon them, and then there would be but two more stages to her journey. For, from the moment she started, Jane never doubted her ultimate destination,—the room where pain and darkness and despair must be waging so terrible a conflict against the moral courage, the mental sanity, and the instinctive hold on life of the man she loved.

That she was going to him, Jane knew; but she felt utterly unable to arrange how or in what way her going could be managed. That it was a complicated problem, her common sense told her; though her yearning arms and aching bosom cried out: "O God, is it not simple? Blind and alone! *My* Garth!"

But she knew an unbiased judgment, steadier than her own, must solve the problem; and that her surest way to Garth lay through the doctor's consulting-room. So she telegraphed to Deryck from Paris, and at present her mind saw no further than Wimpole Street.

At Dover she bought a paper, and hastily scanned its pages as she walked along the platform in the wake of the capable porter who had taken possession of her rugs and hand baggage. In the personal column she found the very paragraph she sought.

"We regret to announce that Mr. Garth Dalmain still lies in a most precarious condition at his house on Deeside, Aberdeenshire, as a result of the shooting accident a fortnight ago. His sight is hopelessly gone, but the injured parts were progressing favourably, and all fear of brain complications seemed over. During the last few days, however, a serious reaction from shock has set in, and it has been considered necessary to summon Sir Deryck Brand, the well-known nerve specialist, in consultation with the oculist and the local practitioner in charge of the case. There is a feeling of wide-spread regret and sympathy in those social and artistic circles where Mr. Dalmain was so well-known and so deservedly popular."

"Oh, thank you, m'lady," said the efficient porter when he had ascertained, by a rapid glance into his palm, that Jane's half-crown was not a penny. He had a sick young wife at home, who had been ordered extra nourishment, and just as the rush on board began, he had put up a simple prayer to the Heavenly Father "who knoweth that ye have need of these things," asking that he might catch the eye of a generous traveller. He felt he had indeed been "led" to this plain, brown-faced, broad-shouldered lady, when he remembered how nearly, after her curt nod from a distance had engaged him, he had responded to the blandishments of a fussy little woman, with many more bags and rugs, and a parrot cage, who was now doling French coppers out of the window of the next compartment. "Seven pence 'apenny of this stuff ain't much for carrying all that along, I *don't* think!" grumbled his mate; and Jane's young porter experienced the double joy of faith confirmed, and willing service generously rewarded.

A telegraph boy walked along the train, saying: "Honrubble Jain Champyun" at intervals. Jane heard her name, and her arm shot out of the window.

"Here, my boy! It is for me."

She tore it open. It was from the doctor.

"Welcome home. Just back from Scotland. Will meet you Charing Cross, and give you all the time you want. Have coffee at Dover. DERYCK."

Jane gave one hard, tearless sob of thankfulness and relief. She had been so lonely.

Then she turned to the window. "Here, somebody! Fetch me a cup of coffee, will you?"

Coffee was the last thing she wanted; but it never occurred to any one to disobey the doctor, even at a distance.

The young porter, who still stood sentry at the door of Jane's compartment, dashed off to the refreshment room; and, just as the train began to move, handed a cup of steaming coffee and a plate of bread-and-butter in at the window.

"Oh, thank you, my good fellow," said Jane, putting the plate on the seat, while she dived into her pocket. "Here! you have done very well for me. No, never mind the change. Coffee at a moment's notice should fetch a fancy price. Good-bye."

The train moved on, and the porter stood looking after it with tears in his eyes. Over the first half-crown he had said to himself: "Milk and new-laid eggs." Now, as he pocketed the second, he added the other two things mentioned by the parish doctor: "Soup and jelly"; and his heart glowed. "Your heavenly Father knoweth that ye have need of these things."

And Jane, seated in a comfortable corner, choked back the tears of relief which threatened to fall, drank her coffee, and was thereby more revived than she could have thought possible. She, also, had need of many things. Not of half-crowns; of those she had plenty. But above all else she needed just now a wise, strong, helpful friend, and Deryck had not failed her.

She read his telegram through once more, and smiled. How like him to think of the coffee; and oh, how like him to be coming to the station.

She took off her hat and leaned back against the cushions. She had been travelling night and day, in one feverish whirl of haste, and at last she had brought herself within reach of Deryck's hand and Deryck's safe control. The turmoil of her soul was stilled; a great calm took its place, and Jane dropped quietly off to sleep. "Your heavenly Father knoweth that ye have need of these things."

Washed and brushed and greatly refreshed, Jane stood at the window of her compartment as the train steamed into Charing Cross.

The doctor was stationed exactly opposite the door when her carriage came to a standstill; mere chance, and yet, to Jane, it seemed so like him to have taken up his position precisely at the right spot on that long platform. An enthusiastic lady patient had once said of Deryck Brand, with more accuracy of definition than of grammar: "You know, he is always so very *just there*." And this characteristic of the doctor had made him to many a very present help in time of trouble.

He was through the line of porters and had his hand upon the handle of Jane's door in a moment. Standing at the window, she took one look at the firm lean face, now alight with welcome, and read in the kind, steadfast eyes of her

175

childhood's friend a perfect sympathy and comprehension. Then she saw behind him her aunt's
footman, and her own maid, who had been given
a place in the duchess's household. In another
moment she was on the platform and her hand
was in Deryck's.

"That is right, dear," he said. "All fit and well, I
can see. Now hand over your keys. I suppose you
have nothing contraband? I telephoned the
duchess to send some of her people to meet your
luggage, and not to expect you herself until dinner
time, as you were taking tea with us. Was that
right? This way. Come outside the barrier. What a
rabble! All wanting to break every possible rule
and regulation, and each trying to be the first
person in the front row. Really the patience and
good temper of railway officials should teach the
rest of mankind a lesson."

The doctor, talking all the time, piloted Jane
through the crowd; opened the door of a neat electric brougham, helped her in, took his seat beside
her, and they glided swiftly out into the Strand,
and turned towards Trafalgar Square.

"Well," said the doctor, "Niagara is a big thing
isn't it? When people say to me, 'Were you not
disappointed in Niagara? *We* were!' I feel tempted
to wish, for one homicidal moment, that the earth
would open her mouth and swallow them up.
People who can be disappointed in Niagara, and
talk about it, should no longer be allowed to crawl

on the face of the earth. And how about the 'Little Mother'? Isn't she worth knowing? I hope she sent me her love. And New York harbour! Did you ever see anything to equal it, as you steam away in the sunset?"

Jane gave a sudden sob; then turned to him, dry-eyed.

"Is there no hope, Deryck?"

The doctor laid his hand on hers. "He will always be blind, dear. But life holds other things beside sight. We must never say: 'No hope.'"

"Will he live?"

"There is no reason he should not live. But how far life will be worth living, largely depends upon what can be done for him, poor chap, during the next few months. He is more shattered mentally than physically."

Jane pulled off her gloves, swallowed suddenly, then gripped the doctor's knee. "Deryck—I love him."

The doctor remained silent for a few moments, as if pondering this tremendous fact. Then he lifted the fine, capable hand resting upon his knee and kissed it with a beautiful reverence,—a gesture expressing the homage of the man to the brave truthfulness of the woman.

"In that case, dear," he said, "the future holds in store so great a good for Garth Dalmain that I think he may dispense with sight.— Meanwhile you have much to say to me, and it is, of course, your right to hear every detail of his case that I can give. And here we are at Wimpole Street. Now come into my consulting-room. Stoddart has orders that we are on no account to be disturbed."

CHAPTER XV

The Consultation

The doctor's room was very quiet. Jane leaned back in his dark green leather arm-chair, her feet on a footstool, her hands gripping the arms on either side.

The doctor sat at his table, in the round pivot-chair he always used,—a chair which enabled him to swing round suddenly and face a patient, or to turn away very quietly and bend over his table.

Just now he was not looking at Jane. He had been giving her a detailed account of his visit to Castle Gleneesh, which he had left only on the previous evening. He had spent five hours with Garth. It seemed kindest to tell her all; but he was looking straight before him as he talked, because he knew that at last the tears were running unchecked down Jane's cheeks, and he wished her to think he did not notice them.

"You understand, dear," he was saying, "the actual wounds are going on well. Strangely enough, though the retina of each eye was pierced, and the sight is irrecoverably gone, there was very little damage done to surrounding parts, and the brain is quite uninjured. The present danger arises from the shock to the nervous system and from the extreme mental anguish caused by the realisation of his loss. The physical suffering during the first days and nights must have been terrible. Poor fellow, he looks shattered by it. But his constitution is excellent, and his life has been so clean, healthy, and normal, that he had every chance of making a good recovery, were it not that as the pain abated and his blindness became more a thing to be daily and hourly realised, his mental torture was so excessive. Sight has meant so infinitely much to him,—beauty of form, beauty of colour. The artist in him was so all-pervading. They tell me he said very little. He is a brave man and a strong one. But his temperature began to vary alarmingly; he showed symptoms of mental trouble, of which I need not give you technical details; and a nerve specialist seemed more necessary than an oculist. Therefore he is now in my hands."

The doctor paused, straightened a few books lying on the table, and drew a small bowl of violets closer to him. He studied these attentively for a few moments, then put them back where his wife had placed them and went on speaking.

"I am satisfied on the whole. He needed a friendly voice to penetrate the darkness. He needed a hand to grasp his, in faithful comprehension. He did not want pity, and those who talked of his loss without understanding it, or being able to measure its immensity, maddened him. He needed a fellow-man to come to him and say: 'It is a fight—an awful, desperate fight. But by God's grace you will win through to victory. It would be far easier to die; but to die would be to lose; you must live to win. It is utterly beyond all human strength; but by God's grace you will come through conqueror.' All this I said to him, Jeanette, and a good deal more; and then a strangely beautiful thing happened. I can tell you, and of course I could tell Flower, but to no one else on earth would I repeat it. The difficulty had been to obtain from him any response whatever. He did not seem able to rouse sufficiently to notice anything going on around him. But those words, 'by God's grace,' appeared to take hold of him and find immediate echo in his inner consciousness. I heard him repeat them once or twice, and then change them to 'with the abundance of Thy grace.' Then he turned his head slowly on the pillow, and what one could see of his face seemed transformed. He said: 'Now I remember it, and the music is this'; and his hands moved on the bedclothes, as if forming chords. Then, in a very low voice, but quite clearly, he repeated the second verse of the *Veni, Creator Spiritus*. I knew it, because I used to sing it as a chorister in my father's church at home. You remember?

" 'Enable with perpetual light
The dulness of our blinded sight.
Anoint and cheer our soiled face
With the abundance of Thy grace.
Keep far our foes; give peace at home;
Where Thou art Guide, no ill can come.'

"It was the most touching thing I ever heard."

The doctor paused, for Jane had buried her face in her hands and was sobbing convulsively. When her sobs grew less violent, the doctor's quiet voice continued: "You see, this gave me something to go upon. When a crash such as this happens, all a man has left to hold on to is his religion. According as his spiritual side has been developed, will his physical side stand the strain. Dalmain has more of the real thing than any one would think who only knew him superficially. Well, after that we talked quite definitely, and I persuaded him to agree to one or two important arrangements. You know, he has no relations of his own, to speak of; just a few cousins, who have never been very friendly. He is quite alone up there; for, though he has hosts of friends, this is a time when friends would have to be very intimate to be admitted; and though he seemed so boyish and easy to know, I begin to doubt whether any of us knew the real Garth—the soul of the man, deep down beneath the surface."

Jane lifted her head. "I did," she said simply.

"Ah," said the doctor, "I see. Well, as I said, ordinary friends could not be admitted. Lady Ingleby went, in her sweet impulsive way, without letting them know she was coming; travelled all the way up from Shenstone with no maid, and nothing but a handbag, and arrived at the door in a fly. Robert Mackenzie, the local medical man, who is an inveterate misogynist, feared at first she was an unsuspected wife of Dal's. He seemed to think unannounced ladies arriving in hired vehicles must necessarily turn out to be undesirable wives. I gather they had a somewhat funny scene. But Lady Ingleby soon got round old Robbie, and came near to charming him—as whom does she not? But of course they did not dare let her into Dal's room; so her ministry of consolation appears to have consisted in letting Dal's old housekeeper weep on her beautiful shoulder. It was somewhat of a comedy, hearing about it, when one happened to know them all, better than they knew each other. But to return to practical details. He has had a fully trained male nurse and his own valet to wait on him. He absolutely refused one of our London hospital nurses, who might have brought a little gentle comfort and womanly sympathy to his sick-room. He said he could not stand being touched by a woman; so there it remained. A competent man was found instead. But we can now dispense with him, and I have insisted upon sending up a lady nurse of my own choosing; not so much to wait on him, or do any of a sick-nurse's ordinary duties—his own man can do these, and he seems a capable fellow—but to sit with him, read to him, attend to his correspondence,—there are piles of unopened letters he ought to hear,—in fact help him to take up life again in his blindness. It will need training; it will require tact; and this afternoon I engaged exactly the right person. She is a gentlewoman by birth, has nursed for me before, and is well up in the special knowledge of mental things which this case requires. Also she is a pretty, dainty little thing; just the kind of elegant young woman poor Dal would have liked to have about him when he could see. He was such a fastidious chap about appearances, and such a connoisseur of good looks. I have written a descriptive account of her to Dr. Mackenzie, and he will prepare his patient for her arrival. She is to go up the day after to-morrow. We are lucky to get her, for she is quite first-rate, and she has only just finished with a long consumptive case, now on the mend and ordered abroad. So you see, Jeanette, all is shaping well.—And now, my dear girl, you have a story of your own to tell me, and my whole attention shall be at your disposal. But first of all I am going to ring for tea, and you and I will have it quietly down here, if you will excuse me for a few minutes while I go upstairs and speak to Flower."

It seemed so natural to Jane to be pouring out the doctor's tea, and to watch him putting a liberal allowance of salt on the thin bread-and-butter, and then folding it over with the careful accuracy which had always characterised his smallest action. In the essentials he had changed so little since the days when as a youth of twenty spending his vacations at the rectory he used to give the lonely girl at the manor so much pleasure by coming up to her school-room tea; and when it proved possible to dispose of her governess's chaperonage and be by themselves, what delightful times they used to have, sitting on the hearth-rug, roasting chestnuts and discussing the many subjects which were of mutual interest. Jane could still remember the painful pleasure of turning hot chestnuts on the bars with her fingers, and how she hastened to do them herself, lest he should be burned. She had always secretly liked and admired his hands, with the brown thin fingers, so delicate in their touch and yet full of such gentle strength. She used to love watching them while he sharpened her pencils or drew wonderful diagrams in her exercise books; thinking how in years to come, when he performed important operations, human lives would depend upon their skill and dexterity. In those early years he had seemed so much older than she. And then came the time when she shot up rapidly into young womanhood and their eyes were on a level and their ages seemed the same. Then, as the years went on, Jane began to feel older than he, and took to calling him "Boy" to emphasise this fact. And then came—Flower;—and complications. And Jane had to see his face grow thin and worn, and his hair whiten on the temples. And she yearned over him, yet dared not offer sympathy. At last things came right for the doctor, and all the highest good seemed his; in his profession; in his standing among men; and, above all, in his heart life, which Flower had always held between her two sweet hands. And Jane rejoiced, but felt still more lonely now she had no companion in loneliness. And still their friendship held, with Flower admitted as a third—a wistful, grateful third, anxious to learn from the woman whose friendship meant so much to her husband, how to succeed where she had hitherto failed. And Jane's faithful heart was generous and loyal to both, though in sight of their perfect happiness her loneliness grew.

And now, in her own hour of need, it had to be Deryck only; and the doctor knew this, and had arranged accordingly; for at last his chance had come, to repay the faithful devotion of a lifetime. The conversation of that afternoon would be the supreme test of their friendship. And so, with a specialist's appreciation of the mental effect of the most trivial external details, the doctor had ordered muffins, and a kettle on the fire, and had asked Jane to make the tea.

By the time the kettle boiled, they had remembered the chestnuts, and were laughing about poor old Fraulein's efforts to keep them in order, and the strategies by which they used to evade her vigilance. And the years rolled back, and Jane felt herself very much at home with the chum of her childhood.

Nevertheless, there was a moment of tension when the doctor drew back the tea-table and they faced each other in easy-chairs on either side of the fireplace. Each noticed how characteristic was the attitude of the other.

Jane sat forward, her feet firmly planted on the hearth-rug, her arms on her knees, and her hands clasped in front of her.

The doctor leaned back, one knee crossed over the other, his elbows on the arms of his chair, the tips of his fingers meeting, in absolute stillness of body and intense concentration of mind.

The silence between them was like a deep, calm pool.

Jane took the first plunge.

"Deryck, I am going to tell you everything. I am going to speak of my heart, and mind, and feelings, exactly as if they were bones, and muscles, and lungs. I want you to combine the offices of doctor and confessor in one."

The doctor had been contemplating his finger-tips. He now glanced swiftly at Jane, and nodded; then turned his head and looked into the fire.

"Deryck, mine has been a somewhat lonely existence. I have never been essential to the life of another, and no one has ever touched the real depths of mine. I have known they were there, but I have known they were unsounded."

The doctor opened his lips, as if to speak; then closed them in a firmer line than before, and merely nodded his head silently.

"I had never been loved with that love which makes one absolutely first to a person, nor had I ever so loved. I had—cared very much; but caring is not loving.—Oh, Boy, I know that now!"

The doctor's profile showed rather white against the dark-green background of his chair; but he smiled as he answered: "Quite true, dear. There is a distinction, and a difference."

"I had heaps of friends, and amongst them a good many nice men, mostly rather younger than myself, who called me 'Miss Champion' to my face, and 'good old Jane' behind my back."

The doctor smiled. He had as often heard the expression, and could recall the whole-hearted affection and admiration in the tones of those who used it.

"Men as a rule," continued Jane, "get on better with me than do women. Being large and solid, and usually calling a spade 'a spade' and not 'a garden implement,' women consider me strong-minded, and are inclined to be afraid of me. The boys know they can trust me; they make a confidante of me, looking upon me as a sort of convenient elder sister who knows less about them than an elder sister would know, and is probably more ready to be interested in those things which they choose to tell. Among my men friends, Deryck, was Garth Dalmain."

Jane paused, and the doctor waited silently for her to continue.

"I was always interested in him, partly because he was so original and vivid in his way of talking, and partly because"—a bright flush suddenly crept up into the tanned cheeks—"well, though I did not realise it then, I suppose I found his extraordinary beauty rather fascinating. And then, our circumstances were so much alike,—both orphans, and well off; responsible to no one for our actions; with heaps of mutual friends, and constantly staying at the same houses. We drifted into a pleasant intimacy, and of all my friends, he was the one who made me feel most like 'a man and a brother.' We discussed women by the dozen, all his special admirations in turn, and the effect of their beauty upon him, and I watched with interest to see who, at last, would fix his roving fancy. But on one eventful day all this was changed in half an hour. We were both staying at Overdene. There was a big house party, and Aunt Georgina had arranged a concert to which half the neighbourhood was coming. Madame Velma failed at the last minute. Aunt 'Gina, in a great state of mind, was borrowing remarks from her macaw. You know how? She always says she is merely quoting 'the dear bird.' Something had to be done. I offered to take Velma's place; and I sang."

"Ah," said the doctor.

"I sang *The Rosary*—the song Flower asked for the last time I was here. Do you remember?"

The doctor nodded. "I remember."

"After that, all was changed between Garth and me. I did not understand it at first. I knew the music had moved him deeply, beauty of sound having upon him much the same effect as beauty of colour; but I thought the effect would pass in the night. But the days went on, and there was always this strange sweet difference; not anything others would notice; but I suddenly became conscious that, for the first time in my whole life, I was essential to somebody. I could not enter a room without realising that he was instantly aware of my presence; I could not leave a room without knowing that he would at once feel and regret my absence. The one fact filled and completed all things; the other left a blank which could not be removed. I knew this, and yet—incredible though it may appear—I did not realise it meant *love*. I thought it was an extraordinarily close bond of sympathy and mutual understanding, brought about principally by our enjoyment of one

189

another's music. We spent hours in the music-room. I put it down to that; yet when he looked at me his eyes seemed to touch as well as see me, and it was a very tender and wonderful touch. And all the while I never thought of love. I was so plain and almost middle-aged; and he, such a beautiful, radiant youth. He was like a young sun-god, and I felt warmed and vivified when he was near; and he was almost always near. Honestly, that was my side of the days succeeding the concert. But *his!* He told me afterwards, Deryck, it had been a sudden revelation to him when he heard me sing *The Rosary*, not of music only, but of *me*. He said he had never thought of me otherwise than as a good sort of chum; but then it was as if a veil were lifted, and he saw, and knew, and felt me as a woman. And—no doubt it will seem odd to you. Boy; it did to me;—but he said, that the woman he found then was his ideal of womanhood, and that from that hour he wanted me for his own as he had never wanted anything before."

Jane paused, and looked into the glowing heart of the fire.

The doctor turned slowly and looked at Jane. He himself had experienced the intense attraction of her womanliness,—all the more overpowering when it was realised, because it did not appear upon the surface. He had sensed the strong mother-tenderness lying dormant within her; had known that her arms would prove a haven of refuge, her bosom a soothing pillow, her love a consolation unspeakable. In his own days of loneliness and disappointment, the doctor had had to flee from this in Jane,—a precious gift, so easy to have taken because of her very ignorance of it; but a gift to which he had no right. Thus the doctor could well understand the hold it would gain upon a man who had discovered it, and who was free to win it for his own.

But he only said, "I do not think it odd, dear."

Jane had forgotten the doctor. She came back promptly from the glowing heart of the fire.

"I am glad you don't," she said. "I did.—Well, we both left Overdene on the same day. I came to you; he went to Shenstone. It was a Tuesday. On the Friday I went down to Shenstone, and we met again. Having been apart for a little while seemed to make this curious feeling of 'togetherness,' deeper and sweeter than ever. In the Shenstone house party was that lovely American girl, Pauline Lister. Garth was enthusiastic about her beauty, and set on painting her. Everybody made sure he was going to propose to her. Deryck, I thought so, too; in fact I had advised him to do it. I felt so pleased and interested over it, though all the while his eyes touched me when he looked at me, and I knew the day did not begin for him until we had met, and was over when we had said good-night. And this experience of being first and most to him made everything so golden, and life so rich, and still I thought of it only as an unusually delightful friendship. But the evening of my arrival at Shenstone he asked me to come out on to the terrace after dinner, as he wanted specially to talk to me. Deryck, I thought it was the usual proceeding of making a confidante of me, and that I was to hear details of his intentions regarding Miss Lister. Thinking that, I walked calmly out beside him; sat down on the parapet, in the brilliant moonlight, and quietly waited for him to begin. Then—oh, Deryck! It happened."

Jane put her elbows on her knees, and buried her face in her clasped hands.

"I cannot tell you—details. His love—it just poured over me like molten gold. It melted the shell of my reserve; it burst through the ice of my convictions; it swept me off my feet upon a torrent of wondrous fire. I knew nothing in heaven or earth but that this love was mine, and was for me. And then—oh, Deryck! I can't explain—I don't know myself how it happened—but this whirlwind of emotion came to rest upon my heart. He knelt with his arms around me, and we held each other in a sudden great stillness; and in that moment I was all his, and he knew it. He might have stayed there hours if he had not moved or spoken; but presently he lifted up his face and looked at me. Then he said two words. I can't repeat them, Boy; but they brought me suddenly to my senses, and made me realise what it all meant. Garth Dalmain wanted me to marry him."

Jane paused, awaiting the doctor's expression of surprise.

"What else could it have meant?" said Deryck Brand, very quietly. He passed his hand over his lips, knowing they trembled a little. Jane's confessions were giving him a stiffer time than he had expected. "Well, dear, so you—?"

"I stood up," said Jane; "for while he knelt there he was master of me, mind and body; and some instinct told me that if I were to be won to wifehood, my reason must say 'yes' before the rest of me. It is 'spirit, soul, and body' in the Word, not 'body, soul, and spirit,' as is so often misquoted; and I believe the inspired sequence to be the right one."

The doctor made a quick movement of interest. "Good heavens, Jane!" he said. "You have got hold of a truth there, and you have expressed it exactly as I have often wanted to express it without being able to find the right words. You have found them, Jeanette."

She looked into his eager eyes and smiled sadly. "Have I, Boy?" she said. "Well, they have cost me dear.—I put my lover from me and told him I must have twelve hours for calm reflection. He was so sure—so sure of me, so sure of himself—that he agreed without a protest. At my request he left me at once. The manner of his going I cannot tell, even to you, Dicky. I promised to meet him at the village church next day and give him my answer. He was to try the new organ at eleven. We knew we should be alone. I came. He sent away the blower. He called me to him at the chancel step. The setting was so perfect. The artist in him sang for joy, and thrilled with expectation. The glory of absolute certainty was in his eyes; though he had himself well in hand. He kept from touching me while he asked for my answer. Then—I refused him, point blank, giving a reason he could not question. He turned from me and left the church, and I have not spoken to him from that day to this."

A long silence in the doctor's consulting-room. One manly heart was entering into the pain of another, and yet striving not to be indignant until he knew the whole truth.

Jane's spirit was strung up to the same pitch as in that fateful hour, and once more she thought herself right.

At last the doctor spoke. He looked at her searchingly now, and held her eyes.

"And why did you refuse him, Jane?" The kind voice was rather stern.

Jane put out her hands to him appealingly. "Ah, Boy, I must make you understand! How could I do otherwise, though, indeed, it was putting away the highest good life will ever hold for me? Deryck, you know Garth well enough to realise how dependent he is on beauty; he must be surrounded by it, perpetually. Before this unaccountable need of each other came to us he had talked to me quite freely on this point, saying of a plain person whose character and gifts he greatly admired, and whose face he grew to like in consequence: 'But of course it was not the sort of face one would have wanted to live with, or to have day after day opposite to one at table; but then one was not called to that sort of discipline, which would be martyrdom to me.' Oh, Deryck! Could I have tied Garth to my plain face? Could I have let myself become a daily, hourly discipline to that radiant, beauty-loving nature? I know they say, 'Love is blind.' But that is before Love has entered into his kingdom. Love desirous, sees only that, in the one beloved, which has awakened the desire. But Love content, regains full vision, and, as time goes on, those powers of vision increase and become, by means of daily, hourly, use,—microscopic and telescopic. Wedded love is not blind. Bah! An outsider staying with married people is apt to hear what love sees, on both sides, and the delusion of love's blindness is dispelled forever. I know Garth was blind, during all those golden days, to my utter lack of beauty, because he wanted *me* so much. But when he had had me, and had steeped himself in all I have to give of soul and spirit beauty; when the daily routine of life began, which after all has to be lived in complexions, and with features to the fore; when he sat down to breakfast and I saw him glance at me and then look away, when I was conscious that I was sitting behind the coffee-pot, looking my very plainest, and that in consequence my boy's discipline had begun; could I have borne it? Should I not, in the miserable sense of failing him day by day, through no fault of my own, have grown plainer and plainer; until bitterness and disappointment, and perhaps jealousy, all combined to make me positively ugly? I ask you, Deryck, could I have borne it?"

The doctor was looking at Jane with an expression of keen professional interest.

"How awfully well I diagnosed the case when I sent you abroad," he remarked meditatively. "Really, with so little data to go upon—"

"Oh, Boy," cried Jane, with a movement of impatience, "don't speak to me as if I were a patient. Treat me as a human being, at least, and tell me—as man to man—could I have tied Garth Dalmain to my plain face? For you know it is plain."

The doctor laughed. He was glad to make Jane a little angry. "My dear girl," he said, "were we speaking as man to man, I should have a few very strong things to say to you. As we are speaking as man to woman,—and as a man who has for a very long time respected, honoured, and admired a very dear and noble woman,—I will answer your question frankly. You are not beautiful, in

196

the ordinary acceptation of the word, and no one who really loves you would answer otherwise; because no one who knows and loves you would dream of telling you a lie. We will even allow, if you like, that you are plain, although I know half a dozen young men who, were they here, would want to kick me into the street for saying so, and I should have to pretend in self-defence that their ears had played them false and I had said, 'You are *Jane,*' which is all they would consider mattered. So long as you are yourself, your friends will be well content. At the same time, I may add, while this dear face is under discussion, that I can look back to times when I have felt that I would gladly walk twenty miles for a sight of it; and in its absence I have always wished it present, and in its presence I have never wished it away."

"Ah, but, Deryck, you did not have to have it always opposite you at meals," insisted Jane gravely.

"Unfortunately not. But I enjoyed the meals more on the happy occasions when it was there."

"And, Deryck—*you did not have to kiss it.*"

The doctor threw back his head and shouted with laughter, so that Flower, passing up the stairs, wondered what turn the conversation could be taking.

But Jane was quite serious; and saw in it no laughing matter.

"No, dear," said the doctor when he had recovered; "to my infinite credit be it recorded, that in all the years I have known it I have never once kissed it."

"Dicky, don't tease! Oh, Boy, it is the most vital question of my whole life; and if you do not now give me wise and thoughtful advice, all this difficult confession will have been for nothing."

The doctor became grave immediately. He leaned forward and took those clasped hands between his.

"Dear," he said, "forgive me if I seemed to take it lightly. My most earnest thought is wholly at your disposal. And now let me ask you a few questions. How did you ever succeed in convincing Dalmain that such a thing as this was an insuperable obstacle to your marriage?"

"I did not give it as a reason."

"What then did you give as your reason for refusing him?"

"I asked him how old he was."

"Jane! Standing there beside him in the chancel, where he had come awaiting your answer?"

"Yes. It did seem awful when I came to think it over afterwards. But it worked."

"I have no doubt it worked. What then?"

"He said he was twenty-seven. I said I was thirty, and looked thirty-five, and felt forty. I also said he might be twenty-seven, but he looked nineteen, and I was sure he often felt nine."

"Well?"

"Then I said that I could not marry a mere boy."

"And he acquiesced?"

"He seemed stunned at first. Then he said of course I could not marry him if I considered him that. He said it was the first time he had given a thought to himself in the matter. Then he said he bowed to my decision, and he walked down the church and went out, and we have not met since."

"Jane," said the doctor, "I wonder he did not see through it. You are so unused to lying, that you cannot have lied, on the chancel step, to the man you loved, with much conviction."

A dull red crept up beneath Jane's tan.

"Oh, Deryck, it was not entirely a lie. It was one of those dreadful lies which are 'part a truth,' of which Tennyson says that they are 'a harder matter to fight.'"

"'A lie which is all a lie
May be met and fought with outright;
But a lie which is part a truth
Is a harder matter to fight,'"

quoted the doctor.

"Yes," said Jane. "And he could not fight this, just because it was partly true. He is younger than I by three years, and still more by temperament. It was partly for his delightful youthfulness that I feared my maturity and staidness. It was part a truth, but oh, Deryck, it was more a lie; and it was altogether a lie to call him—the man whom I had felt complete master of me the evening before—'a mere boy.' Also he could not fight it because it took him so utterly by surprise. He had been all the time as completely without self-consciousness, as I had been morbidly full of it. His whole thought had been of me. Mine had been of him and—of myself."

"Jane," said the doctor, "of all that you have suffered since that hour, you deserved every pang."

Jane bent her head. "I know," she said.

"You were false to yourself, and not true to your lover. You robbed and defrauded both. Cannot you now see your mistake? To take it on the lowest ground, Dalmain, worshipper of beauty as he was, had had a surfeit of pretty faces. He was like the confectioner's boy who when first engaged is allowed to eat all the cakes and sweets he likes, and who eats so many in the first week, that ever after he wants only plain bread-and-butter. *You* were Dal's bread-and-butter. I am sorry if you do not like the simile."

Jane smiled. "I do like the simile," she said.

"Ah, but you were far more than this, my dear girl. You were his ideal of womanhood. He believed in your strength and tenderness, your graciousness and truth. You shattered this ideal; you failed this faith in you. His fanciful, artistic, eclectic nature with all its unused possibilities of faithful and passionate devotion, had found its haven in your love; and in twelve hours you turned it adrift. Jane—it was a crime. The magnificent strength of the fellow is shown by the way he took it. His progress in his art was not arrested. All his best work has been done since. He has made no bad mad marriage, in mockery of his own pain; and no grand loveless one, to spite you. He might have done both—I mean either. And when I realise that the poor fellow I was with yesterday—making such a brave fight in the dark, and turning his head on the pillow to say with a gleam of hope on his drawn face: 'Where Thou art Guide, no ill can come'—had already been put through all this by you—Jane, if you were a man, I'd horsewhip you!" said the doctor.

Jane squared her shoulders and lifted her head with more of her old spirit than she had yet shown.

"You have lashed me well, Boy," she said, "as only words spoken in faithful indignation can lash. And I feel the better for the pain.— And now I think I ought to tell you that while I was on the top of the Great Pyramid I suddenly saw the matter from a different standpoint. You remember that view, with its sharp line of demarcation? On one side the river, and verdure, vegetation, fruitfulness, a veritable 'garden enclosed'; on the other, vast space as far as the eye could reach; golden liberty, away to the horizon, but no sign of vegetation, no hope of cultivation, just barren, arid, loneliness. I felt this was an exact picture of my life as I live it now. Garth's love, flowing through it, as the river, could have made it a veritable 'garden of the Lord.' It would have meant less liberty, but it would also have meant no loneliness. And, after all, the liberty to live for self alone becomes in time a weary bondage. Then I realised that I had condemned him also to this hard desert life. I came down and took counsel of the old Sphinx. Those calm, wise eyes, looking on into futurity, seemed to say: 'They only live who love.' That evening I resolved to give up the Nile trip, return home immediately, send for Garth, admit all to him, asking him to let us both begin again just where we were three years ago in the moonlight on the terrace at Shenstone. Ten minutes after I had formed this decision, I heard of his accident."

The doctor shaded his face with his hand. "The wheels of time," he said in a low voice, "move forward—always; backward, never."

"Oh, Deryck," cried Jane, "sometimes they do. You and Flower know that sometimes they do."

The doctor smiled sadly and very tenderly. "I know," he said, "that there is always one exception which proves every rule." Then he added quickly: "But, unquestionably, it helps to mend matters, so far as your own mental attitude is concerned, that before you knew of Dalmain's blindness you should have admitted yourself wrong, and made up your mind to trust him."

"I don't know that I was altogether clear about having been wrong," said Jane, "but I was quite convinced that I couldn't live any longer without him, and was therefore prepared to risk it. And of course now, all doubt or need to question is swept away by my poor boy's accident, which simplifies matters, where that particular point is concerned."

The doctor looked at Jane with a sudden raising of his level brows. "Simplifies matters?" he said.

Then, as Jane, apparently satisfied with the expression, did not attempt to qualify it, he rose and stirred the fire; standing over it for a few moments in silent thought. When he sat down again, his voice was very quiet, but there was an alertness about his expression which roused Jane. She felt that the crisis of their conversation had been reached.

"And now, my dear Jeanette," said the doctor, "suppose you tell me what you intend doing."

"Doing?" said Jane. "Why, of course, I shall go straight to Garth. I only want you to advise me how best to let him know I am coming, and whether it is safe for him to have the emotion of my arrival. Also I don't want to risk being kept from him by doctors or nurses. My place is by his side. I ask no better thing of life than to be always beside him. But sick-room attendants are apt to be pig-headed; and a fuss under these circumstances would be unbearable. A wire from you will make all clear."

"I see," said the doctor slowly. "Yes, a wire from me will undoubtedly open a way for you to Garth Dalmain's bedside. And, arrived there, what then?"

A smile of ineffable tenderness parted Jane's lips. The doctor saw it, but turned away immediately. It was not for him, or for any man, to see that look. The eyes which should have seen it were sightless evermore.

"What then, Deryck? Love will know best what then. All barriers will be swept away, and Garth and I will be together."

The doctor's finger-tips met very exactly before he spoke again; and when he did speak, his tone was very level and very kind.

"Ah, Jane," he said, "that is the woman's point of view. It is certainly the simplest, and perhaps the best. But at Garth's bedside you will be confronted with the man's point of view; and I should be failing the trust you have placed in me did I not put that before you now.—From the man's point of view, your own mistaken action three years ago has placed you now in an almost impossible position. If you go to Garth with the simple offer of your love—the treasure he asked three years ago and failed to win—he will naturally conclude the love now given is mainly pity; and Garth Dalmain is not the man to be content with pity, where he has thought to win love, and failed. Nor would he allow any woman—least of all his crown of womanhood—to tie herself to his blindness unless he were sure such binding was her deepest joy. And how could you expect him to believe this in face of the fact that, when he was all a woman's heart could desire, you refused him and sent him from you?—If, on the other hand, you explain, as no doubt you intend to do, the reason of that refusal, he can but say one thing: 'You could not trust me to be faithful when I had my sight. Blind, you come to me, when it is no longer in my power to prove my fidelity. There is no virtue in necessity. I can never feel I possess your trust, because you come to me only when accident has put it out of my power either to do the thing you feared, or to prove myself better than your doubts.' My dear girl, that is how matters stand from the man's point of view; from his, I make no doubt, even more than from mine; for I recognise in Garth Dalmain a stronger man than myself. Had it been I that day in the church, wanting you as he did, I should have grovelled at your feet and promised to grow up. Garth Dalmain had the iron strength to turn and go, without a protest, when the woman who had owned him mate the evening before, refused him on the score of inadequacy the next morning. I fear there is no question of the view he would take of the situation as it now stands."

Jane's pale, startled face went to the doctor's heart.

"But Deryck—he—loves—"

"Just because he loves, my poor old girl, where you are concerned he could never be content with less than the best."

"Oh, Boy, help me! Find a way! Tell me what to do!" Despair was in Jane's eyes.

The doctor considered long, in silence. At last he said: "I see only one way out. If Dal could somehow be brought to realise your point of view at that time as a possible one, without knowing it had actually been the cause of your refusal of him, and could have the chance to express himself clearly on the subject—to me, for instance—in a way which might reach you without being meant to reach you, it might put you in a better position toward him. But it would be difficult to manage. If you could be in close contact with his mind, constantly near him unseen—ah, poor chap, that is easy now—I mean unknown to him; if, for instance, you could be in the shoes of this nurse-companion person I am sending him, and get at his mind on the matter; so that he could feel when you eventually made your confession, he had already justified himself to you, and thus gone behind his blindness, as it were."

Jane bounded in her chair. "Deryck, I have it! Oh, send *me* as his nurse-companion! He would never dream it was I. It is three years since he heard my voice, and he thinks me in Egypt. The society column in all the papers, a few weeks ago, mentioned me as wintering in Egypt and Syria and remaining abroad until May. Not a soul knows I have come home. You are the best judge as to whether I have had training and experience; and all through the war our work was fully as much mental and spiritual, as surgical. It was not up to much otherwise. Oh, Dicky, you could safely recommend me; and I still have my uniforms stowed away in case of need. I could be ready in twenty-four hours, and I would go as Sister—anything, and eat in the kitchen if necessary."

"But, my dear girl," said the doctor quietly, "you could not go as Sister Anything, unfortunately. You could only go as Nurse Rosemary Gray; for I engaged her this morning, and posted a full and explicit account of her to Dr. Mackenzie, which he will read, to our patient. I never take a case from one nurse and give it to another, excepting for incompetency. And Nurse Rosemary Gray could more easily fly, than prove incompetent. She will not be required to eat in the kitchen. She is a gentlewoman, and will be treated as such. I wish indeed you could be in her shoes, though I doubt whether you could have carried it through—And now I have something to tell you. Just before I left him, Dalmain asked after you. He sandwiched you most carefully in between the duchess and Flower; but he could not keep the blood out of his thin cheeks, and he gripped the bedclothes in his effort to keep his voice steady. He asked where you were. I said, I believed, in Egypt. When you were coming home. I told him I had heard you intended returning to Jerusalem for Easter, and I supposed we might expect you home at the end of April or early in May. He inquired how you were. I replied that you were not a good correspondent, but I gathered from occasional cables and post-cards that you were very fit and having a good time. I then volunteered the statement that it was I who had sent you abroad because you were going all to pieces. He made a quick movement with his hand as if he would have struck me for using the expression. Then he said: 'Going to pieces? *She!*' in a tone of most utter contempt for me and my opinions. Then he hastily made minute inquiries for Flower. He had already asked about the duchess all the questions he intended asking about you. When he had ascertained that Flower was at home and well, and had sent him her affectionate sympathy, he begged me to glance through a pile of letters which were waiting until he felt able to have them read to him, and to tell him any of the handwritings known to me. All the world seemed to have sent him letters of sympathy, poor chap. I told him a dozen or so of the names I knew,—a royal handwriting among them. He asked whether there were any from abroad. There were two or three. I knew them all, and named them. He could not bear to hear any of them read; even the royal letter remained unopened, though he asked to have it in his hand, and fingered the tiny crimson crown. Then he asked. 'Is there one from the duchess?' There was. He wished to hear that one, so I opened and read it. It was very characteristic of her Grace; full of kindly sympathy, heartily yet tactfully expressed. Half-way through she said: 'Jane will be upset. I shall write and tell her next time she sends me an address. At present I have no idea in which quarter of the globe my dear niece is to be found. Last time I heard of her she seemed in a fair way towards marrying a little Jap and settling in Japan. Not a bad idea, my dear Dal, is it? Though, if Japan is at all like the paper screens, I don't know where in that Liliputian country they will find a house, or a husband, or a what-do-you-call-'em thing they ride in, solid enough for our good Jane!' With intuitive tact of a very high order, I omitted this entire passage about marrying the Jap. When your aunt's letter was finished, he asked point blank whether there was one from you. I said No, but that it was unlikely the news had reached you, and I felt sure you would write when it did. So I hope you will, dear; and Nurse Rosemary Gray will have instructions to read all his letters to him."

"Oh, Deryck," said Jane brokenly, "I can't bear it! I must go to him!"

The telephone bell on the doctor's table whirred sharply. He went over and took up the receiver.

"Hullo! . . . Yes, it is Dr. Brand. . . . Who is speaking? . . . Oh, is it you, Matron?"—Jane felt quite sorry the matron could not see the doctor's charming smile into the telephone.—"Yes? What name did you say? . . . Undoubtedly. This morning; quite definitely. A most important case. She is to call and see me to-night . . . What? . . . Mistake on register? Ah, I see . . . Gone where? . . . Where? . . . Spell it, please . . . Australia! Oh, quite out of reach! . . . Yes, I heard he was ordered there . . . Never mind, Matron. You are in no way to blame . . . Thanks, I think not. I have someone in view . . . Yes. . . . Yes. . . . No doubt she might do . . . I will let you know if I should require her . . . Good-bye, Matron, and thank you."

The doctor hung up the receiver. Then he turned to Jane; a slow, half-doubtful smile gathering on his lips.

"Jeanette," he said, "I do not believe in chance. But I do believe in a Higher Control, which makes and unmakes our plans. You shall go."

CHAPTER XVI

The Doctor Finds a Way

"And now as to ways and means," said the doctor, when Jane felt better. "You must leave by the night mail from Euston, the day after to-morrow. Can you be ready?"

"I am ready," said Jane.

"You must go as Nurse Rosemary Gray."

"I don't like that," Jane interposed. "I should prefer a fictitious name. Suppose the real Rosemary Gray turned up, or some one who knows her."

"My, dear girl, she is half-way to Australia by now, and you will see no one up there but the household and the doctor. Any one who turned up would be more likely to know you. We must take these risks. Besides, in case of complications arising, I will give you a note, which you can produce at once, explaining the situation, and stating that in agreeing to fill the breach you consented at my request to take the name in order to prevent any necessity for explanations to the patient, which at this particular juncture would be most prejudicial. I can honestly say this, it being even more true than appears. So you must dress the part, Jane, and endeavour to look the part, so far as your five foot eleven will permit; for please remember that I have described you to Dr. Mackenzie as 'a pretty, dainty little thing, refined and elegant, and considerably more capable than she looks.'"

"Dicky! He will instantly realise that I am not the person mentioned in your letter."

"Not so, dear. Remember we have to do with a Scotchman, and a Scotchman never realises anything 'instantly.' The Gaelic mind works slowly, though it works exceeding sure. He will be exceeding sure, when he has contemplated you for a while, that I am a 'verra poor judge o' women,' and that Nurse Gray is a far finer woman than I described. But he will have already created for Dalmain, from my letter, a mental picture of his nurse; which is all that really matters. We must trust to Providence that old Robbie does not proceed to amend it by the original. Try to forestall any such conversation. If the good doctor seems to mistrust you, take him on one side, show him my letter, and tell him the simple truth. But I do not suppose this will be necessary. With the patient, you must remember the extreme sensitiveness of a blind man's hearing. Tread lightly. Do not give him any opportunity to judge of your height. Try to remember that you are not supposed to be able to reach the top shelf of an eight-foot bookcase without the aid of steps or a chair. And when the patient begins to stand and walk, try to keep him from finding out that his nurse is slightly taller than himself. This should not be difficult; one of his fixed ideas being that in his blindness he will not be touched by a woman. His valet will lead him about. And, Jane, I cannot imagine any one who has ever had your hand in his, failing to recognise it. So I advise you, from the first, to avoid shaking hands. But all these precautions do not obviate the greatest difficulty of all,—your voice. Do you suppose, for a moment, he will not recognise that?"

"I shall take the bull by the horns in that case," said Jane, "and you must help me. Explain the fact to me now, as you might do if I were really Nurse Rosemary Gray, and had a voice so like my own."

The doctor smiled. "My dear Nurse Rosemary," he said, "you must not be surprised if our patient detects a remarkable similarity between your voice and that of a mutual friend of his and mine. I have constantly noticed it myself."

"Indeed, sir," said Jane. "And may I know whose voice mine so closely resembles?"

"The Honourable Jane Champion's," said the doctor, with the delightful smile with which he always spoke to his nurses. "Do you know her?"

"Slightly," said Jane, "and I hope to know her better and better as the years go by."

Then they both laughed. "Thank you, Dicky. Now I shall know what to say to the patient.—Ah, but the misery of it! Think of it being possible thus to deceive Garth,—Garth of the bright, keen all-perceiving vision! Shall I ever have the courage to carry it through?"

"If you value your own eventual happiness and his you will, dear. And now I must order the brougham and speed you to Portland Place, or you will be late—for dinner, a thing the duchess cannot overlook 'as you very well know,' even in a traveller returned from round the world. And if you take my advice, you will tell your kind, sensible old aunt the whole story, omitting of course all moonlight details, and consult her about this plan. Her shrewd counsel will be invaluable, and you may be glad of her assistance later on."

They rose and faced each other on the hearth-rug.

"Boy," said Jane with emotion, "you have been so good to me, and so faithful. Whatever happens, I shall be grateful always."

"Hush," said the doctor. "No need for gratitude when long-standing debts are paid.—To-morrow I shall not have a free moment, and I foresee the next day as very full also. But we might dine together at Euston at seven, and I will see you off. Your train leaves at eight o'clock, getting you to Aberdeen soon after seven the next morning, and out to Gleneesh in time for breakfast. You will enjoy arriving in the early morning light; and the air of the moors braces you wonderfully.—Thank you, Stoddart. Miss Champion is ready. Hullo, Flower! Look up, Jane. Flower, and Dicky, and Blossom, are hanging over the topmost banisters, dropping you showers of kisses. Yes, the river you mentioned does produce a veritable 'garden of the Lord.' God send you the same, dear. And now, sit well back, and lower your veil. Ah, I remember, you don't wear them. Wise girl! If all women followed your example it would impoverish the opticians. Why? Oh, constant focussing on spots, for one thing. But lean back, for you must not be seen if you are supposed to be still in Cairo, waiting to go up the Nile. And, look here"—the doctor put his head in at the carriage window—"very plain luggage, mind. The sort of thing nurses speak of as 'my box'; with a very obvious R. G. on it!"

"Thank you, Boy," whispered Jane. "You think of everything."

"I think of *you,*" said the doctor. And in all the hard days to come, Jane often found comfort in remembering those last quiet words.

CHAPTER XVII

Enter—Nurse Rosemary

Nurse Rosemary Gray had arrived at Gleneesh.

When she and her "box" were deposited on the platform of the little wayside railway station, she felt she had indeed dropped from the clouds; leaving her own world, and her own identity, on some far-distant planet.

A motor waited outside the station, and she had a momentary fear lest she should receive deferential recognition from the chauffeur. But he was as solid and stolid as any other portion of the car, and paid no more attention to her than he did to her baggage. The one was a nurse; the other, a box, both common nouns, and merely articles to be conveyed to Gleneesh according to orders. So he looked straight before him, presenting a sphinx-like profile beneath the peak of his leather cap,

215

while a slow and solemn porter helped Jane and her luggage into the motor. When she had rewarded the porter with threepence, conscientiously endeavouring to live down to her box, the chauffeur moved foot and hand with the silent precision of a machine, they swung round into the open, and took the road for the hills.

Up into the fragrant heather and grey rocks; miles of moor and sky and solitude. More than ever Jane felt as if she had dropped into another world, and so small an incident as the omission of the usual respectful salute of a servant, gave her a delightful sense of success and security in her new role.

She had often heard of Garth's old castle up in the North, an inheritance from his mother's family, but was hardly prepared for so much picturesque beauty or such stateliness of archway and entrance. As they wound up the hillside and the grey turrets came into view, with pine woods behind and above, she seemed to hear Garth's boyish voice under the cedar at Overdene, with its ring of buoyant enjoyment, saying: "I should like you to see Castle Gleneesh. You would enjoy the view from the terrace; and the pine woods, and the moor." And then he had laughingly declared his intention of getting up a "best party" of his own, with the duchess as chaperon; and she had promised to make one of it. And now he, the owner of all this loveliness, was blind and helpless; and she was entering the fair portals of Gleneesh, unknown to him, unrecognised by any, as a nurse-secretary sort of person. Jane had said at Overdene: "Yes, ask us, and see what happens." And now this was happening. What would happen next?

Garth's man, Simpson, received her at the door, and again a possible danger was safely passed. He had entered Garth's service within the last three years and evidently did not know her by sight.

Jane stood looking round the old hall, in the leisurely way of one accustomed to arrive for the first time as guest at the country homes of her friends; noting the quaint, large fireplace, and the shadowy antlers high up on the walls. Then she became aware that Simpson, already half-way up the wide oak staircase, was expecting the nurse to hurry after him. This she did, and was received at the top of the staircase by old Margery. It did not require the lawn kerchief, the black satin apron, and the lavender ribbons, for Jane to recognise Garth's old Scotch nurse, housekeeper, and friend. One glance at the grave, kindly face, wrinkled and rosy,—a beautiful combination of perfect health and advancing years,—was enough. The shrewd, keen eyes, seeing quickly beneath the surface, were unmistakable. She conducted Jane to her room, talking all the time in a kindly effort to set her at her ease, and to express a warm welcome with gentle dignity, not forgetting the cloud of sadness which hung over the house and rendered her presence necessary. She called her "Nurse Gray" at the conclusion of every sentence, with an upward inflection and pretty rolling of the r's, which charmed Jane. She longed to say: "You old dear! How I shall enjoy being in the house with you!" but remembered in time that a remark which would have been gratifying condescension on the part of the Honourable Jane Champion, would be little short of impertinent familiarity from Nurse Rosemary Gray. So she followed meekly into the pretty room prepared for her; admired the chintz; answered questions about her night journey; admitted that she would be very glad of breakfast, but still more of a bath if convenient.

And now bath and breakfast were both over, and Jane was standing beside the window in her room, looking down at the wonderful view, and waiting until the local doctor should arrive and summon her to Garth's room.

She had put on the freshest-looking and most business-like of her uniforms, a blue print gown, linen collar and cuffs, and a white apron with shoulder straps and large pockets. She also wore the becoming cap belonging to one of the institutions to which she had once been for training. She did not intend wearing this later on, but just this morning she omitted no detail which could impress Dr. Mackenzie with her extremely professional appearance. She was painfully conscious that the severe simplicity of her dress tended rather to add to her height, notwithstanding her low-heeled ward shoes with their noiseless rubber soles. She could but hope Deryck would prove right as to the view Dr. Mackenzie would take.

And then far away in the distance, along the white ribbon of road, winding up from the valley, she saw a high gig, trotting swiftly; one man in it, and a small groom seated behind. Her hour had come.

Jane fell upon her knees, at the window, and prayed for strength, wisdom, and courage. She could realise absolutely nothing. She had thought so much and so continuously, that all mental vision was out of focus and had become a blur. Even his dear face had faded and was hidden from her when she frantically strove to recall it to her mental view. Only the actual fact remained clear, that in a few short minutes she would be taken to the room where he lay. She would see the face she had not seen since they stood together at the chancel step—the face from which the glad confidence slowly faded, a horror of chill disillusion taking its place.

> "Anoint and cheer our soiled face
> With the abundance of Thy grace."

She would see that dear face, and he, sightless, would not see hers, but would be easily deluded into believing her to be someone else.

The gig had turned the last bend of the road, and

passed out of sight on its way to the front of the house.

Jane rose and stood waiting. Suddenly she remembered two sentences of her conversation with Deryck. She had said: "Shall I ever have the courage to carry it through?" And Deryck had answered, earnestly: "If you value your own eventual happiness and his, you will."

A tap came at her door. Jane walked across the room, and opened it.

Simpson stood on the threshold.

"Dr. Mackenzie is in the library, nurse," he said, "and wishes to see you there."

"Then, will you kindly take me to the library, Mr. Simpson," said Nurse Rosemary Gray.

CHAPTER XVIII

The Napoleon of the Moors

On the bear-skin rug, with his back to the fire, stood Dr. Robert Mackenzie, known to his friends as "Dr. Rob" or "Old Robbie," according to their degrees of intimacy.

Jane's first impression was of a short, stout man, in a sealskin waistcoat which had seen better days, a light box-cloth overcoat three sizes too large for him, a Napoleonic attitude,—little spindle legs planted far apart, arms folded on chest, shoulders hunched up,—which led one to expect, as the eye travelled upwards, an ivory-white complexion, a Roman nose, masterful jaw, and thin lips folded in a line of conscious power. Instead of which one found a red, freckled face, a nose which turned cheerfully skyward, a fat pink chin, and drooping sandy moustache. The only striking feature of the face was a pair of keen blue eyes, which, when turned upon any one intently, almost disappeared beneath bushy red eyebrows and became little points of turquoise light.

Jane had not been in his presence two minutes before she perceived that, when his mind was working, he was entirely unconscious of his body, which was apt to do most peculiar things automatically; so that his friends had passed round the remark: "Robbie chews up dozens of good penholders, while Dr. Mackenzie is thinking out excellent prescriptions."

When Jane entered, his eyes were fixed upon an open letter, which she instinctively knew to be Deryck's, and he did not look up at once. When he did look up, she saw his unmistakable start of surprise. He opened his mouth to speak, and Jane was irresistibly reminded of a tame goldfish at Overdene, which used to rise to the surface when the duchess dropped crumbs. He closed it without uttering a word, and turned again to Deryck's letter; and Jane felt herself to be the crumb, or rather the camel, which he was finding it difficult to swallow.

She waited in respectful silence, and Deryck's words passed with calming effect through the palpitating suspense of her brain. "The Gaelic mind works slowly, though it works exceeding sure. He will be exceeding sure that I am a verra poor judge o' women."

At last the little man on the hearth-rug lifted his eyes again to Jane's; and, alas, how high he had to lift them!

"Nurse—er?" he said inquiringly, and Jane thought his searching eyes looked like little bits of broken blue china in a hay-stack.

"Rosemary Gray," replied Jane meekly, with a curtsey in her voice; feeling as if they were rehearsing amateur theatricals at Overdene, and the next minute the duchess's cane would rap the floor and they would be told to speak up and not be so slow.

"Ah," said Dr. Robert Mackenzie, "I see."

He stared hard at the carpet in a distant corner of the room, then walked across and picked up a spline broken from a bass broom; brought it back to the hearth-rug; examined it with minute attention; then put one end between his teeth and began to chew it.

Jane wondered what was the correct thing to do at this sort of interview, when a doctor neither sat down himself nor suggested that the nurse should do so. She wished she had asked Deryck. But he could not possibly have enlightened her, because the first thing he always said to a nurse was: "My dear Nurse So-and-So, pray sit down. People who have much unavoidable standing to do should cultivate the habit of seating themselves comfortably at every possible opportunity."

But the stout little person on the hearth-rug was not Deryck. So Jane stood at attention, and watched the stiff bit of bass wag up and down, and shorten, inch by inch. When it had finally disappeared, Dr. Robert Mackenzie spoke again.

"So you have arrived, Nurse Gray," he said.

"Truly the mind of a Scotchman works slowly," thought Jane, but she was thankful to detect the complete acceptance of herself in his tone. Deryck was right; and oh the relief of not having to take this unspeakable little man into her confidence in this matter of the deception to be practised on Garth.

"Yes, sir, I have arrived," she said.

Another period of silence. A fragment of the bass broom reappeared and vanished once more, before Dr. Mackenzie spoke again.

"I am glad you have arrived, Nurse Gray," he said.

"I am glad *to* have arrived, sir," said Jane gravely, almost expecting to hear the duchess's delighted "Ha, ha!" from the wings. The little comedy was progressing.

Then suddenly she became aware that during the last few minutes Dr. Mackenzie's mind had been concentrated upon something else. She had not filled it at all. The next moment it was turned upon her and two swift turquoise gleams from under the shaggy brows swept over her, with the rapidity and brightness of search-lights. Dr. Mackenzie commenced speaking quickly, with a wonderful rolling of r's.

"I understand, Miss Gray, you have come to minister to the patient's mind rather than to his body. You need not trouble to explain. I have it from Sir Deryck Brand, who prescribed a nurse-companion for the patient, and engaged you. I fully agreed with his prescription; and, allow me to say, I admire its ingredients."

Jane bowed, and realised how the duchess would be chuckling. What an insufferable little person! Jane had time to think this, while he walked across to the table-cloth, bent over it, and examined an ancient spot of ink. Finding a drop of candle grease near it, he removed it with his thumb nail; brought it carefully to the fire, and laid it on the coals. He watched it melt, fizzle, and flare, with an intense concentration of interest; then jumped round on Jane, and caught her look of fury.

"And I think there remains very little for me to say to you about the treatment, Miss Gray," he finished calmly. "You will have received minute instructions from Sir Deryck himself. The great thing now is to help the patient to take an interest in the outer world. The temptation to persons who suddenly become totally blind, is to form a habit of living entirely in a world within; a world of recollection, retrospection, and imagination; the only world, in fact, in which they can see."

Jane made a quick movement of appreciation and interest. After all she might learn something useful from this eccentric little Scotchman. Oh to keep his attention off rubbish on the carpet, and grease spots on the table-cloth!

"Yes?" she said. "Do tell me more."

"This," continued Dr. Mackenzie, "is our present difficulty with Mr. Dalmain. There seems to be no possibility of arousing his interest in the outside world. He refuses to receive visitors; he declines to hear his letters. Hours pass without a word being spoken by him. Unless you hear him speak to me or to his valet, you will easily suppose yourself to have a patient who has lost the power of speech as well as the gift of sight. Should he express a wish to speak to me alone when we are with him, do not leave the room. Walk over to the fireplace and remain there. I desire that you should hear, that when he chooses to rouse and make an effort, he is perfectly well able to do so. The most important part of your duties, Nurse Gray, will be the aiding him day by day to resume life,—the life of a blind man, it is true; but not therefore necessarily an inactive life. Now that all danger of inflammation from the wounds has subsided, he may get up, move about, learn to find his

way by sound and touch. He was an artist by profession. He will never paint again. But there are
other gifts which may form reasonable outlets to
an artistic nature."

He paused suddenly, having apparently caught
sight of another grease spot, and walked over to
the table; but the next instant jumped round on
Jane, quick as lightning, with a question.

"Does he play?" said Dr. Rob.

But Jane was on her guard, even against accidental surprises.

"Sir Deryck did not happen to mention to me,
Dr. Mackenzie, whether Mr. Dalmain is musical
or not."

"Ah, well," said the little doctor, resuming his
Napoleonic attitude in the centre of the hearth-
rug; "you must make it your business to find out.
And, by the way, Nurse, do you play yourself?"

"A little," said Jane.

"Ah," said Dr. Rob. "And I dare say you sing a
little, too?"

Jane acquiesced.

"In that case, my dear lady, I leave most explicit
orders that you neither sing a little nor play a little
to Mr. Dalmain. We, who have our sight, can just
endure while people who 'play a little' show us
how little they can play; because we are able to
look round about us and think of other things. But
to a blind man, with an artist's sensitive soul, the
experience might culminate in madness. We must

not risk it. I regret to appear uncomplimentary, but a patient's welfare must take precedence of all other considerations."

Jane smiled. She was beginning to like Dr. Rob.

"I will be most careful," she said, "neither to play nor to sing to Mr. Dalmain."

"Good," said Dr. Mackenzie. "But now let me tell you what you most certainly may do, by-and-by. Lead him to the piano. Place him there upon a seat where he will feel secure; none of your twirly, rickety stools. Make a little notch on the key-board by which he can easily find middle C. Then let him relieve his pent-up soul by the painting of sound-pictures. You will find this will soon keep him happy for hours. And, if he is already something of a musician,—as that huge grand piano, with no knick-knacks on it indicates,—he may begin that sort of thing at once, before he is ready to be worried with the Braille system, or any other method of instructing the blind. But contrive an easy way—a little notch in the wood-work below the note—by means of which, without hesitation or irritation, he can locate himself instantly at middle C. Never mind the other notes. It is all the *seeing* he will require when once he is at the piano. Ha, ha! Not bad for a Scotchman, eh, Nurse Gray?"

But Jane could not laugh; though somewhere in her mental background she seemed to hear laughter and applause from the duchess. This was no comedy to Jane,—her blind Garth at the piano, his dear beautiful head bent over the keys, his fingers feeling for that pathetic little notch, to be made by herself, below middle C. She loathed this individual who could make a pun on the subject of Garth's blindness, and, in the back of her mind, Tommy seemed to join the duchess, flapping up and down on his perch and shrieking: "Kick him out! Stop his jaw!"

"And now," said Dr. Mackenzie unexpectedly, "the next thing to be done, Nurse Gray, is to introduce you to the patient."

Jane felt the blood slowly leave her face and concentrate in a terrible pounding at her heart. But she stood her ground, and waited silently.

Dr. Mackenzie rang the bell. Simpson appeared.

"A decanter of sherry, a wine-glass, and a couple of biscuits," said Dr. Rob.

Simpson vanished.

"Little beast!" thought Jane. "At eleven o'clock in the morning!"

Dr. Rob stood, and waited; tugging spitefully at his red moustache, and looking intently out of the window.

Simpson reappeared, placed a small tray on the table, and went quietly out, closing the door behind him.

Dr. Rob poured out a glass of sherry, drew up a chair to the table, and said: "Now, Nurse, sit down and drink that, and take a biscuit with it."

Jane protested. "But, indeed, doctor, I never—"

"I have no doubt you 'never,'" said Dr. Rob, "especially at eleven o'clock in the morning. But you will to-day; so do not waste any time in discussion. You have had a long night journey; you are going upstairs to a very sad sight indeed, a strain on the nerves and sensibilities. You have come through a trying interview with me, and you are praising Heaven it is over. But you will praise Heaven with more fervency when you have drunk the sherry. Also you have been standing during twenty-three minutes and a half. I always stand to speak myself, and I prefer folk should stand to listen. I can never talk to people while they loll around. But you will walk upstairs all the more steadily, Nurse Rosemary Gray, if you sit down now for five minutes at this table."

Jane obeyed, touched and humbled. So, after all, it was a kind, comprehending heart under that old sealskin waistcoat; and a shrewd understanding of men and matters, in spite of the erratic, somewhat objectionable exterior. While she drank the wine and finished the biscuits, he found busy occupation on the other side of the room, polishing the window with his silk pocket-handkerchief; making a queer humming noise all the time, like a bee buzzing up the pane. He seemed to have forgotten her presence; but, just as she put down the empty glass, he turned and, walking straight across the room, laid his hand upon her shoulder.

"Now, Nurse," he said, "follow me upstairs,

and, just at first, speak as little as possible. Remember, every fresh voice intruding into the still depths of that utter blackness, causes an agony of bewilderment and disquietude to the patient. Speak little and speak low, and may God Almighty give you tact and wisdom."

There was a dignity of conscious knowledge and power in the small quaint figure which preceded Jane up the staircase. As she followed, she became aware that her spirit leaned on his and felt sustained and strengthened. The unexpected conclusion of his sentence, old-fashioned in its wording, yet almost a prayer, gave her fresh courage. "May God Almighty give you tact and wisdom," he had said, little guessing how greatly she needed them. And now another voice, echoing through memory's arches to organ-music, took up the strain: "Where Thou art Guide, no ill can come." And with firm though noiseless step, Jane followed Dr. Mackenzie into the roam where Garth was lying, helpless, sightless, and disfigured.

CHAPTER XIX

The Voice in the Darkness

Just the dark head upon the pillow. That was all Jane saw at first, and she saw it in sunshine. Somehow she had always pictured a darkened room, forgetting that to him darkness and light were both alike, and that there was no need to keep out the sunlight, with its healing, purifying, invigorating powers.

He had requested to have his bed moved into a corner—the corner farthest from door, fireplace, and windows—with its left side against the wall, so that he could feel the blank wall with his hand and, turning close to it, know himself shut away from all possible prying of unseen eyes. This was how he now lay, and he did not turn as they entered.

Just the dear dark head upon the pillow. It was all Jane saw at first. Then his right arm in the sleeve of a blue silk sleeping-suit, stretched slightly behind him as he lay on his left side, the thin white hand limp and helpless on the coverlet.

Jane put her hands behind her. The impulse was so strong to fall on her knees beside the bed, take that poor hand in both her strong ones, and cover it with kisses. Ah surely, surely then, the dark head would turn to her, and instead of seeking refuge in the hard, blank wall, he would hide that sightless face in the boundless tenderness of her arms. But Deryck's warning voice sounded, grave and persistent: "If you value your own eventual happiness and his—" So Jane put her hands behind her back.

Dr. Mackenzie advanced to the side of the bed and laid his hand upon Garth's shoulder. Then, with an incredible softening of his rather strident voice, he spoke so slowly and quietly, that Jane could hardly believe this to be the man who had jerked out questions, comments, and orders to her, during the last half-hour.

"Good morning, Mr. Dalmain. Simpson tells me it has been an excellent night, the best you have yet had. Now that is good. No doubt you were relieved to be rid of Johnson, capable though he was, and to be back in the hands of your own man again. These trained attendants are never content with doing enough; they always want to do just a little more, and that little more is a weariness to the patient.—Now I have brought you to-day one who is prepared to do all you need, and yet who, I feel sure, will never annoy you by attempting more than you desire. Sir Deryck Brand's prescription, Nurse Rosemary Gray, is here; and I believe she is prepared to be companion, secretary, reader, anything you want, in fact a new pair of eyes for you, Mr. Dalmain, with a clever brain behind them, and a kind, sympathetic, womanly heart directing and controlling that brain. Nurse Gray arrived this morning, Mr. Dalmain."

No response from the bed. But Garth's hand groped for the wall; touched it, then dropped listlessly back.

Jane could not realise that *she* was "Nurse Gray." She only longed that her poor boy need not be bothered with the woman! It all seemed, at this moment, a thing apart from herself and him.

Dr. Mackenzie spoke again. "Nurse Rosemary Gray is in the room, Mr. Dalmain."

Then Garth's instinctive chivalry struggled up through the blackness. He did not turn his head, but his right hand made a little courteous sign of greeting, and he said in a low, distinct voice: "How do you do? I am sure it is most kind of you to come so far. I hope you had an easy journey."

Jane's lips moved, but no sound would pass them.

Dr. Rob made answer quickly, without looking at her: "Miss Gray had a very good journey, and looks as fresh this morning as if she had spent the night in bed. I can see she is a cold-water young lady."

"I hope my housekeeper will make her comfortable. Please give orders," said the tired voice; and Garth turned even closer to the wall, as if to end the conversation.

Dr. Rob attacked his moustache, and stood looking down at the blue silk shoulder for a minute, silently.

Then he turned and spoke to Jane. "Come over to the window, Nurse Gray. I want to show you a special chair we have obtained for Mr. Dalmain, in which he will be most comfortable as soon as he feels inclined to sit up. You see? Here is an adjustable support for the head, if necessary; and these various trays and stands and movable tables can be swung round into any position by a touch.

I consider it excellent, and Sir Deryck approved it. Have you seen one of this kind before, Nurse Gray?"

"We had one at the hospital, but not quite so complete as this," said Jane.

In the stillness of that sunlit chamber, the voice from the bed broke upon them with startling suddenness; and in it was the cry of one lost in an abyss of darkness, but appealing to them with a frantic demand for instant enlightenment.

"*Who* is in the room?" cried Garth Dalmain.

His face was still turned to the wall; but he had raised himself on his left elbow, in an attitude which betokened intent listening.

Dr. Mackenzie answered. "No one is in the room, Mr. Dalmain, but myself and Nurse Gray."

"There *is* some one else in the room!" said Garth violently. "How dare you lie to me! Who was speaking?"

Then Jane came quickly to the side of the bed. Her hands were trembling, but her voice was perfectly under control.

"It was I who spoke, sir," she said; "Nurse Rosemary Gray. And I feel sure I know why my voice startled you. Dr. Brand warned me it might do so. He said I must not be surprised if you detected a remarkable similarity between my voice and that of a mutual friend of yours and his. He said he had often noticed it."

Garth, in his blindness, remained quite still; listening and considering. At length he asked slowly: "Did he say whose voice?"

"Yes, for I asked him. He said it was Miss Champion's."

Garth's head dropped back upon the pillow. Then without turning he said in a tone which Jane knew meant a smile on that dear hidden face: "You must forgive me, Miss Gray, for being so startled and so stupidly, unpardonably agitated. But, you know, being blind is still such a new experience, and every fresh voice which breaks through the black curtain of perpetual night, means so infinitely more than the speaker realises. The resemblance in your voice to that of the lady Sir Deryck mentioned is so remarkable that, although I know her to be at this moment in Egypt, I could scarcely believe she was not in the room. And yet the most unlikely thing in the world would be that she should have been in this room. So I owe you and Dr. Mackenzie most humble apologies for my agitation and unbelief."

He stretched out his right hand, palm upwards, towards Jane.

Jane clasped her shaking hands behind her.

"Now, Nurse, if you please," broke in Dr. Mackenzie's rasping voice from the window, "I have a few more details to explain to you over here."

They talked together for a while without interruption, until Dr. Rob remarked: "I suppose I will have to be going."

Then Garth said: "I wish to speak to you alone, doctor, for a few minutes."

"I will wait for you downstairs, Dr. Mackenzie," said Jane, and was moving towards the door, when an imperious gesture from Dr. Rob stopped her, and she turned silently to the fireplace. She could not see any need now for this subterfuge, and it annoyed her. But the freckled little Napoleon of the moors was not a man to be lightly disobeyed. He walked to the door, opened and closed it; then returned to the bedside, drew up a chair, and sat down.

"Now, Mr. Dalmain," he said.

Garth sat up and turned towards him eagerly.

Then, for the first time, Jane saw his face.

"Doctor," he said, "tell me about this nurse. Describe her to me."

The tension in tone and attitude was extreme. His hands were clasped in front of him, as if imploring sight through the eyes of another. His thin white face, worn with suffering, looked so eager and yet so blank.

"Describe her to me, doctor," he said; "this Nurse Rosemary Gray, as you call her."

"But it is not a pet name of mine, my dear sir," said Dr. Rob deliberately. "It is the young lady's own name, and a pretty one, too. 'Rosemary for remembrance.' Is not that Shakespeare?"

"Describe her to me," insisted Garth, for the third time.

Dr. Mackenzie glanced at Jane. But she had turned her back, to hide the tears which were streaming down her cheeks. Oh, Garth! Oh, beautiful Garth of the shining eyes!

Dr. Rob drew Deryck's letter from his pocket and studied it.

"Well," he said slowly, "she is a pretty, dainty little thing; just the sort of elegant young woman you would like to have about you, could you see her."

"Dark or fair?" asked Garth.

The doctor glanced at what he could see of Jane's cheek, and at the brown hands holding on to the mantelpiece.

"Fair," said Dr. Rob, without a moment's hesitation.

Jane started and glanced round. Why should this little man be lying on his own account?

"Hair?" queried the strained voice from the bed.

"Well," said Dr. Rob deliberately, "it is mostly tucked away under a modest little cap; but, were it not for that wise restraint, I should say it might be that kind of fluffy, fly-away floss-silk, which puts the finishing touch to a dainty, pretty woman."

Garth lay back, panting, and pressed his hands over his sightless face.

"Doctor," he said, "I know I have given you heaps of trouble, and to-day you must think me a fool. But if you do not wish me to go mad in my blindness, send that girl away. Do not let her enter my room again."

"Now, Mr. Dalmain," said Dr. Mackenzie patiently; "let us consider this thing. We may take it you have nothing against this young lady excepting a chance resemblance in her voice to that of a friend of yours now far away. Was not this other lady a pleasant person?"

Garth laughed suddenly, bitterly; a laugh like a hard, sob. "Oh, yes," he said, "she was quite a pleasant person."

" 'Rosemary for remembrance,' " quoted Dr. Rob. "Then why should not Nurse Rosemary call up a pleasant remembrance? Also it seems to me to be a kind, sweet, womanly voice, which is something to be thankful for nowadays, when so many women talk, fit to scare the crows; cackle, cackle, cackle—like stones rattling in a tin canister."

"But can't you understand, doctor," said Garth wearily, "that it is just the remembrance and the resemblance which, in my blindness, I cannot bear? I have nothing against her voice, Heaven knows! But I tell you, when I heard it first I thought it was—it was she—the other—come to me—here—and—" Garth's voice ceased suddenly.

"The pleasant lady?" suggested Dr. Rob. "I see. Well now, Mr. Dalmain, Sir Deryck said the best thing that could happen would be if you came to wish for visitors. It appears you have many friends ready and anxious to come any distance in order to bring you help or cheer. Why not let me send for this pleasant lady? I make no doubt she would come. Then when she herself had sat beside you, and talked with you, the nurse's voice would trouble you no longer."

Garth sat up again, his face wild with protest. Jane turned on the hearth-rug, and stood watching it.

"No, doctor," he said. "Oh, my God, no! In the whole world, she is the last person I would have enter this room!"

Dr. Mackenzie bent forward to examine minutely a microscopic darn in the sheet. "And why?" he asked very low.

"Because," said Garth, "that pleasant lady, as you rightly call her, has a noble, generous heart, and it might overflow with pity for my blindness; and pity from her I could not accept. It would be the last straw upon my heavy cross. I can bear the cross, doctor; I hope in time to carry it manfully, until God bids me lay it down. But that last straw—*her* pity—would break me. I should fall in the dark, to rise no more."

"I see," said Dr. Rob gently. "Poor laddie! The pleasant lady must not come."

He waited silently a few minutes, then pushed back his chair and stood up.

"Meanwhile," he said, "I must rely on you, Mr.

Dalmain, to be agreeable to Nurse Rosemary Gray, and not to make her task too difficult. I dare not send her back. She is Dr. Brand's choice. Besides—think of the cruel blow to her in her profession. Think of it, man!—sent off at a moment's notice, after spending five minutes in her patient's room, because, forsooth, her voice maddened him! Poor child! What a statement to enter on her report! See her appear before the matron with it! Can't you be generous and unselfish enough to face whatever trial there may be for you in this bit of a coincidence?"

Garth hesitated. "Dr. Mackenzie," he said at last, "will you swear to me that your description of this young lady was accurate in every detail?"

" 'Swear not at all,' " quoted Dr. Rob unctuously. "I had a pious mother, laddie. Besides I can do better than that. I will let you into a secret. I was reading from Sir Deryck's letter. I am no authority on women myself, having always considered dogs and horses less ensnaring and more companionable creatures. So I would not trust my own eyes, but preferred to give you Sir Deryck's description. You will allow him to be a fine judge of women. You have seen Lady Brand?"

"Seen her? Yes," said Garth eagerly, a slight flush tinting his thin cheeks, "and more than that, I've painted her. Ah, such a picture!—standing at a table, the sunlight in her hair, arranging golden daffodils in an old Venetian vase. Did you see it, doctor, in the New Gallery, two years ago?"

"No," said Dr. Rob. "I am not finding myself in galleries, new or old. But"—he turned a swift look of inquiry on Jane, who nodded—"Nurse Gray was telling me she had seen it."

"Really?" said Garth, interested. "Somehow one does not connect nurses with picture galleries."

"I don't know why not," said Dr. Rob. "They must go somewhere for their outings. They can't be everlastingly nosing shop windows in all weathers; so why not go in and have a look at your pictures? Besides, Miss Rosemary is a young lady of parts. Sir Deryck assures me she is a gentlewoman by birth, well-read and intelligent.—Now, laddie, what is it to be?"

Garth considered silently.

Jane turned away and gripped the mantelpiece. So much hung in the balance during that quiet minute.

At length Garth spoke, slowly, hesitatingly. "If only I could quite disassociate the voice from the—from that other personality. If I could be quite sure that, though her voice is so extraordinarily like, she herself is not—" he paused, and Jane's heart stood still. Was a description of herself coming?—"is not at all like the face and figure which stand clear in my remembrance as associated with that voice."

"Well," said Dr. Rob, "I'm thinking we can

241

manage that for you. These nurses know their patients must be humoured. We will call the young lady back, and she shall kneel down beside your bed—Bless you! She won't mind, with me to play old Gooseberry!—and you shall pass your hands over her face and hair, and round her little waist, and assure yourself, by touch, what an elegant, dainty little person it is, in a blue frock and white apron."

Garth burst out laughing, and his voice had a tone it had not yet held. "Of all the preposterous suggestions!" he said. "Good heavens! What an ass I must have been making of myself! And I begin to think I have exaggerated the resemblance. In a day or two, I shall cease to notice it. And, look here, doctor, if she really was interested in that portrait—Here, I say—where are you going?"

"All right, sir," said Dr. Rob. "I was merely moving a chair over to the fireside, and taking the liberty of pouring out a glass of water. Really you are becoming abnormally quick of hearing. Now I am all attention. What about the portrait?"

"I was only going to say, if she the nurse, you know—is really interested in my portrait of Lady Brand, there are studies of it up in the studio, which she might care to see. If she brought them here and described them to me I could explain—But, I say, doctor. I can't have dainty young ladies in and out of my room while I'm in bed. Why shouldn't I get up and try that chair of yours? Send

Simpson along; and tell him to look out my brown lounge-suit and orange tie. Good heavens! what a blessing to have the *memory* of colours and of how they blend! Think of the fellows who are *born* blind. And please ask Miss Gray to go out in the pine wood, or on the moor, or use the motor, or rest, or do anything she likes. Tell her to make herself quite at home; but on no account to come up here until Simpson reports me ready."

"You may rely on Nurse Gray to be most discreet," said Dr. Rob; whose voice had suddenly become very husky. "And as for getting up, laddie, don't go too fast. You will not find your strength equal to much. But I am bound to tell you there is nothing to keep you in bed if you feel like rising."

"Good-bye, doctor," said Garth, groping for his hand; "and I am sorry I shall never be able to offer to paint Mrs. Mackenzie!"

"You'd have to paint her with a shaggy head, four paws, and the softest amber eyes in the world," said Dr. Rob tenderly; "and, looking out from those eyes, the most faithful, loving dog-heart in creation. In all the years we've kept house together she has never failed to meet me with a welcome, never contradicted me or wanted the last word, and never worried me for so much as the price of a bonnet. There's a woman for you!— Well, good-bye, lad, and God Almighty bless you. And be careful how you go. Do not be surprised if

I look in again on my way back from my rounds to see how you like that chair."

Dr. Mackenzie held open the door. Jane passed noiselessly out before him. He followed, signing to her to precede him down the stairs.

In the library, Jane turned and faced him. He put her quietly into a chair and stood before her. The bright blue eyes were moist, beneath the shaggy brows.

"My dear," he said, "I feel myself somewhat of a blundering old fool. You must forgive me. I never contemplated putting you through such an ordeal. I perfectly understand that, while he hesitated, you must have felt your whole career at stake. I see you have been weeping; but you must not take it too much to heart that our patient made so much of your voice resembling this Miss Champion's. He will forget all about it in a day or two, and you will be worth more to him than a dozen Miss Champions. See what good you have done him already. Here he is wanting to get up and explain his pictures to you. Never you fear. You will soon win your way, and I shall be able to report to Sir Deryck what a fine success you have made of the case. Now I must see the valet and give him very full instructions. And I recommend you to go for a blow on the moor and get an appetite for lunch. Only put on something warmer than that. You will have no sick-room work to do; and having duly impressed me with your washableness and serviceableness, you may as well wear something comfortable to protect you from our Highland nip. Have you warmer clothing with you?"

"It is the rule of our guild to wear uniform," said Jane; "but I have a grey merino."

"Ah, I see. Well, wear the grey merino. I shall return in two hours to observe how he stands that move. Now, don't let me keep you."

"Dr. Mackenzie," said Jane quietly, "may I ask why you described me as fair; and my very straight, heavy, plainly coiled hair, as fluffy, fly-away floss-silk?"

Dr. Rob had already reached the bell, but at her question he stayed his hand and, turning, met Jane's steadfast eyes with the shrewd turquoise gleam of his own.

"Why certainly you may ask, Nurse Rosemary Gray," he said, "though I wonder you think it necessary to do so. It was of course perfectly evident to me that, for reasons of his own, Sir Deryck wished to paint an imaginary portrait of you to the patient, most likely representing some known ideal of his. As the description was so different from the reality, I concluded that, to make the portrait complete, the two touches unfortunately left to me to supply, had better be as unlike what I saw before me as the rest of the picture. And now, if you will be good enough—" Dr. Rob rang the bell violently.

"And why did you take the risk of suggesting that he should feel me?" persisted Jane.

"Because I knew he was a gentleman," shouted Dr. Rob angrily. "Oh, come in, Simpson—come in, my good fellow—and shut that door! And God Almighty be praised that He made you and me *men,* and not women!"

A quarter of an hour later, Jane watched him drive away, thinking to herself: "Deryck was right. But what a queer mixture of shrewdness and obtuseness, and how marvellously it worked out to the furtherance of our plans."

But as she watched the dog-cart start off at a smart trot across the moor, she would have been more than a little surprised could she have overheard Dr. Rob's muttered remarks to himself, as he gathered up the reins and cheered on his sturdy cob. He had a habit of talking over his experiences, half aloud, as he drove from case to case; the two sides of his rather complex nature apparently comparing notes with each other. And the present conversation opened thus:

"Now what has brought the Honourable Jane up here?" said Dr. Rob.

"Dashed if I know," said Dr. Mackenzie.

"You must not swear, laddie," said Dr. Rob; "you had a pious mother."

CHAPTER XX

Jane Reports Progress

Letter from the Honourable Jane Champion to Sir Deryck Brand.
Castle Gleneesh, N. B.

My dear Deryck: My wires and post-cards have not told you much beyond the fact of my safe arrival. Having been here a fortnight, I think it is time I sent you a report. Only you must remember that I am a poor scribe. From infancy it has always been difficult to me to write anything beyond that stock commencement: "I hope you are quite well;" and I approach the task of a descriptive letter with an effort which is colossal. And yet I wish I might, for once, borrow the pen of a ready writer; because I cannot help knowing that I have been passing through experiences such as do not often fall to the lot of a woman.

Nurse Rosemary Gray is getting on capitally. She is making herself indispensable to the patient, and he turns to her with a completeness of confidence which causes her heart to swell with professional pride.

Poor Jane has got no further than hearing, from his own lips, that she is the very last person in the whole world he would wish should come near him in his blindness. When she was suggested as a possible visitor, he said: "Oh, my God, NO!" and his face was one wild, horrified protest. So Jane is getting her horsewhipping, Boy, and—according to the method of a careful and thoughtful judge, who orders thirty lashes of the "cat," in three applications of ten—so is Jane's punishment laid on at intervals; not more than she can bear at a time; but enough to keep her heart continually sore, and her spirit in perpetual dread. And you, dear, clever doctor, are proved perfectly right in your diagnosis of the sentiment of the case. He says her pity would be the last straw on his already heavy cross; and the expression is an apt one, her pity for him being indeed a thing of straw. The only pity she feels is pity for herself, thus hopelessly caught in the meshes of her own mistake. But how to make him realise this, is the puzzle.

Do you remember how the Israelites were shut in, between Migdol and the sea? I knew Migdol meant "towers," but I never understood the passage, until I stood upon that narrow wedge of desert, with the Red Sea in front and on the left; the rocky range of Gebel Attaka on the right, towering up against the sky, like the weird shapes of an impregnable fortress; the sole outlet or inlet behind, being the route they had just travelled from Egypt, and along which the chariots and horsemen of Pharaoh were then thundering in hot pursuit. Even so, Boy, is poor Jane now tramping her patch of desert, which narrows daily to the measure of her despair. Migdol is *his* certainty that *her* love could only be pity. The Red Sea is the confession into which she must inevitably plunge, to avoid scaling Migdol; in the chill waters of which, as she drags him in with her, his love is bound to drown, as waves of doubt and mistrust sweep over its head,— doubts which he has lost the power of removing; mistrust which he can never hope to prove to have been false and mistaken. And behind come galloping the hosts of Pharaoh; chance, speeding on the wheels of circumstance. At any moment some accident may compel a revelation; and instantly *he* will be scaling rocky Migdol, with torn hands and bleeding feet; and she—poor Jane—floundering in the depths of the Red Sea. O for a Moses, with divine commission, to stretch out the rod of understanding love, making a safe way through; so that together they might reach the Promised Land! Dear wise old Boy, dare you undertake the role of Moses!

But here am I writing like a page of Baedeker, and failing to report on actual facts.

As you may suppose, Jane grows haggard

and thin in spite of old Margery's porridge—which is "put on" every day after lunch, for the next morning's breakfast, and anybody passing "gives it a stir." Did you know that was the right way to make porridge, Deryck? I always thought it was made in five minutes, as wanted. Margery says that must be the English stuff which profanely goes by the name. (N.B. Please mark the self-control with which I repeat Scotch remarks, without rushing into weird spelling; a senseless performance, it seems to me. For if you know already how old Margery pronounces "porridge," you can read her pronunciation into the sentence; and if you do not know it, no grotesque spelling on my part could convey to your mind any but a caricatured version of the pretty Scotch accent with which Margery says: "Stir the porridge, Nurse Gray." In fact, I am agreeably surprised at the ease with which I understand the natives, and the pleasure I derive from their conversation; for, after wrestling with one or two modern novels dealing with the Highlands, I had expected to find the language an unknown tongue. Instead of which, lo! and behold, old Margery, Maggie the housemaid, Macdonald the gardener, and Macalister the game-keeper, all speak a rather purer English than I do; far more carefully pronounced, and with every *R* sounded and rolled. Their idioms are more characteristic than their accent. They say "whenever" for "when," and use in their verbs several quaint variations of tense.)

But what a syntactical digression! Oh, Boy, the wound at my heart is so deep and so sore that I dread the dressings, even by your delicate touch. Where was I? Ah, the porridge gave me my loophole of escape. Well, as I was saying, Jane grows worn and thin, old Margery's porridge notwithstanding; but Nurse Rosemary Gray is flourishing, and remains a pretty, dainty little thing, with the additional charm of fluffy, fly-away floss-silk, for hair,—Dr. Rob's own unaided contribution to the fascinating picture. By the way, I was quite unprepared to find him such a charac ter. I learn much from Dr. Mackenzie, and I love Dr. Rob, excepting on those occasions when I long to pick him up by the scruff of his fawn overcoat and drop him out of the window.

On the point of Nurse Rosemary's personal appearance, I found it best to be perfectly frank with the household. You can have no conception how often awkward moments arose; as, for instance, in the library, the first time Garth came downstairs; when he ordered Simpson to bring the steps for Miss Gray, and Simpson opened his lips to remark that Nurse Gray could reach to the top shelf on her own tiptoes with the greatest ease, he having just seen her do it. Mercifully, the perfect training of an English man-servant saved the situation, and he merely said: "Yessir; certainly sir," and looked upon me, standing silently by, as a person who evidently delighted in giving unnecessary trouble. Had it been dear old Margery with her Scotch tongue, which starts slowly, but gathers momentum as it rolls, and can never be arrested until the full flood of her thought has been poured forth, I should have been constrained to pick her up bodily in my dainty arms and carry her out.

So I sent for Simpson and Margery to the dining-room that evening, when the master was safely out of ear-shot, and told them that, for reasons which I could not fully explain, a very incorrect description of my appearance had been given him. He thought me small and slim; fair and very pretty; and it was most important, in order to avoid long explanations and mental confusion for him, that he should not at present be undeceived. Simpson's expression of polite attention did not vary, and his only comment was: "Certainly, miss. Quite so." But across old Margery's countenance, while I was speaking, passed many shades of opinion, which, fortunately, by the time I had finished, crystallized into an approving smile of acquiescence. She even added her own commentary: "And a very good thing, too, I am thinking. For Master Garth, poor laddie, was always so set upon having beauty about him. 'Master Garthie,' I would say to him, when he had friends coming, and all his ideas in talking over the dinner concerned the cleaning up of the old silver, and putting out of Valentine glass and Worstered china; 'Master Garthie,' I would say, feeling the occasion called for the apt quoting of Scripture, 'it appears to me your attention is given entirely to the outside of the cup and platter, and you care nothing for all the good things that lie within.' So it is just as well to keep him deceived, Miss Gray." And then, as Simpson coughed tactfully behind his hand, and nudged her very obviously with his elbow, she added, as a sympathetic after-thought: "For, though a homey face may indeed be redeemed by its kindly expression, you cannot very well explain expression to the blind." So you see, Deryck, this shrewd old body, who has known Garth from boyhood, would have entirely agreed with the decision of three years ago.

Well, to continue my report. The voice gave us some trouble, as you foresaw, and the whole plan hung in the balance during a few awful moments; for, though he easily accepted the explanation we had planned, he sent me out, and told Dr. Mackenzie my voice in his room would madden him. Dr. Rob was equal to the occasion, and won the day; and Garth, having once given in, never mentioned the matter again. Only, sometimes I see him listening and remembering.

But Nurse Rosemary Gray has beautiful hours when poor anxious, yearning Jane is shut out. For her patient turns to her, and depends on her, and talks to her, and tries to reach her mind, and shows her his, and is a wonderful person to live with and know. Jane, marching about in the cold, outside, and hearing them talk, realises how little she understood the beautiful gift which was laid at her feet; how little she had grasped the nature and mind of the man whom she dismissed as "a mere boy." Nurse Rosemary, sitting beside him during long sweet hours of companionship, is learning it; and Jane, ramping up and down her narrowing strip of desert, tastes the sirocco of despair.

And now I come to the point of my letter, and, though I am a woman, I will not put it in a postscript.

Deryck, can you come up soon, to pay him a visit, and to talk to me? I don't think I can bear it, unaided, much longer; and he would so enjoy having you, and showing you how he had got on, and all the things he had already learned to do. Also you might put in a word for Jane; or at all events, get at his mind on the subject. Oh, Boy, if you *could* spare forty-eight hours! And a breath of the moors would be good for you. Also I have a little private plan, which depends largely for its fulfilment on your coming. Oh, Boy—come!

Yours, needing you,

Jeanette.

From Sir Deryck Brand
to Nurse Rosemary Gray,
Castle Gleneesh, N. B.
Wimpole Street.

My dear Jeanette: Certainly I will come. I will leave Euston on Friday evening. I can spend the whole of Saturday and most of Sunday at Gleneesh, but must be home in time for Monday's work.

I will do my best, only, alas! I am not Moses, and do not possess his wonder-working rod. Moreover, latest investigations have proved that the Israelites could not have crossed at the place you mention, but further north at the Bitter Lakes; a mere matter of detail, in no way affecting the extreme appositeness of your illustration, rather, adding to it; for I fear there are bitter waters ahead of you, my poor girl.

Still I am hopeful, nay, more than hopeful,— confident. Often of late, in connection with you, I have thought of the promise about all things working together for good. Any one can make *good* things work together for good: but only the Heavenly Father can bring good out of evil; and, taking all our mistakes and failings and foolishnesses, cause them to work to our most perfect well-being. The more intricate and involved this problem of human existence becomes, the greater the need to take as our own clear rule of life: "Trust in the Lord with all thine heart; and lean not unto thine own understanding. In all thy ways acknowledge Him, and He shall direct thy paths." Ancient marching orders, and simple; but true, and therefore eternal.

I am glad Nurse Rosemary is proving so efficient, but I hope we may not have to face yet another complication in our problem. Suppose our patient falls in love with dainty little Nurse Rosemary, where will Jane be then? I fear the desert would have to open its mouth and swallow her up. We must avert such a catastrophe. Could not Rosemary be induced to drop an occasional H, or to confess herself as rather "gone" on Simpson?

Oh, my poor old girl! I could not jest thus, were I not coming shortly to your aid.

How maddening it is! And you so priceless! But most men are either fools or blind, and one is both. Trust me to prove it to him,—to my own satisfaction and his,—if I get the chance. Yours always devotedly,
Deryck Brand.

From Sir Deryck Brand
to Dr. Robert Mackenzie.

Dear Mackenzie: Do you consider it to be advisable that I should shortly pay a visit to our patient at Gleneesh and give an opinion on his progress?

I find I can make it possible to come north this week-end.

I hope you are satisfied with the nurse I sent up.

Yours very faithfully,
Deryck Brand.

From Dr. Robert Mackenzie
to Sir Deryck Brand.

Dear Sir Deryck: Every possible need of the patient's is being met by the capable lady you sent to be his nurse. I am no longer needed. Nor are you—for the patient. But I deem it exceedingly advisable that you should shortly pay a visit to the nurse, who is losing more flesh than a lady of her proportions can well afford.

Some secret care, besides the natural anxiety of having the responsibility of this case, is wearing her out. She may confide in you. She cannot quite bring herself to trust in

Your humble servant,
Robert Mackenzie.

CHAPTER XXI

Hard on the Secretary

Nurse Rosemary sat with her patient in the sunny library at Gleneesh. A small table was between them, upon which lay a pile of letters—his morning mail—ready for her to open, read to him, and pass across, should there chance to be one among them he wished to touch or to keep in his pocket.

They were seated close to the French window opening on to the terrace; the breeze, fragrant with the breath of spring flowers, blew about them, and the morning sun streamed in.

Garth, in white flannels, wearing a green tie and a button-hole of primroses, lay back luxuriously, enjoying, with his rapidly quickening senses, the scent of the flowers and the touch of the sun-beams.

Nurse Rosemary finished reading a letter of her own, folded it, and put it in her pocket with a feeling of thankful relief. Deryck was coming. He had not failed her.

"A man's letter, Miss Gray," said Garth unexpectedly.

"Quite right," said Nurse Rosemary. "How did you know?"

"Because it was on one sheet. A woman's letter

on a matter of great importance would have run to two, if not three. And that letter was on a matter of importance."

"Right again," said Nurse Rosemary, smiling. "And again, how did you know?"

"Because you gave a little sigh of relief after reading the first line, and another, as you folded it and replaced it in the envelope."

Nurse Rosemary laughed. "You are getting on so fast, Mr. Dalmain, that soon we shall be able to keep no secrets. My letter was from—"

"Oh, don't tell me," cried Garth quickly, putting out his hand in protest. "I had no idea of seeming curious as to your private correspondence, Miss Gray. Only it is such a pleasure to report progress to you in the things I manage to find out without being told."

"But I meant to tell you anyway," said Nurse Rosemary. "The letter is from Sir Deryck, and, amongst other things, he says he is coming up to see you next Saturday."

"Ah, good!" said Garth. "And what a change he will find! And I shall have the pleasure of reporting on the nurse, secretary, reader, and unspeakably patient guide and companion he provided for me." Then he added, in a tone of suddenly awakened anxiety: "He is not coming to take you away, is he?"

"No," said Nurse Rosemary, "not yet. But, Mr. Dalmain, I was wanting to ask whether you could

259

spare me just during forty-eight hours; and Dr. Brand's visit would be an excellent opportunity. I could leave you more easily, knowing you would have his companionship. If I may take the week-end, leaving on Friday night, I could return early on Monday morning, and be with you in time to do the morning letters. Dr. Brand would read you Saturday's and Sunday's—Ah, I forgot; there is no Sunday post. So I should miss but one; and he would more than take my place in other ways."

"Very well," said Garth, striving not to show disappointment. "I should have liked that we three should have talked together. But no wonder you want a time off. Shall you be going far?"

"No; I have friends near by. And now, do you wish to attend to your letters?"

"Yes," said Garth, reaching out his hand. "Wait a minute. There is a newspaper among them. I smell the printing ink. I don't want that. But kindly give me the rest."

Nurse Rosemary took out the newspaper; then pushed the pile along, until it touched his hand.

Garth took them. "What a lot!" he said, smiling in pleasurable anticipation. "I say, Miss Gray, if you profit as you ought to do by the reading of so many epistles written in every possible and impossible style, you ought to be able to bring out a pretty comprehensive 'Complete Letter-writer.' Do you remember the condolences of Mrs. Parker-Bangs? I think that was the first time we really laughed together. Kind old soul! But she should not have mentioned blind Bartimaeus dipping seven times in the pool of Siloam. It is always best to avoid classical allusions, especially if sacred, unless one has them accurately. Now—" Garth paused.

He had been handling his letters, one by one; carefully fingering each, before laying it on the table beside him. He had just come to one written on foreign paper, and sealed. He broke off his sentence abruptly, held the letter silently for a moment, then passed his fingers slowly over the seal.

Nurse Rosemary watched him anxiously. He made no remark, but after a moment laid it down and took up the next. But when he passed the pile across to her, he slipped the sealed letter beneath the rest, so that she should come to it last of all.

Then the usual order of proceedings commenced. Garth lighted a cigarette—one of the first things he had learned to do for himself—and smoked contentedly, carefully placing his ashtray, and almost unfailingly locating the ash, in time and correctly.

Nurse Rosemary took up the first letter, read the postmark, and described the writing on the envelope. Garth guessed from whom it came, and was immensely pleased if, on opening, his surmise proved correct. There were nine to-day, of varying interest,—some from men friends, one or two from charming women who professed themselves ready to come and see him as soon as he wished for visitors, one from a blind asylum asking for a subscription, a short note from the doctor heralding his visit, and a bill for ties from a Bond Street shop.

Nurse Rosemary's fingers shook as she replaced the eighth in its envelope. The last of the pile lay on the table. As she took it up, Garth with a quick movement flung his cigarette-end through the window, and lay back, shading his face with his hand.

"Did I shoot straight, nurse?" he asked.

She leaned forward and saw the tiny column of blue smoke rising from the gravel.

"Quite straight," she said. "Mr. Dalmain, this letter has an Egyptian stamp, and the postmark is Cairo. It is sealed with scarlet sealing-wax, and the engraving on the seal is a plumed helmet with the visor closed."

"And the writing?" asked Garth, mechanically and very quietly.

"The handwriting is rather bold and very clear, with no twirls or flourishes. It is written with a broad nib."

"Will you kindly open it, nurse, and tell me the signature before reading the rest of the letter."

Nurse Rosemary fought with her throat, which threatened to close altogether and stifle her voice. She opened the letter, turned to the last page, and found the signature.

"It is signed 'Jane Champion,' Mr. Dalmain," said Nurse Rosemary.

"Read it, please," said Garth quietly. And Nurse Rosemary began.

Dear Dal: What *can* I write? If I were with you, there would be so much I could say; but writing is so difficult, so impossible.

I know it is harder for you than it would have been for any of us; but you will be braver over it than we should have been, and you will come through splendidly, and go on thinking life beautiful, and making it seem so to other people. *I* never thought it so until that summer at Overdene and Shenstone when you taught me the perception of beauty. Since then, in every sunset and sunrise, in the blue-green of the Atlantic, the purple of the mountains, the spray of Niagara, the cherry blossom of Japan, the golden deserts of Egypt, I have thought of you, and understood them better, because of you. Oh, Dal! I should like to come and tell you all about them, and let you see them through my eyes; and then you would widen out my narrow understanding of them, and show them again to me in greater loveliness.

I hear you receive no visitors; but cannot you make just one exception, and let me come?

I was at the Great Pyramid when I heard. I

was sitting on the piazza after dinner. The moonlight called up memories. I had just made up my mind to give up the Nile, and to come straight home, and write asking you to come and see me; when General Loraine turned up, with an English paper and a letter from Myra, and—I heard. Would you have come, Garth?

And now, my friend, as you cannot come to me, may I come to you? If you just say: *"come,"* I will come from any part of the world where I may chance to be when the message reaches me. Never mind this Egyptian address. I shall not be there when you are hearing this. Direct to me at my aunt's town house. All my letters go there, and are forwarded unopened.

Let me come. And oh, do believe that I know something of how hard it is for you. But God can "enable."
Believe me to be,
Yours, more than I can write,
Jane Champion.

Garth removed the hand which had been shielding his face.

"If you are not tired, Miss Gray, after reading so many letters, I should like to dictate my answer to that one immediately, while it is fresh in my mind. Have you paper there? Thank you.

264

May we begin?—Dear Miss Champion . . . I am deeply touched by your kind letter of sympathy . . . It was especially good of you to write to me from so far away amid so much which might well have diverted your attention from friends at home."

A long pause. Nurse Rosemary Gray waited, pen in hand, and hoped the beating of her heart was only in her own ears, and not audible across the small table.

"I am glad you did not give up the Nile trip but—"

An early bee hummed in from the hyacinths and buzzed against the pane. Otherwise the room was very still.

—"but of course, if you had sent for me I should have come."

The bee fought the window angrily, up and down, up and down, for several minutes; then found the open glass and whirled out into the sunshine, joyfully.

Absolute silence in the room, until Garth's quiet voice broke it as he went on dictating.

"It is more than kind of you to suggest coming to see me, but—"

Nurse Rosemary dropped her pen. "Oh, Mr. Dalmain," she said, "let her come."

Garth turned upon her a face of blank surprise.

"I do not wish it," he said, in a tone of absolute finality.

"But think how hard it must be for any one to want so much to be near a—a friend in trouble, and to be kept away."

"It is only her wonderful kindness of heart makes her offer to come, Miss Gray. She is a friend and comrade of long ago. It would greatly sadden her to see me thus."

"It does not seem so to her," pleaded Nurse Rosemary. "Ah, cannot you read between the lines? Or does it take a woman's heart to understand a woman's letter? Did I read it badly? May I read it over again?"

A look of real annoyance gathered upon Garth's face. He spoke with quiet sternness, a frown bending his straight black brows.

"You read it quite well," he said, "but you do not do well to discuss it. I must feel able to dictate my letters to my secretary, without having to explain them."

"I beg your pardon, sir," said Nurse Rosemary humbly. "I was wrong."

Garth stretched his hand across the table, and left it there a moment; though no responsive hand was placed within it.

"Never mind," he said, with his winning smile, "my kind little mentor and guide. You can direct me in most things, but not in this. Now let us conclude. Where were we? Ah—'to suggest coming to see me.' Did you put 'It is most kind' or 'It is more than kind?'"

" 'More than kind,' " said Nurse Rosemary, brokenly.

"Right, for it is indeed more than kind. Only she and I can possibly know how much more. Now let us go on . . . But I am receiving no visitors, and do not desire any until I have so mastered my new circumstances that the handicap connected with them shall neither be painful nor very noticeable to other people. During the summer I shall be learning step by step to live this new life, in complete seclusion at Gleneesh. I feel sure my friends will respect my wish in this matter. I have with me one who most perfectly and patiently is helping— Ah, wait!" cried Garth suddenly. "I will not say that. She might think—she might misunderstand. Had you begun to write it? No? What was the last word? 'Matter?' Ah yes. That is right. Full stop after 'matter.' Now let me think."

Garth dropped his face into his hands, and sat for a long time absorbed in thought.

Nurse Rosemary waited. Her right hand held the pen poised over the paper. Her left was pressed against her breast. Her eyes rested on that dark bowed head, with a look of unutterable yearning and of passionate tenderness. At last Garth lifted his face. "Yours very sincerely, Garth Dalmain;" he said. And, silently, Nurse Rosemary wrote it.

CHAPTER XXII

Dr. Rob to the Rescue

Into the somewhat oppressive silence which followed the addressing and closing of the envelope, broke the cheery voice of Dr. Rob.

"Which is the patient to-day? The lady or the gentleman? Ah, neither, I see. Both flaunt the bloom of perfect health and make the doctor shy. It is spring without, but summer within," ran on Dr. Rob gaily, wondering why both faces were so white and perturbed, and why there was in the air a sense of hearts in torment. "Flannels seem to call up boating and picnic parties; and I see you have discarded the merino, Nurse Gray, and returned to the pretty blue washables. More becoming, undoubtedly; only, don't take cold; and be sure you feed up well. In this air people must eat plenty, and you have been perceptibly losing weight lately. We don't want *too* airy-fairy dimensions."

"Why do you always chaff Miss Gray about being small, Dr. Rob?" asked Garth, in a rather vexed tone. "I am sure being short is in no way detrimental to her."

"I will chaff her about being tall if you like," said Dr. Rob, looking at her with a wicked twinkle, as she stood in the window, drawn up to her full height, and regarding him with cold disapproval.

"I would sooner no comments of any kind were made upon her personal appearance," said Garth shortly; then added, more pleasantly: "You see, she is just a voice to me—a kind, guiding voice. At first I used to form mental pictures of her, of a hazy kind; but now I prefer to appropriate in all its helpfulness what I *do* know, and leave unimagined what I do not. Did it ever strike you that she is the only person—bar that fellow Johnson, who belongs to a nightmare time I am quickly forgetting—I have yet had near me, in my blindness, whom I had not already seen; the only voice I have ever heard to which I could not put a face and figure? In time, of course, there will be many. At present she stands alone to me in this."

Dr. Rob's observant eye had been darting about during this explanation, seeking to focus itself upon something worthy of minute examination. Suddenly he spied the foreign letter lying close beside him on the table.

"Hello!" he said. "Pyramids? The Egyptian stamp? That's interesting. Have you friends out there, Mr. Dalmain?"

"That letter came from Cairo," Garth replied; "but I believe Miss Champion has by now gone on to Syria." Dr. Rob attacked his moustache, and stared at the letter meditatively. "Champion?" he repeated. "Champion? It's an uncommon name. Is

269

your correspondent, by any chance, the Honourable Jane?"

"Why, that letter is from her," replied Garth, surprised. "Do you know her?" His voice vibrated eagerly.

"Well," answered Dr. Rob, with slow deliberation, "I know her face, and I know her voice; I know her figure, and I know a pretty good deal of her character. I know her at home, and I know her abroad. I've seen her under fire, which is more than most men of her acquaintance can claim. But there is one thing I never knew until to-day and that is her handwriting. May I examine this envelope?" He turned to the window;—yes, this audacious little Scotchman had asked the question of Nurse Rosemary. But only a broad blue back met his look of inquiry. Nurse Rosemary was studying the view. He turned back to Garth, who had evidently already made a sign of assent, and on whose face was clearly expressed an eager desire to hear more, and an extreme disinclination to ask for it.

Dr. Mackenzie took up the envelope and pondered it.

"Yes," he said, at last, "it is like her,—clear, firm, unwavering; knowing what it means to say, and saying it; going where it means to go, and getting there. Ay, lad, it's a grand woman that; and if you have the Honourable Jane for your friend, you can be doing without a few other things."

A tinge of eager colour rose in Garth's thin cheeks. He had been so starved in his darkness for want of some word concerning her, from that outer light in which she moved. He had felt so hopelessly cut off from all chance of hearing of her. And all the while, if only he had known it, old Robbie could have talked of her. He had had to question Brand so cautiously, fearing to betray his secret and hers; but with Dr. Rob and Nurse Gray no such precautions were needed. He could safely guard his secret, and yet listen and speak.

"Where—when?" asked Garth.

"I will tell you where, and I will tell you when," answered Dr. Rob, "if you feel inclined for a war tale on this peaceful spring morning."

Garth was aflame with eagerness. "Have you a chair, doctor?" he said. "And has Miss Gray a chair?"

"I have no chair, sir," said Dr. Rob, "because when I intend thoroughly to enjoy my own eloquence it is my custom to stand. Nurse Gray has no chair, because she is standing at the window absorbed in the view. She has apparently ceased to pay any heed to you and me. You will very rarely find one woman take much interest in tales about another. But you lean back in your own chair, laddie, and light a cigarette. And a wonderful thing it is to see you do it, too, and better than pounding the wall. Eh? All of which we may consider we owe to the lady who disdains us and prefers the scenery. Well, I'm not much to look at, goodness knows; and she can see you all the rest of the day. Now that's a brand worth smoking. What do you call it—'Zenith'? Ah, and 'Marcovitch.' Yes; you can't better that for drawing-room and garden purposes. It mingles with the flowers. Lean back and enjoy it, while I smell gun-powder. For I will tell you where I first saw the Honourable Jane. Out in South Africa, in the very thick of the Boer war. I had volunteered for the sake of the surgery experience. She was out there, nursing; but the real thing, mind you. None of your dabbling in eau-de-cologne with lace handkerchiefs, and washing handsome faces when the orderlies had washed them already; making charming conversation to men who were getting well, but fleeing in dread from the dead or the dying. None of that, you may be sure, and none of that allowed in her hospital; for Miss Champion was in command there, and I can tell you she made them scoot. She did the work of ten, and expected others to do it too. Doctors and orderlies adored her. She was always called 'The Honourable Jane,' most of the men sounding the H and pronouncing the title as four syllables. Ay, and the wounded soldiers! There was many a lad out there, far from home and friends, who, when death came, died with a smile on his lips, and a sense of mother and home quite near, because the Honourable Jane's arm was around him, and his dying head rested against her womanly breast. Her voice when she talked to them? No,—that I shall never forget. And to hear her snap at the women, and order along the men; and then turn and speak to a sick Tommy as his mother or his sweetheart would have wished to hear him spoken to, was a lesson in quick-change from which I am profiting still. And that big, loving heart must often have been racked; but she was always brave and bright. Just once she broke down. It was over a boy whom she tried hard to save—quite a youngster. She had held him during the operation which was his only chance; and when it proved no good, and he lay back against her unconscious, she quite broke down and said: 'Oh, doctor,—a mere boy—and to suffer so, and then die like this!' and gathered him to her, and wept over him, as his own mother might have done. The surgeon told me of it himself. He said the hardest hearts in the tent were touched and softened. But, it was the only time the Honourable Jane broke down."

Garth shielded his face with his hand. His half-smoked cigarette fell unheeded to the floor. The hand that had held it was clenched on his knee. Dr. Rob picked it up, and rubbed the scorched spot on the carpet carefully with his foot. He glanced towards the window. Nurse Rosemary had turned and was leaning against the frame. She did not look at him, but her eyes dwelt with troubled anxiety on Garth.

"I came across her several times, at different centres," continued Dr. Rob; "but we were not in the same departments, and she spoke to me only once. I had ridden in, from a temporary overflow sort of place where we were dealing with the worst cases straight off the field, to the main hospital in the town for a fresh supply of chloroform. While they fetched it, I walked round the ward, and there in a corner was Miss Champion, kneeling beside a man whose last hour was very near, talking to him quietly, and taking measures at the same time to ease his pain. Suddenly there came a crash—a deafening rush—and another crash, and the Honourable Jane and her patient were covered with dust and splinters. A Boer shell had gone clean through the roof just over their heads. The man sat up, yelling with fear. Poor chap, you couldn't blame him; dying, and half under morphine. The Honourable Jane never turned a hair. 'Lie down, my man,' she said, 'and keep still.' 'Not here,' sobbed the man. 'All right,' said the Honourable Jane; 'we will soon move you.' Then she turned and saw me. I was in the most nondescript khaki, a non-com's jacket which I had caught up on leaving the tent, and various odds and ends of my outfit which had survived the wear and tear of the campaign. Also I was dusty with a long gallop. 'Here, serjeant,' she said, 'lend a hand with this poor fellow. I can't have him disturbed just now.' That was Jane's only comment on the passing of a shell within a few yards of her own head. Do you wonder the men adored her? She placed her hands beneath his shoulders, and signed to me to take him under the knees, and together we carried him round a screen, out of the ward, and down a short passage; turning unexpectedly into a quiet little room, with a comfortable bed, and photographs and books arranged on the tiny dressing-table. She said: 'Here, if you please, serjeant,' and we laid him on the bed. 'Whose is it?' I asked. She looked surprised at being questioned, but seeing I was a stranger, answered civilly: 'Mine.' And then, noting that he had dozed off while we carried him, added: 'And he will have done with beds, poor chap, before I need it.' There's nerve for you!—Well, that was my only conversation out there with the Honourable Jane. Soon after I had had enough and came home."

Garth lifted his head. "Did you ever meet her at home?" he asked.

"I did," said Dr. Rob. "But she did not remember me. Not a flicker of recognition. Well, how could I expect it? I wore a beard out there; no time to shave; and my jacket proclaimed me a serjeant, not a surgeon. No fault of hers if she did not expect to meet a comrade from the front in the wilds of—of Piccadilly," finished Dr. Rob lamely. "Now, having spun so long a yarn, I must be off to your gardener's cot in the wood, to see his good wife, who has had what he pathetically calls 'an increase.' I should think a decrease would have better suited the size of his house. But first I must interview Mistress Margery in the dining-room. She is anxious about herself just now because she 'canna eat bacon.' She says it flies between her shoulders. So erratic a deviation from its normal route on the part of the bacon, undoubtedly requires investigation. So, by your leave, I will ring for the good lady."

"Not just yet, doctor," said a quiet voice from the window. "I want to see you in the dining-room, and will follow you there immediately. And afterwards, while you investigate Margery, I will run up for my bonnet, and walk with you through the woods, if Mr. Dalmain will not mind an hour alone."

When Jane reached the dining-room, Dr. Robert Mackenzie was standing on the hearth-rug in a Napoleonic attitude, just as on the morning of their first interview. He looked up uncertainly as she came in.

"Well?" he said. "Am I to pay the piper?"

Jane came straight to him, with both hands extended.

"Ah, serjeant!" she said. "You dear faithful old serjeant! See what comes of wearing another man's coat. And my dilemma comes from taking another woman's name. So you knew me all the time, from the first moment I came into the room?"

"From the first moment you entered the room," assented Dr. Rob.

"Why did you not say so?" asked Jane.

"Well, I concluded you had your reasons for being 'Nurse Rosemary Gray,' and it did not come within my province to question your identity."

"Oh, you dear!" said Jane. "Was there ever anything so shrewd, and so wise, and so bewilderingly far-seeing, standing on two legs on a hearth-rug before! And when I remember how you said: 'So you have arrived, Nurse Gray?' and all the while you might have been saying. 'How do you do, Miss Champion? And what brings you up here under somebody else's name?'"

"I might have so said," agreed Dr. Rob reflectively; "but praise be, I did not."

"But tell me," said Jane, "why let it out now?"

Dr. Rob laid his hand on her arm. "My dear, I am an old fellow, and all my life I have made it my business to know, without being told. You have been coming through a strain,—a prolonged period of strain, sometimes harder, sometimes easier, but never quite relaxed,—a strain such as few women could have borne. It was not only with him; you had to keep it up towards us all. I knew, if it were to continue, you must soon have the relief of someone with whom to share the secret,—someone towards whom you could be yourself occasionally. And when I found you had been writing to him here, sending the letter to be posted in Cairo (how like a woman, to strain at a gnat, after swallowing such a camel!), awaiting its return day after day, then obliged to read it to him yourself, and take down his dictated answer, which I gathered from your faces when I entered was his refusal of your request to come and see him, well, it seemed to me about time you were made to realise that you might as well confide in an old fellow who, in common with all the men who knew you in South Africa, would gladly give his right hand for the Honourable Jane."

Jane looked at him, her eyes full of gratitude. For the moment she could not speak.

"But tell me, my dear," said Dr. Rob, "tell me, if you can: why does the lad put from him so firmly that which, if indeed it might be his for the asking, would mean for him so great, so wonderful, so comforting a good?"

"Ah, doctor," said Jane, "thereby hangs a tale of sad mistrust and mistake, and the mistrust and mistake, alas, were mine. Now, while you see Margery, I will prepare for walking; and as we go through the wood I will try to tell you the woeful thing which came between him and me and placed our lives so far apart. Your wise advice will help me, and your shrewd knowledge of men and of the human heart may find us a way out, for indeed we are shut in between Migdol and the sea."

As Jane crossed the hall and was about to mount

the stairs, she looked towards the closed library door. A sudden fear seized her, lest the strain of listening to that tale of Dr. Rob's had been too much for Garth. None but she could know all it must have awakened of memory to be told so vividly of the dying soldiers whose heads were pillowed on her breast, and the strange coincidence of those words, "A mere boy—and to suffer so!" She could not leave the house without being sure he was safe and well. And yet she instinctively feared to intrude when he imagined himself alone for an hour.

Then Jane, in her anxiety, did a thing she had never done before. She opened the front door noiselessly, passed round the house to the terrace, and when approaching the open window of the library, trod on the grass border, and reached it without making the faintest sound.

Never before had she come upon him unawares, knowing he hated and dreaded the thought of an unseen intrusion on his privacy.

But now—just this once—

Jane looked in at the window.

Garth sat sideways in the chair, his arms folded on the table beside him, his face buried in them. He was sobbing as she had sometimes heard men sob after agonising operations, borne without a sound until the worst was over. And Garth's sob of agony was this: *"Oh, my wife—my wife—my wife!"*

Jane crept away. How she did it she never knew. But some instinct told her that to reveal herself then, taking him at a disadvantage, when Dr. Rob's story had unnerved and unmanned him, would be to ruin all. *"If you value your ultimate happiness and his,"* Deryck's voice always sounded in warning. Besides, it was such a short postponement. In the calm earnest thought which would succeed this storm, his need of her, would win the day. The letter, not yet posted, would be rewritten. He would say *"come"*—and the next minute he would be in her arms.

So Jane turned noiselessly away.

Coming in, an hour later, from her walk with Dr. Rob, her heart filled with glad anticipation, she found him standing in the window, listening to the countless sounds he was learning to distinguish. He looked so slim and tall and straight in his white flannels, both hands thrust deep into the pockets of his coat, that when he turned at her approach it seemed to her as if the shining eyes *must* be there.

"Was it lovely in the woods?" he asked. "Simpson shall take me up there after lunch. Meanwhile, is there time, if you are not tired, Miss Gray, to finish our morning's work?"

Five letters were dictated and a cheque written. Then Jane noticed that hers to him had gone from among the rest. But his to her lay on the table ready for stamping. She hesitated.

"And about the letter to Miss Champion?" she said. "Do you wish it to go as it is, Mr. Dalmain?"

"Why certainly," he said. "Did we not finish it?"

"I thought," said Jane nervously, looking away from his blank face, "I thought perhaps—after Dr. Rob's story—you might—"

"Dr. Rob's story could make no possible difference as to whether I should let her come here or not," said Garth emphatically; then added more gently: "It only reminded me—"

"Of what?" asked Jane, her hands upon her breast.

"Of what a glorious woman she is," said Garth Dalmain, and blew a long, steady cloud of smoke into the summer air.

CHAPTER XXIII

The Only Way

When Deryck Brand alighted at the little northern wayside station, he looked up and down the gravelled platform, more than half expecting to see Jane. The hour was early, but she invariably said "So much the better" to any plan which involved rising earlier than usual. Nothing was to be seen, however, but his portmanteau in the distance—looking as if it had taken up a solitary and permanent position where the guard had placed it—and one slow porter, who appeared to be overwhelmed by the fact that he alone was on duty to receive the train.

There were no other passengers descending; there was no other baggage to put out. The guard swung up into his van as the train moved off.

The old porter, shading his eyes from the slanting rays of the morning sun, watched the train glide round the curve and disappear from sight; then slowly turned and looked the other way,—as if to make sure there was not another coming,—saw the portmanteau, and shambled towards it. He stood looking down upon it pensively, then moved slowly round, apparently reading the names and particulars of all the various continental hotels at which the portmanteau had recently stayed with its owner.

Dr. Brand never hurried people. He always said: "It answers best, in the long run, to let them take their own time. The minute or two gained by hurrying them is lost in the final results." But this applied chiefly to patients in the consulting-room; to anxious young students in hospital; or to nurses, too excitedly conscious at first of the fact that he was talking to them, to take in fully what he was saying. His habit of giving people, even in final moments, the full time they wanted, had once lost him an overcoat, almost lost him a train, and won him the thing in life he most desired. But that belongs to another story.

Meanwhile he wanted his breakfast on this fresh

spring morning. And he wanted to see Jane. Therefore, as porter and portmanteau made no advance towards him, the doctor strode down the platform.

"Now then, my man!" he called.

"I beg your pardon?" said the Scotch porter.

"I want my portmanteau."

"Would this be your portmanteau?" inquired the porter doubtfully.

"It would," said the doctor. "And it and I would be on our way to Castle Gleneesh, if you would be bringing it out and putting it into the motor, which I see waiting outside."

"I will be fetching a truck," said the porter. But when he returned, carefully trundling it behind him, the doctor, the portmanteau, and the motor were all out of sight.

The porter shaded his eyes and gazed up the road.

"I will be hoping it *was* his portmanteau," he said, and went back to his porridge.

Meanwhile the doctor sped up into the hills, his mind alight with eagerness to meet Jane and to learn the developments of the last few days. Her non-appearance at the railway station filled him with an undefinable anxiety. It would have been so like Jane to have been there, prompt to seize the chance of a talk with him alone before he reached the house. He had called up, in anticipation, such a vivid picture of her, waiting on the platform,—

bright, alert, vigorous, with that fresh and healthy vigour which betokens a good night's rest, a pleasant early awakening, and a cold tub recently enjoyed,—and the disappointment of not seeing her had wrought in him a strange foreboding. What if her nerve had given way under the strain?

They turned a bend in the winding road, and the grey turrets of Gleneesh came in sight, high up on the other side of the glen, the moor stretching away behind and above it. As they wound up the valley to the moorland road which would bring them round to the house, the doctor could see, in the clear morning light, the broad lawn and terrace of Gleneesh, with its gay flower-beds, smooth gravelled walks, and broad stone parapet, from which was a drop almost sheer down into the glen below.

Simpson received him at the hall door; and he just stopped himself in time, as he was about to ask for Miss Champion. This perilous approach to a slip reminded him how carefully he must guard words and actions in this house, where Jane had successfully steered her intricate course. He would never forgive himself if he gave her away.

"Mr. Dalmain is in the library, Sir Deryck," said Simpson; and it was a very alert, clear-headed doctor who followed the man across the hall.

Garth rose from his chair and walked forward to meet him, his right hand outstretched, a smile of welcome on his face, and so direct and unhesitating a course that the doctor had to glance at the sightless face to make sure that this lithe, graceful, easy-moving figure was indeed the blind man he had come to see. Then he noticed a length of brown silk cord stretched from an arm of the chair Garth had quitted to the door. Garth's left hand had slipped lightly along it as he walked.

The doctor put his hand into the one out-stretched, and gripped it warmly.

"My dear fellow! What a change!"

"Isn't it?" said Garth delightedly. "And it is entirely she who has worked it,—the capital little woman you sent up to me. I want to tell you how first-rate she is." He had reached his chair again, and found and drew forward for the doctor the one in which Jane usually sat, "this is her own idea." He unhitched the cord, and let it fall to the floor, a fine string remaining attached to it and to the chair, by which he could draw it up again at will. "There is one on this side leading to the piano, and one here to the window. Now how should you know them apart?"

"They are brown, purple, and orange," replied the doctor.

"Yes," said Garth. "You know them by the colours, but I distinguish them by a slight differ-ence in the thickness and in the texture, which you could not see, but which I can feel. And I enjoy thinking of the colours, too. And sometimes I wear ties and things to match them. You see, I know exactly how they look; and it was so like her to remember that. An ordinary nurse would have put red, green, and blue, and I should have sat and hated the thought of them knowing how vilely they must be clashing with my Persian carpet. But she understands how much colours mean to me, even though I cannot see them."

"I conclude that by 'she' you mean Nurse Rosemary," said the doctor. "I am glad she is a success."

"A success!" exclaimed Garth. "Why, she helped me to live again! I am ashamed to remember how at the bottom of all things I was when you came up before, Brand,—just pounding the wall, as old Robbie expresses it. You must have thought me a fool and a coward."

"I thought you neither, my dear fellow. You were coming through a stiffer fight than any of us have been called to face. Thank God, you have won."

"I owe a lot to you, Brand, and still more to Miss Gray. I wish she were here to see you. She is away for the week-end."

"Away! J—just now?" exclaimed the doctor, almost surprised into another slip.

"Yes; she went last night. She is week-ending in the neighbourhood. She said she was not going far, and should be back with me early on Monday morning. But she seemed to want a change of scene, and thought this a good opportunity, as I shall have you here most of the time. I say, Brand,

I do think it is extraordinarily good of you to come all this way to see me. You know, from such a man as yourself it is almost overwhelming."

"You must not be overwhelmed, my dear chap; and, though I very truly came to see you, I am also up, about another old friend in the near neighbourhood in whom I am interested. I only mention this in order to be quite honest, and to lift from off you any possible burden of feeling yourself my only patient."

"Oh, thanks!" said Garth. "It lessens my compunction without diminishing my gratitude. And now you must be wanting a brush up and breakfast, and here am I selfishly keeping you from both. And I say, Brand,"—Garth coloured hotly, boyishly, and hesitated,—"I am awfully sorry you will have no companion at your meals, Miss Gray being away. I do not like to think of you having them alone, but I—I always have mine by myself. Simpson attends to them."

He could not see the doctor's quick look of comprehension, but the understanding sympathy of the tone in which he said: "Ah, yes. Yes, of course," without further comment, helped Garth to add: "I couldn't even have Miss Gray with me. We always take our meals apart. You cannot imagine how awful it is chasing your food all round your plate, and never sure it is not on the cloth, after all, or on your tie, while you are hunting for it elsewhere."

"No, I can't imagine," said the doctor. "No one could who had not been through it. But can you bear it better with Simpson than with Nurse Rosemary? She is trained to that sort of thing, you know."

Garth coloured again. "Well, you see, Simpson is the chap who shaves me, and gets me into my clothes, and takes me about; and, though it will always be a trial, it is a trial to which I am growing accustomed. You might put it thus: Simpson is eyes to my body; Miss Gray is vision to my mind. Simpson's is the only touch which cores to me in the darkness. Do you know, Miss Gray has never touched me,—not even to shake hands. I am awfully glad of this. I will tell you why presently, if I may. It makes her just a *mind* and *voice* to me, and nothing more; but a wonderfully kind and helpful voice. I feel as if I could not live without her."

Garth rang the bell and Simpson appeared.

"Take Sir Deryck to his room; and he will tell you what time he would like breakfast. And when you have seen to it all, Simpson, I will go out for a turn. Then I shall be free, Brand, when you are. But do not give me any more time this morning if you ought to be resting, or out on the moors having a holiday from minds and men."

The doctor tubbed and got into his knicker-bockers and an old Norfolk jacket; then found his way to the dining-room, and did full justice to an excellent breakfast. He was still pondering the problem of Jane, and at the same time wondering in another compartment of his mind in what sort of machine old Margery made her excellent coffee, when that good lady appeared, enveloped in an air of mystery, and the doctor immediately propounded the question.

"A jug," said old Margery. "And would you be coming with me, Sir Deryck,—and softly, whenever you have finished your breakfast?

"Softly," said Margery again, as they crossed the hall, the doctor's tall figure closely following in her portly wake. After mounting a few stairs she turned to whisper impressively: "It is not what ye make it *in;* it is *how* ye make it." She ascended a few more steps, then turned to say: "It all hangs upon the word *fresh,*" and went on mounting. "Freshly roasted—freshly ground—water—freshly-boiled—" said old Margery, reaching the topmost stair somewhat breathless; then turning, bustled along a rather dark passage, thickly carpeted, and hung with old armour and pictures.

"Where are we going, Mistress Margery?" asked the doctor, adapting his stride to her trot—one to two.

"You will be seeing whenever we get there, Sir Deryck," said Margery. "And never touch it with metal, Sir Deryck. Pop it into an earthenware jug, pour your boiling water straight upon it, stir it with a wooden spoon, set it on the hob ten minutes to settle; the grounds will all go to the bottom, though you might not think it; and you pour it out—fragrant, strong, and clear. But the secret is, fresh, fresh, fresh, and don't stint your coffee."

Old Margery paused before a door at the end of the passage, knocked lightly; then looked up at the doctor with her hand on the door-handle, and an expression of pleading earnestness in her faithful Scotch eyes.

"And you will not forget the wooden spoon, Sir Deryck?"

The doctor looked down into the kind old face raised to his in the dim light. "I will not forget the wooden spoon, Mistress Margery," he said, gravely. And old Margery, turning the handle whispered mysteriously into the half-opened doorway: "It will be Sir Deryck, Miss Gray," and ushered the doctor into a cosy little sitting-room.

A bright fire burned in the grate. In a high-backed arm-chair in front of it sat Jane, with her feet on the fender. He could only see the top of her head, and her long grey knees; but both were unmistakably Jane's.

"Oh, Dicky!" she said, and a great thankfulness was in her voice, "is it you? Oh, come in, Boy, and shut the door. Are we alone? Come round here quick and shake hands, or I shall be plunging about trying to find you."

In a moment the doctor had reached the hearth-rug, dropped on one knee in front of the large chair, and took the vaguely groping hands held out to him.

"Jeanette?" he said. "Jeanette!" And then surprise and emotion silenced him.

Jane's eyes were securely bandaged. A black silk scarf, folded in four thicknesses, was firmly tied at the back of her smooth coils of hair. There was a pathetic helplessness about her large capable figure, sitting alone, in this bright little sitting-room, doing nothing.

"Jeanette!" said the doctor, for the third time. "And you call this week-ending?"

"Dear," said Jane, "I have gone into Sightless Land for my week-end. Oh, Deryck, I had to do it. The only way really to help him is to know exactly what it means, in all the small, trying details. I never had much imagination, and I have exhausted what little I had. And he never complains, or explains how things come hardest. So the only way to find out is to have forty-eight hours of it one's self. Old Margery and Simpson quite enter into it, and are helping me splendidly. Simpson keeps the coast clear if we want to come down or go out; because with two blind people about, it would be a complication if they ran into one another. Margery helps me with all the things in which I am helpless; and, oh Dicky, you would never believe how many they are! And the awful, awful dark—a black curtain always in front of you, sometimes seeming hard and firm, like a wall of coal, within an inch of your face; sometimes sinking away into soft depths of blackness—miles and miles of distant, silent, horrible darkness; until you feel you must fall forward into it and be submerged and overwhelmed. And out of that darkness come voices. And if they speak loudly, they hit you like tapping hammers; and if they murmur indistinctly, they madden you because you can't *see* what is causing it. You can't see that they are holding pins in their mouths, and that therefore they are mumbling; or that they are half under the bed, trying to get out something which has rolled there, and therefore the voice seems to come from somewhere beneath the earth. And, because you cannot see these things to account for it, the variableness of sound torments you. Ah!— and the waking in the morning to the same blackness as you have had all night! I have experienced it just once,—I began my darkness before dinner last night,—and I assure you, Deryck, I dread to-morrow morning. Think what it must be to wake to that always, with no prospect of ever again seeing the sunlight! And then the meals—"

"What! You keep it on?" The doctor's voice sounded rather strained.

"Of course," said Jane. "And you cannot imagine the humiliation of following your food all round the plate, and then finding it on the table-cloth; of being quite sure there was a last bit somewhere, and when you had given up the search and gone on to another course, discovering it, eventually, in your lap. I do not wonder my poor boy would not let me come to his meals. But after this I believe he will, and I shall know exactly how to help him and how to arrange so that very soon he will have no difficulty. Oh, Dicky, I had to do it! There was no other way."

"Yes," said the doctor quietly, "you had to do it." And Jane in her blindness could not see the working of his face, as he added below his breath: "You being *you,* dear, there was no other way."

"Ah, how glad I am you realise the necessity, Deryck! I had so feared you might think it useless or foolish. And it was now or never; because I trust—if he forgives me—this will be the only week-end I shall ever have to spend away from him. Boy, do you think he will forgive me?"

It was fortunate Jane was blind: The doctor swallowed a word, then: "Hush, dear," he said. "You make me sigh for the duchess's parrot. And I shall do no good here, if I lose patience with Dalmain. Now tell me; you really never remove that bandage?"

"Only to wash my face," replied Jane, smiling. "I can trust myself not to peep for two minutes. And last night I found it made my head so hot that I could not sleep; so I slipped it off for an hour or two, but woke and put it on again before dawn."

"And you mean to wear it until to-morrow morning?"

Jane smiled rather wistfully. She knew what was involved in that question.

"Until to-morrow night, Boy," she answered gently.

"But, Jeanette," exclaimed the doctor, in indignant protest; "surely you will see me before I go! My dear girl, would it not be carrying the experiment unnecessarily far?"

"Ah, no," said Jane, leaning towards him with her pathetic bandaged eyes. "Don't you see, dear, you give me the chance of passing through what will in time be one of his hardest experiences, when his dearest friends will come and go, and be to him only voice and touch; their faces unseen and but dimly remembered? Deryck, just because this hearing and not seeing you *is* so hard, I realise how it is enriching me in what I can share with him. He must not have to say: 'Ah, but you saw him before he left.' I want to be able to say: 'He came and went,—my greatest friend,—and I did not see him at all.' "

The doctor walked over to the window and stood there, whistling softly. Jane knew he was fighting down his own vexation. She waited patiently. Presently the whistling stopped and she heard him laugh. Then he came back and sat down near her.

"You always were a *thorough* old thing!" he said.

"No half-measures would do. I suppose I must agree."

Jane reached out for his hand. "Ah, Boy," she said, "now you will help me. But I never before knew you so nearly selfish."

"The 'other man' is always a problem," said the doctor. "We male brutes, by nature, always want to be first with all our women; not merely with the one, but with all those in whom we consider, sometimes with egregious presumption, that we hold a right. You see it everywhere,—fathers towards their daughters, brothers as regards their sisters, friends in a friendship. The 'other man,' when he arrives, is always a pill to swallow. It is only natural, I suppose; but it is fallen nature and therefore to be surmounted. Now let me go and forage for your hat and coat, and take you out upon the moors. No? Why not? I often find things for Flower, so really I know likely places in which to search. Oh, all right! I will send Margery. But don't be long. And you need not be afraid of Dalmain hearing us, for I saw him just now walking briskly up and down the terrace, with only an occasional touch of his cane against the parapet. How much you have already accomplished! We shall talk more freely out on the moor; and, as I march you along, we can find out tips which may be useful when the time comes for you to lead the 'other man' about. Only do be careful how you come downstairs with old Margery. Think if you fell upon her, Jane! She does make such excellent coffee!"

CHAPTER XXIV

The Man's Point of View

A deep peace reigned in the library at Gleneesh. Garth and Deryck sat together and smoked in complete fellowship, enjoying that sense of calm content which follows an excellent dinner and a day spent in moorland air.

Jane, sitting upstairs in her self-imposed darkness, with nothing to do but listen, fancied she could hear the low hum of quiet voices in the room beneath, carrying on a more or less continuous conversation.

It was a pity she could not see them as they sat together, each looking his very best,—Garth in the dinner jacket which suited his slight upright figure so well; the doctor in immaculate evening clothes of the latest cut and fashion, which he had taken the trouble to bring, knowing Jane expected the men of her acquaintance to be punctilious in the matter of evening dress, and little dreaming she would have, literally, no eyes for him.

And indeed the doctor himself was fastidious to a degree where clothes were concerned, and always well groomed and unquestionably correct in cut and fashion, excepting in the case of his favourite old Norfolk jacket. This he kept for occasions when he intended to be what he called "happy and glorious," though Lady Brand made gentle but persistent attempts to dispose of it.

The old Norfolk jacket had walked the moors that morning with Jane. She had recognised the feel of it as he drew her hand within his arm, and they had laughed over its many associations. But now Simpson was folding it and putting it away, and a very correctly clad doctor sat in an armchair in front of the library fire, his long legs crossed the one over the other, his broad shoulders buried in the depths of the chair.

Garth sat where he could feel the warm flame of the fire, pleasant in the chill evening which succeeded the bright spring day. His chair was placed sideways, so that he could, with his hand, shield his face from his visitor should he wish to do so.

"Yes," Dr. Brand was saying thoughtfully, "I can easily see that all things which reach you in that darkness assume a different proportion and possess a greatly enhanced value. But I think you will find, as time goes on, and you come in contact with more people, there will be a great readjustment, and you will become less consciously sensitive to sound and touch from others. At present your whole nervous system is highly strung, and responds with an exaggerated vibration to every impression made upon it. A highly strung nervous system usually exaggerates. And the medium of sight having been taken away, the other means of communication with the outer world, hearing and touch, draw to themselves an overplus of nervous force, and have become painfully sensitive. Eventually things will right themselves, and they will only be usefully keen and acute. What was it you were going to tell me about Nurse Rosemary not shaking hands?"

"Ah, yes," said Garth. "But first I want to ask, is it a rule of her order, or guild, or institution, or whatever it is to which she belongs, that the nurses should never shake hands with their patients?"

"Not that I have ever heard," replied the doctor.

"Well, then, it must have been Miss Gray's own perfect intuition as to what I want, and what I don't want. For from the very first she has never shaken hands, nor in any way touched me. Even in passing across letters, and handing me things, as she does scores of times daily, never once have I felt her fingers against mine."

"And this pleases you?" inquired the doctor, blowing smoke rings into the air, and watching the blind face intently.

"Ah, I am so grateful for it," said Garth earnestly. "Do you know, Brand, when you suggested sending me a lady nurse and secretary, I felt I could not possibly stand having a woman touch me."

"So you said," commented the doctor quietly.

"No! Did I? What a bear you must have thought me."

"By no means," said the doctor, "but a distinctly unusual patient. As a rule, men——"

"Ah, I dare say," Garth interposed half impatiently. "There was a time when I should have liked a soft little hand about me. And I dare say by now I should often enough have caught it and held it, perhaps kissed it—who knows? I used to do such things, lightly enough. But, Brand, when a man has known the touch of The Woman, and when that touch has become nothing but a memory; when one is dashed into darkness, and that memory becomes one of the few things which remain, and, remaining, brings untold comfort, can you wonder if one fears another touch which might in any way dim that memory, supersede it, or take away from its utter sacredness?"

"I understand," said the doctor slowly. "It does not come within my own experience, but I understand. Only—my dear boy, may I say it?—if the One Woman exists—and it is excusable in your case to doubt it, because there were so many—surely her place should be here; her actual touch, one of the things which remain."

"Ah, say it," answered Garth, lighting another cigarette. "I like to hear it said, although as a matter of fact you might as well say that if the view from the terrace exists, I ought to be able to see it. The view is there, right enough, but my own deficiency keeps me from seeing it."

"In other words," said the doctor, leaning forward and picking up the match which, not being thrown so straight as usual, had just missed the fire; "in other words, though She was the One Woman, you were not the One Man?"

"Yes," said Garth bitterly, but almost beneath his breath. "I was 'a mere boy.'"

"Or you thought you were not," continued the doctor, seeming not to have heard the last remark. "As a matter of fact, you are always the One Man to the One Woman, unless another is before you in the field. Only it may take time and patience to prove it to her."

Garth sat up and turned a face of blank surprise towards the doctor. "What an extraordinary statement!" he said. "Do you really mean it?"

"Absolutely," replied the doctor in a tone of quiet conviction. "If you eliminate all other considerations, such as money, lands, titles, wishes of friends, attraction of exteriors—that is to say, admiration of mere physical beauty in one another, which is after all just a question of comparative anatomy; if, freed of all this social and habitual environment, you could place the man and the woman in a mental Garden of Eden, and let them face one another, stripped of all shams and conventionalities, soul viewing soul, naked and unashamed; if under those circumstances she is so truly his mate, that all the noblest of the man cries out: 'This is the One Woman!' then I say, so truly is he her mate, that he cannot fail to be the

One Man; only he must have the confidence required to prove it to her. On him it bursts, as a revelation; on her it dawns slowly, as the breaking of the day."

"Oh, my God," murmured Garth brokenly, "it was just that! The Garden of Eden, soul to soul, with no reservations, nothing to fear, nothing to hide. I realised her my *wife,* and called her so. And the next morning she called *me* 'a mere boy,' whom she could not for a moment think of marrying. So what becomes of your fool theory, Brand?"

"Confirmed," replied the doctor quietly. "Eve, afraid of the immensity of her bliss, doubtful of herself, fearful of coming short of the marvel of his ideal of her, fleeing from Adam, to hide among the trees of the garden. Don't talk about fool theories, my boy. The fool-fact was Adam, if he did not start in prompt pursuit."

Garth sat forward, his hands clutching the arms of his chair. That quiet, level voice was awakening doubts as to his view of the situation, the first he had had since the moment of turning and walking down the Shenstone village church three years ago. His face was livid, and as the firelight played upon it the doctor saw beads of perspiration gleam on his forehead.

"Oh, Brand," he said, "I am blind. Be merciful. Things mean so terribly much in the dark."

The doctor considered. Could his nurses and

students have seen the look on his face at that moment, they would have said that he was performing a most critical and delicate operation, in which a slip of the scalpel might mean death to the patient. They would have been right; for the whole future of two people hung in the balance; depending, in this crisis, upon the doctor's firmness and yet delicacy of touch. This strained white face in the firelight, with its beads of mental agony and its appealing "I am blind," had not entered into the doctor's calculations. It was a view of "the other man" upon which he could not look unmoved. But the thought of that patient figure with bandaged eyes sitting upstairs in suspense, stretching dear helpless hands to him, steadied the doctor's nerve. He looked into the fire.

"You may be blind, Dalmain, but I do not want you to be a fool," said the doctor quietly.

"Am I—was I—a fool?" asked Garth.

"How can I judge?" replied the doctor. "Give me a clear account of the circumstances from your point of view, and I will give you my opinion of the case."

His tone was so completely dispassionate and matter-of-fact, that it had a calming effect on Garth, giving him also a sense of security. The doctor might have been speaking of a sore throat, or a tendency to sciatica.

Garth leaned back in his chair, slipped his hand

into the breast-pocket of his jacket, and touched a letter lying there. Dare he risk it? Could he, for once take for himself the comfort of speaking of his trouble to a man he could completely trust, and yet avoid the danger of betraying her identity to one who knew her so intimately?

Garth weighed this, after the manner of a chess-player looking several moves ahead. Could the conversation become more explicit, sufficiently so to be of use, and yet no clue be given which would reveal Jane as the One Woman?

Had the doctor uttered a word of pressure or suggestion, Garth would have decided for silence. But the doctor did not speak. He leaned forward and reached the poker, mending the fire with extreme care and method. He placed a fragrant pine log upon the springing flame, and as he did so he whistled softly the closing bars of *Veni, Creator Spiritus*.

Garth, occupied with his own mental struggle, was, for once, oblivious to sounds from without, and did not realise why, at this critical moment, these words should have come with gentle insistence into his mind:

"Keep far our foes; give peace at home;
Where Thou art Guide, no ill can come."

He took them as an omen. They turned the scale. "Brand," he said, "if, as you are so kind as to suggest, I give myself the extreme relief of confiding in you, will you promise me never to attempt to guess at the identity of the One Woman?"

The doctor smiled; and the smile in his voice as he answered, added to Garth's sense of security.

"My dear fellow," he said, "I never guess at other people's secrets. It is a form of mental recreation which does not appeal to me, and which I should find neither entertaining nor remunerative. If I know them already, I do not require to guess them. If I do not know them, and their possessors wish me to remain in ignorance, I would as soon think of stealing their purse as of filching their secret."

"Ah, thanks," said Garth. "Personally, I do not mind what you know. But I owe it to her, that her name should not appear."

"Undoubtedly," said the doctor. "Except in so far as she herself, chooses to reveal it, the One Woman's identity should always remain a secret. Get on with your tale, old chap. I will not interrupt."

"I will state it as simply and as shortly as I can," began Garth. "And you will understand that there are details of which no fellow could speak.—I had known her several years in a friendly way, just staying at the same houses, and meeting at Lord's and Henley and all the places where those in the same set do meet. I always liked her, and always felt at my best with her, and thought no end of her opinion, and so forth. She was a friend and a real chum to me, and to lots of other fellows. But one never thought of love-making in connection with her. All the silly things one says to ordinary women she would have laughed at. If one had sent her flowers to wear, she would have put them in a vase and wondered for whom they had really been intended. She danced well, and rode straight; but the man she danced with had to be awfully good at it, or he found himself being guided through the giddy maze; and the man who wanted to be in the same field with her, must be prepared for any fence or any wall. Not that I ever saw her in the hunting-field; her love of life and of fair play would have kept her out of that. But I use it as a descriptive illustration. One was always glad to meet her in a house party, though one could not have explained why. It is quite impossible to describe her. She was just—well, just—"

The doctor saw "just Jane" trembling on Garth's lips, and knew how inadequate was every adjective to express this name. He did not want the flood of Garth's confidences checked, so he supplied the needed words.

"Just a good sort. Yes, I quite understand. Well?"

"I had had my infatuations, plenty of them," went on the eager young voice. "The one thing I thought of in women was their exteriors. Beauty of all kinds—of any kind—crazed me for the moment. I never wanted to marry them, but I always wanted to paint them. Their mothers, and aunts, and other old dowagers in the house parties used to think I meant marriage, but the girls themselves knew better. I don't believe a girl now walks this earth who would accuse me of flirting. I admired their beauty, and they knew it, and they knew that was all my admiration meant. It was a pleasant experience at the time, and, in several instances, helped forward good marriages later on. Pauline Lister was apportioned to me for two whole seasons, but she eventually married the man on whose jolly old staircase I painted her. Why didn't I come a cropper over any of them? Because there were too many, I suppose. Also, the attraction was skin-deep. I don't mind telling you quite frankly: the only one whose beauty used to cause me a real pang was Lady Brand. But when I had painted it and shown it to the world in its perfection, I was content. I asked no more of any woman than to paint her, and find her paintable. I could not explain this to the husbands and mothers and chaperons, but the women themselves understood it well enough; and as I sit here in my darkness not a memory rises up to reproach me."

"Good boy," said Deryck Brand, laughing. "You were vastly misunderstood, but I believe you."

"You see," resumed Garth, "that sort of thing being merely skin-deep, I went no deeper. The only women I really knew were my mother, who died when I was nineteen, and Margery Graem, whom I always hugged at meeting and parting, and always shall hug until I kiss the old face in its coffin, or she straightens me in mine. Those ties of one's infancy and boyhood are among the closest and most sacred life can show. Well, so things were until a certain evening in June several years ago. She—the One Woman—and I were in the same house party at a lovely old place in the country. One afternoon we had been talking intimately, but quite casually and frankly. I had no more thought of wanting to marry her than of proposing to old Margery. Then—something happened,—I must not tell you what; it would give too clear a clue to her identity. But it revealed to me, in a few marvellous moments, the woman in her; the wife, the mother; the strength, the tenderness; the exquisite perfection of her true, pure soul. In five minutes there awakened in me a hunger for her which nothing could still, which nothing ever will still, until I stand beside her in the Golden City, where they shall hunger no more, neither thirst any more; and there shall be no more darkness, or depending upon sun, moon, or candle, for the glory of God shall lighten it; and there shall be no more sorrow, neither shall there be any more pain, for former things shall have passed away."

The blind face shone in the firelight. Garth's

retrospection was bringing him visions of things to come.

The doctor sat quite still and watched the vision fade. Then he said: "Well?"

"Well," continued the young voice in the shadow, with a sound in it of having dropped back to earth and finding it a mournful place; "I never had a moment's doubt as to what had happened to me. I knew I loved her; I knew I wanted her; I knew her presence made my day and her absence meant chill night; and every day was radiant, for she was there."

Garth paused for breath and to enjoy a moment of silent retrospection.

The doctor's voice broke in with a question, clear, incisive. "Was she a pretty woman; handsome, beautiful?"

"A pretty woman?" repeated Garth, amazed: "Good heavens, no! Handsome? Beautiful? Well you have me there, for, 'pon my honour, I don't know."

"I mean, would you have wished to paint her?"

"I *have* painted her," said Garth very low, a moving tenderness in his voice; "and my two paintings of her, though done in sadness and done from memory, are the most beautiful work I ever produced. No eye but my own has ever seen them, and now none ever will see them, excepting those of one whom I must perforce trust to find them for me, and bring them to me for destruction."

"And that will be—?" queried the doctor.

"Nurse Rosemary Gray," said Garth.

The doctor kicked the pine log, and the flames darted up merrily. "You have chosen well," he said, and had to make a conscious effort to keep the mirth in his face from passing into his voice. "Nurse Rosemary will be discreet. Very good. Then we may take it the One Woman was beautiful?"

But Garth looked perplexed. "I do not know," he answered slowly. "I cannot see her through the eyes of others. My vision of her, in that illuminating moment, followed the inspired order of things,—spirit, soul, and body. Her spirit was so pure and perfect, her soul so beautiful, noble, and womanly, that the body which clothed soul and spirit partook of their perfection and became unutterably dear."

"I see," said the doctor, very gently. "Yes, you dear fellow, I see." (Oh, Jane, Jane! You were blind, without a bandage, in those days!)

"Several glorious days went by," continued Garth. "I realise now that I was living in the glow of my own certainty that she was the One Woman. It was so clear and sweet and wonderful to me, that I never dreamed of it not being equally clear to her. We did a lot of music together for pure enjoyment; we talked of other people for the fun of it; we enjoyed and appreciated each other's views and opinions; but we did not talk of ourselves, because we *knew,* at least *I* knew, and, before God, I thought she did. Every time I saw her she seemed more grand and perfect. I held the golden key to trifling matters not understood before. We young fellows, who all admired her, used nevertheless to joke a bit about her wearing collars and stocks, top boots and short skirts; whacking her leg with a riding-whip, and stirring the fire with her toe. But after that evening, I understood all this to be a sort of fence behind which she hid her exquisite womanliness, because it was of a deeper quality than any man looking upon the mere surface of her had ever fathomed or understood. And when she came trailing down in the evening, in something rich and clinging and black, with lots of soft old lace covering her bosom and moving with the beating of her great tender heart; ah, then my soul rejoiced and my eyes took their fill of delight! I saw her, as all day long I had known her to be,—perfect in her proud, sweet womanliness."

"Is he really unconscious," thought the doctor, "of how unmistakable a word-picture of Jane he is painting?"

"Very soon," continued Garth, "we had three days apart, and then met again at another house, in a weekend party. One of the season's beauties was there, with whom my name was being freely coupled, and something she said on that subject, combined with the fearful blankness of those three interminable days, made me resolve to speak without delay. I asked her to come out on to the terrace that evening. We were alone. It was a moonlight night."

A long silence. The doctor did not break it. He knew his friend was going over in his mind all those things of which a man does not speak to another man.

At last Garth said simply, "I told her."

No comment from the doctor, who was vividly reminded of Jane's "Then—it happened," when *she* had reached this point in the story. After a few moments of further silence, steeped in the silver moonlight of reminiscence for Garth; occupied by the doctor in a rapid piecing in of Jane's version; the sad young voice continued:

"I thought she understood completely. Afterwards I knew she had not understood at all. Her actions led me to believe I was accepted, taken into her great love, even as she was wrapped around by mine. Not through fault of hers,—ah, no; she was blameless throughout; but because she did not, could not, understand what any touch of hers must mean to me. In her dear life, there had never been another man; that much I knew by unerring instinct and by her own admission. I have sometimes thought that she may have had an ideal in her girlish days, against whom, in after years, she measured others, and, finding them come short, held them at arm's length. But, if I am right in this surmise, he must have been a blind fool, unconscious of the priceless love which might have been his, had he tried to win it. For I am certain that, until that night, no man's love had ever flamed about her; she had never felt herself enveloped in a cry which was all one passionate, inarticulate, inexplicable, boundless need of herself. While I thought she understood and responded,—Heaven knows I *did* think it,— she did not in the least understand, and was only trying to be sympathetic and kind."

The doctor stirred in his chair, slowly crossed one leg over the other, and looked searchingly into the blind face. He was finding these confidences of the "other man" more trying than he had expected.

"Are you sure of that?" he asked rather huskily.

"Quite sure," said Garth. "Listen. I called her— what she was to me just then, what I wanted her to be always, what she is forever, so far as my part goes, and will be till death and beyond. That one word,—no, there were two,—those two words made her understand. I see that now. She rose at once and put me from her. She said I must give her twelve hours for quiet thought, and she would come to me in the village church next morning with her answer. Brand, you may think me a fool; you cannot think me a more egregious ass than I now think myself; but I was absolutely certain she was mine; so sure that, when she came, and we

312

were alone together in the house of God, instead of going to her with the anxious haste of suppliant and lover, I called her to me at the chancel step as if I were indeed her husband and had the right to bid her come. She came, and, just as a sweet formality before taking her to me, I asked for her answer. It was this: 'I cannot marry a mere boy.'"

Garth's voice choked in his throat on the last word. His head was bowed in his hands. He had reached the point where most things stopped for him; where all things had ceased forever to be as they were before.

The room seemed strangely silent. The eager voice had poured out into it such a flow of love and hope and longing; such a revealing of a soul in which the true love of beauty had created perpetual youth; of a heart held free by high ideals from all playing with lesser loves, but rising to volcanic force and height when the true love was found at last.

The doctor shivered at that anticlimax, as if the chill of an empty church were in his bones. He knew how far worse it had been than Garth had told. He knew of the cruel, humiliating question: "How old are you?" Jane had confessed to it. He knew how the outward glow of adoring love had faded as the mind was suddenly turned inward to self-contemplation. He had known it all as abstract fact. Now he saw it actually before him. He saw Jane's stricken lover, bowed beside him in his blindness, living again through those sights and sounds which no merciful curtain of oblivion could ever hide or veil.

The doctor had his faults, but they were not Peter's. He never, under any circumstances, spoke *because* he wist not what to say.

He leaned forward and laid a hand very tenderly on Garth's shoulder. "Poor chap," he said. "Ah, poor old chap."

And for a long while they sat thus in silence.

CHAPTER XXV

The Doctor's Diagnosis

"So you expressed no opinion? explained nothing? let him go on believing that? Oh, Dicky! And you might have said so much!"

In the quiet of the Scotch Sabbath morning, Jane and the doctor had climbed the winding path from the end of the terrace, which zigzagged up to a clearing amongst the pines. Two fallen trees at a short distance from each other provided convenient seats in full sunshine, facing a glorious view,—down into the glen, across the valley, and away to the purple hills beyond. The doctor had guided Jane to the sunnier of the two trunks, and seated himself beside her. Then he had quietly recounted practically the whole of the conversation of the previous evening.

"I expressed no opinion. I explained nothing. I let him continue to believe what he believes; because it is the only way to keep you on the pinnacle where he has placed you. Let any other reason for your conduct than an almost infantine ignorance of men and things be suggested and accepted, and down you will come, my poor Jane, and great will be the fall. Mine shall not be the hand thus to hurl you headlong. As you say, I might have said so much, but I might also have lived to regret it."

"I should fall into his arms," said Jane recklessly, "and I would sooner be there than on a pinnacle."

"Excuse me, my good girl," replied the doctor. "It is more likely you would fall into the first express going south. In fact, I am not certain you would wait for an express. I can almost see the Honourable Jane quitting yonder little railway station, seated in an empty coal-truck. No! Don't start up and attempt to stride about among the pine needles," continued the doctor, pulling Jane down beside him again. "You will only trip over a fir cone and go headlong into the valley. It is no use forestalling the inevitable fall."

"Oh, Dicky," sighed Jane, putting her hand through his arm; and leaning her bandaged eyes against the rough tweed of his shoulder; "I don't know what has come to you to-day. You are not kind to me. You have harrowed my poor soul by repeating all Garth said last night; and, thanks to that terribly good memory of yours, you have reproduced the tones of his voice in every inflection. And then, instead of comforting me, you leave me entirely in the wrong, and completely in the lurch."

"In the wrong—yes," said Deryck; "in the lurch—no. I did not say I would do nothing to-day. I only said I could do nothing last night. You cannot take up a wounded thing and turn it about and analyse it. When we bade each other good-night, I told him I would think the matter over and give him my opinion to-day. I will tell you what has happened to me if you like. I have looked into the inmost recesses of a very rare and beautiful nature, and I have seen what havoc a woman can work in the life of the man who loves her. I can assure you, last night was no pastime. I woke this morning feeling as if I had, metaphorically, been beaten black and blue."

"Then what do you suppose *I* feel?" inquired Jane pathetically.

"You still feel yourself in the right—partly," replied Deryck. "And so long as you think you have a particle of justification and cling to it, your case is hopeless. It will have to be: 'I confess. Can you forgive?'"

"But I acted for the best," said Jane. "I thought of him before I thought of myself. It would have been far easier to have accepted the happiness of the moment, and chanced the future."

"That is not honest, Jeanette. You thought of yourself first. You dared not face the possibility of the pain to you if his love cooled or his admiration waned. When one comes to think of it, I believe every form of human love—a mother's only excepted—is primarily selfish. The best chance for Dalmain is that his helpless blindness may awaken the mother love in you. Then self will go to the wall."

"Ah me!" sighed Jane. "I am lost and weary and perplexed in this bewildering darkness. Nothing seems clear; nothing seems right. If I could see your kind eyes, Boy, your hard voice would hurt less."

"Well, take off the bandage and look," said the doctor.

"I will not!" cried Jane furiously. "Have I gone through all this to fail at the last?"

"My dear girl, this self-imposed darkness is getting on your nerves. Take care it does not do more harm than good. Strong remedies—"

"Hush!" whispered Jane. "I hear footsteps."

"You can always hear footsteps in a wood if you hearken for them," said the doctor; but he spoke low, and then sat quiet, listening.

"I hear Garth's step," whispered Jane. "Oh, Dicky, go to the edge and look over. You can see the windings of the path below."

The doctor stepped forward quietly and looked down upon the way they had ascended. Then he came back to Jane.

"Yes," he said. "Fortune favours us. Dalmain is coming up the path with Simpson. He will be here in two minutes."

"Fortune favours us? My dear Dicky! Of all mis-chances!" Jane's hand flew to her bandage, but the doctor stayed her just in time.

"Not at all," he said. "And do not fail at the last in your experiment. I ought to be able to keep you two blind people apart. Trust me, and keep dark—I mean, sit still. And can you not understand why I said fortune favours us? Dalmain is coming for my opinion on the case. You shall hear it together. It will be a saving of time for me, and most enlightening for you to mark how he takes it. Now keep quiet. I promise he shall not sit on your lap. But if you make a sound, I shall have to say you are a bunny or a squirrel, and throw fir cones at you."

The doctor rose and sauntered round the bend of the path.

Jane sat on in darkness.

"Hullo, Dalmain," she heard Deryck say. "Found your way up here? An ideal spot. Shall we dispense with Simpson? Take my arm."

"Yes," replied Garth. "I was told you were up here, Brand, and followed you."

They came round the bend together, and out into the clearing.

"Are you alone?" asked Garth standing still. "I thought I heard voices."

"You did," replied the doctor. "I was talking to a young woman."

"What sort of young woman?" asked Garth.

"A buxom young person," replied the doctor, "with a decidedly touchy temper."

"Do you know her name?"

"Jane," said the doctor recklessly.

"Not 'Jane,'" said Garth quickly,—"Jean. I know her,—my gardener's eldest daughter. Rather weighed down by family cares, poor girl."

"I saw she was weighed down," said the doctor. "I did not know it was by family cares. Let us sit on this trunk. Can you call up the view to mind?"

"Yes," replied Garth; "I know it so well. But it terrifies me to find how my mental pictures are fading; all but one."

"And that is—?" asked the doctor.

"The face of the One Woman," said Garth in his blindness.

"Ah, my dear fellow," said the doctor, "I have not forgotten my promise to give you this morning my opinion on your story. I have been thinking it over carefully, and have arrived at several conclusions. Shall we sit on this fallen tree? Won't you smoke? One can talk better under the influence of the fragrant weed."

Garth took out his cigarette case, chose a cigarette, lighted it with care, and flung the flaming match straight on to Jane's clasped hands.

Before the doctor could spring up, Jane had smilingly flicked it off.

"What nerve!" thought Deryck, with admiration. "Ninety-nine women out of a hundred would have said 'Ah!' and given away the show. Really, she deserves to win."

Suddenly Garth stood up. "I think we shall do better on the other log," he said unexpectedly. "It is always in fuller sunshine." And he moved towards Jane.

With a bound the doctor sprang in front of him, seized Jane with one strong hand and drew her behind him; then guided Garth to the very spot where she had been sitting.

"How accurately you judge distance," he remarked, backing with Jane towards the further trunk. Then he seated himself beside Garth in the sunshine. "Now for our talk," said the doctor, and he said it rather breathlessly.

"Are you sure we are alone?" asked Garth. "I seem conscious of another presence."

"My dear fellow," said the doctor, "is one ever alone in a wood? Countless little presences surround us. Bright eyes peep down from the branches; furry tails flick in and out of holes; things unseen move in the dead leaves at our feet. If you seek solitude, shun the woods."

"Yes," replied Garth, "I know, and I love listening to them. I meant a human presence. Brand, I am often so tried by the sense of an unseen

320

human presence near me. Do you know, I could have sworn the other day that she—the One Woman—came silently, looked upon me in my blindness, pitied me, as her great tender heart would do, and silently departed."

"When was that?" asked the doctor.

"A few days ago. Dr. Rob had been telling us how he came across her in—Ah! I must not say where. Then he and Miss Gray left me alone, and in the lonely darkness and silence I felt her eyes upon me."

"Dear boy," said the doctor, "you must not encourage this dread of unseen presences. Remember, those who care for us very truly and deeply can often make us conscious of their mental nearness, even when far away, especially if they know we are in trouble and needing them. You must not be surprised if you are often conscious of the nearness of the One Woman, for I believe—and I do not say it lightly, Dalmain—I believe her whole heart and love and life are yours."

"Good Lord!" exclaimed Garth, and springing up, strode forward aimlessly.

The doctor caught him by the arm. In another moment he would have fallen over Jane's feet.

"Sit down, man," said the doctor, "and listen to me. You gain nothing by dashing about in the dark in that way. I am going to prove my words. But you must give me your calm attention. Now listen.

We are confronted in this case by a psychological problem, and one which very likely has not occurred to you. I want you for a moment to picture the One Man and the One Woman facing each other in the Garden of Eden, or in the moonlight— wherever it was—if you like better. Now will you realise this? The effect upon a man of falling in love is to create in him a complete unconsciousness of self. On the other hand, the effect upon a woman of being loved and sought, and of responding to that love and seeking, is an accession of intense self-consciousness. He, longing to win and take, thinks of her only. She, called upon to yield and give, has her mind turned at once upon herself. Can she meet his need? Is she all he thinks her? Will she be able to content him completely, not only now but in the long vista of years to come? The more natural and unconscious of self she had been before, the harder she would be hit by this sudden, overwhelming attack of self-consciousness."

The doctor glanced at Jane on the log six yards away. She had lifted her clasped hands and was nodding towards him, her face radiant with relief and thankfulness.

He felt he was on the right tack. But the blind face beside him clouded heavily, and the cloud deepened as he proceeded.

"You see, my dear chap, I gathered from yourself she was not of the type of feminine loveliness you were known to admire. Might she not have feared that her appearance would, after a while, have failed to content you?"

"No," replied Garth with absolutely finality of tone. "Such a suggestion is unworthy. Besides, had the idea by any possibility entered her mind, she would only have had to question me on the point. My decision would have been final; my answer would have fully reassured her."

"Love is blind," quoted the doctor quietly.

"They lie who say so," cried Garth violently. "Love is so far-seeing that it sees beneath the surface and delights in beauties unseen by other eyes."

"Then you do not accept my theory?" asked the doctor.

"Not as an explanation of my own trouble," answered Garth; "because I know the greatness of her nature would have lifted her far above such a consideration. But I do indeed agree as to the complete oblivion to self of the man in love. How else could we ever venture to suggest to a woman that she should marry us? Ah, Brand, when one thinks of it, the intrusion into her privacy; the asking the right to touch, even her hand, at will; it could not be done unless the love of her and the thought of her had swept away all thoughts of self. Looking back upon that time I remember how completely it was so with me. And when she said to me in the church: 'How old are you?'—ah, I did not tell you that last night—the revulsion of feeling brought about by being turned at that moment in upon myself was so great, that my joy seemed to shrivel and die in horror at my own unworthiness."

Silence in the wood. The doctor felt he was playing a losing game. He dared not look at the silent figure opposite. At last he spoke.

"Dalmain, there are two possible solutions to your problem. Do you think it was a case of Eve holding back in virginal shyness, expecting Adam to pursue?"

"Ah, no," said Garth emphatically. "We had gone far beyond all that. Nor could you suggest it, did you know her. She is too honest, too absolutely straight and true, to have deceived me. Besides, had it been so, in all these lonely years, when she found I made no sign, she would have sent me word of what she really meant."

"Should you have gone to her then?" asked the doctor.

"Yes," said Garth slowly. "I should have gone and I should have forgiven—because she is my own. But it could never have been the same. It would have been unworthy of us both."

"Well," continued the doctor, "the other solution remains. You have admitted that the One Woman came somewhat short of the conventional standard of beauty. Your love of loveliness was so well known. Do you not think, during the long hours of that night,—remember how new it was to her to be so worshipped and wanted,—do you not think her courage failed her? She feared she might come short of what eventually you would need in the face and figure always opposite you at your table; and, despite her own great love and yours, she thought it wisest to avoid future disillusion by rejecting present joy. Her very love for you would have armed her to this decision."

The silent figure opposite nodded, and waited with clasped hands. Deryck was pleading her cause better than she could have pleaded it herself.

Silence in the woods. All nature seemed to hush and listen for the answer.

Then:—"No," said Garth's young voice unhesitatingly. "In that case she would have told me her fear, and I should have reassured her immediately. Your suggestion is unworthy of my beloved."

The wind sighed in the trees. A cloud passed before the sun. The two who sat in darkness, shivered and were silent.

Then the doctor spoke. "My dear boy," he said, and a deep tenderness was in his voice: "I must maintain my unalterable belief that to the One Woman you are still the One Man. In your blindness her rightful place is by your side. Perhaps even now she is yearning to be here. Will you tell me her name, and give me leave to seek her out, hear from herself her version of the story; and, if it be as I think, bring her to you, to prove, in your affliction, her love and tenderness?"

"Never!" said Garth. "Never, while life shall last! Can you not see that if when I had sight, and fame, and all heart could desire, I could not win her love, what she might feel for me now, in my helpless blindness, could be but pity? And pity from her I could never accept. If I was 'a mere boy' three years ago, I am 'a mere blind man' now, an object for kind commiseration. If indeed you are right, and she mistrusted my love and my fidelity, it is now out of my power forever to prove her wrong and to prove myself faithful. But I will not allow the vision of my beloved to be dimmed by these suggestions. For her completion, she needed so much more than I could give. She refused me because I was not fully worthy. I prefer it should be so. Let us leave it at that."

"It leaves you to loneliness," said the doctor sadly.

"I prefer loneliness," replied Garth's young voice, "to disillusion. Hark! I hear the first gong, Brand. Margery will be grieved if we keep her Sunday dishes waiting."

He stood up and turned his sightless face towards the view.

"Ah, how well I know it," he said. "When Miss Gray and I sit up here, she tells me all she sees, and I tell her what she does not see, but what I know is there. She is keen on art, and on most of the things I care about. I must ask for an arm, Brand, though the path is wide and good. I cannot risk a tumble. I have come one or two awful croppers, and I promised Miss Gray—The path is wide. Yes, we can walk two abreast, three abreast if necessary. It is well we had this good path made. It used to be a steep scramble."

"Three abreast," said the doctor. "So we could—if necessary." He stepped back and raised Jane from her seat, drawing her cold hand through his left arm. "Now, my dear fellow, my right arm will suit you best; then you can keep your stick in your right hand."

And thus they started down through the wood, on that lovely Sabbath morn of early summer; and the doctor walked erect between those two severed hearts, uniting, and yet dividing them.

Just once Garth paused and listened. "I seem to hear another footstep," he said, "besides yours and mine."

"The wood is full of footsteps," said the doctor, "just as the heart is full of echoes. If you stand still and listen you can hear what you will in either."

"Then let us not stand still," said Garth, "for in old days, if I was late for lunch, Margery used to spank me."

CHAPTER XXVI

Hearts Meet in Sightless Land

"It will be absolutely impossible, Miss Gray, for me ever to tell you what I think of this that you have done for my sake."

Garth stood at the open library window. The morning sunlight poured into the room. The air was fragrant with the scent of flowers, resonant with the songs of birds. As he stood there in the sunshine, a new look of strength and hopefulness was apparent in every line of his erect figure. He held out eager hands towards Nurse Rosemary, but more as an expression of the outgoing of his appreciation and gratitude than with any expectation of responsive hands being placed within them.

"And here was I, picturing you having a gay weekend, and wondering where, and who your friends in this neighbourhood could be. And all the while you were sitting blindfold in the room over my head. Ah, the goodness of it is beyond words! But did you not feel somewhat of a deceiver, Miss Gray?"

She always felt that—poor Jane. So she readily answered: "Yes. And yet I told you I was not going far. And my friends in the neighbourhood were Simpson and Margery, who aided and abetted. And it was true to say I was going, for was I not going into darkness? and it is a different world from the land of light."

"Ah, how true that is!" cried Garth. "And how difficult to make people understand the loneliness of it, and how they seem suddenly to arrive close to one from another world; stooping from some distant planet, with sympathetic voice and friendly touch; and then away they go to another sphere, leaving one to the immensity of solitude in Sightless Land."

"Yes," agreed Nurse Rosemary, "and you almost dread the coming, because the going makes the darkness darker, and the loneliness more lonely."

"Ah, so *you* experienced that?" said Garth. "Do you know, now you have week-ended in Sightless Land, I shall not feel it such a place of solitude. At every turn I shall be able to say:—'A dear and faithful friend has been here.'"

He laughed a laugh of such almost boyish pleasure, that all the mother in Jane's love rose up and demanded of her one supreme effort. She looked at the slight figure in white flannels, leaning against the window frame, so manly, so beautiful still, and yet so helpless and so needing the wealth of tenderness which was hers to give. Then, standing facing him, she opened her arms, as if the great preparedness of that place of rest, so close to him must, magnet-like, draw him to her; and standing thus in the sunlight, Jane spoke.

Was she beautiful? Was she paintable? Would a man grow weary of such a look turned on him, of such arms held out? Alas! Too late! On that point no lover shall ever be able to pass judgment. That look is for one man alone. He only will ever bring it to that loving face. And he cannot pronounce upon its beauty in voice of rapturous content. He cannot judge. He cannot see. He is blind!

"Mr. Dalmain, there are many smaller details; but before we talk of those I want to tell you the greatest of all the lessons I learned in Sightless Land." Then, conscious that her emotion was producing in her voice a resonant depth which might remind him too vividly of notes in *The Rosary*, she paused, and resumed in the high, soft edition of her own voice which it had become second nature to her to use as Nurse Rosemary: "Mr. Dalmain, it seems to me I learned to understand how that which is loneliness unspeakable to *one* might be Paradise of a very perfect kind for *two*. I realised that there might be circumstances in which the dark would become a very wonderful meeting-place for souls. If I loved a man who lost his sight, I should be glad to have mine in order to be eyes for him when eyes were needed; just as, were I rich and he poor, I should value my money simply as a thing which might be useful to him. But I know the daylight would often be a trial to me, because it would be something he could not share; and when evening came, I should long to say: 'Let us put out the lights and shut away the moonlight and sit together in the sweet soft darkness, which is more uniting than the light.'"

While Jane was speaking, Garth paled as he listened, and his face grew strangely set. Then, as if under a reaction of feeling, a boyish flush spread to the very roots of his hair. He visibly shrank from the voice which was saying these things to him. He fumbled with his right hand for the orange cord which would guide him to his chair.

"Nurse Rosemary," he said, and at the tone of his voice Jane's outstretched arms dropped to her sides; "it is kind of you to tell me all these beautiful thoughts which came to you in the darkness. But I hope the man who is happy enough to possess your love, or who is going to be fortunate enough to win it, will neither be so unhappy nor so unfortunate as to lose his sight. It will be better for him to live with you in the light, than to be called upon to prove the kind way in which you would be willing to adapt yourself to his darkness. How about opening our letters?" He slipped his hand along the orange cord and walked over to his chair.

Then, with a sense of unutterable dismay, Jane saw what she had done. She had completely forgotten Nurse Rosemary, using her only as a means of awakening in Garth an understanding of how much her—Jane's—love might mean to him in his blindness. She had forgotten that, to Garth, Nurse

331

Rosemary's was the only personality which counted in this conversation; she, who had just given him such a proof of her interest and devotion. And—O poor dear Garth! O bold, brazen Nurse Rosemary!—he very naturally concluded she was making love to him. Jane felt herself between Scylla and Charybdis, and she took a very prompt and characteristic plunge.

She came across to her place on the other side of the small table and sat down. "I believe it was the thought of him made me realise this," she said; "but just now I and my young man have fallen out. He does not even know I am here."

Garth unbent at once, and again that boyish heightening of colour indicated his sense of shame at what he had imagined.

"Ah, Miss Gray," he said eagerly, "you will not think it impertinent or intrusive on my part, but do you know I have wondered sometimes whether there was a happy man."

Nurse Rosemary laughed. "Well, we can't call him a happy man just now," she said, "so far as his thoughts of me are concerned. My whole heart is his, if he could only be brought to believe it. But a misunderstanding has grown up between us,—my fault entirely,—and he will not allow me to put it right."

"What a fool!" cried Garth. "Are you and he engaged?"

Nurse Rosemary hesitated. "Well—not exactly

engaged," she said, "though it practically amounts to that. Neither of us would give a thought to any one else."

Garth knew there was a class of people whose preliminary step to marriage was called "keeping company," a stage above the housemaid's "walking out," both expressions being exactly descriptive of the circumstances of the case; for, whereas pretty Phyllis and her swain go walking out of an evening in byways and between hedges, or along pavements and into the parks,—these keep each other company in the parlours and arbours of their respective friends and relations. Yet, somehow, Garth had never thought of Nurse Rosemary as belonging to any other class than his own. Perhaps this ass of a fellow, whom he already cordially disliked, came of a lower stratum; or perhaps the rules of her nursing guild forbade a definite engagement, but allowed "an understanding." Anyway the fact remained that the kind-hearted, clever, delightful little lady, who had done so much for him, had "a young man" of her own; and this admitted fact lifted a weight from Garth's mind. He had been so afraid lately of not being quite honest with her and with himself. She had become so necessary to him, nay, so essential, and by her skill and devotion had won so deep a place in his gratitude. Their relation was of so intimate a nature, their companionship so close and continuous; and into this rather ideal state of things had heavily trodden Dr. Rob the other day with a suggestion. Garth, alone with him, had been explaining how indispensable Miss Gray had become to his happiness and comfort, and how much he dreaded a recall from her matron.

"I fear they do not let them go on indefinitely at one case; but perhaps Sir Deryck can arrange that this should be an exception," said Garth.

"Oh, hang the matron, and blow Sir Deryck," said Dr. Rob breezily. "If you want her as a permanency, make sure of her. Marry her, my boy! I'll warrant she'd have you!"

Thus trod Dr. Rob, with heavily nailed boots, upon the bare toes of a delicate situation.

Garth tried to put the suggestion out of his mind and failed. He began to notice thoughts and plans of Nurse Rosemary's for his benefit, which so far exceeded her professional duties that it seemed as if there must be behind them the promptings of a more tender interest. He put the thought away again and again, calling Dr. Rob an old fool, and himself a conceited ass. But again and again there came about him, with Nurse Rosemary's presence, the subtle surrounding atmosphere of a watchful love.

Then, one night, he faced and fought a great temptation.

After all why should he not do as Dr. Rob suggested? Why not marry this charming, capable, devoted nurse, and have her constantly about him in his blindness? *She* did not consider him "a mere boy." . . . What had he to offer her? A beautiful home, every luxury, abundant wealth, a companionship she seemed to find congenial . . . But then the Tempter overreached himself, for he whispered: "And the voice would be always Jane's. You have never seen the nurse's face; you never will see it. You can go on putting to the voice the face and form you adore. You can marry the little nurse, and go on loving Jane." . . . Then Garth cried out in horror: "Avaunt, Satan!" and the battle was won.

But it troubled his mind lest by any chance her peace of heart should be disturbed through him. So it was with relief, and yet with an unreasonable smouldering jealousy, that he heard of the young man to whom she was devoted. And now it appeared she was unhappy through her young man, just as he was unhappy through—no, because of—Jane.

A sudden impulse came over him to do away forever with the thought which in his own mind had lately come between them, and to establish their intimacy on an even closer and firmer basis, by being absolutely frank with her on the matter.

"Miss Gray," he said, leaning towards her with that delightful smile of boyish candour which many women had found irresistible, "it is good of you to have told me about yourself; and, although I confess to feeling unreasonably jealous of the fortunate fellow who possesses your whole heart, I am glad he exists, because we all miss something unless we have in our lives the wonderful experience of the One Woman or the One Man. And I want to tell you something, dear sweet friend of mine, which closely touches you and me; only, before I do so, put your hand in mine, that I may realise you in a closer intimacy than heretofore. You, who have been in Sightless Land, know how much a hand clasp means down here."

Garth stretched his hand across the table, and his whole attitude was tense with expectation.

"I cannot do that, Mr. Dalmain," said Nurse Rosemary, in a voice which shook a little. "I have burned my hands. Oh, not seriously. Do not look so distressed. Just a lighted match. Yes; while I was blind. Now tell me the thing which touches you and me."

Garth withdrew his hand and clasped both around his knee. He leaned back in his chair, his face turned upwards. There was upon it an expression so pure, the exaltation of a spirit so lifted above the temptations of the lower nature, that Jane's eyes filled with tears as she looked at him. She realised what his love for her, supplemented by the discipline of suffering, had done for her lover.

He began to speak softly, not turning towards her. "Tell me," he said, "is he—very much to you?"

Jane's eyes could not leave the dear face and figure in the chair. Jane's emotion trembled in Nurse Rosemary's voice.

"He is all the world to me," she said.

"Does he love you as you deserve to be loved?"

Jane bent and laid her lips on the table where his outstretched hand had rested. Then Nurse Rosemary answered: "He loved me far, *far* more than I ever deserved."

"Why do you say 'loved'? Is not 'loves' the truer tense?"

"Alas, no!" said Nurse Rosemary, brokenly; "for I fear I have lost his love by my own mistrust of it and my own wrong-doing."

"Never!" said Garth. "'Love never faileth.' It may for a time appear to be dead, even buried. But the Easter morn soon dawns, and lo, Love ariseth! Love grieved, is like a bird with wet wings. It cannot fly; it cannot rise. It hops about upon the ground, chirping anxiously. But every flutter shakes away more drops; every moment in the sunshine is drying the tiny feathers; and very soon it soars to the tree top, all the better for the bath, which seemed to have robbed it of the power to rise."

"Ah,—if my beloved could but dry his wings," murmured Nurse Rosemary. "But I fear I did more than wet them. I clipped them. Worse still,—I broke them."

"Does he know you feel yourself so in the wrong?" Garth asked the question very gently.

"No," replied Nurse Rosemary. "He will give me no chance to explain, and no opportunity to tell him how he wrongs himself and me by the view he now takes of my conduct."

"Poor girl!" said Garth in tones of sympathy and comprehension. "My own experience has been such a tragedy that I can feel for those whose course of true love does not run smooth. But take my advice, Miss Gray. Write him a full confession. Keep nothing back. Tell him just how it all happened. Any man who truly loves would believe, accept your explanation, and be thankful. Only, I hope he would not come tearing up here and take you away from me!"

Jane smiled through a mist of tears.

"If he wanted me, Mr. Dalmain, I should have to go to him," said Nurse Rosemary.

"How I dread the day," continued Garth, "when you will come and say to me: 'I have to go.' And, do you know, I have sometimes thought—you have done so much for me and become so much to me—I have sometimes thought—I can tell you frankly now—it might have seemed as if there were a very obvious way to try to keep you always. You are so immensely worthy of all a man could offer, of all the devotion a man could give. And because, to one so worthy, I never could have offered less than the best, I want to tell you that in my heart I hold shrined forever one beloved face. All others are gradually fading.

Now, in my blindness, I can hardly recall clearly the many lovely faces I have painted and admired. All are more or less blurred and indistinct. But this one face grows clearer, thank God, as the darkness deepens. It will be with me through life, I shall see it in death, *the face of the woman I love*. You said 'loved' of your lover, hesitating to be sure of his present state of heart. I can neither say 'love' nor 'loved' of my beloved. She never loved me. But I love her with a love which makes it impossible for me to have any 'best' to offer to another woman. If I could bring myself, from unworthy motives and selfish desires, to ask another to wed me, I should do her an untold wrong. For her unseen face would be nothing to me; always that one and only face would be shining in my darkness. Her voice would be dear, only in so far as it reminded me of the voice of the woman I love. Dear friend, if you ever pray for me, pray that I may never be so base as to offer to any woman such a husk as marriage with me would mean."

"But—" said Nurse Rosemary. "She—she who has made it a husk for others; she who might have the finest of the wheat, the full corn in the ear, herself?"

"She," said Garth, "has refused it. It was neither fine enough nor full enough. It was not worthy. O my God, little girl—! What it means, to appear inadequate to the woman one loves!"

Garth dropped his face between his hands with a groan.

Silence unbroken reigned in the library.

Suddenly Garth began to speak, low and quickly, without lifting his head.

"Now," he said, "now I feel it, just as I told Brand, and never so clearly before, excepting once, when I was alone. Ah, Miss Gray! Don't move! Don't stir! But look all round the room and tell me whether you see anything. Look at the window. Look at the door. Lean forward and look behind the screen. I cannot believe we are alone. I will not believe it. I am being deceived in my blindness. And yet—I am *not* deceived. I am conscious of the presence of the woman I love. Her eyes are fixed upon me in pity, sorrow, and compassion. Her grief at my woe is so great that it almost enfolds me, as I had dreamed her love would do . . . O my God! She is so near—and it is so terrible, because I do not wish her near. I would sooner a thousand miles were between us—and I am certain there are not many yards! . . . Is it psychic? or is it actual? or am I going mad? . . . Miss Gray! *You* would not lie to me. No persuasion or bribery or confounded chicanery could induce *you* to deceive me on this point. Look around, for God's sake, and tell me! Are we alone? And if not, *who is in the room* besides you and me?"

Jane had been sitting with her arms folded upon

340

the table, her yearning eyes fixed upon Garth's bowed head. When he wished her a thousand miles away she buried her face upon them. She was so near him that had Garth stretched out his right hand again, it would have touched the heavy coils of her soft hair. But Garth did not raise his head, and Jane still sat with her face buried.

There was silence in the library for a few moments after Garth's question and appeal. Then Jane lifted her face.

"There is no one in the room, Mr. Dalmain," said Nurse Rosemary, "but *you*—and *me*."

CHAPTER XXVII

The Eyes Garth Trusted

"So you enjoy motoring, Miss Gray?"

They had been out in the motor together for the first time, and were now having tea together in the library, also for the first time; and, for the first time, Nurse Rosemary was pouring out for her patient. This was only Monday afternoon, and already her week-end experience had won for her many new privileges.

"Yes, I like it, Mr. Dalmain; particularly in this beautiful air."

"Have you had a case before in a house where they kept a motor?"

Nurse Rosemary hesitated. "Yes, I have stayed

in houses where they had motors, and I have been in Dr. Brand's. He met me at Charing Cross once with his electric brougham."

"Ah, I know," said Garth. "Very neat. On your way to a case, or returning from a case?"

Nurse Rosemary smiled, then bit her lip. "To a case," she replied quite gravely. "I was on my way to his house to talk it over and receive instructions."

"It must be splendid working under such a fellow as Brand," said Garth; "and yet I am certain most of the best things you do are quite your own idea. For instance, he did not suggest your week-end plan, did he? I thought not. Ah, the difference it has made! Now tell me. When we were motoring we never slowed up suddenly to pass anything, or tooted to make something move out of the way, without your having already told me what we were going to pass or what was in the road a little way ahead. It was: 'We shall be passing a hay cart at the next bend; there will be just room, but we shall have to slow up'; or, 'An old red cow is in the very middle of the road a little way on. I think she will move if we hoot.' Then, when the sudden slow down and swerve came, or the toot toot of the horn, I knew all about it and was not taken unawares. Did you know how trying it is in blindness to be speeding along and suddenly alter pace without having any idea why, or swerve to one side, and not know what one has just been avoiding? This afternoon our spin was pure pleasure, because not once did you let these things happen. I knew all that was taking place, as soon as I should have known it had I had my sight."

Jane pressed her hand over her bosom. Ah, how able she was always to fill her boy's life with pure pleasure. How little of the needless suffering of the blind should ever be his if she won the right to be beside him always.

"Well, Mr. Dalmain," said Nurse Rosemary, "I motored to the station with Sir Deryck yesterday afternoon, and I noticed all you describe. I have never before felt nervous in a motor, but I realised yesterday how largely that is owing to the fact that all the time one keeps an unconscious look-out; measuring distances, judging speed, and knowing what each turn of the handle means. So when we go out you must let me be eyes to you in this."

"How good you are!" said Garth, gratefully. "And did you see Sir Deryck off?"

"No. I did not *see* Sir Deryck at all. But he said good-bye, and I felt the kind, strong grip of his hand as he left me in the car. And I sat there and heard his train start and rush away into the distance."

"Was it not hard to you to let him come and go and not to see his face?"

Jane smiled. "Yes, it was hard," said Nurse

Rosemary; "but I wished to experience that hardness."

"It gives one an awful blank feeling, doesn't it?" said Garth.

"Yes. It almost makes one wish the friend had not come."

"Ah—" There was a depth of contented comprehension in Garth's sigh; and the brave heart, which had refused to lift the bandage to the very last, felt more than recompensed.

"Next time I reach the Gulf of Partings in Sightless Land," continued Garth, "I shall say: 'A dear friend has stood here for my sake.'"

"Oh, and one's meals," said Nurse Rosemary laughing. "Are they not grotesquely trying?"

"Yes, of course; I had forgotten you would understand all that now. I never could explain to you before why I must have my meals alone. You know the hunt and chase?"

"Yes," said Nurse Rosemary, "and it usually resolves itself into 'gone away,' and turns up afterwards unexpectedly! But, Mr. Dalmain, I have thought out several ways of helping so much in that and making it all quite easy. If you will consent to have your meals with me at a small table, you will see how smoothly all will work. And later on, if I am still here, when you begin to have visitors, you must let me sit at your left, and all my little ways of helping would be so unobtrusive, that no one would notice."

"Oh, thanks," said Garth. "I am immensely grateful. I have often been reminded of a silly game we used to play at Overdene, at dessert, when we were a specially gay party. Do you know the old Duchess of Meldrum? Or anyway, you may have heard of her? Ah, yes, of course, Sir Deryck knows her. She called him in once to her macaw. She did not mention the macaw on the telephone, and Sir Deryck, thinking he was wanted for the duchess, threw up an important engagement and went immediately. Luckily she was at her town house. She would have sent just the same had she been at Overdene. I wish you knew Overdene. The duchess gives perfectly delightful 'best parties,' in which all the people who really enjoy meeting one another find them-selves together, and are well fed and well housed and well mounted, and do exactly as they like; while the dear old duchess tramps in and out, with her queer beasts and birds, shedding a kindly and exciting influence wherever she goes. Last time I was there she used to let out six Egyptian jerboas in the drawing-room every evening after dinner, awfully jolly little beggars, like miniature kanga-roos. They used to go skipping about on their hind legs, frightening some of the women into fits by hiding under their gowns, and making young footmen drop trays of coffee cups. The last impor-tation is a toucan,—a South American bird, with a beak like a banana, and a voice like an old sheep in despair. But Tommy, the scarlet macaw, remains prime favourite, and I must say he is clever and knows more than you would think.

"Well, at Overdene we used to play a silly game at dessert with muscatels. We each put five raisins at intervals round our plates, then we shut our eyes and made jabs at them with forks. Whoever succeeded first in spiking and eating all five was the winner. The duchess never would play. She enjoyed being umpire, and screaming at the people who peeped. Miss Champion and I—she is the duchess's niece, you know—always played fair, and we nearly always made a dead heat of it."

"Yes," said Nurse Rosemary, "I know that game. I thought of it at once when I had my blindfold meals."

"Ah," cried Garth, "had I known, I would not have let you do it!"

"I knew that," said Nurse Rosemary. "That was why I week-ended."

Garth passed his cup to be refilled, and leaned forward confidentially.

"Now," he said, "I can venture to tell you one of my minor trials. I am always so awfully afraid of there being a *fly* in things. Ever since I was a small boy I have had such a horror of inadvertently eating flies. When I was about six, I heard a lady visitor say to my mother: 'Oh, one *has* to swallow a fly—about once a year! I have just swallowed mine, on the way here!' This terrible idea of an annual fly took possession of my small mind. I used to be thankful when it happened, and I got it over. I remember quickly finishing a bit of bread in which I had seen signs of legs and wings, feeling it was an easy way of taking it and I should thus be exempt for twelve glad months; but I had to run up and down the terrace with clenched hands while I swallowed it. And when I discovered the fallacy of the annual fly, I was just as particular in my dread of an accidental one. I don't believe I ever sat down to sardines on toast at a restaurant without looking under the toast for my bugbear, though as I lifted it I felt rather like the old woman who always looks under the bed for a burglar. Ah, but since the accident this foolishly small thing *has* made me suffer! I cannot say: 'Simpson, are you sure there is not a fly in this soup?' Simpson would say: 'No—sir; no fly—sir,' and would cough behind his hand, and I could never ask him again."

Nurse Rosemary leaned forward and placed his cup where he could reach it easily, just touching his right hand with the edge of the saucer. "Have all your meals with me," she said, in a tone of such complete understanding, that it was almost a caress; "and I can promise there shall never be any flies in anything. Could you not trust my eyes for this?"

And Garth replied, with a happy, grateful smile: "I could trust your kind and faithful eyes for anything. Ah! and that reminds me: I want to intrust to them a task I could confide to no one else. Is it twilight yet, Miss Gray, or is an hour of daylight left to us?"

Nurse Rosemary glanced out of the window and looked at her watch. "We ordered tea early," she said, "because we came in from our drive quite hungry. It is not five o'clock yet, and a radiant afternoon. The sun sets at half-past seven."

"Then the light is good," said Garth. "Have you finished tea? The sun will be shining in at the west window of the studio. You know my studio at the top of the house? You fetched the studies of Lady Brand from there. I dare say you noticed stacks of canvases in the corners. Some are unused; some contain mere sketches or studies; some are finished pictures. Miss Gray, among the latter are two which I am most anxious to identify and to destroy. I made Simpson guide me up the other day and leave me there alone. And I tried to find them by touch; but I could not be sure, and I soon grew hopelessly confused amongst all the canvases. I did not wish to ask Simpson's help, because the subjects are—well, somewhat unusual, and if he found out I had destroyed them it might set him wondering and talking, and one hates to awaken curiosity in a servant. I could not fall back on Sir Deryck because he would have recognised the portraits. The principal figure is known to him. When I painted those pictures I never dreamed of any eye but my own seeing them. So you, my dear and trusted secretary, are the one person to whom I can turn. Will you do what I ask? And will you do it now?"

Nurse Rosemary pushed back her chair. "Why of course, Mr. Dalmain. I am here to do anything and everything you may desire; and to do it when you desire it."

Garth took a key from his waistcoat pocket, and laid it on the table. "There is the studio latch-key. I think the canvases I want are in the corner furthest from the door, behind a yellow Japanese screen. They are large—five feet by three and a half. If they are too cumbersome for you to bring down, lay them face to face, and ring for Simpson. But do not leave him alone with them."

Nurse Rosemary picked up the key, rose, and went over to the piano, which she opened. Then she tightened the purple cord, which guided Garth from his chair to the instrument.

"Sit and play," she said, "while I am upstairs, doing your commission. But just tell me one thing. You know how greatly your work interests me. When I find the pictures, is it your wish that I give them a mere cursory glance, just sufficient for identification; or may I look at them, in the beautiful studio light? You can trust me to do whichever you desire."

The artist in Garth could not resist the wish to have his work seen and appreciated. "You may look at them of course, if you wish," he said.

"They are quite the best work I ever did, though I painted them wholly from memory. That is—I mean, that used to be—a knack of mine. And they are in no sense imaginary. I painted exactly what I saw—at least, so far as the female face and figure are concerned. And they make the pictures. The others are mere accessories." He stood up, and went to the piano. His fingers began to stray softly amongst the harmonies of the *Veni*.

Nurse Rosemary moved towards the door. "How shall I know them?" she asked, and waited.

The chords of the *Veni* hushed to a murmur, Garth's voice from the piano came clear and distinct, but blending with the harmonies as if he were reciting to music.

"A woman and a man . . . alone, in a garden—but the surroundings are only indicated. She is in evening dress; soft, black, and trailing; with lace at her breast. It is called: 'The Wife.'"

"Yes?"

"The same woman; the same scene; but without the man, this time. No need to paint the man; for now—visible or invisible—to her, he is always there. In her arms she holds"—the low murmur of chords ceased; there was perfect silence in the room—"a little child. It is called: 'The Mother.'"

The *Veni* burst forth in an unrestrained upbearing of confident petition:

"Keep far our foes; give peace at home"—and the door closed behind Nurse Rosemary.

CHAPTER XXVIII

In the Studio

Jane mounted to the studio; unlocked the door, and, entering, closed it after her.

The evening sun shone through a western window, imparting an added richness to the silk screens and hangings; the mauve wistaria of a Japanese embroidery; or the golden dragon of China on a deep purple ground, wound up in its own interminable tail, and showing rampant claws in unexpected places.

Several times already Jane had been into Garth's studio, but always to fetch something for which he waited eagerly below; and she had never felt free to linger. Margery had a duplicate key; for she herself went up every day to open the windows, dust tenderly all special treasures; and keep it exactly as its owner had liked it kept, when his quick eyes could look around it. But this key was always on Margery's bunch; and Jane did not like to ask admission, and risk a possible refusal.

Now, however, she could take her own time; and she seated herself in one of the low and very deep wicker lounge-chairs, comfortably upholstered; so exactly fitting her proportions, and supporting arms, knees, and head, just rightly, that it seemed as if all other chairs would in future appear inadequate, owing to the absolute perfection of this one. Ah, to be just that to her beloved! To so fully meet his need, at every point, that her presence should be to him always a source of strength, and rest, and consolation.

She looked around the room. It was so like Garth; every detail perfect; every shade of colour enhancing another, and being enhanced by it. The arrangements for regulating the light, both from roof and windows; the easels of all kinds and sizes; clean bareness, where space, and freedom from dust, were required; the luxurious comfort round the fireplace, and in nooks and corners; all were so perfect. And the plain brown wall-paper, of that beautiful quiet shade which has in it no red, and no yellow; a clear nut-brown. On an easel near the further window stood an unfinished painting; palette and brushes beside it, just as Garth had left them when he went out on that morning, nearly three months ago; and, vaulting over a gate to protect a little animal from unnecessary pain, was plunged himself into such utter loss and anguish.

Jane rose, and took stock of all his quaint treasures on the mantelpiece. Especially her mind was held and fascinated by a stout little bear in brass, sitting solidly yet jauntily on its haunches, its front paws clasping a brazen pole; its head turned sideways; its small, beady, eyes, looking straight before it. The chain, from its neck to the pole denoted captivity and possible fierceness. Jane had no doubt its head would lift, and its body prove a receptacle for matches; but she felt equally certain that, should she lift its head and look, no matches would be within it. This little bear was unmistakably Early Victorian; a friend of childhood's days; and would not be put to common uses. She lifted the head. The body was empty. She replaced it gently on the mantelpiece, and realised that she was deliberately postponing an ordeal which must be faced.

Deryck had told her of Garth's pictures of the One Woman. Garth, himself, had now told her even more. But the time had come when she must see them for herself. It was useless to postpone the moment. She looked towards the yellow screen.

Then she walked, over to the western window, and threw it wide open. The sun was dipping gently towards the purple hills. The deep blue of the sky began to pale, as a hint of lovely rose crept into it. Jane looked heavenward and, thrusting her hands deeply into her pockets, spoke aloud. "Before God" she said,—"in case I am never able to say or think it again, I will say it now—*I believe I was right*. I considered Garth's future happiness, and I considered my own. I decided as I did for both our sakes, at terrible cost to present joy. But, before God, I believed I was right; and—*I believe it still*."

Jane never said it again.

CHAPTER XXIX

Jane Looks into Love's Mirror

Behind the yellow screen, Jane found a great confusion of canvases, and unmistakable evidence of
the blind hands which had groped about in a vain
search, and then made fruitless endeavours to sort
and rearrange. Very tenderly, Jane picked up each
canvas from the fallen heap; turning it the right
way up, and standing it with its face to the wall.
Beautiful work was there; some of it finished;
some, incomplete. One or two faces she knew,
looked out at her in their pictured loveliness. But
the canvases she sought were not there.

She straightened herself, and looked around. In
a further corner, partly concealed by a Cairo
screen, stood another pile. Jane went to them.

Almost immediately she found the two she
wanted; larger than the rest, and distinguishable at
a glance by the soft black gown of the central
figure.

Without giving them more than a passing look,
she carried them over to the western window,
and placed them in a good light. Then she drew
up the chair in which she had been sitting; took
the little brass bear in her left hand, as a talisman
to help her through what lay before her; turned
the second picture with its face to the easel; and

sat down to the quiet contemplation of the first.

The noble figure of a woman, nobly painted, was the first impression which leapt from eye to brain. Yes, nobility came first, in stately pose, in uplifted brow, in breadth of dignity. Then—as you marked the grandly massive figure, too well-proportioned to be cumbersome, but large and full, and amply developed; the length of limb; the firmly planted feet; the large capable hands,—you realised the second impression conveyed by the picture, to be strength;—strength to do; strength to be; strength to continue. Then you looked into the face. And there you were confronted with a great surprise. The third thought expressed by the picture was Love—love, of the highest, holiest, most ideal, kind; yet, withal, of the most tenderly human order; and you found it in that face.

It was a large face, well proportioned to the figure. It had no pretensions whatever to ordinary beauty. The features were good; there was not an ugly line about them; and yet, each one just missed the beautiful; and the general effect was of a good-looking plainness; unadorned, uncon-cealed, and unashamed. But the longer you looked, the more desirable grew the face; the less you noticed its negations; the more you admired its honesty, its purity, its immense strength of pur-pose; its noble simplicity. You took in all these outward details; you looked away for a moment, to consider them; you looked back to verify them;

and then the miracle happened. Into the face had stolen the "light that never was on sea or land." It shone from the quiet grey eyes,—as, over the head of the man who knelt before her, they looked out of the picture—with an expression of the sublime surrender of a woman's whole soul to an emotion which, though it sways and masters her, yet gives her the power to be more truly herself than ever before. The startled joy in them; the marvel at a mystery not yet understood; the passionate tenderness; and yet the almost divine compassion for the unrestrained violence of feeling, which had flung the man to his knees, and driven him to the haven of her breast; the yearning to soothe, and give, and content;—all these were blended into a look of such exquisite sweetness, that it brought tears to the eyes of the beholder.

The woman was seated on a broad marble parapet. She looked straight before her. Her knees came well forward, and the long curve of the train of her black gown filled the foreground on the right. On the left, slightly to one side of her, knelt a man, a tall slight figure in evening dress, his arms thrown forward around her waist; his face completely hidden in the soft lace at her bosom; only the back of his sleek dark head, visible. And yet the whole figure denoted a passion of tense emotion. She had gathered him to her with what you knew must have been an exquisite gesture, combining the utter self-surrender of the woman, with the tender throb of maternal solicitude; and now her hands were clasped behind his head, holding him closely to her. Not a word was being spoken. The hidden face was obviously silent; and her firm lips above his dark head were folded in a line of calm self-control; though about them hovered the dawning of a smile of bliss ineffable.

A crimson rambler rose climbing some woodwork faintly indicated on the left, and hanging in a glowing mass from the top left-hand corner, supplied the only vivid colour in the picture.

But, from taking in these minor details, the eye returned to that calm tender face, alight with love; to those strong capable hands, now learning for the first time to put forth the protective passion of a woman's tenderness; and the mind whispered the only possible name for that picture: The Wife.

Jane gazed at it long, in silence. Had Garth's little bear been anything less solid than Early Victorian brass; it must have bent and broken under the strong pressure of those clenched hands.

She could not doubt, for a moment, that she looked upon herself; but, oh, merciful heavens! how unlike the reflected self of her own mirror! Once or twice as she looked, her mind refused to work, and she simply gazed blankly at the minor details of the picture. But then again, the expression of the grey eyes drew her, recalling so vividly every feeling she had experienced when that dear head had come so unexpectedly to its resting-place upon her bosom. "It is true," she whispered; and again: "Yes; it is true. I cannot deny it. It is as I felt; it must be as I looked."

And then, suddenly; she fell upon her knees before the picture. "Oh, my God! Is that as I looked? And the next thing that happened was my boy lifting his shining eyes and gazing at me in the moonlight. Is *this* what he saw? Did I look *so?* And did the woman who looked so; and who, looking so, pressed his head down again upon her breast, refuse next day to marry him, on the grounds of his youth, and her superiority? . . . Oh, Garth, Garth! . . . O God, help him to understand! . . . help him to forgive me!"

In the work-room just below, Maggie the house-maid was singing as she sewed. The sound floated through the open window, each syllable distinct in the clear Scotch voice, and reached Jane where she knelt. Her mind, stunned to blankness by its pain, took eager hold upon the words of Maggie's hymn. And they were these.

> "O Love, that will not let me go,
> I rest my weary soul in Thee;
> I give Thee back the life I owe,
> That in Thine ocean depths its flow
> May richer, fuller be.

"O Light, that followest all my way,
I yield my flick'ring torch to Thee;
My heart restores its borrowed ray,
That in Thy sunshine's blaze its day
May brighter, fairer be."

Jane took the second picture, and placed it in front of the first.

The same woman, seated as before; but the man was not there; and in her arms, its tiny dark head pillowed against the fulness of her breast, lay a little child. The woman did not look over that small head, but bent above it, and gazed into the baby face.

The crimson rambler had grown right across the picture, and formed a glowing arch above mother and child. A majesty of tenderness was in the large figure of the mother. The face, as regarded contour and features, was no less plain; but again it was transfigured, by the mother-love thereon depicted. You knew "The Wife" had more than fulfilled her abundant promise. The wife was there in fullest realisation; and, added to wifehood, the wonder of motherhood. All mysteries were explained; all joys experienced; and the smile on her calm lips, bespoke ineffable content.

A rambler rose had burst above them, and fallen in a shower of crimson petals upon mother and child. The baby-fingers clasped tightly the soft lace at her bosom. A petal had fallen upon the tiny wrist. She had lifted her hand to remove it; and, catching the baby-eyes, so dark and shining, paused for a moment, and smiled.

Jane, watching them, fell to desperate weeping. The "mere boy" had understood her potential possibilities of motherhood far better than she understood them herself. Having had one glimpse of her as "The Wife," his mind had leaped on, and seen her as "The Mother." And again she was forced to say: "It is true—yes; it is true."

And then she recalled the old line of cruel reasoning:

"It was not the sort of face one would have wanted to see always in front of one at table." Was this the sort of face—this, as Garth had painted it, after a supposed year of marriage? Would any man weary of it, or wish to turn away his eyes?

Jane took one more long look. Then she dropped the little bear, and buried her face in her hands; while a hot blush crept up to the very roots of her hair, and tingled to her finger-tips.

Below, the fresh young voice was singing again.

"O Joy, that seekest me through pain,
I cannot close my heart to Thee;
I trace the rainbow through the rain,
And feel the promise is not vain
That morn shall tearless be."

After a while Jane whispered: "Oh, my darling, forgive me. I was altogether wrong. I will confess; and, God helping me, I will explain; and, oh, my darling, you will forgive me?"

Once more she lifted her head and looked at the picture. A few stray petals of the crimson rambler lay upon the ground; reminding her of those crushed roses, which, falling from her breast, lay scattered on the terrace at Shenstone, emblem of the joyous hopes and glory of love which her decision of that night had laid in the dust of disillusion. But crowning this picture, in rich clusters of abundant bloom, grew the rambler rose. And through the open window came the final verse of Maggie's hymn.

"O Cross, that liftest up my head,
I dare not ask to fly from Thee;
I lay in dust life's glory dead,
And from the ground there blossoms red
Life that shall endless be."

Jane went to the western window, and stood, with her arms stretched above her, looking out upon the radiance of the sunset. The sky blazed into gold and crimson at the horizon; gradually as the eye lifted, paling to primrose, flecked with rosy clouds; and, overhead, deep blue—fathomless, boundless, blue.

Jane gazed at the golden battlements above the

purple hills, and repeated, half aloud: "And the city was of pure gold;—and had no need of the sun, neither of the moon to shine in it: for the glory of God did lighten it. And there shall be no more death; neither sorrow, nor crying, neither shall there be any more pain: for the former things are passed away."

Ah, how much had passed away since she stood at that western window, not an hour before. All life seemed readjusted; its outlook altered; its per-spective changed. Truly Garth had "gone behind his blindness."

Jane raised her eyes to the blue; and a smile of unspeakable anticipation parted her lips. "Life, that shall endless be," she murmured. Then, turning, found the little bear, and restored him to his place upon the mantelpiece; put back the chair; closed the western window; and, picking up the two canvases, left the studio, and made her way carefully downstairs.

CHAPTER XXX

"The Lady Portrayed"

"It has taken you long, Miss Gray. I nearly sent Simpson up, to find out what had happened."

"I am glad you did not do that, Mr. Dalmain. Simpson would have found me weeping on the studio floor; and to ask his assistance under those circumstances, would have been more humbling than inquiring after the fly in the soup!"

Garth turned quickly in his chair. The artist-ear had caught the tone which meant comprehension of his work.

"Weeping!" he said. "Why?"

"Because," answered Nurse Rosemary, "I have been entranced. These pictures are so exquisite. They stir one's deepest depths. And yet they are so pathetic—ah, *so* pathetic; because you have made a plain woman, beautiful."

Garth rose to his feet, and turned upon her a face which would have blazed, had it not been sightless.

"A *what?*" he exclaimed.

"A plain woman," repeated Nurse Rosemary, quietly. "Surely you realised your model to be that. And therein lies the wonder of the pictures. You have so beautified her by wifehood, and glorified her by motherhood, that the longer one looks the more one forgets her plainness; seeing her as loving and loved; lovable, and therefore lovely. It is a triumph of art."

Garth sat down, his hands clasped before him.

"It is a triumph of truth," he said. "I painted what I saw."

"You painted her soul," said Nurse Rosemary, "and it illuminated her plain face."

"I *saw* her soul," said Garth, almost in a whisper; "and that vision was so radiant that it

363

illumined my dark life. The remembrance lightens my darkness, even now."

A very tender silence fell in the library.

The twilight deepened.

Then Nurse Rosemary spoke, very low. "Mr. Dalmain, I have a request to make of you. I want to beg you not to destroy these pictures."

Garth lifted his head. "I must destroy them, child," he said. "I cannot risk their being seen by people who would recognise my—the—the lady portrayed."

"At all events, there is one person who must see them, before they are destroyed."

"And that is?" queried Garth.

"The lady portrayed," said Nurse Rosemary, bravely.

"How do you know she has not seen them?"

"Has she?" inquired Nurse Rosemary.

"No," said Garth, shortly; "and she never will."

"She must."

Something in the tone of quiet insistence struck Garth.

"Why?" he asked; and listened with interest for the answer.

"Because of all it would mean to a woman who knows herself plain, to see herself thus beautified."

Garth sat very still for a few moments. Then: "A woman who—knows—herself—plain?" he repeated, with interrogative amazement in his voice.

"Yes," proceeded Nurse Rosemary, encouraged. "Do you suppose, for a moment, that that lady's mirror has ever shown her a reflection in any way approaching what you have made her in these pictures? When we stand before our looking-glasses, Mr. Dalmain, scowling anxiously at hats and bows, and partings, we usually look our very worst; and that lady, at her very worst, would be of a most discouraging plainness."

Garth sat perfectly silent.

"Depend upon it," continued Nurse Rosemary, "she never sees herself as 'The Wife'—'The Mother.' Is she a wife?"

Garth hesitated only the fraction of a second. "Yes," he said, very quietly.

Jane's hands flew to her breast. Her heart must be held down, or he would hear it throbbing.

Nurse Rosemary's voice had in it only a slight tremor, when she spoke again.

"Is she a mother?"

"No," said Garth. "I painted what might have been."

"If—?"

"If it *had* been," replied Garth, curtly.

Nurse Rosemary felt rebuked. "Dear Mr. Dalmain," she said, humbly; "I realise how officious I must seem to you, with all these questions, and suggestions. But you must blame the hold these wonderful paintings of yours have taken on my mind. Oh, they are beautiful—beautiful!"

"Ah," said Garth, the keen pleasure of the artist springing up once more. "Miss Gray, I have somewhat forgotten them. Have you them here? That is right. Put them up before you, and describe them to me. Let me hear how they struck you, as pictures." Jane rose, and went to the window. She threw it open; and as she breathed in the fresh air, breathed out a passionate prayer that her nerve, her voice, her self-control might not fail her, in this critical hour. She herself had been convicted by Garth's pictures. Now she must convince Garth, by her description of them. He must be made to believe in the love he had depicted.

Then Nurse Rosemary sat down; and, in the gentle, unemotional voice, which was quite her own, described to the eager ears of the blind artist, exactly what Jane had seen in the studio.

It was perfectly done. It was mercilessly done. All the desperate, hopeless, hunger for Jane, awoke in Garth; the maddening knowledge that she had been his, and yet not his; that, had he pressed for her answer that evening, it could not have been a refusal; that the cold calculations of later hours, had no place in those moments of ecstasy. Yet—he lost her—lost her! Why? Ah, why? Was there any possible reason other than the one she gave?

Nurse Rosemary's quiet voice went on, regardless of his writhings. But she was drawing to a close. "And it is such a beautiful crimson rambler,

Mr. Dalmain," she said. "I like the idea of its being small and in bud, in the first picture; and blooming in full glory, in the second."

Garth pulled himself together and smiled. He must not give way before this girl.

"Yes," he said; "I am glad you noticed that. And, look here. We will not destroy them at once. Now they are found, there is no hurry. I am afraid I am giving you a lot of trouble; but will you ask for some large sheets of brown paper, and make a package, and write upon it: 'Not to be opened,' and tell Margery to put them back in the studio. Then, when I want them, at any time, I shall have no difficulty in identifying them."

"I am so glad," said Nurse Rosemary. "Then perhaps the plain lady——"

"I cannot have her spoken of so," said Garth, hotly. "I do not know what she thought of herself—I doubt if she ever gave a thought to self at all. I do not know what you would have thought of her. I can only tell you that, to me, hers is the one face which is visible in my darkness. All the loveliness I have painted, all the beauty I have admired, fades from my mental vision, as wreaths of mist; flutters from memory's sight, as autumn leaves. Her face alone abides; calm, holy, tender, beautiful,—it is always before me. And it pains me that one who has only seen her as *my* hand depicted her should speak of her as plain."

"Forgive me," said Nurse Rosemary, humbly. "I

did not mean to pain you, sir. And, to show you what your pictures have done for me, may I tell you a resolution I made in the studio? I cannot miss what they depict—the sweetest joys of life—for want of the courage to confess myself wrong; pocket my pride; and be frank and humble. I am going to write a full confession to my young man, as to my share of the misunderstanding which has parted us. Do you think he will understand? Do you think he will forgive?"

Garth smiled. He tried to call up an image of a pretty troubled face, framed in a fluffy setting of soft fair hair. It harmonised so little with the voice; but it undoubtedly was Nurse Rosemary Gray, as others saw her.

"He will be a brute if he doesn't, child," he said.

CHAPTER XXXI

In Lighter Vein

Dinner that evening, the first at their small round table, was a great success. Nurse Rosemary's plans all worked well; and Garth delighted in arrangements which made him feel less helpless.

The strain of the afternoon brought its reaction of merriment. A little judicious questioning drew forth further stories of the duchess and her pets; and Miss Champion's name came in with a frequency which they both enjoyed.

It was a curious experience for Jane, to hear herself described in Garth's vivid word-painting. Until that fatal evening at Shenstone, she had been remarkably free from self-consciousness; and she had no idea that she had a way of looking straight into people's eyes when she talked to them, and that that was what muddled up "the silly little minds of women who say they are afraid of her, and that she makes them nervous! You see she looks right into their shallow shuffling little souls, full of conceited thoughts about themselves, and nasty ill-natured thoughts about her; and no wonder they grow panic-stricken, and flee; and talk of her as 'that formidable Miss Champion.' I never found her formidable; but, when I had the chance of a real talk with her, I used to be thankful I had nothing of which to be ashamed. Those clear eyes touched bottom every time, as our kindred over the water so expressively put it."

Neither had Jane any idea that she always talked with a poker, if possible; building up the fire while she built up her own argument; or attacking it vigorously, while she demolished her opponent's; that she stirred the fire with her toe, but her very smart boots never seemed any the worse; that when pondering a difficult problem, she usually stood holding her chin in her right hand, until she had found the solution. All these small characteristics Garth described with vivid touch, and dwelt upon with a tenacity of remembrance, which astonished Jane, and revealed him, in his relation to herself three years before, in a new light.

His love for her had been so suddenly disclosed, and had at once had to be considered as a thing to be either accepted or put away; so that when she decided to put it away, it seemed not to have had time to become in any sense part of her life. She had viewed it; realised all it might have meant; and put it from her.

But now she understood how different it had been for Garth. During the week which preceded his declaration, he had realised, to the full, the meaning of their growing intimacy; and, as his certainty increased, he had more and more woven her into his life; his vivid imagination causing her to appear as his beloved from the first; loved and wanted, when as yet they were merely acquaintances; kindred spirits; friends.

To find herself thus shrined in his heart and memory was infinitely touching to Jane; and seemed to promise, with sweet certainty, that it would not be difficult to come home there to abide, when once all barriers between them were removed.

After dinner, Garth sat long at the piano, filling the room with harmony. Once or twice the theme of *The Rosary* crept in, and Jane listened anxiously for its development; but almost immediately it gave way to something else. It seemed rather to haunt the other melodies, than to be actually there itself.

When Garth left the piano, and, guided by the purple cord, reached his chair, Nurse Rosemary said gently, "Mr. Dalmain, can you spare me for a few days at the end of this week?"

"Oh, why?" said Garth. "To go where? And for how long? Ah, I know I ought to say: 'Certainly! Delighted!' after all your goodness to me. But I really cannot! You don't know what life was without you, when you week-ended! That week-end seemed months, even though Brand was here. It is your own fault for making yourself so indispensable."

Nurse Rosemary smiled. "I daresay I shall not be away for long," she said. "That is, if you want me, I can return. But, Mr. Dalmain, I intend to-night to write that letter of which I told you. I shall post it to-morrow. I must follow it up almost immediately. I must be with him when he receives it, or soon afterwards. I think—I hope—he will want me at once. This is Monday. May I go on Thursday?"

Poor Garth looked blankly dismayed.

"Do nurses, as a rule, leave their patients, and rush off to their young men in order to find out how they have liked their letters?" he inquired, in mock protest.

"Not as a rule, sir," replied Nurse Rosemary, demurely. "But this is an exceptional case."

"I shall wire to Brand."

"He will send you a more efficient and more dependable person."

"Oh you wicked little thing!" cried Garth. "If Miss Champion were here, she would shake you! You know perfectly well that nobody could fill your place!"

"It is good of you to say so, sir," replied Nurse Rosemary, meekly. "And is Miss Champion much addicted to shaking people?"

"Don't call me 'sir'! Yes; when people are tiresome she often says she would like to shake them; and one has a mental vision of how their teeth would chatter. There is a certain little lady of our acquaintance whom we always call 'Mrs. Do-and-don't.' She isn't in our set; but she calls upon it; and sometimes it asks her to lunch, for fun. If you inquire whether she likes a thing, she says: 'Well, I do, and I don't.' If you ask whether she is going to a certain function, she says: 'Well, I am, and I'm not.' And if you send her a note, imploring a straight answer to a direct question, the answer comes back: 'Yes *and* no.' Miss Champion used to say she would like to take her up by the scruff of her feather boa, and shake her, asking at intervals: 'Shall I stop?' so as to wring from Mrs. Do-and-don't a definite affirmative, for once."

"Could Miss Champion carry out such a threat? Is she a very massive person?"

"Well, she could, you know; but she wouldn't.

She is most awfully kind, even to little freaks she laughs at. No, she isn't massive. That word does not describe her at all. But she is large, and very finely developed. Do you know the Venus of Milo? Yes; in the Louvre. I am glad you know Paris. Well, just imagine the Venus of Milo in a tailor-made coat and skirt,—and you have Miss Champion."

Nurse Rosemary laughed, hysterically. Either the Venus of Milo, or Miss Champion, or this combination of both, proved too much for her.

"Little Dicky Brand summed up Mrs. Do-and-don't rather well," pursued Garth. "She was calling at Wimpole Street, on Lady Brand's 'at home' day. And Dicky stood talking to me, in his black velvets and white waistcoat, a miniature edition of Sir Deryck. He indicated Mrs. Do-and-don't on a distant lounge, and remarked: '*That* lady never *knows;* she always *thinks*. I asked her if her little girl might come to my party, and she said: "I think so." Now if she had asked *me* if I was coming to *her* party, I should have said: "Thank you; I am." It is very trying when people only *think* about important things, such as little girls and parties; because their thinking never amounts to much. It does not so much matter what they think about other things—the weather, for instance; because that all happens, whether they think or not. Mummie asked that lady whether it was raining when she got here; and she said: "I *think* not." I can't imagine why Mummie always wants to know what her friends think about the weather. I have heard her ask seven ladies this afternoon whether it is raining. Now if father or I wanted to know whether it was raining we should just step over to the window, and look out; and then come back and go do with really interesting conversation. But Mummie asks them whether it is raining, or whether they think it has been raining, or is going to rain; and when they have told her, she hurries away and asks somebody else. I asked the thinking lady in the feather thing, whether she knew who the father and mother were, of the young lady whom Cain married; and she said: "Well, I do; and I don't." I said: "If you *do,* perhaps you will tell me. And if you *don't,* perhaps you would like to take my hand, and we will walk over together and ask the Bishop—the one with the thin legs, and the gold cross, talking to Mummie." But she thought she had to go, quite in a hurry. So I saw her off; and then asked the Bishop alone. Bishops are most satisfactory kind of people; because they are quite sure about everything; and you feel safe in quoting them to Nurse. Nurse told Marsdon that this one is in "sheep's clothing," because he wears a gold cross. I saw the cross; but I saw no sheep's clothing. I was looking out for the kind of woolly thing our new curate wears on his back in church. Should you call that "sheep's clothing"? I asked father, and he said: "No. Bunny-skin." And mother seemed as shocked as if father and I had spoken in church, instead of just as we came out. And she said: "It is a B.A. hood." Possibly she thinks "baa" is spelled with only one "a." Anyway father and I felt it best to let the subject drop.'"

Nurse Rosemary laughed. "How exactly like Dicky," she said. "I could hear his grave little voice, and almost see him pull down his small waistcoat!"

"Why, do you know the little chap?" asked Garth.

"Yes," replied Nurse Rosemary; "I have stayed with them. Talking to Dicky is an education; and Baby Blossom is a sweet romp. Here comes Simpson. How quickly the evening has flown. Then may I be off on Thursday?"

"I am helpless," said Garth. "I cannot say 'no.' But suppose you do not come back?"

"Then you can wire to Dr. Brand."

"I believe you want to leave me," said Garth reproachfully.

"I do, and I don't!" laughed Nurse Rosemary; and fled from his outstretched hands.

When Jane had locked the letter-bag earlier that evening, and handed it to Simpson, she had slipped in two letters of her own. One was addressed to Georgina, Duchess of Meldrum, Portland Place.

The other, to Sir Deryck Brand, Wimpole Street.

Both were marked: URGENT. IF ABSENT, FORWARD IMMEDIATELY.

CHAPTER XXXII

An Interlude

Tuesday passed uneventfully, to all outward seeming.

There was nothing to indicate to Garth that his secretary had sat up writing most of the night; only varying that employment by spending long moments in silent contemplation of his pictures, which had found a temporary place of safety, on their way back to the studio, in a deep cupboard in her room, of which she had the key.

If Nurse Rosemary marked, with a pang of tender compunction, the worn look on Garth's face, telling how mental suffering had chased away sleep; she made no comment thereupon.

Thus Tuesday passed, in uneventful monotony.

Two telegrams had arrived for Nurse Gray in the course of the morning. The first came while she was reading a *Times* leader aloud to Garth. Simpson brought it in, saying: "A telegram for you, miss."

It was always a source of gratification to

Simpson afterwards, that, almost from the first, he had been led, by what he called his "unHaided HintuHition," to drop the "nurse," and address Jane with the conventional "miss." In time he almost convinced himself that he had also discerned in her "a Honourable"; but this, Margery Graem firmly refused to allow. She herself had had her "doots," and kept them to herself; but all Mr. Simpson's surmisings had been freely expressed and reiterated in the housekeeper's room; and never a word about any honourable lead passed Mr. Simpson's lips. Therefore Mrs. Graem berated him for being so ready to "go astray and speak lies." But Maggie, the housemaid, had always felt sure Mr. Simpson knew more than he said. "Said more than he knew, you mean," prompted old Margery. "No," retorted Maggie, "I know what I said; and I said what I meant." "You may have said what you meant, but you did not mean what you knew," insisted Margery; "and if anybody says another word on the matter, *I* shall say grace and dismiss the table," continued old Margery, exercising the cloture, by virtue of her authority, in a way which Simpson and Maggie, who both wished for cheese, afterwards described as "mean."

But this was long after the uneventful Tuesday, when Simpson entered, with a salver; and, finding Jane enveloped in the *Times*, said: "A telegram for you, miss."

Nurse Rosemary took it; apologised for the interruption, and opened it. It was from the duchess, and ran thus:

MOST INCONVENIENT, AS YOU VERY WELL KNOW; BUT AM LEAVING EUSTON TO-NIGHT. WILL AWAIT FURTHER ORDERS AT ABERDEEN.

Nurse Rosemary smiled, and put the telegram into her pocket. "No answer, thank you, Simpson."

"Not bad news, I hope?" asked Garth.

"No," replied Nurse Rosemary; "but it makes my departure on Thursday imperative. It is from an old aunt of mine, who is going to my 'young man's' home. I must be with him before she is, or there will be endless complications."

"I don't believe he will ever let you go again, when once he gets you back," remarked Garth, moodily.

"You think not?" said Nurse Rosemary, with a tender little smile, as she took up the paper, and resumed her reading.

The second telegram arrived after luncheon. Garth was at the piano, thundering Beethoven's *Funeral March on the Death of a Hero*. The room was being rent asunder by mighty chords; and Simpson's smug face and side-whiskers appearing noiselessly in the doorway, were an insupportable anticlimax. Nurse Rosemary laid her finger on her lips; advanced with her firm noiseless tread, and took the telegram. She returned to her seat and waited until the hero's obsequies were over, and the last roll of the drums had died away. Then she opened the orange envelope. And as she opened it, a strange thing happened. Garth began to play *The Rosary*. The string of pearls dropped in liquid sound from his fingers; and Nurse Rosemary read her telegram. It was from the doctor, and said: SPECIAL LICENSE EASILY OBTAINED. FLOWER AND I WILL COME WHENEVER YOU WISH. WIRE AGAIN.

The Rosary drew to a soft melancholy close.

"What shall I play next?" asked Garth, suddenly.

"Veni, Creator Spiritus," said Nurse Rosemary; and bowed her head in prayer.

CHAPTER XXXIII

"Something Is Going to Happen!"

Wednesday dawned; an ideal First of May: Garth was in the garden before breakfast. Jane heard him singing, as he passed beneath her window.

"It is not mine to sing the stately grace,
    The great soul beaming in my lady's face."

She leaned out.

He was walking below in the freshest of white flannels; his step so light and elastic; his every movement so lithe and graceful; the only sign of his blindness the Malacca cane he held in his hand, with which he occasionally touched the grass border, or the wall of the house. She could only see the top of his dark head. It might have been on the terrace at Shenstone, three years before. She longed to call from the window; "Darling—my Darling! Good morning! God bless you to-day."

Ah what would to-day bring forth;—the day when her full confession, and explanation, and plea for pardon, would reach him? He was such a boy in many ways; so light-hearted, loving, artistic, poetic, irrepressible; ever young, in spite of his great affliction. But where his manhood was concerned; his love; his right of choice and of decision; of maintaining a fairly-formed opinion, and setting aside the less competent judgment of others; she knew him rigid, inflexible. His very pain seemed to cool him, from the molten lover, to the bar of steel.

As Jane knelt at her window that morning, she had not the least idea whether the evening would find her travelling to Aberdeen, to take the night mail south; or at home forever in the heaven of Garth's love.

And down below he passed again, still singing:

"But mine it is to follow in her train;
Do her behests in pleasure or in pain;

Burn at her altar love's sweet frankincense,
And worship her in distant reverence."

"Ah, beloved!" whispered Jane, "not 'distant.' If you want her, and call her, it will be to the closest closeness love can devise. No more distance between you and me."

And then, in the curious way in which inspired words will sometimes occur to the mind quite apart from their inspired context, and bearing a totally different meaning from that which they primarily bear, these words came to Jane: "For He is our peace, Who hath made both one, and hath broken down the middle wall of partition between us . . . that He might reconcile both . . . by the cross." "Ah, dear Christ!" she whispered. "If Thy cross could do this for Jew and Gentile, may not my boy's heavy cross, so bravely borne, do it for him and for me? So shall we come at last, indeed, to 'kiss the cross.' "

The breakfast gong boomed through the house. Simpson loved gongs. He considered them "Haristocratic." He always gave full measure.

Nurse Rosemary went down to breakfast.

Garth came in, through the French window, humming "The thousand beauties that I know so well." He was in his gayest, most inconsequent mood. He had picked a golden rosebud in the conservatory and wore it in his buttonhole. He carried a yellow rose in his hand.

"Good day, Miss Rosemary," he said. "What a May Day! Simpson and I were up with the lark; weren't we, Simpson? Poor Simpson felt like a sort of 'Queen of the May,' when my electric bell trilled in his room, at 5 A.M. But I couldn't stay in bed. I woke with my something-is-going-to-happen feeling; and when I was a little chap and woke with that, Margery used to say: 'Get up quickly then, Master Garth, and it will happen all the sooner.' You ask her if she didn't, Simpson. Miss Gray, did you ever learn: 'If you're waking call me early, call me early, mother dear'? I always hated that young woman! I should think, in her excited state, she would have been waking long before her poor mother, who must have been worn to a perfect rag, making all the hussy's May Queen–clothes, overnight."

Simpson had waited to guide him to his place at the table. Then he removed the covers, and left the room.

As soon as he had closed the door behind him, Garth leaned forward, and with unerring accuracy laid the opening rose upon Nurse Rosemary's plate.

"Roses for Rosemary," he said. "Wear it, if you are sure the young man would not object. I have been thinking about him and the aunt. I wish you could ask them both here, instead of going away on Thursday. We would have the 'maddest, merriest time!' I would play with the aunt, while you had it out with the young man. And I could easily keep the aunt away from nooks and corners, because my hearing is sharper than any aunt's eyes could be, and if you gave a gentle cough, I would promptly clutch hold of auntie, and insist upon being guided in the opposite direction. And I would take her out in the motor; and you and the young man could have the gig. And then when all was satisfactorily settled, we could pack them off home, and be by ourselves again. Ah, Miss Gray, do send for them, instead of leaving me on Thursday."

"Mr. Dalmain," said Nurse Rosemary, reprovingly, as she leaned forward and touched his right hand with the rim of his saucer, "this May-Day morning has gone to your head. I shall send for Margery. She may have known the symptoms, of old."

"It is not that," said Garth. He leaned forward and spoke confidentially. "Something is going to happen to-day, little Rosemary. Whenever I feel like this, something happens. The first time it occurred, about twenty-five years ago, there was a rocking-horse in the hall, when I ran downstairs! I have never forgotten my first ride on that rocking-horse. The fearful joy when he went backward; the awful plunge when he went forward; and the proud moment when it was possible to cease clinging to the leather pommel. I nearly killed the cousin who pulled out his tail. I thrashed him, then and there, *with* the tail; which was such a silly thing to do; because, though it damaged the cousin, it also spoiled the tail. The next time—ah, but I am boring you!"

"Not at all," said Nurse Rosemary, politely; "but I want you to have some breakfast; and the letters will be here in a few minutes."

He looked so brown and radiant, this dear delightful boy, with his gold-brown tie, and yellow rose. She was conscious of her pallor, and oppressive earnestness, as she said: "The letters will be here."

"Oh, bother the letters!" cried Garth. "Let's have a holiday from letters on May Day! You shall be Queen of the May; and Margery shall be the old mother. I will be Robin, with the breaking heart, leaning on the bridge beneath the hazel tree; and Simpson can be the 'bolder lad.' And we will all go and 'gather knots of flowers, and buds, and garlands gay.' "

"Mr. Dalmain," said Nurse Rosemary, laughing, in spite of herself, "you really must be sensible, or I shall go and consult Margery. I have never seen you in such a mood."

"You have never seen me, on a day when something was going to happen," said Garth; and Nurse Rosemary made no further attempt to repress him.

After breakfast, he went to the piano, and played two-steps, and rag-time music, so infectiously, that Simpson literally tripped as he cleared the

table; and Nurse Rosemary, sitting pale and preoc-
cupied, with a pile of letters before her, had hard
work to keep her feet still.

Simpson had two-stepped to the door with the
cloth, and closed it after him. Nurse Rosemary's
remarks about the post-bag, and the letters, had
remained unanswered. "Shine little glowworm
glimmer" was pealing gaily through the room,
like silver bells,—when the door opened, and old
Margery appeared, in a black satin apron, and a
blue print sunbonnet. She came straight to the
piano, and laid her hand gently on Garth's arm.

"Master Garthie," she said, "on this lovely May
morning, will you take old Margery up into the
woods?"

Garth's hands dropped from the keys. "Of
course I will, Margie," he said. "And, I say
Margie, *something is going to happen.*"

"I know it, laddie," said the old woman, tenderly; and the expression with which she looked
into the blind face filled Jane's eyes with tears. "I
woke with it too, Master Garthie; and now we
will go into the woods, and listen to the earth,
and trees, and flowers, and they will tell us
whether it is for joy, or for sorrow. Come, my
own laddie."

Garth rose, as in a dream. Even in his blindness
he looked so young, and so beautiful, that Jane's
watching heart stood still.

At the window he paused. "Where is that secretary person?" he said, vaguely. "She kept trying to shut me up."

"I know she did, laddie," said old Margery, curtseying apologetically towards Jane. "You see she does not know the 'something-is-going-to-happen-to-day' awakening."

"Ah, doesn't she?" thought Jane, as they disappeared through the window. "But as my Garth has gone off his dear head, and been taken away by his nurse, the thing that is going to happen, can't happen just yet." And Jane sat down to the piano, and very softly ran through the accompaniment of *The Rosary*. Then,—after shading her eyes on the terrace, and making sure that a tall white figure leaning on a short dark one, had almost reached the top of the hill,—still more softly, she sang it.

Afterwards she went for a tramp on the moors, and steadied her nerve by the rapid swing of her walk, and the deep inbreathing of that glorious air. Once or twice she took a telegram from her pocket, stood still and read it; then tramped on, to the wonder of the words: "Special license easily obtained." Ah, the license might be easy to obtain; but how about his forgiveness? That must be obtained first. If there were only this darling boy to deal with, in his white flannels and yellow roses, with a May-Day madness in his veins, the license might come at once; and all he could wish should happen without delay. But this is a passing phase of Garth. What she has to deal with is the white-faced man, who calmly said: "I accept the cross," and walked down the village church leaving her—for all these years. Loving her, as he loved her; and yet leaving her,—without word or sign, for three long years. To hire, was the confession; his would be the decision; and, somehow, it did not surprise her, when she came down to luncheon, a little late, to find *him* seated at the table.

"Miss Gray," he said gravely, as he heard her enter, "I must apologise for my behaviour this morning. I was what they call up here 'fey.' Margery understands the mood; and together she and I have listened to kind Mother Earth, laying our hands on her sympathetic softness, and she has told us her secrets. Then I lay down under the fir trees and slept; and awakened calm and sane, and ready for what to-day must bring. For it *will* bring something. That is no delusion. It is a day of great things. That much, Margery knows, too."

"Perhaps," suggested Nurse Rosemary, tentatively, "there may be news of interest in your letters."

"Ah," said Garth, "I forgot. We have not even opened this morning's letters. Let us take time for them immediately after lunch. Are there many?"

"Quite a pile," said Nurse Rosemary.

"Good. We will work soberly through them."

Half an hour later Garth was seated in his chair, calm and expectant; his face turned towards his secretary. He had handled his letters, and amongst them he had found one sealed; and the seal was a plumed helmet, with visor closed. Nurse Rosemary saw him pale, as his fingers touched it. He made no remark; but, as before, slipped it beneath the rest, that it might come up for reading, last of all.

When the others were finished, and Nurse Rosemary took up this letter, the room was very still. They were quite alone. Bees hummed in the garden. The scent of flowers stole in at the window. But no one disturbed their solitude.

Nurse Rosemary took up the envelope.

"Mr. Dalmain, here is a letter, sealed with scarlet wax. The seal is a helmet with visor—"

"I know," said Garth. "You need not describe it further. Kindly open it."

Nurse Rosemary opened it. "It is a very long letter, Mr. Dalmain."

"Indeed? Will you please read it to me, Miss Gray."

A tense moment of silence followed. Nurse Rosemary lifted the letter; but her voice suddenly refused to respond to her will. Garth waited without further word.

Then Nurse Rosemary said: "Indeed, sir, it seems a most private letter. I find it difficult to read it to you."

Garth heard the distress in her voice, and turned to her kindly.

"Never mind, my dear child. It in no way concerns you. It is a private letter to me; but my only means of hearing it is through your eyes, and from your lips. Besides, the lady, whose seal is a plumed helmet, can have nothing of a very private nature to say to me."

"Ah, but she has," said Nurse Rosemary, brokenly.

Garth considered this in silence.

Then: "Turn over the page," he said, "and tell me the signature."

"There are many pages," said Nurse Rosemary.

"Turn over the pages then," said Garth, sternly. "Do not keep me waiting. How is that letter signed?"

"Your wife," whispered Nurse Rosemary.

There was a petrifying quality about the silence which followed. It seemed as if those two words, whispered into Garth's darkness, had turned him to stone.

At last he stretched out his hand. "Will you give me that letter, if you please, Miss Gray? Thank you. I wish to be alone for a quarter of an hour. I shall be glad if you will be good enough to sit in the dining-room, and stop any one from coming into this room. I must be undisturbed. At the end of that time kindly return."

He spoke so quietly that Jane's heart sank within her. Some display of agitation would have been reassuring. This was the man who, bowing his dark head towards the crucifixion window, said: "I accept the cross." This was the man whose footsteps never once faltered as he strode down the aisle and left her. This was the man who had had the strength, ever since, to treat that episode between her and himself as completely closed; no word of entreaty; no sign of remembrance; no hint of reproach. And this was the man to whom she had signed herself: "Your wife."

In her whole life, Jane had never known fear. She knew it now.

As she silently rose and left him, she stole one look at his face. He was sitting perfectly still; the letter in his hand. He had not turned his head toward her as he took it. His profile might have been a beautiful carving in white ivory. There was not the faintest tinge of colour in his face; just that ivory pallor, against the ebony lines of his straight brows, and smooth dark hair.

Jane softly left the room, closing the door behind her.

Then followed the longest fifteen minutes she had ever known. She realised what a tremendous conflict was in progress in that quiet room. Garth was arriving at his decision without having heard any of her arguments. By the strange fatality of his own insistence, he had heard only two words of her letter, and those the crucial words; the two words to which the whole letter carefully led up. They must have revealed to him instantly, what the character of the letter would be; and what was the attitude of mind towards himself, of the woman who wrote them.

Jane paced the dining-room in desperation, remembering the hours of thought which had gone to the compiling of sentences, cautiously preparing his mind to the revelation of the signature.

Suddenly, in the midst of her mental perturbation, there came to her the remembrance of a conversation between Nurse Rosemary and Garth over the pictures. The former had said: "Is she a wife?" And Garth had answered: "Yes." Jane had instantly understood what that answer revealed and implied. Because Garth had so felt her his during those wonderful moments on the terrace at Shenstone, that he could look up into her face and say, "My wife"—not as an interrogation, but as an absolute statement of fact,—he still held her this, as indissolubly as if priest, and book, and ring, had gone to the wedding of their union. To him, the union of souls came before all else; and if that had taken place, all that might follow was but the outward indorsement of an accomplished fact. Owing to her fear, mistrust, and deception, nothing had followed. Their lives had been sundered; they had gone different ways. He regarded himself as being no more to her than any other man of her acquaintance. During these years he had believed, that her part in that evening's wedding of souls had existed in his imagination, only;

and had no binding effect upon her. But his remained. Because those words were true to him then, he had said them; and, because he had said them, he would consider her his wife, through life,—and after. It was the intuitive understanding of this, which had emboldened Jane so to sign her letter. But how would he reconcile that signature with the view of her conduct which he had all along taken, without ever having the slightest conception that there could be any other?

Then Jane remembered, with comfort, the irresistible appeal made by Truth to the soul of the artist; truth of line; truth of colour; truth of values; and, in the realm of sound, truth of tone, of harmony, of rendering, of conception. And when Nurse Rosemary had said of his painting of "The Wife": "It is a triumph of art"; Garth had replied: "It is a triumph of truth." And Jane's own verdict on the look he had seen and depicted was: "It is true—yes, it is true!" Will he not realise now the truth of that signature; and, if he realises it, will he not be glad in his loneliness, that his wife should come to him; unless the confessions and admissions of the letter cause him to put her away as wholly unworthy?

Suddenly Jane understood the immense advantage of the fact that he would hear every word of the rest of her letter, knowing the conclusion, which she herself could not possibly have put first. She saw a Higher Hand in this arrangement;

and said, as she watched the minutes slowly pass: "He hath broken down the middle wall of partition between us"; and a sense of calm assurance descended, and garrisoned her soul with peace.

The quarter of an hour was over.

Jane crossed the hall with firm, though noiseless, step; stood a moment on the threshold relegating herself completely to the background; then opened the door; and Nurse Rosemary re-entered the library.

CHAPTER XXXIV

"Love Never Faileth"

Garth was standing at the open window, when Nurse Rosemary re-entered the library; and he did not turn, immediately.

She looked anxiously for the letter, and saw it laid ready on her side of the table. It bore signs of having been much crumpled; looking almost as a letter might appear which had been crushed into a ball, flung into the waste-paper basket, and afterwards retrieved. It had, however, been carefully smoothed out; and lay ready to her hand.

When Garth turned from the window and passed to his chair, his face bore the signs of a great struggle. He looked as one who, sightless, has yet been making frantic efforts to see. The ivory pallor was gone. His face was flushed; and his thick hair, which grew in beautiful curves low upon his forehead and temples, and was usually carefully brushed back in short-cropped neatness, was now ruffled and disordered. But his voice was completely under control, as he turned towards his secretary.

"My dear Miss Gray," he said, "we have a difficult task before us. I have received a letter, which it is essential I should hear. I am obliged to ask you to read it to me, because there is absolutely no one else to whom I can prefer such a request. I cannot but know that it will be a difficult and painful task for you, feeling yourself an intermediary between two wounded and sundered hearts. May I make it easier, my dear little girl, by assuring you that I know of no one in this world from whose lips I could listen to the contents of that letter with less pain; and, failing my own, there are no eyes beneath which I could less grudgingly let it pass, there is no mind I could so unquestioningly trust, to judge kindly, both of myself and of the writer; and to forget faithfully, all which was not intended to come within the knowledge of a third person."

"Thank you, Mr. Dalmain," said Nurse Rosemary.

Garth leaned back in his chair, shielding his face with his hand.

"Now, if you please," he said. And, very clearly and quietly, Nurse Rosemary began to read.

"DEAR GARTH, As you will not let me come to you, so that I could say, between you and me alone, that which must be said, I am compelled to write it. It is your own fault, Dal; and we both pay the penalty. For how can I write to you freely when I know, that as you listen, it will seem to you of every word I am writing, that I am dragging a third person into that which ought to be, most sacredly, between you and me alone. And yet, I must write freely; and I must make you fully understand; because the whole of your future life and mine will depend upon your reply to this letter. I must write as if you were able to hold the letter in your own hands, and read it to yourself. Therefore, if you cannot completely trust your secretary, with the private history of your heart and mine, bid her give it you back without turning this first page; and let me come myself, Garth, and tell you all the rest."

"That is the bottom of the page," said Nurse Rosemary; and waited.

Garth did not remove his hand. "I do completely trust; and she must not come," he said.

Nurse Rosemary turned the page, and went on reading.

"I want you to remember, Garth, that every word I write, is the simple unvarnished truth.

395

If you look back over your remembrance of me, you will admit that I am not naturally an untruthful person, nor did I ever take easily to prevarication. But, Garth, I told you one lie; and that fatal exception proves the rule of perfect truthfulness, which has always otherwise held, between you and me; and, please God, always will hold. The confession herein contained, concerns that one lie; and I need not ask you to realise how humbling it is to my pride to have to force the hearing of a confession upon the man who has already refused to admit me to a visit of friendship. You will remember that I am not naturally humble; and have a considerable amount of proper pride; and, perhaps, by the greatness of the effort I have had to make, you will be able to gauge the greatness of my love. God help you to do so—my darling; my beloved; my poor desolate boy!"

Nurse Rosemary stopped abruptly; for, at this sudden mention of love, and at these words of unexpected tenderness from Jane, Garth had risen to his feet, and taken two steps towards the window; as if to escape from something too immense to be faced. But, in a moment he recovered himself, and sat down again, completely hiding his face with his hand.

Nurse Rosemary resumed the reading of the letter.

"Ah, what a wrong I have done, both to you, and to myself! Dear, you remember the evening on the terrace at Shenstone, when you asked me to be—when you called me—when *I was—your wife?* Garth, I leave this last sentence as it stands, with its two attempts to reach the truth. I will not cross them out, but leave them to be read to you; for, you see Garth, I finally arrived! I *was* your wife. I did not understand it then. I was intensely surprised; unbelievably inexperienced in matters of feeling; and bewildered by the flood of sensation which swept me off my feet and almost engulfed me. But even then I knew that my soul arose and proclaimed you mate and master. And when you held me, and your dear head lay upon my heart, I knew, for the first time the meaning of the word ecstasy; and I could have asked no kinder gift of heaven, than to prolong those moments into hours."

Nurse Rosemary's quiet voice broke, suddenly; and the reading ceased.

Garth was leaning forward, his head buried in his hands. A dry sob rose in his throat, just at the very moment when Nurse Rosemary's voice gave way.

Garth recovered first. Without lifting his head, with a gesture of protective affection and sympathy, he stretched his hand across the table.

"Poor little girl," he said, "I am so sorry. It is rough on you. If only it had come when Brand was here! I am afraid you *must* go on; but try to read without realising. Leave the realising to me."

And Nurse Rosemary read on.

"When you lifted your head in the moonlight and gazed long and earnestly at me—Ah, those dear eyes!—your look suddenly made me self-conscious. There swept over me a sense of my own exceeding plainness, and of how little there was in what those dear eyes saw, to provide reason, for that adoring look. Overwhelmed with a shy shame I pressed your head back to the place where the eyes would be hidden; and I realise now what a different construction you must have put upon that action. Garth, I assure you, that when you lifted your head the second time, and said, 'My wife,' it was the first suggestion to my mind that this wonderful thing which was happening meant—marriage. I know it must seem almost incredible, and more like a child of eighteen, than a woman of thirty. But you must remember, all my dealings with men up to that hour had been handshakes, heartiest comradeship, and an occasional clap on the shoulder given and received. And don't forget, dear King of my heart, that, until one short week before, you had been amongst the boys who called me 'good old Jane,' and addressed me in intimate conversation as 'my dear fellow'! Don't forget that I had always looked upon you as *years* younger than myself; and though a strangely sweet tie had grown up between us, since the evening of the concert at Overdene, I had never realised it as love. Well—you will remember how I asked for twelve hours to consider my answer; and you yielded, immediately; (you were so perfect, all the time, Garth) and left me, when I asked to be alone; left me, with a gesture I have never forgotten. It was a revelation of the way in which the love of a man such as you exalts the woman upon whom it is outpoured. The hem of that gown has been a sacred thing to me, ever since. It is always with me, though I never wear it.—A detailed account of the hours which followed, I shall hope to give you some day, my dearest. I cannot write it. Let me hurl on to paper, in all its crude ugliness, the miserable fact which parted us; turning our dawning joy to disillusion and sadness. Garth—it was this. I did not believe your love would stand the test of my plainness. I knew what a worshipper of beauty you were; how you must have it, in one form or another, always around you. I got out my diary in which I had recorded verbatim our conversation about the ugly preacher, whose face became illumined into beauty, by the inspired glory within. And you added that you never thought him ugly again; but he would always be plain. And you said it was not the sort of face one would want to have always before one at meals; but that you were not called upon to undergo that discipline, which would be sheer martyrdom to you.

"I was so interested, at the time; and so amused at the unconscious way in which you stood and explained this, to quite the plainest woman of your acquaintance, that I recorded it very fully in my journal.—Alas! On that important night, I read the words, over and over, until they took morbid hold upon my brain. Then—such is the self-consciousness awakened in a woman by the fact that she is loved and sought—I turned on all the lights around my mirror, and critically and carefully examined the face you would have to see every day behind your coffee-pot at breakfast, for years and years, if I said 'Yes,' on the morrow. Darling, I did not see myself through your eyes, as, thank God, I have done since. And *I did not trust your love to stand the test.* It seemed to me, I was saving both of us from future disappointment and misery, by bravely putting away present joy, in order to avoid certain disenchantment. My beloved, it will seem to you so coolly calculating, and so mean; so unworthy of the great love you were even then lavishing upon me. But remember, for years, your remarkable personal grace and beauty had been a source of pleasure to me; and I had pictured you wedded to Pauline Lister, for instance, in her dazzling whiteness, and soft radiant youth. So my morbid self-conscious-ness said: 'What! This young Apollo, tied to my ponderous plainness; growing handsomer every year, while I grow older and plainer?' Ah, darling! It sounds so unworthy, now we know what our love is. But it sounded sensible and right that night; and at last, with a bosom that ached, and arms that hung heavy at the thought of being emptied of all that joy, I made up my mind to say 'no.' Ah, believe me, I had no idea what it already meant to you. I thought you would pass on at once to another fancy; and transfer your love to one more able to meet your needs, at every point. Honestly, Garth, I thought I should be the only one left desolate.—Then came the question: how to refuse you. I knew if I gave the true reason, you would argue it away, and prove me wrong, with glowing words, before which I should perforce yield. So—as I really meant not to let you run the risk, and not to run it myself—I lied to you, my beloved. To you, whom my whole being acclaimed King of my heart, Master of my will; supreme to me, in love and life,—to *you* I said: 'I cannot marry a mere boy.' Ah, darling! I do not excuse it. I do not defend it. I merely confess it; trusting to your generosity to admit, that no other answer would have sent you away. Ah, your poor Jane, left desolate! If you could have seen her in the little church, calling you back; retracting and promising; listening for your returning footsteps, in an agony of longing. But my Garth is not made of the stuff which stands waiting on the door-mat of a woman's indecision.

"The lonely year which followed so broke my nerve, that Deryck Brand told me I was going all to pieces, and ordered me abroad. I went, as you know; and in other, and more vigorous, surroundings, there came to me a saner view of life. In Egypt last March, on the summit of the Great Pyramid, I made up my mind that I could live without you no longer. I did not see myself wrong; but I yearned so for your love, and to pour mine upon you, my beloved, that I concluded it was worth the risk. I made up my mind to take the next boat home, and send for you. Then—oh, my own boy—I heard. I wrote to you; and you would not let me come.

"Now I know perfectly well, that you might say: 'She did not trust me when I had my sight. Now that I cannot see, she is no longer

402

afraid.' Garth, you might say that; but it would not be true. I have had ample proof lately that I was wrong, and ought to have trusted you all through. What it is, I will tell you later. All I can say now is: that, if your dear shining eyes could see, they would see, *now,* a woman who is, trustfully and unquestioningly, all your own. If she is doubtful of her face and figure, she says quite simply: 'They pleased *him;* and they are just *his.* I have no further right to criticise them. If he wants them, they are not mine, but his.' Darling, I cannot tell you now, how I have arrived at this assurance. But I have had proofs beyond words of your faithfulness and love.

"The question, therefore, simply resolves itself into this: Can you forgive me? If you can forgive me, I can come to you at once. If this thing is past forgiveness, I must make up my mind to stay away. But, oh, my own Dear,— the bosom on which once you laid your head waits for you with the longing ache of lonely years. If you need it, do not thrust it from you."

"Write me one word by your own hand: 'Forgiven.' It is all I ask. When it reaches me, I will come to you at once. Do not dictate a letter to your secretary. I could not bear it. Just write—if you can truly write it—*'forgiven'*; and send it to 'Your Wife.' "

The room was very still, as Nurse Rosemary finished reading; and, laying down the letter, silently waited. She wondered for a moment whether she could get herself a glass of water, without disturbing him; but decided to do without it.

At last Garth lifted his head.

"She has asked me to do a thing impossible," he said; and a slow smile illumined his drawn face.

Jane clasped her hands upon her breast.

"*Can* you not write 'forgiven'?" asked Nurse Rosemary, brokenly.

"No," said Garth. "I cannot. Little girl, give me a sheet of paper, and a pencil."

Nurse Rosemary placed them close to his hand.

Garth took up the pencil. He groped for the paper; felt the edges with his left hand; found the centre with his fingers; and, in large firm letters, wrote one word.

"Is that legible?" he asked, passing it across to Nurse Rosemary.

"Quite legible," she said; for she answered before it was blotted by her tears.

Instead of "forgiven," Garth had written: *"loved."*

"Can you post it at once?" Garth asked, in a low, eager voice. "And she will come—oh, my God, she will come! If we catch to-night's mail, she may be here the day after to-morrow!"

Nurse Rosemary took up the letter; and, by an almost superhuman effort, spoke steadily.

"Mr. Dalmain," she said; "there is a postscript to this letter. It says: 'Write to The Palace Hotel, Aberdeen.'"

Garth sprang up, his whole face and figure alive with excitement.

"In Aberdeen?" he cried. "Jane, in Aberdeen! Oh, my God! If she gets this paper to-morrow morning, she may be here any time in the day. Jane! Jane! Dear little Rosemary, do you hear? Jane will come to-morrow! Didn't I tell you something was going to happen? You and Simpson were too British to understand; but Margery knew; and the woods told us it was Joy coming through Pain. Could that be posted at once, Miss Gray?"

The May-Day mood was upon him again. His face shone. His figure was electric with expectation. Nurse Rosemary sat at the table watching him; her chin in her hands. A tender smile dawned on her lips, out of keeping with her supposed face and figure; so full was it of the glorious expectation of a mature and perfect love.

"I will go to the post-office myself, Mr. Dalmain," she said. "I shall be glad of the walk; and I can be back by tea-time."

At the post-office she did not post the word in Garth's handwriting. That lay hidden in her bosom. But she sent off two telegrams. The first to

The Duchess of Meldyum,
Palace Hotel, Aberdeen.
"COME HERE BY 5.50 TRAIN WITHOUT
FAIL THIS EVENING."

The second to

Sir Deryck Brand,
Wimpole Sheet, London.
"ALL IS RIGHT."

CHAPTER XXXV

Nurse Rosemary Has Her Reward

"Mr. Dalmain," said Nurse Rosemary, with patient insistence, "I really do want you to sit down, and give your mind to the tea-table. How can you remember where each thing is placed, if you keep jumping up, and moving your chair into different positions? And last time you pounded the table to attract my attention, which was already anxiously fixed upon you, you nearly knocked over your own tea, and sent floods of mine into the saucer. If you cannot behave better, I shall ask Margery for a pinafore, and sit you up on a high chair!"

Garth stretched his legs in front of him, and his arms over his head; and lay back in his chair, laughing joyously.

"Then I should have to say: 'Please, Nurse, may I get down?' What a cheeky little thing you are becoming! And you used to be quite oppressively polite. I suppose you would answer: 'If you say your grace nicely, Master Garth, you may.' Do you know the story of 'Tommy, you should say Your Grace'?"

"You have told it to me twice in the last forty-eight hours," said Nurse Rosemary, patiently.

"Oh, what a pity! I felt so like telling it now. If you had really been the sort of sympathetic person Sir Deryck described, you would have said: 'No; and I should so *love* to hear it!'"

"No; and I should so *love* to hear it!" said Nurse Rosemary.

"Too late! That sort of thing, to have any value should be spontaneous. It need not be true; but it *must* be spontaneous. But, talking of a high chair,—when you say those chaffy things in a voice like Jane's, and just as Jane would have said them—oh, my wig!—Do you know, that is the duchess's only original little swear. All the rest are quotations. And when she says: 'My wig!' we all try not to look at it. It is usually slightly awry. The toucan tweaks it. He is so very *loving,* dear bird!"

"Now hand me the buttered toast," said Nurse Rosemary; "and don't tell me any more naughty stories about the duchess. No! That is the thin bread-and-butter. I told you you would lose your bearings. The toast is in a warm plate on your right. Now let us make believe I am Miss Champion, and hand it to me, as nicely as you will be handing it to her, this time to-morrow."

"It is easy to make believe you are Jane, with that voice," said Garth; "and yet—I don't know. I have never really associated you with her. One little sentence of old Rob's made all the difference to me. He said you had fluffy floss-silk sort of hair. No one could ever imagine Jane with fluffy floss-silk sort of hair! And I believe that one sentence saved the situation. Otherwise, your voice would have driven me mad, those first days. As it was, I used to wonder sometimes if I could possibly bear it. You understand why, now; don't you? And yet, in a way, it is *not* like hers. Hers is deeper; and she often speaks with a delicious kind of drawl, and uses heaps of slang; and you are such a very proper little person; and possess what the primers call 'perfectly correct diction.' What fun it would be to hear you and Jane talk together! And yet—I don't know. I should be on thorns, all the time."

"Why?"

"I should be so awfully afraid lest you should not like one another. You see, *you* have really, in a way, been more to me than any one else in the world; and *she*—well, she *is* my world," said Garth, simply. "And I should be so afraid lest she should not fully appreciate you; and you should not quite understand her. She has a sort of way of standing and looking people up and down, and, women hate it; especially pretty fluffy little women. They feel she spots all the things that come off."

"Nothing of mine comes off," murmured Nurse Rosemary, "excepting my patient, when he will not stay on his chair."

"Once," continued Garth, with the gleeful enjoyment in his voice which always presaged a story in which Jane figured, "there was a fearfully silly little woman staying at Overdene, when a lot of us were there. We never could make out why she was included in one of the duchess's 'best parties,' except that the dear duchess vastly enjoyed taking her off, and telling stories about her; and we could not appreciate the cleverness of the impersonation, unless we had seen the original. She was rather pretty, in a fussy, curling-tongs, wax-doll sort of way; but she never could let her appearance alone, or allow people to forget it. Almost every sentence she spoke, drew attention to it. We got very sick of it, and asked Jane to make her shut up. But Jane said: 'It doesn't hurt you, boys; and it pleases her. Let her be.' Jane was always extra nice to people, if she suspected they were asked down in order to make sport for the duchess afterwards. Jane hated that sort of thing. She couldn't say much to her aunt; but we had to be very careful how we egged the duchess on, if Jane was within hearing. Well— one evening, after tea, a little group of us were waiting around the fire in the lower hall, to talk to

409

Jane. It was Christmas time. The logs looked so jolly on the hearth. The red velvet curtains were drawn right across, covering the terrace door and the windows on either side. Tommy sat on his perch, in the centre of the group, keeping a keen lookout for cigarette ends. Outside, the world was deep in snow; and that wonderful silence reigned; making the talk and laughter within all the more gay by contrast—you know, that *penetrating* silence; when trees, and fields, and paths, are covered a foot thick in soft sparkling whiteness. I always look forward, just as eagerly, each winter to the first sight—ah, I forgot! . . . Fancy never seeing snow again! . . . Never mind. It is something to remember *having* seen it; and I shall hear the wonderful snow-silence more clearly than ever. Perhaps before other people pull up the blinds, I shall be able to say: 'There's been a fall of snow in the night.' What was I telling you? Yes, I remember. About little Mrs. Fussy. Well— all the women had gone up to dress for dinner; excepting Jane, who never needed more than half an hour; and Fussy, who was being sprightly, in a laboured way; and fancied herself the centre of attraction which kept us congregated in the hall. As a matter of fact, we were waiting to tell Jane some private news we had just heard about a young chap in the guards, who was in fearful hot water for ragging. His colonel was an old friend of Jane's, and we thought she could put in a word, and improve matters for Billy. So Mrs. Fussy was very much de trop, and didn't know it. Jane was sitting with her back to all of us, her feet on the fender, and her skirt turned up over her knees. Oh, there was another one, underneath; a handsome silk thing, with rows of little frills,—which you would think should have gone on outside. But Jane's best things are never paraded; always hidden. I don't mean clothes, now; but her splendid self. Well—little Fussy was 'chatting'— she never talked—about herself and her conquests; quite unconscious that we all wished her at Jericho. Jane went on reading the evening paper; but she felt the atmosphere growing restive. Presently—ah, but I must not tell you the rest. I have just remembered. Jane made us promise never to repeat it. She thought it detrimental to the other woman. But we just had time for our confab; and Jane caught the evening post with the letter which got Billy off scot-free; and yet came down punctually to dinner, better dressed than any of them. We felt it rather hard luck to have to promise; because we had each counted on being the first to tell the story to the duchess. But, you know, you always have to do as Jane says."

"Why?"

"Oh, I don't know! I can't explain why. If you knew her, you would not need to ask. Cake, Miss Gray?"

"Thank you. Right, this time."

"There! That is exactly as Jane would have said: 'Right, this time.' Is it not strange that after having for weeks thought your voice so like hers, to-morrow I shall be thinking her voice so like yours?"

"Oh, no, you will not," said Nurse Rosemary. "When she is with you, you will have no thoughts for other people."

"Indeed, but I shall!" cried Garth. "And, dear little Rosemary, I shall miss you, horribly. No one—not even she—can take your place. And, do you know," he leaned forward, and a troubled look clouded the gladness of his face, "I am beginning to feel anxious about it. She has not seen me since the accident. I am afraid it will give her a shock. Do you think she will find me much changed?"

Jane looked at the sightless face turned so anxiously toward her. She remembered that morning in his room, when he thought himself alone with Dr. Rob; and, leaving the shelter of the wall, sat up to speak, and she saw his face for the first time. She remembered turning to the fireplace, so that Dr. Rob should not see the tears raining down her cheeks. She looked again at Garth—now growing conscious, for the first time, of his disfigurement; and then, only for her sake—and an almost overwhelming tenderness gripped her heart. She glanced at the clock. She could not hold out much longer.

"Is it very bad?" said Garth; and his voice shook.

"I cannot answer for another woman," replied Nurse Rosemary; "but I should think your face, just as it is, will always be her joy."

Garth flushed; pleased and relieved, but slightly surprised. There was a quality in Nurse Rosemary's voice, for which he could not altogether account.

"But then, she will not be accustomed to my blind ways," he continued. "I am afraid I shall seem so helpless and so blundering. She has not been in Sightless Land, as you and I have been. She does not know all our plans of cords, and notches, and things. Ah, little Rosemary! Promise not to leave me to-morrow. I want Her—only God knows how I want her; but I begin to be half afraid. It will be so wonderful, for the great essentials; but, for the little every-day happenings, which are so magnified by the darkness, oh, my kind unseen guide, how I shall need you. At first, I thought it lucky you had settled to go, just when she is coming; but now, just because she is coming, I cannot let you go. Having her will be wonderful beyond words; but it will not be the same as having you."

Nurse Rosemary was receiving her reward, and she appeared to find it rather overwhelming.

As soon as she could speak, she said, gently: "Don't excite yourself over it, Mr. Dalmain.

Believe me, when you have been with her for five minutes, you will find it just the same as having me. And how do you know she has not also been in Sightless Land? A nurse would do that sort of thing, because she was very keen on her profession, and on making a success of her case. The woman who loves you would do it for love of you."

"It would be like her," said Garth; and leaned back, a look of deep contentment gathering on his face. "Oh, Jane! Jane! She is coming! She is coming!"

Nurse Rosemary looked at the clock.

"Yes; she is coming," she said; and though her voice was steady, her hands trembled. "And, as it is our last evening together under quite the same circumstances as during all these weeks, will you agree to a plan of mine? I must go upstairs now, and do some packing, and make a few arrangements. But will you dress early? I will do the same; and if you could be down in the library by half-past six, we might have some music before dinner."

"Why certainly," said Garth. "It makes no difference to me at what time I dress; and I am always ready for music. But, I say: I wish you were not packing, Miss Gray."

"I am not exactly packing up," replied Nurse Rosemary. "I am packing things away."

"It is all the same, if it means leaving. But you have promised not to go until she comes?"

"I will not go—until she comes."

"And you will tell her all the things she ought to know?"

"She shall know all I know, which could add to your comfort."

"And you will not leave me, until I am really—well, getting on all right?"

"I will never leave you, while you need me," said Nurse Rosemary. And again Garth detected that peculiar quality in her voice. He rose, and came towards where he heard her to be standing.

"Do you know, you are no end of a brick," he said, with emotion. Then he held out both hands towards her. "Put your hands in mine just for once, little Rosemary. I want to try to thank you."

There was a moment of hesitation. Two strong capable hands—strong and capable, though, just then, they trembled—nearly went home to his; but were withdrawn just in time. Jane's hour was not yet. This was Nurse Rosemary's moment of triumph and success. It should not be taken from her.

"This evening," she said, softly, "after the music, we will—shake hands. Now be careful, sir. You are stranded. Wait. Here is the garden-cord, just to your left. Take a little air on the terrace; and sing again the lovely song I heard under my window this morning. And now that you know what it is that is 'going to happen,' this exquisite May-Day evening will fill you with tender expectation. Good-bye, sir—for an hour."

"What has come to little Rosemary?" mused Garth, as he felt for his cane, in its corner by the window. "We could not have gone on indefinitely quite as we have been, since she came in from the post-office."

He walked on; a troubled look clouding his face: Suddenly it lifted, and he stood still, and laughed. "Duffer!" he said. "Oh, what a conceited duffer! She is thinking of her 'young man.' She is going to him to-morrow; and her mind is full of him; just as mine is full of Jane. Dear, good, clever, little Rosemary! I hope he is worthy of her. No; that he cannot be. I hope he knows he is *not* worthy of her. That is more to the point. I hope he will receive her as she expects. Somehow, I hate letting her go to him. Oh, hang the fellow!—as Tommy would say."

CHAPTER XXXVI

The Revelation of the Rosary

Simpson was crossing the hall just before half-past six o'clock. He had left his master in the library. He heard a rustle just above him; and, looking up, saw a tall figure descending the wide oak staircase.

Simpson stood transfixed. The soft black evening-gown, with its trailing folds, and old lace at the bosom, did not impress him so much as the quiet look of certainty and power on the calm face above them.

"Simpson," said Jane, "my aunt, the Duchess of Meldrum, and her maid, and her footman, and a rather large quantity of luggage, will be arriving from Aberdeen, at about half-past seven. Mrs. Graem knows about preparing rooms; and I have given James orders for meeting the train with the brougham, and the luggage-cart. The duchess dislikes motors. When her Grace arrives, you can show her into the library. We will dine in the dining-room at a quarter past eight. Meanwhile, Mr. Dalmain and myself are particularly engaged just now, and must not be disturbed on any account, until the duchess's arrival. You quite understand?"

"Yes, miss-m'lady," stammered Simpson. He had been boot-boy in a ducal household early in his career; and he considered duchesses' nieces to be people before whom one should bow down.

Jane smiled. "'Miss' is quite sufficient, Simpson," she said; and swept towards the library.

Garth heard her enter, and close the door; and his quick ear caught the rustle of a train.

"Hullo, Miss Gray," he said. "Packed your uniform?"

"Yes," said Jane. "I told you I was packing."

She came slowly across the room, and stood on the hearth-rug looking down at him. He was in full evening-dress; just as at Shenstone on that

417

memorable night; and, as he sat well back in his deep arm-chair, one knee crossed over the other, she saw the crimson line of his favourite silk socks.

Jane stood looking down upon him. Her hour had come at last. But even now she must, for his sake, be careful and patient.

"I did not hear the song," she said.

"No," replied Garth. "At first, I forgot. And when I remembered, I had been thinking of other things, and somehow—ah, Miss Gray! I cannot sing to-night. My soul is dumb with longing."

"I know," said Jane, gently; "and I am going to sing to you."

A faint look of surprise crossed Garth's face. "Do you sing?" he asked. "Then why have you not sung before?"

"When I arrived," said Jane, "Dr. Rob asked me whether I played. I said: 'A little.' Thereupon he concluded I sang a little, too; and he forbade me, most peremptorily, either to play a little; or sing a little, to you. He said he did not want you driven altogether mad."

Garth burst out laughing.

"How like old Robbie," he said. "And, in spite of his injunctions, are you going to take the risk, and 'sing a little,' to me, to-night?"

"No," said Jane. "I take no risks. I am going to sing you one song. Here is the purple cord, at your right hand. There is nothing between you and the

418

piano; and you are facing towards it. If you want to stop me—you can come."

She walked to the instrument, and sat down.

Over the top of the grand piano, she could see him, leaning back in his chair; a slightly amused smile playing about his lips. He was evidently still enjoying the humour of Dr. Rob's prohibition.

The Rosary has but one opening chord. She struck it; her eyes upon his face. She saw him sit up, instantly; a look of surprise, expectation, bewilderment, gathering there.

Then she began to sing. The deep rich voice, low and vibrant, as the softest tone of 'cello, thrilled into the startled silence.

> "The hours I spent with thee, dear heart,
> Are as a string of pearls to me;
> I count them over, ev'ry one apart,
> My rosary,—my rosary.
> Each hour a pearl—"

Jane got no further.

Garth had risen. He spoke no word; but he was coming blindly over to the piano. She turned on the music-stool, her arms held out to receive him. Now he had found the woodwork. His hand crashed down upon the bass. Now he had found her. He was on his knees, his arms around her. Hers enveloped him—, yearning, tender, hungry with the repressed longing of all those hard weeks.

He lifted his sightless face to hers, for one moment. "You?" he said. "*You?* You—all the time?"

Then he hid his face in the soft lace at her breast.

"Oh, my boy, my darling!" said Jane, tenderly; holding the dear head close. "Yes; I, all the time; all the time near him, in his loss and pain. Could I have stopped away? But, oh, Garth! What it is, at last to hold you, and touch you, and feel you here! . . . Yes, it is I. Oh, my beloved, are you not quite sure? Who else could hold you thus? . . . Take care, my darling! Come over to the couch, just here; and sit beside me."

Garth rose, and raised her, without loosing her; and she guided herself and him to a safer seat close by. But there again he flung himself upon his knees, and held her; his arms around her waist; his face hidden in the shelter of her bosom.

"Ah,—darling, darling," said Jane softly, and her hands stole up behind his head, with a touch of unspeakable protective tenderness; "it has been so sweet to wait upon my boy; and help him in his darkness; and shield him from unnecessary pain; and be always there, to meet his every need. But I could not come myself—until he knew; and understood; and had forgiven—no, not 'forgiven'; understood, and yet still *loved*. For he does now understand? And he does forgive? . . . Oh, Garth! . . . Oh—hush, my darling! . . . You frighten me! . . . No, I will never leave you; never, never! . . .

420

Oh, can't you understand, my beloved? . . . Then I must tell you more plainly. Darling,—do be still, and listen. Just for a few days we must be as we have been; only my boy will know it is I who am near him. Aunt 'Gina is coming this evening. She will be here in half an hour. Then, as soon as possible we will get a special license; and we will be married, Garth; and then—" Jane paused; and the man who knelt beside her, held his breath to listen—"and then," continued Jane in a low tender voice, which gathered in depth of sacred mystery, yet did not falter—"then it will be my highest joy, to be always with my husband, night and day."

A long sweet silence. The tempest of emotion in her arms was hushed to rest. The eternal voice of perfect love had whispered: "Peace, be still"; and there was a great calm.

At last Garth lifted his head. "Always? Always together?" he said. "Ah, that will be 'perpetual light!'"

When Simpson, pale with importance, flung open the library door, and announced: "Her Grace, the Duchess of Meldrum," Jane was seated at the piano, playing soft dreamy chords; and a slim young man, in evening dress, advanced with eager hospitality to greet his guest.

The duchess either did not see, or chose to ignore the guiding cord. She took his outstretched hand warmly in both her own.

"Goodness gracious, my dear Dal! How you surprise me! I expected to find you blind! And here you are striding about, just your old handsome self!"

"Dear Duchess," said Garth, and stooping, kissed the kind old hands still holding his; "I cannot see you, I am sorry to say; but I don't feel very blind to-night. My darkness has been lightened by a joy beyond expression."

"Oh ho! So that's the way the land lies! Now which are you going to marry? The nurse,—who, I gather, is a most respectable young person, and highly recommended; or that hussy, Jane; who, without the smallest compunction, orders her poor aunt from one end of the kingdom to the other, to suit her own convenience?"

Jane came over from the piano, and slipped her hand through her lover's arm.

"Dear Aunt 'Gina," she said; "you know you loved coming; because you enjoy a mystery, and like being a dear old 'deus ex machina,' at the right moment. And he is going to marry them both; because they both love him far too dearly ever to leave him again; and he seems to think he cannot do without either."

The duchess looked at the two radiant faces; one sightless; the other, with glad proud eyes for both; and her own filled with tears.

"Hoity-toity!" she said. "Are we in Salt Lake City? Well, we always thought one girl would not do for Dal; he would need the combined perfections of several; and he appears to think he has found them. God bless you both, you absurdly happy people; and I will bless you, too; but not until I have dined. Now, ring for that very nervous person, with side-whiskers; and tell him I want my maid, and my room, and I want to know where they have put my toucan. I had to bring him, Jane. He is so *loving,* dear bird! I knew you would think him in the way; but I really could not leave him behind."

CHAPTER XXXVII

"In the Face of This Congregation"

The society paragraphs would have described it as "a very quiet wedding," when Garth and Jane, a few days later, were pronounced "man and wife together," in the little Episcopal church among the hills.

Perhaps, to those who were present, it stands out rather as an unusual wedding, than as a quiet one.

To Garth and Jane the essential thing was to be married, and left to themselves, with as little delay as possible. They could not be induced to pay any attention to details as to the manner in which this desired end was to be attained. Jane left it entirely to the doctor, in one practical though casual sentence: "Just make sure it is valid, Dicky; and send us in the bills."

The duchess, being a true conservative, early began mentioning veils, orange-blossom, and white satin; but Jane said: "My dear Aunt! Fancy me—in orange-blossom! I should look like a Christmas pantomime. And I never wear veils, even in motors; and white satin is a form of clothing I have always had the wisdom to avoid."

"Then in what do you intend to be married, unnatural girl?" inquired the duchess.

"In whatever I happen to put on, that morning," replied Jane, knotting the silk of a soft crimson cord she was knitting; and glancing out of the window, to where Garth sat smoking, on the terrace.

"Have you a time-table?" inquired her Grace of Meldrum, with dangerous calmness. "And can you send me to the station this afternoon?"

"We can always send to the station, at a moment's notice," said Jane, working in a golden strand, and considering the effect. "But where are you going, dear Aunt 'Gina? You know Deryck and Flower arrive this evening."

"I am washing my hands of you, and going South," said the duchess, wrathfully.

"Don't do that, dear," said Jane, placidly. "You have washed your hands of me so often; and, like the blood of King Duncan of Scotland, I am upon them still. 'All the perfumes of Arabia will not sweeten this little hand.'" Then, raising her voice: "Garth, if you want to walk, just give a call. I am here, talking over my trousseau with Aunt 'Gina."

"What is a trousseau?" came back in Garth's happy voice.

"A thing you get into to be married," said Jane.

"Then let's get into it quickly," shouted Garth, with enthusiasm.

"Dear Aunt," said Jane, "let us make a compromise. I have some quite nice clothes upstairs, including Redfern tailor-mades, and several uniforms. Let your maid look through them, and whatever you select, and she puts out in readiness on my wedding morning, I promise to wear."

This resulted in Jane appearing at the church in a long blue cloth coat and skirt, handsomely embroidered with gold, and suiting her large figure to perfection; a deep yellow vest of brocaded silk; and old lace ruffles at neck and wrists.

Garth was as anxious about his wedding garments, as Jane had been indifferent over hers; but he had so often been in requisition as best-man at town weddings, that Simpson had no difficulty in turning him out in the acme of correct bridal attire. And very handsome he looked, as he stood waiting at the chancel steps; not watching for his bride; but obviously listening for her; for, as Jane came up the church on Deryck's arm, Garth slightly turned his head and smiled.

The duchess—resplendent in purple satin and

ermine, with white plumes in her bonnet, and many jewelled chains depending from her, which rattled and tinkled, in the silence of the church, every time she moved—was in a front pew on the left, ready to give her niece away.

In a corresponding seat, on the opposite side, as near as possible to the bridegroom, sat Margery Graem, in black silk, with a small quilted satin bonnet, and a white lawn kerchief folded over the faithful old heart which had beaten in tenderness for Garth since his babyhood. She turned her head anxiously, every time the duchess jingled; but otherwise kept her eyes fixed on the marriage service, in a large-print prayer-book in her lap. Margery was not used to the Episcopal service, and she had her "doots" as to whether it could possibly be gone through correctly, by all parties concerned. In fact this anxiety of old Margery's increased so painfully when the ceremony actually commenced, that it took audible form; and she repeated all the answers of the bridal pair, in an impressive whisper, after them.

Dr. Rob, being the only available bachelor, did duty as best-man; Jane having stipulated that he should not be intrusted with the ring; her previous observations leading her to conclude that he would most probably slip it unconsciously on to his finger, and then search through all his own pockets and all Garth's; and begin taking up the church matting, before it occurred to him to look at his hand. Jane would not have minded the diversion, but she did object to any delay. So the ring went to church in Garth's waistcoat pocket, where it had lived since Jane brought it out from Aberdeen; and, without any fumbling or hesitation, was quietly laid by him upon the open book.

Dr. Rob had charge of the fees for clerk, verger, bell-ringers, and every person, connected with the church, who could possibly have a tip pressed upon them.

Garth was generous in his gladness, and eager to do all things in a manner worthy of the great gift made fully his that day. So Dr. Rob was well provided with the wherewithal; and this he jingled in his pockets as soon as the exhortation commenced, and his interest in the proceedings resulted in his fatal habit of unconsciousness of his own actions. Thus he and the duchess kept up a tinkling duet, each hearing the other, and not their own sounds. So the duchess glared at Dr. Rob; and Dr. Rob frowned at the duchess; and old Margery looked tearfully at both.

Deryck Brand, the tallest man in the church, his fine figure showing to advantage in the long frock coat with silk facings, which Lady Brand had pronounced indispensable to the occasion, retired to a seat beside his wife, just behind old Margery, as soon as he had conducted Jane to Garth's side. As Jane removed her hand from his arm, she turned and smiled at him; and a long look passed between them. All the memories, all the comprehension, all the trust and affection of years, seemed to concentrate in that look; and Lady Brand's eyes dropped to her dainty white and gold prayer-book. She had never known jealousy; the doctor had never given her any possible reason for acquiring that cruel knowledge. His Flower bloomed for him; and her fragrance alone made his continual joy. All other lovely women were mere botanical specimens, to be examined and classified. But Flower had never quite understood the depth of the friendship between her husband and Jane, founded on the associations and aspirations of childhood and early youth, and a certain similarity of character which would not have wedded well, but which worked out into a comradeship, providing a source of strength for both. Of late, Flower had earnestly tried to share, even while failing to comprehend it.

Perhaps she, in her pale primrose gown, with daffodils at her waist, and sunbeams in her golden hair, was the most truly bridal figure in the church. As the doctor turned from the bride, and sought his place beside her in the pew, he looked at the sweet face, bent so demurely over the prayer-book, and thought he had never seen his wife look more entrancingly lovely. Unconsciously his hand strayed to the white rosebud she had fastened in his coat as they strolled round the conservatory together that morning. Flower, glancing up, surprised his look. She did not think it right to smile in church; but a delicate wave of colour swept over her face, and her cheek leaned as near the doctor's shoulder, as the size of her hat would allow. Flower felt quite certain that was a look the doctor had never given Jane.

The service commenced. The short-sighted clergyman, very nervous, and rather overwhelmed by the unusual facts of a special license, a blind bridegroom, and the reported presence of a duchess, began reading very fast, in an undertone, which old Margery could not follow, though her finger, imprisoned in unwonted kid, hurried along the lines. Then conscious of his mistake, he slowed down, and became too impressive; making long nerve-straining pauses, fled in by the tinkling of the duchess, and the chinking in Dr. Rob's trousers-pockets.

Thus they arrived at the demand upon the congregation, if they could show any just cause why these two persons might not lawfully be joined together, *now* to speak—and the pause here was so long, and so over-powering, that old Margery said "nay"; and then gave a nervous sob. The bridegroom turned and smiled in the direction of the voice; and the doctor, leaning forward, laid his hand on the trembling shoulder, and whispered: "Steady, old friend. It is all right."

There was no pause whatever after the solemn charge to the couple; so if Garth and Jane had any secrets to disclose, they had perforce to keep them for after discussion.

Then Jane found her right hand firmly clasped in Garth's; and no inadequacy of the Church's mouth-piece could destroy the exquisite beauty of the Church's words, in which Garth was asked if he would take her to be his own.

To this, Garth, and old Margery, said they would; with considerable display of emotion.

Then the all-comprehensive question was put to Jane; the Church seeming to remind her gently, that she took him in his blindness, with all which that might entail.

Jane said: "I will"; and the deep, tender voice, was the voice of *The Rosary*.

When the words were uttered, Garth lifted the hand he held, and reverently kissed it.

This was not in the rubric, and proved disconcerting to the clergyman. He threw up his head suddenly, and inquired: "Who giveth this woman to be married to this man?" And as, for the moment, there was no response, he repeated, the question wildly; gazing into distant corners of the church.

Then the duchess, who up to that time had been feeling a little bored, realised that her moment had come, and rejoiced. She sailed out of her pew, and advanced to the chancel step. "My dear good man," she said; "*I* give my niece away; having come north at considerable inconvenience for that express purpose. Now, go on. What do we do next?"

Dr. Rob broke into an uncontrollable chuckle. The duchess lifted her lorgnette, and surveyed him. Margery searched her prayer-book in vain for the duchess's response. It did not appear to be there.

Flower looked in distressed appeal at the doctor. But the doctor was studying, with grave intentness, a stencilled pattern on the chancel roof; and paid no attention to Flower's nudge.

The only people completely unconscious of anything unusual in the order of proceedings appeared to be the bride and bridegroom. They were taking each other "in the sight of God, and in the face of this congregation." They were altogether absorbed in each other, standing together in the sight of God; and the deportment of "this congregation" was a matter they scarcely noticed. "People always behave grotesquely at weddings," Jane had said to Garth, beforehand; "and ours will be no exception to the general rule. But we can close our eyes, and stand together in Sightless Land; and Deryck will take care it is valid."

"Not in Sightless Land, my beloved," said Garth; "but in the Land where they need no candle neither light of the sun. However, and wherever, I take *you* as my wife, I shall be standing on the summit of God's heaven."

So they stood; and in their calmness the church

431

hushed to silence. The service proceeded; and the minister, who had not known how to keep them from clasping hands when the rubric did not require it, found no difficulty in inducing them to do so again.

So they took each other—these two, who were so deeply each other's already—solemnly, reverently, tenderly, in the sight of God, they took each other, according to God's holy ordinance; and the wedding ring, type of that eternal love which has neither beginning nor ending, passed from Garth's pocket, over the Holy Book, on to Jane's finger.

When it was over, she took his arm; and leaning upon it, so that he could feel she leaned, guided him to the vestry.

Afterwards, in the brougham, for those few precious minutes, when husband and wife find themselves alone for the first time, Garth turned to Jane with an eager naturalness, which thrilled her heart as no studied speech could have done. He did not say: "My wife." That unique moment had been theirs, three years before.

"Dearest," he said, "how soon will they all go? How soon shall we be quite alone? Oh, why couldn't they drive to the station from the church?"

Jane looked at her watch. "Because we must lunch them, dear," she said. "Think how good they have all been. And we could not start our married life by being inhospitable. It is just one

432

o'clock; and we ordered luncheon at half-past. Their train leaves the station at half-past four. In three hours, Garth, we shall be alone."

"Shall I be able to behave nicely for three hours?" exclaimed Garth, boyishly.

"You must," said Jane, "or I shall fetch Nurse Rosemary."

"Oh hush!" he said. "All that is too precious, to-day, for chaff. Jane"—he turned suddenly, and laid his hand on hers—"Jane! Do you understand that you are now—actually—my wife?"

Jane took his hand, and held it against her heart, just where she so often had pressed her own, when she feared he would hear it throbbing.

"My darling," she said, "I do not understand it. But I know—ah, thank God!—I know it to be true."

CHAPTER XXXVIII

Perpetual Light

Moonlight on the terrace—silvery, white, serene. Garth and Jane had stepped out into the brightness; and, finding the night so warm and still, and the nightingales filling the woods and hills with soft-throated music, they moved their usual fireside chairs close to the parapet, and sat there in restful comfort, listening to the sweet sounds of the quiet night.

The solitude was so perfect; the restfulness so complete. Garth had removed the cushion seat from his chair, and placed it on the gravel; and sat at his wife's feet leaning against her knees. She stroked his hair and brow softly, as they talked; and every now and then he put up his hand, drew hers to his lips, and kissed the ring he had never seen.

Long tender silences fell between them. Now that they were at last alone, thoughts too deep, joys too sacred for words, trembled about them; and silence seemed to express more than speech. Only, Garth could not bear Jane to be for a moment out of reach of his hand. What to another would have been: "I cannot let her out of my sight," was, to him, "I cannot let her be beyond my touch." And Jane fully understood this; and let him feel her every moment within reach. And the bliss of this was hers as well as his; for sometimes it had seemed to her as if the hunger in her heart, caused by those long weeks of waiting, when her arms ached for him, and yet she dared not even touch his hand, would never be appeased.

"Sweet, sweet, sweet—thrill," sang a nightingale in the wood. And Garth whistled an exact imitation.

"Oh, darling," said Jane, "that reminds me; there is something I do so want you to sing to me. I don't know what it is; but I think you will remember. It was on that Monday evening, after I had seen the pictures, and Nurse Rosemary had described them to you. Both our poor hearts were on the rack; and I went up early in order to begin my letter of confession; but you told Simpson not to come for you until eleven. While I was writing in the room above, I could hear you playing in the library. You played many things I knew—music we had done together, long ago. And then a theme I had never heard crept in, and caught my ear at once, because it was quite new to me, and so marvellously sweet. I put down my pen and listened. You played it several times, with slight variations, as if trying to recall it. And then, to my joy, you began to sing. I crossed the room; softly opened my window, and leaned out. I could hear some of the words; but not all. Two lines, however, reached me distinctly, with such penetrating, tender sadness, that I laid my head against the window-frame, feeling as if I could write no more, and wait no longer, but must go straight to you at once."

Garth drew down the dear hand which had held the pen that night; turned it over, and softly kissed the palm.

"What were they, Jane?" he said.

" 'Lead us, O Christ, when all is gone,
Safe home at last.'

"And oh, my darling, the pathos of those words, 'when all is gone'! Whoever wrote that music, had been through suffering such as ours. Then came a theme of such inspiring hopefulness and joy, that I arose, armed with fresh courage; took up my pen, and went on with my letter. Again two lines had reached me:

> " 'Where Thou, Eternal Light of Light,
> Art Lord of All.'

"What is it, Garth? And whose? And where did you hear it? And will you sing it to me now, darling? I have a sudden wish that you should sing it, here and now; and I can't wait!"

Garth sat up, and laughed—a short happy laugh, in which all sorts of emotions were mingled.

"Jane! I like to hear you say you can't wait. It isn't like you; because you are so strong and patient. And yet it is so deliciously like you, if you *feel* it, to *say* it. I found the words in the Anthem-book at Worcester Cathedral, this time last year, at even-song. I copied them into my pocket-book, during the reading of the first lesson, I am ashamed to say; but it was all about what Balak said unto Balaam, and Balaam said unto Balak,— so I hope I may be forgiven! They seemed to me some of the most beautiful words I had ever read; and, fortunately, I committed them to memory. Of course, I will sing them to you, if you wish, here and now. But I am afraid the air will sound rather poor without the accompaniment. However, not for worlds would I move from here, at this moment."

So sitting up; in the moonlight, with his back to Jane, his face uplifted, and his hands clasped around one knee, Garth sang. Much practice had added greatly to the sweetness and flexibility of his voice; and he rendered perfectly the exquisite melody to which the words were set.

Jane listened with an overflowing heart.

> "The radiant morn hath passed away,
> And spent too soon her golden store;
> The shadows of departing day
> Creep on once more.

> "Our life is but a fading dawn,
> Its glorious noon, how quickly past!
> Lead us, O Christ, when all is gone,
> Safe home at last.

> "Where saints are clothed in spotless white,
> And evening shadows never fall;
> where Thou, Eternal Light of Light,
> Art Lord of All."

The triumphant worship of the last line rang out into the night, and died away. Garth loosed his hands, and leaned back, with a sigh of vast content, against his wife's knees.

"Beautiful!" she said. "Beautiful! Garthie—perhaps it is because *you* sang it; and to-night;—but it seems to me the most beautiful thing I ever heard. Ah, and how appropriate for us; on this day, of all days."

"Oh, I don't know," said Garth, stretching his legs in front of him, and crossing his feet the one over the other. "I certainly feel 'Safe home at last'—not because 'all is gone'; but because I *have* all, in having you, Jane."

Jane bent, and laid her cheek upon his head. "My own boy," she said, "you have all I have to give—all, *all*. But, darling, in those dark days which are past, all seemed gone, for us both. 'Lead us, O Christ'—It was He who led us safely through the darkness, and has brought us to this. And Garth, I love to know that He is Lord of All—Lord of our joy; Lord of our love; Lord of our lives—our wedded lives, my husband. We could not be so safely, so blissfully, each other's, were we not *one, in him*. Is this true for you also, Garth?"

Garth felt for her left hand, drew it down, and laid his cheek against it; then gently twisted the wedding ring that he might kiss it all round.

"Yes, my wife," he said. "I thank God, that I can say in all things: 'Thou, Eternal Light of Light, art Lord of All.'"

A long sweet silence. Then Jane said, suddenly: "Oh, but the music, Garthie! That exquisite setting. Whose is it? And where did you hear it?"

Garth laughed again; a laugh of half-shy pleasure.

"I am glad you like it, Jane," he said, "because I must plead guilty to the fact that it is my own. You see, I knew no music for it; the Anthem-book gave the words only. And on that awful night, when little Rosemary had mercilessly rubbed it in, about 'the lady portrayed'; and what her love *must* have been, and *would* have been, and *could* have been; and had made me *see* 'The Wife' again, and 'The—' the other picture; I felt so bruised, and sore, and lonely. And then those words came to my mind: 'Lead us, O Christ, when all is gone, safe home at last.' All seemed gone indeed; and there seemed no home to hope for, in this world." He raised himself a little, and then leaned back again; so that his head rested against her bosom. "Safe home at last," he said, and stayed quite still for a moment, in utter content. Then remembered what he was telling her, and went on eagerly.

"So those words came back to me; and to get away from despairing thoughts, I began reciting them, to an accompaniment of chords.

> " 'The radiant morn hath passed away,
> And spent too soon her golden store;
> The shadows of departing day—'

"And then—suddenly, Jane—I *saw* it, pictured in sound! Just as I used to *see* a sunset, in light and shadow, and then transfer it to my canvas in shade and colour,—so I heard a *sunset* in harmony, and I felt the same kind of tingle in my fingers as I used to feel when inspiration came, and I could catch up my brushes and palette. So I played the sunset. And then I got the theme for life fading, and what one feels when the glorious noon is suddenly plunged into darkness; and then the prayer. And then, I *heard* a vision of heaven, where evening shadows never fall: And after that came the end; just certainty, and worship, and peace. You see the eventual theme, worked out of all this. It was like making studies for a picture. That was why you heard it over and over. I wasn't trying to remember. I was gathering it into final form. I am awfully glad you like it, Jane; because if I show you how the harmonies go, perhaps you could write it down. And it would mean such a lot to me, if you thought it worth singing. I could play the accompaniment—Hullo! Is it beginning to rain? I felt a drop on my cheek, and another on my hand."

No answer. Then he felt the heave, with which Jane caught her breath; and realised that she was weeping.

In a moment he was on his knees in front of her. "Jane! Why, what is the matter; Sweet? What on earth—? Have I said anything to trouble you? Jane, what is it? O God, why can't I see her!"

Jane mastered her emotion; controlling her

voice, with an immense effort. Then drew him down beside her.

"Hush, darling, hush! It is only a great joy—a wonderful surprise. Lean against me again, and I will try to tell you. Do you know that you have composed some of the most beautiful music in the world? Do you know, my own boy, that not only your proud and happy wife, but *all* women who can sing, will want to sing your music? Garthie, do you realise what it means? The creative faculty is so strong in you, that when one outlet was denied it, it burst forth through another. When you had your sight, you created by the hand and *eye*. Now, you will create by the hand and *ear*. The power is the same. It merely works through another channel. But oh, think what it means! Think! The world lies before you once more!"

Garth laughed, and put up his hand to the dear face, still wet with thankful tears.

"Oh, bother the world!" he said. "I don't want the world. I only want my wife."

Jane put her arms around him. Ah, what a boy he was in some ways! How full of light-hearted, irrepressible, essential youth. Just then she felt so much older than he; but how little that mattered. The better could she wrap him round with the greatness of her tenderness; shield him from every jar or disillusion; and help him to make the most of his great gifts.

"I know, darling," she said. "And you have her. She is just *all yours*. But think of the wonderful future. Thank God, I know enough of the technical part, to write the scores of your compositions. And, Garth,—fancy going together to noble cathedrals, and hearing your anthems sung; and to concerts where the most perfect voices in the world will be doing their utmost adequately to render your songs. Fancy thrilling hearts with pure harmony, stirring souls with tone-pictures; just as before you used to awaken in us all, by your wonderful paintings, an appreciation and comprehension of beauty."

Garth raised his head. "Is it really as good as that, Jane?" he said.

"Dear," answered Jane, earnestly, "I can only tell you, that when you sang it first, and I had not the faintest idea it was yours, I said to myself: 'It is the most beautiful thing I ever heard.'"

"I am glad," said Garth, simply. "And now, let's talk of something else. Oh, I say, Jane! The present is too wonderful, to leave any possible room for thoughts about the future. Do talk about the present."

Jane smiled; and it was the smile of "The Wife"—mysterious; compassionate; tender; self-surrendering. She leaned over him, and rested her cheek upon his head.

"Yes, darling. We will talk of this very moment, if you wish. You begin."

"Look at the house, and describe it to me, as you see it in the moonlight."

"Very grey, and calm, and restful-looking. And so home-like, Garthie."

"Are there lights in the windows?"

"Yes. The library lights are just as we left them. The French window is standing wide open. The pedestal lamp, under a crimson silk shade, looks very pretty from here, shedding a warm glow over the interior. Then, I can see one candle in the dining-room. I think Simpson is putting away silver."

"Any others, Jane?"

"Yes, darling. There is a light in the Oriel chamber. I can see Margery moving to and fro. She seems to be arranging my things, and giving final touches. There is also a light in your room, next door. Ah, now she has gone through. I see her standing and looking round to make sure all is right. Dear faithful old heart! Garth, how sweet it is to be at home to-day; served and tended by those who really love us."

"I am so glad you feel that," said Garth. "I half feared you might regret not having an ordinary honeymoon—And yet, no! I wasn't really afraid of that, or of anything. Just, together at last, was all we wanted. Wasn't it, my wife?"

"All."

A clock in the house struck nine.

"Dear old clock," said Garth, softly. "I used to

443

hear it strike nine, when I was a little chap in my crib, trying to keep awake until my mother rustled past; and went into her room. The door between her room and mine used to stand ajar, and I could see her candle appear in a long streak upon my ceiling. When I saw that streak, I fell asleep immediately. It was such a comfort to know she was there; and would not go down again. Jane, do you like the Oriel chamber?"

"Yes, dear. It is a lovely room; and very sacred because it was hers. Do you know, Aunt Georgina insisted upon seeing it, Garth; and said it ought to be whitened and papered. But I would not hear of that; because the beautiful old ceiling is hand-painted, and so are the walls; and I was certain you had loved those paintings, as a little boy; and would remember them now."

"Ah, yes," said Garth, eagerly. "A French artist stayed here, and did them. Water and rushes, and the most lovely flamingoes; those on the walls standing with their feet in the water; and those on the ceiling, flying with wings outspread, into a pale green sky, all over white billowy clouds. Jane, I believe I could walk round that room, blindfold—no! I mean, as I am now; and point out the exact spot where each flamingo stands."

"You shall," said Jane, tenderly. These slips when he talked, momentarily forgetting his blindness, always wrung her heart. "By degrees you must tell me all the things you specially did and

444

loved, as a little boy. I like to know them. Had you always that room, next door to your mother's?"

"Ever since I can remember," said Garth. "And the door between was always open. After my mother's death, I kept it locked. But the night before my birthday, I used to open it; and when I woke early and saw it ajar, I would spring up, and go quickly in; and it seemed as if her dear presence was there to greet me, just on that one morning. But I had to go quickly, and immediately I wakened; just as you must go out early to catch the rosy glow of sunrise on the fleeting clouds; or to see the gossamer webs on the gorse, outlined in diamonds, by the sparkling summer dew. But, somehow, Margery found out about it; and the third year there was a sheet of writing-paper firmly stuck to the pincushion by a large black-headed pin, saying, in Margery's careful caligraphy: 'Many happy returns of the day, Master Garthie.' It was very touching, because it was meant to be so comforting and tactful. But it destroyed the illusion! Since then the door has been kept closed."

Another long sweet silence. Two nightingales, in distant trees, sang alternately; answering one another in liquid streams of melody.

Again Garth turned the wedding ring; then spoke, with his lips against it.

"You said Margery had 'gone through.' Is it open to-night?" he asked.

Jane clasped both hands behind his head—strong, capable hands, though now they trembled a little—and pressed his face against her, as she had done on the terrace at Shenstone, three years before.

"Yes, my own boy," she said; "it is."

"Jane! Oh, Jane—" He released himself from the pressure of those restraining hands, and lifted his adoring face to hers.

Then, suddenly, Jane broke down. "Ah, darling," she said, "take me away from this horrible white moonlight! I cannot bear it. It reminds me of Shenstone. It reminds me of the wrong I did you. It seems a separating thing between you and me—this cruel brightness which you cannot share."

Her tears fell on his upturned fate.

Then Garth sprang to his feet. The sense of manhood and mastery; the right of control, the joy of possession, arose within him. Even in his blindness, he was the stronger. Even in his helplessness, for the great essentials, Jane must lean on him. He raised her gently, put his arms about her, and stood there, glorified by his great love.

"Hush, sweetest wife," he said. "Neither light nor darkness can separate between you and me: This quiet moonlight cannot take you from me; but in the still, sweet darkness you will feel more completely my own, because it will hold nothing we cannot share. Come with me to the library, and we will send away the lamps, and close the curtains; and you shall sit on the couch near the piano, where you sat, on that wonderful evening when I found you, and when I almost frightened my brave Jane. But she will not be frightened now, because she is so my own; and I may say what I like; and do what I will; and she must not threaten me with Nurse Rosemary; because it is Jane I want—Jane, Jane; just *only* Jane! Come in, beloved; and I, who see as clearly in the dark as in the light, will sit and play *The Rosary* for you; and then *Veni, Creator Spiritus*; and I will sing you the verse which has been the secret source of peace, and the sustaining power of my whole inner life, through the long, hard years, apart."

"Now," whispered Jane. "Now, as we go."

So Garth drew her hand through his arm; and, as they walked, sang softly:

"Enable with perpetual light,
The dulness of our blinded sight;
Anoint and cheer our soiled face
With the abundance of Thy grace.
Keep far our foes; give peace at home;
Where Thou art Guide, no ill can come."

Thus, leaning on her husband; yet guiding him as she leaned; Jane passed to the perfect happiness of her wedded home.

447

Center Point Publishing

600 Brooks Road ● PO Box 1
Thorndike ME 04986-0001 USA

(207) 568-3717

US & Canada:
1 800 929-9108
www.centerpointlargeprint.com